HEART OF REDEMPTION

A HOCKEY ROMANCE NOVEL

THE HEART SERIES

BOOK TWO

LIANA TIAMZON

LT

DEDICATION

For the people that love so hard that it just bites you back.
To my friends who stayed with me through the toughest times,
Sophie and Julia.
To my roommate, Lexi who kept bugging me to finish writing.
To my parents, again if you are reading this, please close the book
and throw it away. This will scar you for eternity.
-Liana

Content Warning

Trigger Warning

This story covers explicit sexual content, profanity, violence, the use of drugs, domestic abuse, alcohol use, disorders, and topics that may be sensitive to some readers.

UPCOMING BOOKS BY LIANA TIAMZON

THE HEART SERIES

THE HEART OF DESIRE
ADRIANNA & GRAYSON

THE HEART OF ABANDON
VERINA & CHRIS

THE HEART OF MERIT
JULIETTE & NEIL

Table Of Contents

Playlist

Apologize (feat. OneRepublic) – Timbaland
Dancing on my Own – Calum Scott
Jar of Hearts – Cristina Perri
Teardrops on my Guitar – Taylor Swift
Good for You – Selena Gomez
Memories – Conan Grey
the 1 – Taylor Swift
The Great War – Taylor Swift
right where you left me – Taylor Swift
Cruel Summer – Taylor Swift
I Won't Apologize – Selena Gomez
bet u wanna – Sabrina Carpenter
things i wish you said – Sabrina Carpenter
Heaven – Julia Michaels
rubberband – Tate McRae
Boyfriend – Arianna Grande & Social House
How You Get the Girl (Taylor's Version) – Taylor Swift
They Don't Know About Us – One Direction
Toxic – Britney Spears
Secret Love Song – Little Mix
Good Looking – Suki Waterhouse

Please Please Please – Sabrina Carpenter
But Daddy I Love Him – Taylor Swift
imgonnagetyouback – Taylor Swift
Guilty as Sin? – Taylor Swift
the grudge – Olivia Rodrigo
we can't be friends (wait for your love) – Ariana Grande
i wish i hated you – Arianna Grande
Dirty Little Secret – Nessa Barrett
That's So True – Gracie Abrams
I Love You, I'm Sorry – Gracie Abrams
Close To You – Gracie Abrams
Another Life – SZA

CHAPTER 1

MARGO

I feel like I am an absolute ornament to society. I am a prize to be won and I'm proud of it.

I think I'm proud to call myself a girl that a boy desires, and a girl that many would love to diminish.

I have no room to complain, I was sitting outside my villa in Greece, counting down the days I could come back to New York. I was tired of attending senseless parties filled with other ornaments to society.

I'm exhausted of extravagant dresses, excessive makeup, people pretending to care about whether I had a great year. I certainly would prefer being in Hawthorne right now. The city noise, the yelling citizens, taxi drivers beeping their horns, and especially the birds attacking old people.

The last one was a joke, I'm not horrible I promise. I yawn, placing my magazine down to the table next to me, feeling a bit sore because of the atrocious sunburn I have graciously acquired.

"Do you have a dress ready for tonight, darling?" I hear a whimsical voice intrude my thoughts.

I take a breath; it was the eighth party I was attending. I've grown irritated to attending the parties that the same repeating cycle of people that had personalities of cardboard boxes.

I groan, sitting up to look at my mother, "You have got to be kidding me." I lark at her as she sends me a condescending scowl.

"You have been laying there, tanning for about two hours, Margo Raine." She stresses as I grimace.

"It was one hour!" I correct her before I fall back to my previous relaxing position.

I could hear her footsteps get louder, meaning she was walking closer to me, she sits next to me as I try and ignore her eyes, which were burning through my skull.

"Come on, Maggie it's not that bad. Besides there was a dress sent in for you to wear." She reasons, I could feel myself cave into my mother's request to start getting ready.

"Don't forget our current situation." She adds on before standing up, putting on her expensive pearls.

I take a loud annoyed breathe, "I know."

My parent's business had been underwater, and it has been looking very hopeless nevertheless, all I could do was be supportive and stick with them through thick and thin.

I am loyal to people I love; it is my number one rule.

"Where's father?" I ask, while getting up.

"He's already down mingling with his many potential business partners. He does not waste time." She turns to look at me.

I couldn't help but frown, but before I could hide it from my own mother, she walks towards me with open arms, that wrap themselves around me.

I always have enjoyed her free spirit and talent of making others feel better. She pulls away from me, but her hands stay on my shoulders, greeting me with a huge smile.

"There is an amazing grand piano at the party, I know you never like to sing and play in front of people but maybe it could be something spontaneous you do in Greece." Her grin reaches both of her eyes.

How could I ever say no to her, "I would love to." I smile thinly as she shakes me, "Amazing! I will let the others know." She rushes to the doorway, whilst pulling my Chanel bag from my closet.

"Hey! I was going to use that!" I yell, but tragically get cut off by the loud slam of the door when she ran out quickly.

I roll my eyes, before walking into my ginormous walk-in closet. My eyes wander around my profligate clothing choices, before landing on the breathtaking black laced, two-piece dress. It was see through and looked very breathable.

The last dress I wore was a green velvet creation, that suffocated me the whole night, I was sweating and constricted. It was the worst fashion choice I had definitely made.

I admire the soft lace and the beautiful patterns all over, I scan the tag that was attached to the dress, with a knowing huff.

"Meet some hot guys! – Verina"

I shake my head with appreciation that she would make this beautiful dress just for my trip. I smell the tag, as it had her signature Burberry scent.

As I slip in the dress, I couldn't help but think about running away, sneaking away from this horrid party that I was supposed to attend. But I wouldn't.

I couldn't.

I would hate to disappoint my mother and father after all they have done for me, how much they have loved me. I would always be there for them.

I would never actually abandon them.

"So, what's your favorite color!" A guy with dorky glasses, and a mullet asks me as I cringe.

I was being awful, and I shouldn't be, he is a genuinely nice boy that shouldn't be ruining his self-esteem by speaking to me, or even approaching me.

"Um, iris." I mutter as he nods with a wide beam. I had been twirling the toothpick that my martini came with for the past thirty minutes.

I wasn't going to lie and say that my face looked absolutely interested in every conversation I've had. Instead, it was noticeable that my face held a wretched and pissed expression.

I had hoped that all the boys that have pulled me in for a conversation would have gotten the hint, but they weren't that smart.

I spot my father's eyes as he makes his way through the crowd over to me, I was so ready for him to save me from this torment.

He pats the guys back that was speaking to me, interrupting him from mid-sentence to a conversation that I wasn't paying attention to.

"May I please borrow my daughter, Eric?" My father asks.

Ohh. That was his name, I completely zoned out when he introduced himself. Speaking of which... I did zone out when the others also introduced themselves.

Eric walks off as I stare mindlessly at the bar, thinking about whether I could hide under the counters and drink the whole night.

"I know what you're thinking." My father looks at me with a frown. I bet he didn't know what the hell was going through my mind.

I think it was a pretty hard thing to do... you know... read my mind, there has only been one person ever that did and did it accurately, and that is my best friend, Adrianna Cassian.

My soulmate, my person, my everything. She always knew what was up with every roaming thought that I had spewed or even if it was just floating in there somewhere, she would know about it.

I never complain, she can stay in my thoughts all she wants, because I know that I was the only person that she ever really opened up to, letting me in her dark thoughts.

She is the strongest person I know; without her I wouldn't be who I am and I'm sure that she would feel the same way.

"You look miserable, Maggie." He voices as I pick at a piece of lint from my top.

"I'm here, father. Is that not what you want?" My father looked absolutely rigid as I throw a bit of attitude his way.

I sigh as his eyes pierce through mine, "I'm sorry, I didn't mean to yell." I admit as he shakes his head, "Maggie, I am sorry to put you in this position. But you know the reason we are here."

I was now zoning out once again, but never once this summer did my parents ever let me forget that the reason we were here. They plan just to marry me off and join companies with my future husband's family.

My family is on the brink of bankruptcy, and they are definitely panicking. My father was practically jumping up and down the moment I spark an interest in anyone remotely interested in merging businesses.

I hear him babbling on and on as I continuously look around to pay attention to anything or anyone else other than my father in front of me.

"Have you sparked an interest in someone?" My father raises his voice as I shake my head, lacking energy to say it out loud.

"Maggie, you really need to get out there." He stresses and I knock my head back, "Father, I am trying very hard."

"And I thank you for that, my love." He comes closer to kiss the top of my head as I lean closer to him.

"Dad, I am just very exhausted, I can't speak to another bobble head right now." I groan as he laughs softly, "You can take your rightful place on the stage and play for everyone."

I pull away from him, with saucers as eyes, excitement practically blasted from my body, "I thought mom only said that to me to get me down here."

He points over at the beautiful Steinway Model B Grand Piano, that had gold rimming and the most beautiful black paint exterior.

"The Grimaldi family has given it to us, a gift from Benjamin, who has kindly asked for your hand in marriage." He pronounces as I look back at the piano once again.

I pull away from his grasps, practically running over to the piano, my hands begin to shake as I touch the beautiful porcelain keys, delicately.

Silence in the room scatters, even if the party sits next to the beach, I could feel the waves calm down and the birds even quiet just to hear my shaky voice.

All eyes on me, horrifying looks from everyone in the room, but mine catch beautiful honey brown glass orbs that studied me intently.

William Brookshire stands within the crowd, his hands down his pockets, while his body leans on one of the pillars, his eyes sinking into my body like a snake bite.

I wipe my sweaty hands on my thighs before placing my hands on the piano. I never sang in front of crowds before, let alone strangers that have studied me like a mannequin in a glass window. This is definitely nerve racking in every type of way I could imagine.

However, I am not easily embarrassed. I used music to calm myself down in stressful situations. I take a long abysmal breath, before opening my mouth to let opening chords spill out.

The rest of the notes flow out as my hands traveled and guided through the major chords of the piano.

Everyone looked absolutely serenaded as I kept singing, I could feel my heart fill up as I continue, a lovely rich baritone of my voice rises through the entire crowd as they stare at me in awe.

I can't help but lean closer to the piano, my mouth closer to the microphone that was attached, my hands flowing nicely through the piano keys.

Minutes later, my final note ends and remains for a while until I see fit for it to end, I take a soft breath, as I await for the whole crowds to look expressionless.

The silence stays and I feel my cheeks redden, as well as my body heat, before I could feel completely stupid for singing in front of everyone, one slow clap from the crowd was at bay.

His penetrating brown eyes narrow at mine, as everyone joins in on his clapping, I can't help but smile at the many people that were showing gratitude and amazement.

But before I could thank Liam, which was something that was not on my bingo card this summer, my parents have ran in front of me complementing my performance.

I didn't want to be rude, so I just thanked them before attempting to brush through the crowd, seeing that Liam was now nowhere to be found.

I take a deep breath before a hand touches my shoulder, I turn quickly to find that it was a man I had never seen before, an old man. I pull away, caution builds through my body as he smiles widely.

"Margo Hamilton?" He asks as I nod, questioning whether to answer him vocally or not.

"I am Rosco Sonata, your parents have mentioned that you were looking for a husband and I would like to take you to dinner some time." He expresses as I cringe away.

Hopefully my face didn't expose my true feelings of this scenario, I am absolutely infuriated at his date invitation.

A man who looks so ancient he probably has dust up his asshole! I mean what the hell, am I really worth this, am I only a prize for every man to fucking want?

I don't want this, even if it breaks my parents heart, I will not be subjected to marry an old fart! I want to have a mind-blowing type of love that makes my heart race. A type of love that makes me see sparks flying across my vision.

Those ones that make my heart skip a beat when I'm near him, butterflies in my stomach, the type of love you would see old people still have.

"I'm sorry, I'm busy." I kindly say to the man as he nods politely, "If you ever need anything I am always here to help." He says with a jolly like voice.

He kind of looks like Santa Clauss if I really think about it, he probably has an empire like the North Pole toy shop, with all his elves, sadly I was not ready to be a Mrs. Clauss whatsoever.

"I will take you up on that." I laugh, so daunting and fake how could people not see it? Do they really think that everyone here enjoys speaking to each other?

He nods before looking to find someone else to ask to be his bride to be. Maybe I can fix him up with a one of the teachers at the university who wasn't getting laid.

Maybe one that can help me get from a B average to an A, yes, I know I could just study but that was Juliette's thing, she's been trying to get the whole group together for a big study session.

I certainly voiced my opinion that no one was going to attend, but Juliette didn't mind, she still studied, but in my head, what's the point?

Juliette has an outstanding IQ of 222, which by the way is estimated to be larger than Einstein, and she still has to study! There is truly no hope for the rest of humanity if you ask me.

And I'm not dumb, I wouldn't be going to an Ivy League if I was, no one in Hawthorne University is stupid, except the selected individuals like... Maya Brown, Brooks Johnson, Victoria Lewinski, and Karen Goldstein.

These people were definitely just off the top of my head, Adrianna of course had to be dating Brooks, so I can't openly be rude to him, but I could do whatever I want when it came to other people I dislike.

Speaking of people I dislike, Liam Brookshire had completely vanished, I shouldn't complain, I just want to make sure he didn't have a video of my voice and send it for the whole world to see.

Before I turn away from everyone and go back to my destined seat at the bar, I notice my family standing around a large table with what seems to be a whole other family. My father looks at his watch then through the crowd, probably looking for me.

But I hide behind a pillar, my breath raged and my pulse quick, damn I really need to get back in shape.

Brings me to the fact that Juliette would always insist on dragging us to the gym to help her train for soccer season, we all kindly denied, except for Verina who doesn't complain at the sight of the shirtless, men that surround the gym and worship her.

Wait why did I say no again?

I hear my name being called by my father's recognizable voice, I bolt to the back exit, away from the party.

I wasn't in the mood to talk to a whole bunch on strangers again, scared that I might lose it, say things I don't mean.

As I look forward, the whole beach was empty, the horizon was beautiful as the sun began to set.

I take in a large, needed breath, while waking closer to the shore, my feet being submersed by the cold relaxing wave of water that left as quickly as it came.

The ocean breeze brushing through me as my hair flies away from my face, I take a seat down on the sand, letting my arms wrap around my legs, I set my head down on my knees, afraid that if I pull my eyes away from the sun it might disappear.

Sure, it would disappear later, but not just yet.

Right now, it was just me and the ocean, what else could I ask for?

CHAPTER 2

LIAM

Earlier Today.

"Come on, Prince." I sigh, as my best friend rejects flying over to Greece to spend time with me.

Grayson pauses before answering, "I'm busy, with a lot of things man, why can't you just find something to distract yourself with, I'm sure that you will find a pretty brunette there to keep yourself occupied." He reasons as I roll my eyes.

"By busy do you mean, you're still trying to win your ex-girlfriend back?" I point out the obvious as he completely ignores my statement.

"I'm just busy." He counters as I give a huff, "Come on, Grayson, so many bombshells here, like damn man, as Princess Ariel from the Little Mermaid would say, *"It's a Whole New World."* I let out with an excited tone before he knocks down my enthusiasm.

"That's Princess Jasmine from Aladdin, you fucking idiot." Grayson sneered as I shake my head, "No I'm pretty sure it was Ariel."

Grayson takes a huff and a half, before responding, "Ariel sings, *A Part of Your World*, I would know." He retorts as I take swing at my glass of whiskey.

"How would you know, you don't sit down and watch Disney Princess movies on your free time, so nice try." I was getting tired of how entitled Grayson always thought of himself.

He could never be wrong in his eyes.

"No of course not it's not like I have a little sister who watched it every day of her childhood." He declares as I pause to think about the lyrics.

"That doesn't matter!" I say to buy time to think.

"Ariel sings "A Part of Your World" because she wants to be with Prince Eric which is in the human world." Grayson calmly explains as I lean back to listen.

I let my mouth open in the moment of epiphany, then a scowl breaches my face to remember that Grayson was sadly correct once again.

"Whatever, I'm just saying instead of wallowing and crying about August dumping you, you should be living your life here in Greece with me." I weigh in as I hear his annoying exhale.

"I am not wallowing or crying, Liam just simply upset at the situation." He pawns as I take a seat on one of the many stools, that the bar by the beach has to offer.

I didn't understand Grayson's thoughts on August, in my head she simply uses Grayson repeatedly and he never batted an eye because he was so focused on keeping her.

It wasn't normal in our society for Grayson Prince to date a girl who doesn't live off her parent's wealth, she has to work for everything she's got.

That's never a bad thing of course, but I can tell Grayson didn't want her because of her hardworking skills and the fact that she gets paid $8.95 per hour.

He likes her because there's a rebellious feel of being with someone who his parents wouldn't necessarily love.

He and I never really see eye to eye on this, it was always him wanting August and me frolicking about.

"Have you met someone there as your summer lover?" Grayson asks as I couldn't help but laugh at his assumption, "It's a cruel summer out here Prince." I shake my head, examining my now empty glass of whiskey.

"Come on Liam, I know you like to play your cards right... but maybe someone you don't expect could be the one you've been waiting for."

"You are such a poet, you ever thing of becoming a song writer?" I lean forward so my elbows could touch the table.

I can practically feel his eyes rolling from the other side of the call, "I'm just trying to help my best friend out, considering you do feel lonely because I'm not there to give you kisses and cuddles." He teases as I look around for a waiter or waitress to get me a refill.

"I don't need help in getting women Prince, trust me when I say that I have been getting a lot of attention, through the entire trip." I point out as he scoffs.

"You are so full of yourself."

"Rightfully so, I didn't work out all my life to get this eight pack for nothing Prince."

Grayson snickers, "I would like to believe that you worked out so hard because of hockey but then again I forgot I'm talking to one of the most narcissistic person I've ever met."

"I'm going to take that as a great compliment, I'm not going to lie to you."

There's a small pause before Grayson speaks, "Have you spoken to Chris?" He mutters, it's a topic that everyone in the group usually strays away from.

"Yeah, every now and then, but I'm visiting Finn and him when I come back, I got them a little something." I add.

"I've tried giving Chris a bit of money, but he's being really stubborn. I just want to help but he won't accept anything man." Grayson whines as I tilt my head to think.

"Gray, how would you feel if it was Amelia who has what Finn has, you have no one to help you. Chris is on a damn scholarship at Hawthorne University and has to feed himself and his brother. His mother is a fucking drug addict that is barely in the house to help out. I know damn well you would want everyone to think you don't need help." I warble as I hear the complete silence on the other end of the call.

Then Grayson finally speaks, "I get it, you want me to lay off." He temporizes as a waiter comes over quickly and refills my beverage.

"I'm just saying to just be supportive to Chris right now, he needs that more than he needs money."

"Yeah, I got it." He wonders for a second as I recline my head backwards.

"When did you get so wise Liam Brookshire?" Grayson teases as I laugh for a second, "I've been wise, your head is just too far up your ass that you've never noticed."

"Right." He sneers as I place the glass of whiskey down on the table.

"How is he doing with the fights?" I ask.

I let the whiskey linger down my throat, feeling the bitterness to my core, I shiver.

"He's doing great with the more lowkey fights, I have a feeling he's thinking about going for more, the money is a big prize."

I wonder for a moment, "How much?"

"Half a million." Grayson says thickly as I roll my tongue, Grayson, and Neil's parents as well as my mine make quadruple that amount every three minutes.

But I had to remember that Chris has a different life, he's had more mature responsibilities than anyone in Hawthorne University, he hides it well.

No one knows half of the real shit he's gone through or is going through.

"How many finalist are allowed from our team?" I ask quickly as Grayson thinks for a moment.

"I think five." He makes note as I nod, "We're helping him get that half million." I say rather quickly as Grayson stays silent.

He didn't have to say anything, I knew he would be on board

the moment I mentioned it because he was definitely thinking the same damn thing.

"The trainings and practices would help a ton with the hockey season." Grayson points out as I roll my eyes.

"You act like the whole team let themselves go when we have a break." I say with nonchalance. I could hear his heavy sigh of annoyance.

"Some do." Grayson voices as I smile, "That reminds me..." I continue.

"Yes, I know." He mutters, "We gotta start looking for the next team captain." A smile worms its way into my lips.

"I've really been thinking about Jacob." I voice as Grayson takes a moment.

"Lawrence?" He asks as I reassure him.

"Yes, Jacob Lawrence, he's shown great leadership during lifting, and always carries a good attitude."

"You shouldn't always appear perfect if you're team captain, it makes it look like your teammates can't mess up." He counters as I groan.

"Okay who do you propose?" I ask with a bit of an attitude.

"Maybe, Zhen Chie." He makes note as my jaw drops, "Seriously Gray? You're thinking about Z as team captain?!"

Grayson sounds irritated through the phone, "It was just a thought, he's doing really good and has the sternly voice I like."

"Well, it's not for you, it's for the team you dip shit." I spat as he grumbles.

"Well how about Ortiz?" I suggest.

"Lazy." He argues.

"Chuck Reynolds?"

"Dramatic."

"Greene?"

"He's mediocre at best." Grayson disputes.

"Then why the fuck are they still in the team, Prince?"

"Because when pre-season starts, they're scared shitless of me which forces them to get their shit together." He shrugs off as I roll my eyes.

"You're a fucking idiot." I taunt as he laughs.

"Well man I got to go help out Amelia with her outfit for school pictures." Grayson warns as I nod, "Tell her I said hi, and make sure she doesn't put a speck of make up on your face."

"I quite enjoy it when she plays make up with me." Grayson admits as I shake my head with a small giggle, "Of course you do."

"Okay, talk to Neil when you can he needs help with his motorcycle repairs." Grayson adds before hanging up abruptly.

I scroll through my phone's contact list to look for Neil's number, catching the thousands of girls that have messaged me from the other night were all ignored.

Doesn't surprise me, I'm a blast to be with but I realize that I'm getting tired of going to multiple different rendezvous.

As I get up, I place eight hundred dollars on the table. While walking away from the bar, I call Neil's cell phone number.

Suspiciously it was declined. But before I could even further care about why he didn't answer, it was like I was being mesmerized by an angelic voice.

Something that I have heard in my fucking dreams before. I can't help but put my phone down only looking for where the voice was coming from.

I wasn't even thinking as my legs lead me to a party full of modern billionaires with extravagant dresses.

I hear chords on the piano blending with the beatific vocals, and I swear my heart skips a beat as I listen, I still can't track down who was singing, all I know is that I'm fucking mesmerized.

Until I hit a wall around two giant pillars, my eyes zone in on the gigantic stage in front of the whole crowd. Beautiful blonde hair falling behind the mysterious beauty's back.

I tilt my head, admiring the singer's beautiful voice, adoring the sun light that shadowed her silhouetted body. I couldn't help but lean back, my hands gripping my pockets as the sun finally came down.

To where I could admire the woman's fa--

--*Margo fucking Hamilton?!*

As I stand within the crowd, my hands down my pockets, her eyes find mine, she looks scared to move. Margo's blue irises mirrored the blue ocean behind her.

Margo wipes down her hands on her model thighs before placing her hands on the piano to make another note. She was like a fucking statue that people were admiring, multiple men staring at her like a golden ticket. It make my hands clench into fists.

She takes a time-consuming dreadful breath, before finally opening her picturesque lips to let the opening chords spill out.

As she continues to sing, the more I had been put in a damn trans, I couldn't pull my eyes away from Margo Hamilton in under two minutes she's created a certain hold over me.

I was regaled like everyone else as she kept singing, it felt like one second before the whole thing was over, she ended on a beautiful note, which felt like ended my happiness.

I wonder if I look like an absolute doofus. The whole crowd stays silence as her cheeks turn bright red, she looked like me when I didn't have a father to walk down with me during senior night in high school. I knew that feeling all too well, so before she completely looked destroyed, I couldn't help but form a slow clap.

My penetrating brown eyes narrow at her ocean blues, as a second passes, the rest of the crowd joins in, Margo smiles at me.

And me only.

I completely forgot about the fact that I was making eyes at Margo Hamilton I had to give myself a thirty second reboot.

My phone rings, seeing Neil's name pop up I take a look back up at Margo once more as she took in the crowd's cheers. I smile to myself seeing her beaming expression.

My phone meets my ear, "Neil?"

I hear nothing before the signal makes a ghastly noise. I look around noticing that this section didn't have the best signal, so I walk off.

Neil hangs up the phone quickly, I text him that I would call him back. Ultimately, I would've already left the party to get a better signal to call Neil back.

But instead, I come back to look for Margo once more before deciding that looking for Margo shouldn't be in my plans for tonight.

It shouldn't even have crossed my mind, but it did, and I think I'm actually losing my mind. But I couldn't help but want her at this very moment.

I decided that it wasn't a great idea if I acted on it, and of course...

She would agree with me.

CHAPTER 3

LIAM

I've scoured every fucking crevice of Greece for her.

Yes, I've made it abundantly clear that I didn't want anything to do with Margo Hamilton but even God himself would fall into his knees with one glance at the angel.

I'm irritated that even with paying millions of euros to securities and guards they didn't know a fucking thing. I might as well have sent out a bounty hunter to find her for me.

Not that she was for me, but I wanted to see her, talk to her, fuck it, she is for me. The stares she gave were practically for me to only see.

I didn't care if I was delusional, I couldn't help it.

Ultimately, with no fucking clue where she was. The large ocean surrounded me while I practically trip over my own feet, vodka in my hand and a banging headache was at bay.

I yawned and thought about how Margo was probably on her way back home to Hawthorne's elite.

I most definitely was ready to give up, since if we were back home there would be no possible way for me and her to ever be in each other's vicinity. Her and Adrianna are basically joined by the hip. The same way that Grayson and I are, but in a cool way.

I took a breath of the sunlight that loomed over the ocean.

Until my eyes caught a scenic blonde body sitting by the shore only a couple feet away, her knees tucked in, long golden hair draped behind her, blown away from her face as her hands played with the sand.

I was drawn, my legs fucking moving before even thinking about it. Then I was next to her, I could smell the ocean breeze, her long dress pooling around her all wet.

I press my lips together, my hand scratching the nape of my neck, not really know what to say.

Hi, I'm Liam.

I'm an idiot, she knows who I am.

Hey, I see you're sitting by yourself.

Of course, she's sitting by herself, she's not stupid.

"Are you going to just stand there and stare at me or are you going to say something to me, Mr. Brookshire." She turned around with an innocent smile laying on her lips.

I coughed out the lump in my throat before I try to open my dry mouth, her eyes crinkled as she looked at me. I could tell there was nothing but pure question in her eyes.

I could still comprehend her diamond blue eyes even as the sun was setting, before noticing the tears that streamed down her face. She continued to glare up at me with teary eyes.

My eyes softened, "Why are you crying, Raine?"

She fidgeted, whilst her eyes widened, "Raine?"

I laughed, I invited myself to take a seat next to her, her eyes narrowed at my bottle of vodka, so as a gentleman I offered her the bottle.

She took a heavy swing, as I shook my head, "Kindergarten, remember I stole your fraction worksheet and that was when you still wrote your name as Margo Raine."

She pulled the bottle down, staring into my eyes, "How could you possibly still remember that."

I looked away, hoped that maybe she wouldn't think too deep about it, I mean how could I not remember that she had the prettiest fucking handwriting ever.

"Just came to me I guess." I sent her a smirk that only the bravest women could survive.

Margo looked at me, her head tilting to the right as my eyebrows wrinkle at the mere idea that she didn't even flinch, instead she looked like she wanted to challenge me.

"Stop smiling at me like that, Charming, it will never work." She made note as I turned over to her.

"Charming?" I mocked as she only let her smile widen even more, like she was proud of herself.

"You don't like that nickname?" She teased as I rolled my eyes, "Raine, I like everything that comes out of your mouth, especially if it has anything to do with me."

Then right there, her walls cracked, one tiny sliver of a crack had just broke, as her eyes sparkled, a bit hesitant to what she wanted to say to me.

"Have you said that to every girl you've hooked up with?" She snapped back as I shook my head, "Brave of you to assume that I'm even remotely thinking of hooking up with you."

Again, she surprised me. Margo moved closer, I could smell her sweet perfume, "Don't you?"

My mouth quivered as her eyes made their way down to my parted lips, dying to move an inch closer. I would've been where paradise was.

But Margo grinned instead, "What are you doing walking down the beach by yourself anyways? As much as I would love it if you had gotten kidnapped and taken away for good, I'm curious."

I've been looking for you.

I wanted to say, but there was no way in hell I would've slightly considered that option. "Partied too hard I guess, I just wanted fresh air."

Margo didn't say anything, only took another drink of the Vodka I had provided. "What about you Raine?" I let my mouth widen.

"What has the infamous Margo Raine Hamilton done to be

in her own little world... away from the party that you were singing at." I asked as she turns her head to lock eyes with me.

"There is no *my* world, this isn't like Gatsby. It's a shithole of a life." She said plainly.

I let my eyes show my emotion as she hits me, "What is it? You think I'm overreacting, don't you?"

"A bit, I mean this life *is* like Gatsby. You have the glamour, the looks, the fucking power. Margo you could be crying at the streets of Brooklyn, which a lot of people do by the way, because they are homeless." I made a point as she shook her head.

"But you aren't. You are in Greece, crying at the private beach that your family has rented, at a villa that your family has owned. You are ruining a dress that could probably feed the entirety of Africa's hungry population." I laughed as she bit her bottom lips.

"You are drinking your problems away with Vodka that could pay off people's mortgages. So, I'm sorry if I might think you are overreacting." I reasoned as she scooted away from me.

"Just because I'm living a better life than most people doesn't mean my problems should just be dismissed." She handed me a longed gaze that ripped my chest apart.

"I'm not saying that--"

Margo gave a harsh scoff, "You have no idea how much I've been dealing with this past summer. How much I am about to give up."

"I might not know, and it's none of my business of course. But Margo, you have the world at the palm of your hand. You are more powerful than you realize, make something of it." I shrugged as she sent me a questionable look.

Mostly searching where I had gotten all my wisdom all of a sudden. I certainly wouldn't know either.

"You know, you're pretty hot when you don't act like such a major dickhead to anything that breathes." Margo snarled as I shook my head.

"Trust me Raine, I'm hot all the time, you are just way too

stubborn to let your heart pick what you really want." I sent her a scorned expression as she licked her lips.

"And what do you *think* I want, Charming?" Her eyes narrowed down on me as her hand landed on my soaked chest from when the water had grazed my body.

"I think you want to kiss me, Raine." I leaned closer as she shook in my hold. Her hand practically searching for something to grab.

I held her up, closer to me than I had ever imagined. "Thanks for being a fan." She laughed softly as I shook my head, my nose had grazed hers.

She had extremely soft skin, porcelain glass. Margo's thumb began to stroke my jawline, I wasn't sure whether she felt my pulse raging.

This girl has completely shook my world in under twenty minutes, she pulled away, I was saddened by the brief moment of her warmth leaving my presence. Margo let her eyes find mine; she studied my face.

She had never been this close to my face and not been side-tracked by something I had said to her to irritate her, she could continue to gawk all she wanted but nothing would ever change my opinion on Margo.

She had been the most stunning looking woman I had ever met in my life. Her ocean blue eyes would signify this moment for ever in my eyes.

I wasn't making fun of her, which I had come to a conclusion was extremely weird, her warm eyes slithered down, looking back at my lips.

I wondered if she was ready to call my bluff.

She wants me. I fucking know it.

She swallowed for a brief moment before wetting her lips, the moonlight now casting a light on her diamond like features.

She was so close, close enough that my breath was warm against her wet lips, and the sensation of it did something giddy to my stomach.

I wanted to close the gap between us with a searing kiss, but it wasn't up to me, it was up to her.

I wanted her to want me.

But she was hesitant, I pulled away, "Hey..." I murmured suddenly, "If you don't want to do it then that's fine, we can stop all you have to say--"

Margo closed the gap between us, and something in me awakened that I didn't even know lived inside me. I lifted my hand to rest on her bare back, which made her startle, her lips stuttered softly against mine.

This had been the perfect formula; she caught up to whatever I had done. She tried to memorize us, our rhythm and motions, keeping up with my tempo, whether I had gone slow or fast she knew.

She pulled me in, by my collar as I laid her on the sand, my kisses had her enthralled and absorbed.

The sun had completely gone away as the moon was the only source of light left... or so I thought.

A large crack of the sky lit up, lightning and thunder had struck almost near us, I pulled away from her as she held on to me, "Pretty electrifying kiss." She joked as I hurried off away from the shore.

"Or you didn't enjoy it?" She looked concerned as I smiled thinly, "No, I enjoyed the kiss quite well. And would love to continue but away from the premises of lightning and thunder." I quickly muttered as she turned around to look at the lightning.

I jolt as another hit, Margo turned her head back to look at me, not hiding the phobia I had. She only walked closer to me, her hands landing on my chest once more.

She plants a small kiss on my lips, "Then where have you been staying?"

CHAPTER 4

MARGO

I wakeup, staring up into the broad white ceilings that were set above me. I feel a wave of chills brush through my skin as I lean over to my right.

I hear a soft breathing pattern next to me as I jolt up from the comfortable bed, my eyes widen at the sight of a Greek god's back muscles that I very much want to touch.

But before I could gawk over him, I realize that the reason I feel such a cold breeze is the fact that I am completely half naked.

I pull the blankets toward my body before turning my head gently over to Liam who's only shielded in the first lining of the covers.

I can't help but smile at him, thinking maybe there's a reason why God led us to each other. Or maybe because I'm so desperate in wishing not to get engaged, I look at him like he was a thrown lifeline by God himself.

Liam fidgets, turning his body towards me but still sound asleep, I let my hand slightly graze his toned arm, then moving closer to his chiseled jawline.

Maybe he is a lifeline thrown by God, or maybe he's just a random rendezvous that God needs to send me before I do need to get engaged.

I've been trying to put it off for the whole summer, but the truth is, time is ticking, and it's been kind and reasonable to me.

Liam's hand softly lands on top of mine, caressing it near his mouth before kissing my palm, "Good morning, Raine."

"Charming..." I respond as he sits up, still holding my hand, he looks at me, up and down and suddenly my face feels like it's scorching red.

"Go back to sleep." I laugh gently as he sends me a wrinkled eyebrow, "I have to get going anyways, my parents are probably worried sick."

Liam rolls his eyes, "No chance I can go back to snoozing, you woke me up from my beauty sleep." He addresses before smiling.

"We're both just lucky that I'm already good looking." He further makes a point while leaning closer to my space slightly to emphasize how good looking he was.

Leave it up to Liam to be the cockiest person in this universe.

I send a sneer over to him as he laughs for a moment, Liam stands up, walking towards the kitchen, still in only a pair of sweatpants that hung so low I could see his happy trail.

I can only stare and admire this man, even if he was cocky, he had reasons to be, he had the money, the looks, and basically everything a man desires.

Everything is at the reach of his hands. Including me.

"You've already taken up a majority of my time." I assert while slipping on my dress and strapping on my heels.

As I see Liam's reflection from the window, his eyes stayed directly on my body, making me shiver.

I turn my head but not my body, "You like what you see?" I ask with a devilish smirk as he coughs out.

"You're not the only good looking one in this room, Charming." I proclaim.

As I finally turn my body to face his, he was leaning onto the fridge, a bowl in his hand and a spoon on the other, "Maybe not." He says calmly.

I walk towards him, his eyes stayed on mine as I came closer, tilting my head before looking up at him, now yes, I consider myself pretty tall, I'm five foot, seven inches.

But Liam towers me at a height of six foot, two inches.

"You want some?" He asks as I look at the box of Fruit Loops that sit out on the counter and a carton of almond milk.

"Almond milk?" I laugh with a questionable tone as he shakes his head, "I'm lactose intolerant!"

I can't help but burst out laughing, I take a small peek of Liam's face, in which ends up looking irritated.

I start to walk away but before I knew it his hands wraps around my waist causing me to still. It was like he could scoop me up with one hand, he probably could.

Liam pulls me closer, flush to his body I could feel his rock-hard abs, and his hands squeezing my waist.

"Fuck Raine, you are a *vision*." He whispers in my ear, causing goosebumps to spread all across my body.

"I'm not falling for whatever you are trying to pull, Charming." I reason as he larks gently, "I'm not pulling anything, I assure you."

I take a deep breath before turning my body to face him, his hands still not releasing my waist as he leans back, "I only came here last night because I didn't want to talk to my parents, don't think it's because I remotely think--"

Before I could finish my sentence, he silences me with a frenzied kiss. I leaned closer than is conceivable, catching his lips. Liam grips my waist tighter pulling me into a clumsy impact that intensifies as he draws me in.

I moan into his mouth, feeling my heart race harder than I thought was even possible.

I feel my body heating up, as well as his, we both pull away at the same time, out of breath I look up at him, "Liam we can't--"

He shakes his head, "--Margo, I've never felt that way when kissing someone, you make me feel electrified, fuck I don't want to stop."

I lick my lips, his hands shaking as well as my body, hoping for more of his touch but now he was hovering over me.

"All you have to say is you don't want it and I will pull away, and you can leave." He alleges as I bite my bottom lip.

I didn't know what to say, nor did I want to stop whatever was going on between the two of us. This was a summer fling and I had about a week before I could never have one ever again.

Why should I say no now?

I sigh, pulling away from him I make my way over to the side table, grabbing my clutch, continuing to walk towards the door, I open it looking back at Liam's smug face.

"What? I have to change my clothes; I can't be seen wearing the same thing twice." I signal to my slightly dried clothes as he beams.

"I'll meet you by the beach in an hour?" He asks so full of hope, it's cute.

I smile, "Bring Vodka, like a good boy."

Then I slam the door shut.

"You are so noisy!" I whisper pretty harshly at Liam who thought it was a magnificent idea to climb up my villa's window.

"I didn't know that your window would be so fucking creaky." He stresses as I fold my arms together with a horrid scowl.

"I don't even know why you thought it would be a good idea to climb up when we were supposed to meet by the beach."

He looks at me with his soft, brown, puppy dog eyes, "I missed you so much already."

I can't help but laugh at him, his gorgeous face.

"You couldn't wait another twenty minutes?"

Liam shakes his head frantically.

Since Liam so graciously climbed up to my room, I feel bad that I have to break the news that he wasn't allowed in my room.

God forbid my mother ever found him in here I would be toast. He's not the ideal eligible bachelor my parents are thinking of to marry me off to.

They want someone responsible and can handle a relationship, Liam's a man that's been plastered all over newspapers and blogs about being a major playboy of Hawthorne.

"You don't miss me?" He questions me with a wild smile that could make my knees buckle.

"No, I don't, I just saw you forty minutes ago." I snap back as he places his hand over his heart like he had been told Santa wasn't real.

"You are so cruel to me, Raine." He wipes a fake tear away from his face, "I thought we had more than this, I thought you were it for me."

I stare at him blankly as he looks around my room, suddenly his character fades as his curiosity strengthens.

The first place he appears to be drawn to is my piano, my guitar stood next to it on its stand, "You have a lot of sheet music here." He picks one up while looking at me.

I nod, "I like to write songs... make music." I fiddle with my hair as he grins, "Write a song about me." He suggests as I let my brown eyes furrow.

"Be careful what you wish for Mr. Brookshire." I say softly as he winks, "I don't care if you Taylor Swift the shit out of me." He notes.

Before looking down at me he whispers, "Don't forget when I told you I like everything that comes out of your mouth, especially if it has anything to do with me."

I felt my hands begin to shake as well as my heart race.

Liam leans down, I could see that he was begging for a kiss and I can't lie saying that I wasn't as well. I wanted to melt on to him, if I just let myself.

As I place my hand on the nape of his neck, my lips so close to his I could feel the warmth, the doorknob rattles uncontrollably.

My body jolts, without even thinking about it, Liam's body crashes into my big pile of clothing, "I'm so sorry baby," I send him an apologetic smile before shutting my closet doors close, slamming his nose he curse quietly.

"Maggie?" I whip my head around, facing my father who looks at me with a grinning face.

"Dad." I address as he takes a seat on the couch, "Where were you last night?" He demanded the question, and it wasn't optional to answer.

"I needed fresh air, so I ended up falling asleep by the beach cabanas." I quickly thought of as he sends a questionable scowl.

"That's dangerous, a girl like you could have ended up in someone's not so delicate hands!" He stands up looking frantic and worried.

"Yes, and I'm sorry but I'm here now, see?" I lift both my hands up in the air, "I am alive and very well."

My father looks at me before smiling, he comes up in front of me, embracing me in his huge arms.

"Dad!" I laugh as he takes his hand and messes up my hair, "I love you, Maggie." He whispers, "Don't ever forget that.

"I won't!" I pull away with a beaming smile that sends him to roll his eyes.

Everyone always tells me I have a face that was very expressive, I displayed exactly how I was feeling.

"And don't forget the dinner tonight with the--" My eyes widen what the rest of his sentence was probably going to be.

"--Yes! I won't forget, I will be there."

I suddenly push him out of my room in a hurry, my heart racing at the mere idea of Liam over hearing about my arranged engagement, well... not engagement yet... but soon."

As soon as the door shuts, I turn to look at my closet, seeing it open suspiciously slow, Liam's broad figure appears slowly as the shadow pulls away from his face.

I can't help but giggle at his irritated expression, his hand on his nose, must be from when I slammed the door shut.

"I'm sorry?" I shrug my shoulders sheepishly before he runs up towards me looking vengeful, "Oh you are *so* going to pay for that." Liam throws me on the bed.

Laughter and chuckles shoot themselves out of both of us. We can't help but want to be near each other's presence.

Liam was on top of me, his hands around my waist once more it was like they were made to fit there, he tickles me as my eyes widen in genuine fear.

"Don't!" I say with a violent warning as he smiles, "Don't what?" He bends his head lower.

And there his hands went, tickling me as I start to squirm and break free, but it was not a possible outcome, "Liam!" I hack as he ends up laughing and rolling next to me.

"My nose needed vengeance." He mutters as I stare up at the ceiling waiting for my body to regulate and calm down.

I roll up, my arm holding up my head as it rested.

My eyes can't help up gaze at his breathtaking face, he was perfect in every way shape or form, had I just not realize it?

It was weird to say the least.

"What is it?" He asks as his hand comes up at the nape of my neck, "It's just weird." I swallow.

"How?"

I shake my head, "I hated you; I just did because well... Grayson and Anna hated each other, and I stand by my best friend." I reason.

"I stand by Grayson too." He adds as I laugh gently, "What I mean to say is... I hated everything about the Elite Four, in classes I hated how you used to interrupt me all the damn time."

Liam turns his head closer to mine, "Everyone hates being interrupted." And he made a great point of course but it was different.

"I hated the instant smirk on your stupid face, I hated that you were aware that girls threw themselves at you, you constantly belittle them."

Liam's eyes widen, "I don't belittle them!"

"You ignore them." I mutter as he nods, "Well I can't give all of them attention, that would be leading them on."

I roll my eyes at his response, while my hand couldn't help but play with his dark hair, "Why do you guys keep your hair longer?" I ask as he shakes his head.

"No... don't change the subject." He gives me a dirty look to continue as I smile, "It's nothing..."

Liam looks more alert than ever, "No tell me, I can take it."

I let my shyness shrivel up as my mouth opens, my hand pulls away from his face, "I hated how you constantly felt that you could simply turn your back away from me without a second glance."

Liam's face falls, he looks away from me to recompose himself before his eyes meet me again, "Raine, we aren't children anymore... if you gave me *your* attention now... fuck I'd be yours."

I pull away, "Why now?"

"Because the guy that you're talking about was freshman to junior in high school that wanted to bang chicks and leave them because he had no time for a relationship and just focused on hockey." He explains, "I can manage both now."

Was Liam somehow hinting at a relationship?

I scoff, "Liam don't bullshit me, you are still that playboy that everyone fucking says when I mention your name."

Liam laughs, "I'm not going to deny that people still preserve me as such," He runs his tongue along his lower lip and bit down, he looked frustrated.

"And if you think that you won't be able to look past the reviews about me then I don't know what we're doing." He gestures at the both of us.

"I can spend my whole life trying to convince you but all you would have to do is let me... and give me a chance."

How can I ever say no to him. His face speaks volume, and I

can't help but feel like my heart is melting, still I'm a bit hesitant to his approach.

"That's a whole lot to ask for, Charming." I pull away from him as he shakes his head, "I'm being serious Raine... I would do fucking *anything* for you to even think about it."

I send him a curious look, "Think about what?" I taunt him a bit.

He gives me a playful look, "You know what I mean."

"I don't know about that William; a lot of girls would be angry at me for finally taming you."

He narrows his eyes, "I am not tamed!" He settles down, "Just overcame by you."

I smile uncontrollably, like God didn't give me a choice in the matter and I sound fucking crazy. I shouldn't be feeling butterflies when he looks at me, I shouldn't be thinking about saving him a seat at the family table. I shouldn't be touching him like he's my boyfriend because, he's not.

He's not my anything. And it was pretty impossible for him to be any part of my life romantically. God, forbid I have a dinner with my maybe future husband.

I thin my lips as he takes his eyes away from me, "I know it isn't the best idea to get with me and I'm not even going to lie to you and say that I don't have the reputation you said."

He stands up, "But I can tell you how much you have made me speechless."

He looks at me like I was his lifeline, the only source of clean water during a war, and I can't help but think that when his eyes meet mine, my eyes look at him the same fucking way.

"There is no way *you* are saying that to me, Mr. Grayson Prince's right-hand man..." I gently tease him as he pulls out his phone, "I have a surprise for you."

I let my eyebrows wrinkle as he holds out his hand for me to take, almost like the simple gesture was sentimental and it meant something a lot more.

I roll my eyes before placing my hand on top of his as he pulls me out of the door, "Wait we have to be quiet!" I let out in a laughing, yet muffling tone.

I wasn't sure which direction this was going, but he wasn't rushing me in making a decision. I was rushing myself, because I have to.

But all I knew was that Liam Brookshire has completely blind-sided me and, I was happy about it.

CHAPTER 5

LIAM

Call me Gordan Ramsey because I was on fucking fire tonight, well I didn't cook... but I ordered people to cook and I tasted it, which is basically what Gordan Ramsey does nowadays... right?

Right by the beach, I had a table set out for us, candlelight dinner, music in the back, and a blanket draped over the sand with wine next to it.

I'm giving myself props due to the fact that I did set it up and I did think of the date... especially the finishing touch. I set a telescope next to the flowers I had bought her.

Margo walks in, complete awe all over her face, "No way you did this for me?" She whips her head back towards me with a bright smile.

It was like sunlight was created by her face when she smiled, she lit the whole fucking place up more than the candles did.

"Well yeah, I kinda like you." I say sheepishly as she runs up to me, wrapping her hands around my neck with a squeal.

"Do you like it?" I laugh as she pulls back with widen eyes.

"Do I like it?!" She gives me an unserious facial expression that answered my question.

"I love it!" She turns around, running up to the flowers, "Are these for me?!" She picks them up like she already knew the answer.

"No, the flowers are actually for the woman I met at the bar, two nights ago." I joke as she conducts me a still expression that made my body shake.

"I'm joking!" I place my hands up in the air to show my innocence.

"What are they?" She smells the bouquet, "I have never seen these before and trust me, I love flowers, and I receive them a lot."

"Modest much?" I roll my eyes as I walk closer to her.

She ignores me as I bend down to smell the bouquet, "It's a wild saffron crocus." I explain, "It's a flower that's been dated back around the mid-second millennium BC, grown in Crete and Attica... I was told you can only buy it in Greece."

Her jaw drops, "How much did this cost you!"

I laugh, "Don't worry about it." I pull her chair out, urging for her to take a seat. She stands there for a moment, looking at me in some sort of awe.

"Don't tell me you're going to leave our date when you haven't even had an appetizer yet." I give a playfully annoyed reaction as she smiles once more, taking her seat, I push her towards the table.

Once I take a seat, the appetizers come out and Margo looks at it like it's a treasure chest, "I've been starving."

"Good thing I'm a mind reader." I mutter as she laughs, taking her fork and stabbing the crab cake.

"Really..." She looks around, "You didn't do bad, Charming... I'll give props when deserved and this... is beautiful."

I can't help but smirk, "You're the breathtaking one."

And there goes her expressional face, turning bright red, she looks down at the flowers on the floor, her hand begins to shake, "You are." I stress as her face calms down to a neutral expression.

"What type of food do you like?" I ask as she ponders for a moment to think.

Her eyes light up as soon as she hits the nail on the head,

"Probably mac and cheese." I let my eyes squint as she bursts of laughing at my sour expression.

"What?!" She says with full defense.

I let my mouth drop lower, "You do understand that you live in the type of lifestyle that you can have caviar with the snap of your fingers, right?"

Margo rolls her eyes, twirling her fingers on the rim of her glass of champagne, "Well not the way Anna makes it, Adrianna is probably the best cook ever."

I highly doubt that. I make a killer chicken risotto if you ask me, but I guess only time can show her that I will make sure to cook her a damn good meal.

I will make her the best mac and cheese ever, straight from fucking scratch.

"How about you, what's your favorite food?"

I smile, and it's almost like she can see it coming, "You're pretty delicious." I lean closer as she blushingly looks at the ground, "You are so cringy." She voices.

I can't help but laugh, a genuine one, that I think everyone on the fucking island could hear.

"But seriously, what's your favorite food, I'm not the greatest cook but I can master one dish pretty well." She reassures me with a slanted smile.

"I'm a pretty picky eater." I shrug as her eyebrows narrow.

"Okay then... what don't you eat?" She adjusts the question to a better and easier understanding.

"I don't eat sushi, avocadoes, shrimp, olives, tofu, liver, beans, carrots, radish, brussels sprouts, raisins, turnips, and beats." I list off as she takes a moment to sit back.

"Well, that's a pretty long list." She judges as I shake my head playfully, "Okay which one are you not okay with?" She asks.

I shrug.

"Avocados are amazing!" She stresses as I shake my head unpleasingly.

"Are all of these foods you just don't like or are you allergic to some?" She asks with an insightful face.

"Why..." I lean back with a smirk, "Are you going to try and poison me, Raine?"

Margo moves closer, her eyes scanning mine with a challenge, "I think you want me to."

I do.

Her face comes to a halt as her nose brushes mine, "You can't hurt me unless your lips taste like kiwi." I mutter as she pulls away suddenly.

"I didn't know being allergic to kiwi was so common." She looks at me, with a puzzling look.

"I didn't think it was." I answer as she goes on her phone, "Yes, Adrianna is allergic too. You guys could be twins."

I laugh at how adorable she looked looking at her phone, the reflection mirrored her eyes like a luminating ocean blue.

"I guess we really could."

Her eyes lift from her screen to my face, her gaze softens like I blew a flame off from inside her, "I've never seen this side of you Charming, it's a good surprise I must say."

"Ask any questions you want honey, I'm all yours." I counter as she looks like she was about to be cozy in her seat.

"Favorite color?"

"Your eyes." I leer as she rolls her eyes once more.

"Favorite sport?" She smiles as I let my eyebrows wrinkle, "C'mon you know it's hockey."

"Favorite singer?"

"Taylor Swift." I let out before I had a moment to think about it. I slap my hand over my mouth as soon as it left my lips.

Margo's face dropped as I shudder, "I didn't say that."

"You so did." She counters with a wide grin.

"Whatever... you can't prove it to anyone." I let a smirk form on my face as she looked at me with disapproval.

"So, you really think you won't sing along to a song if I put one on." She looks at me with an evil twinkle in her eyes.

"I won't say." I pull my eyes away from hers, "But if you do, I ask that you play Taylor's Version."

"You're such a swiftie and I didn't know."

I narrow my eyes at her, "And you're the only one that knows so... keep it down." I whisper as she laughs coolly.

"Anyways..." She ponders for a second, "You and Amelia Burns during junior year of high school in the dining hall during midnight?"

I shake my head denying, "Never happened but she got popular so whatever."

"Sadie Andrews and you French kissing at church?"

I wink at her as she folds her arms together in front of herself.

"Madelyn Monroe, sex in the swimming pool during Ivy week?"

She got me there, but to be fair, Madelyn and I did like each other for some time before she told me she was more into women which in all honesty hurt me but, good for her for coming out.

"Truth." I muster as she looked about done.

"You and me, this summer?" She calms her breath as I look into her eyes, "Is this real?"

I nod, slowly but surely, I nod, "This is so real."

"But, what's the catch?" She sighs.

"What?"

She begins to look around, "You know... The cameras... this is a prank, right? I mean really Liam I can't believe that you just all of a sudden change your mind about relationships because of me."

I fidget in my seat, suddenly my hands sweating, and I wasn't sure if my face was showing the full nervous breakdown I was about to have.

"Margo." I mutter, feeling my hands shake, "There's no joke. There is no prank, no games. I can't describe the way I'm feeling because I've never felt it before. All I know is that I'm feeling this way because of you." I begin to tap my foot, as she didn't form a new face for me to decipher.

"Liam, you've known me for years... are you telling me that after one night, you're ready to just-- drop every girl you have connections with because of me?" She was asking in a way that she needs to hear a yes.

"It was a hell of a night." I counter as she forms a smile.

"Liam, if I say yes, I don't think you know what you're committing to." She says warily, "And if I do say yes, it is a commitment for both of us. I want a boyfriend, I want someone to want me and only me. I'm not doing the friends with benefits."

She runs out of breath and takes a pause, "I am a girlfriend girl. I am not a friends with benefits girl." She deepens her gaze, "I need you to know that."

My eyes widen, "I understand."

But I can tell that Margo was still unsure and I'm positive that she would always be wary of the idea of me and her.

Margo takes a look at the sky above us, a cold breeze brushing through.

"This." She gestures to the both of us.

"If this is going to happen, it's not just a summer fling, Charming."

She forms a ridged posture, "You're mine." She bellows in a sharp tone.

I can't help but form a smile, "I'm asking you to just... give me the benefit of the doubt Raine." I look deep into her eyes, "What's it going to take for you to trust me?"

She takes a second, "I don't know."

I nod, understanding, "I'll wait forever for you to let me know."

She grins... a small one but it was so visible, even if I wasn't supposed to see it... I did and then... just then, her walls break, they come crumbling down to the fucking ground.

She rolls her eyes, looking behind her, the telescope sits nicely ready to be used, "And who's bright idea was it to buy this?"

I stand up, laughing, holding out my hand for her to hold.

"It was all me." I bow, "No need for appreciation, I know I'm amazing." I reply as she pushes me off playfully.

Margo runs up to the telescope quickly, I stay back to admire her joyful laugh and her sunshine hair that stuck out at night.

"Look there's a shooting star!" She aligns her eye with the telescope looking through and pointing at the shooting light.

I check my watch seeing that the time was 11:11 P.M.

I approach her slowly, "It's 11:11," I mutter.

She thinks for a moment, before saying, "I wish you the best."

I send her a confusing expression, "You're supposed to make a wish for yourself, Raine." I explain as Margo shakes her head.

"You might do it that way... but every time someone sees an angel number and tells me, I always wish the person who told me the best." She looks down at the telescope once more.

This girl is it for me.

"But the shooting star, did you wish for anything?" She whips her head towards me with a shimmering smile.

"Yeah, I did."

She wiggles her eyebrow, "You want to tell me?"

I shake my head, "Well, Mrs. Wishing connoisseur, you out of everyone should know that you never tell people what you are wishing for... it might not come true."

Margo forms a smirk, "Okay Mr. Brookshire... lets both act like you didn't wish for me, we both know you're obsessed."

"Well, if you did wish for something, not pertaining to this..." I watched her as a smile fell on her lips.

I leer to myself, as she directs her attention back to the telescope.

"I would really like to own a cat one day." She answered.

"What would you name it?' I asked.

She looked up at the sky, then back down at me.

"Coco." She grinned.

I didn't know a lot of things... but one thing I'm sure about is that I am obsessed. There was no denying it.

CHAPTER 6

MARGO

It had been a month since I had met Liam out on the beach, I never thought such a small exchange could turn my entire summer around. Every time I had to meet up with other contending families that my parents want to marry me off to, Liam would secretly whisk me away.

The stolen kisses in secret, the looks that he would shower me with from a far. And every time he did, I felt guilt that I had been hiding such a big secret to my mother and father. That I had been falling hard for Liam.

He would take me out on dates, sneak up from the balcony, running around in the back paths in the rain, privately swimming by a beautiful water fall.

He even taught me how to backflip, and I taught him how to tan.

He would send me gifts, letters, bracelets, necklaces by making a waitress slip in my purse.

As more and more dates have gone by, I got used to his presence. I got used to the attention he gave me, the love and admiration I got back.

From the very first date he knew what he wanted and made sure to let me know.

He brought me flowers, he set up a fancy dinner and basically told me he wanted to be with me. He would do whatever it takes.

Don't blame me, I'm convinced that I had turned crazy because of him. Would this mean that I wouldn't have to get married to someone I didn't want to be with?

I mean it's Liam Brookshire for God's sake. His mother is practically made of money, and he can help with my family... surely... right?

But I would never ask him to help. I would never let him. Liam is a guy I like; I wouldn't use him. I hope my parents would understand that he means more to me than normal, as a girl that has come from wealth. I'm not going to give a sob story on that fact that men are attracted to not only me but my wealth.

I party like no other, maybe one person would beat me in the party aspect and that would be Verina.

I don't think she would ever pick a guy over having a good time. I was notorious for getting my friends in the best of the best clubs in the city.

To be fair my father does own half of the clubs in the country. At least my parents know my ways. Verina on the other hand, loves to party but has to show her family a different type of herself. Verina's family is the limelight of Hawthorne, politics type of famous.

I think she mentioned something about her father running for senator.

Now New York limelight and full-on country limelight would be Grayson Prince's family, same with Adrianna's father. At the end of the day, the majority of people that live in Hawthorne come from old money. Only a couple have gotten in from scholarships. It was extremely rare, but some people are just like that, smart and deserving.

Usually everything would be going great, but my family and I have reached mirky waters. The role of being a good daughter, I was supposed to help. But now what am I supposed to say.

"Hey mom, hey dad, I want to leave you both high and dry! I no longer want to get married and help you and the business."

There is nothing more to say other than the fact that I am a horrible daughter. Choosing a boy over my parents is not going to be an easy decision to make. It was a decision that I can never come back from.

I don't know if Liam would be worth it enough to lose the trust of my family. The fact that I am even thinking about this is making my head explode. The thought of picking a man over my family sickened me... only that I really want to pick Liam.

It's going to be a big risk that I'm not sure I am willing to make.

I have not moved in my chair for twenty minutes, contemplating on what I want to say. They had been having conversations in front of me and I found myself reaching the bottom of the wine bottle.

My parents with wide grins, they always looked pleased, but I didn't know if they looked happy enough to hear bad news and still be happy later.

"I am so glad you have asked us to go to dinner, we thought you were angry with us!" My father consulted as I took a gulp of my nervousness.

"I am so glad you have come to your senses and finally came home to us. We are so happy to tell that the Grimaldi family will be joining us for dinner and discuss your future possibility with Benjamin." My father added as I failed to say anything else.

"He is a great man, Maggie."

I flinched at his words. I certainly couldn't help it; I've always knew that I didn't want to marry by the arrangements of my parents. It wasn't what I wanted, I felt guilty. I have led them to believe that I did and that I wouldn't back down the moment it counted.

It counted now. And I wanted to back down. I'm horrible, because now it truly does count, and I am a complete asshole for keeping the secret.

"Mother." I breathe. "Father." I addressed calmly.

"Yes Maggie?" My father slowly chopped his steak and placed it in his mouth to devour.

I took a deep breath, "I don't want to marry."

So it goes, my mother's wine glass dropped to the floor, shattering, the purple liquid stained her suede heels as it continued to spread. My father's face turned bright red.

Silence settled in the room as my heart stopped for a moment. "What?" My mother's voice breaks. My father took a moment to pull back and took a calm breath.

I sat all fucking silent, scared that if I move something else might shatter. But my father's head turned, "What has caused you to change your mind?" He said it in a way where he physically looked pained to anything.

My lip quivered, "I've met someone else that I would really like to date," My hands shake, while my mother stands up.

"Is he marriage material?"

I shake my head, "I would like to experience a relationship first before marriage, mother."

She starts to cry, "No. You will stay away from him, and you will go to this dinner with Benjamin."

I couldn't feel it until now, but tears had gathered down my cheeks.

"Daddy?" My voice broke, my heart aching, breath hitching. I didn't have to say anything else because I knew that I didn't need to say anything for my father to understand that I needed him to take my side.

My father stood as well, breaking a barrier never crossed before, "You can date him, Maggie." He calmly suggested.

I looked at my disappointed mother, then back at my father, "But not under my fucking roof."

"You are not our daughter." My mother spat as I let my tears fall.

My whole world fell, my heart broke and yet the only person I wanted to console me was Liam.

Now. I had nowhere to go. I only had him.

"You..." I muttered, "You don't mean that..." I asked with a little bit of hope as my parents faces hadn't moved an inch.

"Margo, we can't even look at you."

They had never called me Margo before, until now.

CHAPTER 7

LIAM

I had gone insane, and I don't regret any of my decisions that I have made.

So why was I in front of *Cartier*?

I questioned myself a lot, but I somehow couldn't stop myself from going inside the store. I wasn't insane, I was going to buy her a gold bracelet, but not just a regular one that many people in our type of pay grade would purchase on a daily.

Something my aunt had made for the kings and queens of the world. I walked inside the gold rimmed out building, the floors were marbled and there was a diamond chandelier hanging from the high ceilings.

I stood around for a moment, looking around, there was an old woman that had a Birken bag made for her fucking dog. A couple teenage girls eyes wandered my way.

A few older ladies blocked my way to the rings, I wasn't stupid. I knew people knew who I am, a lot of people knew my family, and I wasn't naïve enough to know that I attract a lot of men and women.

I've always struggled to think that many people were interested in anything that I did, anything my friends had done. Our faces on newspapers, articles, new deals, new relationships, new reputations.

Even Grayson and Neil's lives are intruded upon. Chris keeps himself in the dark, he always had and I'm quite sure he will keep up the shy boy aesthetic.

He was a genius now that I've thought of it, girls always went crazy for that emo boy shit. We were more lowkey, but Margo's friends– the girls on the other hand are a whole different story, they lived for the paparazzi, they lived for the news outlets, front page on Vogue.

Personalities clash, we didn't get along. Grayson and Adrianna have hated each other since birth. But as his best friend I can't fail to mention that when he doesn't think she's looking, he admires her from a far. Grayson got injured his freshman year of high school, only a minor concussion, but Adrianna sent one of her minions to spy on him every practice to see if he got any better.

I've always rooted for them in some way, even if it was a long shot.

Verina has always been in her own world, and never noticed other world problems. Chris was far too busy to do anything other than work, go to school, and play hockey, his life was a fucking simulation.

Neil's family is too far up his ass to even let him date who he wants, or who he can converse with.

None of us or the girls would really interact unless Grayson decided to be a dick to Adrianna. Margo and I would stay away from each other, due to the fact that Adrianna and Grayson would always be near us, and they can't be near each other.

As I walked over to the bracelets, a man stood next to me, he looked far too happy and cheerful for me to like but, that didn't stop him from sparking a conversation with me.

"You shopping for a special girl?" He beamed.

I nodded.

The man's smile turned upside down, I just realized how rude

I was, and if Margo wants me to be a better man, I could definitely be a better man.

I take a heavy breath, "Yeah, I'm just trying to prove to a girl how much I want to change and be with her."

The man smiled, his cheeks turned bright red, "That's so sweet of you."

I began to look at the bracelets that were being displayed in front of me, but none of them really caught my eye.

"Can I please ask you a question?" I asked the worker that stood across from me.

They nodded; I rolled my eyes.

"Could I possibly ask if I can look at the summer collection by Odessa Brookshire?" I look up at the woman who then started to smirk at me.

"Yes, I will work on getting that out for you."

I looked around to wait, only to be invested at the fact that the man that stood next to me looking at rings was about my age, buying a fucking ring?

I couldn't hide my concerned face, I just had to ask.

"Are you getting engaged?" I blurted out as the man's head turned to face me.

He smiled widely, "Yes I am, my name is Benjamin Grimaldi."

My eyes narrowed at the familiar name. I placed my hand out in front of me.

I couldn't help but smirk, "You just looked about my age, so I was just confused–" He cuts me off.

"I'm twenty." He looked giddy as I tried not to show a soured expression.

Instead, I smiled thickly, "So you are my age... and looking to propose?" I questioned his methods, betting on the fact that he was about to scare his girl away.

Benjamin looked absolutely ecstatic, "Not looking... the proposal is already confirmed. I'm just reevaluating the rings, she's beautiful and amazing so I need the right ring."

I wanted to roll my eyes, yet he seemed so excited, I couldn't judge him, he seemed to have his whole life figured out.

"Who's the lucky girl?" I leaned back on the counter in front of us.

He laughed like we were best friends; he was lucky Grayson wasn't here, otherwise he would've been punted by now.

"Her name is Margo. Margo Hamilton."

Then. Just fucking then. He punched my gut when he said Margo's name. I turned around from him, something in my torso hurt, something I hadn't felt before.

I should call a fucking doctor. I felt fucking blindsided. He looked at me in a way of cockiness which made my blood change fucking temperature.

Benjamin fucking Grimaldi had something I wanted.

Something I fucking yearned for and I snapped quietly., my jaw hardened my eyes pierced, and I felt blood rush to my fucking head.

If I took one fucking lookback at him my anger would've ripped through me. My muscles rippled, until I closed both my fists, trying not to break his nose, but after I had come to the decision of making his nosebleed... I turned around.

I felt the same fucking thing in my stomach tug, a rip through my heart, I felt as though I couldn't breathe, I was suffocating, and I kept the brave face on.

Then the memories came rushing back to me.

Benjamin fucking Grimaldi. He's got to be fucking kidding. Brookshires and Grimaldi's don't get along. They never had and I can assure you right now they fucking won't.

It was a long time ago, but I didn't forget anything, his family killed my grandfather. It was all over the fucking news.

I couldn't help but smile, right at his face. A fucking evil smirk that I only saved for my enemies, "Well Benjamin I'm so glad that you are getting married. Hopefully the Brookshire's will be invited?"

I pull my sleeve back to check the time, "My family would love to congratulate you and your... *future wife.*"

Benjamin's smile depleted, looked fucking dead.

"Oh Liam, how are you... you know... since the incident?"

I scowled, "Great Benny, glad to know you are now engaged to Margo Hamilton, nevertheless."

He nodded, "She's a great woman." He straightened up his posture, as well as making should he fixed his tie.

I physically fidgeted, Margo was more than fucking great, she was– no is, the most down to earth woman on the fucking planet, the most jaw dropping girl that captured me. She's fucking everything.

He didn't know a damn thing about her, and I know I've never voiced on the fact that she was always on my mind but, to be fair, liking a girl that is associated with Adrianna Cassian was a fucking death wish.

Grayson would have my head on a damn stick. Besides, I wasn't an idiot, I knew that she was on the market at Hawthorne, every guy wanted a piece of her, thank God she has taste and was pretty selective.

But then again Grayson fucking Prince was right, she was playing me. Like a damn fiddle. She's fucking engaged.

"Mr. Brookshire?" I look back at the lady who came back with the summer collection. I stared at the beautiful bracelet.

"Do you still want the bracelet?" I look away from it, letting my eyes travel to Benjamin's God-awful fucking ring.

I didn't need to be Margo's fucking boyfriend to know that she would hate it.

I smiled thickly, "No. It's okay I've changed my mind."

I pulled away from the jewelry case, disappointed that I didn't have a ring at hand. But he fucking did.

Is this how it fucking felt to not get want I wanted? To try for something and have it right in the palm of my hands then dropping the ball when it really counted?

To get blindsided?

I should've known better, shouldn't I?

She's me after all. This was something I would pull, but I didn't. She did. And I didn't know why I was feeling like someone had stomped on my damn heart.

This was all new, I didn't know how to stop it. Ironically, Margo's name pops up on my phone and my heart sank even more. I couldn't possibly talk to her, not after this.

I felt anger ripple through my skin and bones. A piece of my heart ripped and tore apart. Her name disappeared, I clicked on her contact and the big red fucking letters that read, "BLOCK."

Grayson's name came up, "When are you coming home?" I let the question linger for a while.

"Hello Brookshire, are you going to answer or what?" Grayson muttered once more.

I took a second breath, "Tonight. I'm about to get in the jet."

Grayson took a second to answer, "What's wrong?" He asked as I shook my head in defeat. I wasn't sure if I should even tell him anything. If I did, I knew Grayson wouldn't fucking shut up about it. But that never stopped me anyway.

I paused, "I'll tell you tonight."

"Yay! We can have a girl's night!" Grayson beams as I roll my eyes.

"Maybe we can even get mani–" But before Grayson could even finish the sentence, I hung up immediately.

CHAPTER 8

MARGO

I had no idea where to go. Somehow, I ended up right in front of Liam's villa, he hadn't been answering any of my calls. I was worried about him, scared that maybe something happened.

After everything I had told my family, I wasn't sure if they would ever talk to me ever again, I had let them down tremendously.

I had never let down my family. And I felt fucking crazy, no guy ever makes me feel this way. The way Liam had made me feel. A way that made me want to be with him regularly, like talking to him felt like the world had stopped.

But I couldn't help but think that his whole pursuance was a joke. That is still is a sick joke. I don't think I could ever forgive him if it was. The trust would be broken, and I wouldn't know how to deal with it.

I felt like a lunatic, like I shouldn't even be thinking of all these negative things about Liam, he has been nothing but good to me for these past days.

But I still stayed thinking about Liam's ideal love life, I don't think I remembered one time he was at a party by himself. Without girls on either sides of him.

I shook off my hesitance to knock on the double doors. My breath shook as I coughed, there was no response.

I pushed the doors open, as they slide out in front of me, they greeted me with a cold harshness and a killer embrace.

"Liam?" I whispered.

I didn't know why I whispered, it wasn't like he was the one hiding our relationship, it was me, but not anymore.

I continued to walk behind, over to the open kitchen, only to be greeted by one of his maids.

"Excuse me, do you know where Liam is?" I smiled at her as she gave a sour expression as if she didn't know what I was talking about.

Maybe she only spoke Greek, I continued to look around and found empty drawers, empty rooms and no signs of Liam ever staying at this villa.

Had he left without telling me? I stood silent, it didn't matter whether he left or not, we were bound to go back eventually, I just hoped he would've told me before he bolted to Hawthorne.

Back to the college of privilege and parties. I turned a corner, only to slam into another woman, who looked shocked to see me, to be fair I committed a breaking and entering crime.

"Oh, I'm so sorry!" I apologized to her as she grinned back.

"It's okay darling, are you looking for Mr. Brookshire?" She asked as my heavy breathing stilled back to a calmed exhale.

"Yes, would you happen to know where he's gone?" I continued to look around, scanning the empty room.

"He left to go shopping, he mentioned that he would be home soon, but then asked someone to pick up all of his belongings and he hasn't come back since." She gave me a measly smile.

She looked at me like I was a crazy ass girlfriend, like I would hunt him down because he left without saying anything, but I wasn't.

I wasn't going to hunt him down, obviously, but it was inevitable that I would return home. I was not allowed to go back to my villa, I basically threw my parents under the bridge for a guy.

My only idea was to go home and hide in the guest house. I wouldn't be welcome to my actual house, not that I would even feel comfortable being in that humongous home.

I turned around to leave Liam's villa, that was a great way to end the summer in Greece.

LIAM

I finally arrived in New York, after a long ass flight I was ready to do my head in. I was never one to sit still for a long amount of time, I always fidgeted when my mother took me to church.

Speaking of mother, as my driver approached the front of my house another car was parked there. Only a black, Rolls-Royce Tail, which only meant that my mother was in the vicinity.

I never understand how she could just pop in anytime she wanted; her whole life was based on traveling. She was always on the move, Paris, Italy, London, and Milan. I guess I got that from her, not that I could really compare myself to anyone else, my father wasn't present. I knew nothing about him, I often wondered if I got some of his traits.

Not that I wasn't grateful for my mother, I love her very much and I know she had sacrificed a lot to give me this lavish life that I often take for granted.

I pull myself out of the car, leaving my driver a tip. A few of the help had rushed out the house the moment I stepped on the concrete.

I checked my phone to see if I got any text from my mother on why she possibly decided to stop by, only to get distracted that the time was 3:33 p.m.

I wondered how long it would take for Margo not to plague my brain anymore. Surely this crush wasn't going to last right?

I shook my head before continuing to walk through the big double door entrance, to be greeted by my mother's beautiful face.

Though I won't judge my mother in anyway shape or form, this was casually the first time I've seen her in sweatpants.

Call me flabbergasted.

"Mom?" I winced while calling her.

She whipped her head back to look at me, she had dark circles under her eyes like she hadn't slept in days, color drained from her skin like she had been hidden in a cave for months.

"William!" She shot up quickly and navigated her way over to my taunt body. She wrapped her lengthy arms around me with a hard squeeze.

She pulled away and took in the view of my very confused face, then she couldn't help but part my hair correctly.

"You should really get a haircut; I never understood the deal with having that type of hair style just because you play hockey." She muttered.

My mother has never been the greatest fan of me playing hockey, she didn't like the idea of me getting injured in anyway shape or form.

"Mother, what are you doing here exactly?" I craned my head slowly as she let go of my face before answering, "Can't I just drop in and see how my only son is doing?"

"You could..." I sheepishly muttered, "But you don't." I continued as she rolled her eyes.

"What are you talking about, I visit a lot of times!" She attempted to defend herself.

She failed miserably and even she knew that.

I sent over a scowl, "That didn't answer my first question." I began to open my luggage as she shoves me out of the way.

My mother suddenly starts to take all my clothes and fold them into nice and neat piles, "Oh you know I just think that we should spend time together, I am starting to realize that I don't have much time in this world and how much I would love to just hold my son in my arms and cradle him."

My eyebrows furrowed, "First and foremost, mom if you even try and pick me up to hold me, I will crush you. Second, knock off that bullshit about you having a midlife crisis, you aren't going to die, and third, when will we have time to hang out, I have school and hockey, you have your whole fashion empire to run in about the whole world."

"Oh Liam, lighten up. You are always so grouchy and over-worked." She groaned, "Live a little, you know when I was your age I was out clubbing and having fun with many people." She wiggled her brow.

I couldn't help but fold my arms in front of myself, "I was planning on partying tonight mother, get black out drunk and get high."

She ignored my comment, "Good, maybe you'll fail the drug test and get kicked from hockey."

I couldn't help but laugh at my mother's pouting face.

"I'm just staying her a for a while, since your stepfather and I are finalizing the divorce, I didn't want to stay with him in Phil-adelphia." She finally lets me in on her game plan.

I approached my mother with open arms and embrace her softly. I was happy she got divorced to that asshole, I never liked him, especially didn't like the way he would hit me when I was too little to fight back.

But now I'm stronger than ever, bigger than ever, I could snap him like a twig. I'm pretty sure my mother would've snapped him like a twig a long time ago if I told her about his abuse towards me.

I kiss the top of my mother's head, "You can stay as long as you want, just don't meddle in my love life or hockey."

She pushes me away; I almost fall over.

"Shut up! You don't mean that!" She looked mortified as I couldn't help but smirk, "No meddling!" I repeat as she looked amused.

"By not meddling... you mean there is something to meddle with, so there's a girl isn't there?" She looked like she just got gifted the most expensive thing in the universe.

I hesitated to answer, I wasn't sure if there was even an anything between me and Margo, I mean she's engaged for heaven's sake.

"I never said that." I muttered before I chose to check my phone to see if Neil had texted me. He hadn't, which forced me to actually converse with my mother.

"You never, *not* said that," She gleamed, "Who is she?!" She pried a bit more as I grew agitated by her attempts.

"She's a no one, I just had a bit of fun while I was away." I muttered quickly while angrily pulling my closet door open.

I turned to look at my mother's reflection on the mirror, obviously she looked devastated at my avoidance of the subject of my love life.

What she didn't know was my feeling or urgency to tell her everything about Margo, how much I adored her and how much I wanted to introduce them to each other. But how could I do that, when there really wasn't anything to tell.

My romance with Margo Hamilton was basically a fucking figment of my imagination.

I simply had to get over it.

CHAPTER 9

MARGO

There was absolutely nothing in my life that was going to my advantage. Liam hasn't spoken to me in a day. My parents have basically shunned me until further notice. Sure, I made it back to New York but to no home I was welcome to.

It would break my heart to ask Adrianna for a place to stay knowing that my explanation was fucking embarrassing.

I found Juliette's dad way too strict and scary, and lastly Verina's father would contact my father immediately and I was not about to let my parents know that I had asked for help.

So, camping out in my family's guest house was the last resort, which I know is far greater than living on the streets. But I had no clothes, only the ones on my back and the ones I brought back from my vacation.

I shouldn't sound so ungrateful, I'm very lucky to even be back in New York but it was the last that I would as my parents for help until they accept Liam and I's–– something.

I wasn't quite sure what we were, what we had or have. Did he still want me like I wanted him, did he still think about me like I thought of him?

It didn't matter, did it? If he did then he would return a fucking call or a text.

I didn't dwell much over it as the only thing that had caught my attention was the fact that my stomach had been grumbling like a god damn tired hound.

I was crossing my fingers before opening the pantry, only to spot boxed mac and cheese and a small box of granola bars.

Well at least there was food, it could help me lose a few pounds, I thought to myself before I shook my head.

No Margo, we don't think like that anymore.

I took a breather, I had hoped for a fucking distraction from this horrible day I had, only to be graced by the ring of my phone.

I was invited to a back to campus party that was being thrown by Maya Brown. Now this was something that I looked forward to, something fun to keep my mind off of Liam, my parents, and the Grimaldi.

I dumped the pieces of clothing I had in my suitcase on top of the bed in front of me, violently snatched the blue silk dress that Liam had gifted me one random night that I had yet to wear.

I had a feeling tonight would be the perfect night to wear it.

LIAM

I clearly didn't know how act or go too in depth about what I was feeling. I found myself riding my motorcycle to Dead Cullen's bar. I was desperate to speak with Christopher.

It was ironic really, he wasn't very active when it came to his love life, but then again, he was mysteriously wise. None of my best friends really could be deciphered by one look.

People could take a look at Grayson and infer that he was an overachiever when it came to hockey, but they have never really seen him sweat blood and tears to get where he was at our age, killing himself every night trying to be the best, but it was never enough for him... it still isn't.

Others could take a glance at Chris and probably spread the word that he didn't talk much or had shown any type of affection but undoubtedly would never talk about how he practically has to work three jobs to put food on the table and pay for his brother's chemotherapy without the help of his absent mother and nonexistent father. He also has to keep a scholarship to stay in Hawthorne, let alone get straight A's to stay on the hockey team.

Now I know damn well the world would take one mere gaze at Neil and make the hypothesis that because of his motorcycle and full sleeve tattoos he was always the one up to no good. Which in ways is correct but you really had to be either Grayson, Chris, or I to know that his whole family detests him for being different than them. Neil was one out of his five siblings who don't want anything to do with politics. This made him the black sheep of the family; he always went an extra mile to piss them off.

Me on the other hand, I feel like people glance at me and the rumors, the news, the suspicion, and the fucking "did you hears" were always right. I was black and white; you get what you see. There was nothing special about me, nothing to gloat about, I wasn't talented at anything so there was nothing to work my fucking bones for. You throw a fucking killer body, and millions of dollars in front of a black-haired dummy and that was me. I'm fucking average really, a fucking loser... maybe it was for the best that Margo was marrying Ben Grimaldi, lord knows he deserves her because I will never really deserve anybody.

Anyways, enough of over analyzing my friend's lives, they all have their own stories and how they want to tell it.

I finally arrived at the bar, parking behind the building. Sam, the security and or bouncer some might call him, nodded his head towards me.

"Hello Samuel."

"Brookshire," He addressed.

I smirked, "Someone should really tell you that shirt you're wearing is not your color." I let out a small laugh.

But Samuel, however, didn't look amused like I was. He gave me a snarky look, "Liam, I wonder who's going to let you know that you're fucking balding."

My eyes widened, both my hands land on top of my head, "You're fucking lying." I groaned with dread.

Sam only leered, "You never know, do you?"

I shook my head, I held out a $100 bill, and he rolled his eyes gladly taking it, "I was joking." He admitted as I couldn't help but grin.

"I know."

Sam chuckled as I took a peek inside, "Is Chris working?" I ask as he lifted one of his eyebrows, "He always is."

He yawned before letting me in, I walked in slowly. I looked around before my eyes zeroed in on Chris who was running around like a mad man, waiting tables.

His eyes caught mine, "What are you doing here, Brookshire?" He greeted me with a welcoming tone.

"I wanted to talk to you, have a little chat, curl your hair and you can paint my nails." I attempted at a joke, but he didn't look pleased.

"Can't you tell I'm busy," He paused to showcase the full bar of impatient people waiting for their food.

I roll my eyes at my friend, "It will only take a second, I promise." I lied through my teeth as he ignored me once more.

"What is it about?" He asked as I couldn't help but form a grin.

"My fun summer." I summarized as he looked like he wanted to throw a fucking plate directly on my head.

"I don't have time for your shit today, Brookshire." He warned as I couldn't help but whine, "You never have time for me anymore Chrissy- Bear!"

His eyes sliced through my soul for a fucking moment when the funny nickname escaped my mouth.

My eyes widened in fear I almost called Grayson to protect me from Chris's wrath at the end of his shift. But Chris's face calmed.

"Don't you have Gray to talk about that type of shit." He sounded annoyed, like he always did.

It was always annoyed or tired. Majorly both.

"Yes, but Grayson isn't answering me right now and it would be inappropriate to show up unannounced to his house." I grumbled.

Chris looked at me like I just slapped his dog– if he had a dog, before he spoke again, "Liam, may I remind you that you showed up here unannounced, how is that better than just going to Grayson."

He didn't ask that like a question but more of a complaint.

"I just wanted your advice on stuff!" I probed once more as he called out an order number to the cooks in the back.

"Fine, if you really want advice and your desperate for it, you can go talk to Finn, I just picked him up from hockey."

My eyes gleamed, "Really?!" I smiled at Chris who threw me his keys to the front door of his apartment.

"Sick!" I celebrate to myself.

But before I turned my body to walk to his apartment, I throw him a serious face, "You're taking off this weekend." I bellowed.

Chris shook his head, "You are joking right?" He stressed as I laughed.

"Chris, if you don't take off, I will buy every business you work for and pay you myself." I made sure to not lose the eye contact that I held with him.

He then looked at the floor in complete defeat, "You're not gonna leave me alone until I say yes?" He looked up just a little bit as I couldn't help but grin.

I throw him a cheeky look of success before I walked to the back of the bar, using his keys to unlock his door, I was welcomed by a small nook, a long and narrow staircase that led up to the kitchen.

I continued to walk up the stairs, each step creaked as I got up higher on the platform.

My eyes zeroed in on the tiny fridge that practically called my name, maybe Chris had something fun for my stomach to enjoy.

I approached the fridge, opening one door to be welcomed by the box full of Capri suns. Fruitpunch, my favorite.

I knew Chris's fridge wouldn't disappoint me. I looked around for the trash can to throw away the plastic that covered the straw before I pierced it through the juice bag.

But before I could enjoy my drink of delicacy, a small monster had made the great decision of jumping on my back which caused me to topple down to the floor.

"Stranger danger!" They screamed.

"Stranger danger!" They yelped even louder that made me wince.

I grunted, as I tried and look for my innocent Capri sun that was a victim of domestic violence. I turned around to make direct eye contact with Finn.

He gave a mischievous smile before I let my head slam down to the ground beneath me.

"You knew it was me." I growled as he got off my body.

"Of course, I knew it was you, I'm not stupid." Finn rolled his eyes before he helped me up from the ground.

I discovered my crushed Capri sun that laid on the tiled flooring. I stared at it longingly; I felt Finn's judgmental eyes that lingered on me.

"Aren't you rich?" He threw himself on top of their small sofa as I craned my head towards him.

"Just comfortable." I answered with a bitter tone as he folds his arms in front of himself.

"So rich." He shook his head, "Why don't you just buy a Capri sun with, I don't know... your own money." He continued as I picked up the plastic from the floor.

"It wouldn't be the same." I mutter before I threw it away.

Finn's one brow shot up, "Oh so taking a Capri sun from the one family that you know can't afford food already is better?"

Without hesitation, I opened up my wallet, throwing him a one-hundred-dollar bill with a frown.

"Pleasure doing business with you William Brookshire." He smiled while flaunting the bill towards me.

"You know you're too good at that." I shook my head before I took a seat right next to him.

"I have other talents that I can gain money from too." He winked as my eyes widened quickly.

"Like what?!" I shot up as he laughed hysterically, "Like listen to people's problems, I'm a really good listener, I think that's a talent."

I nodded as he tilted his head with concern, "Why are you looking so blue, Will?"

Finn has never failed to make anyone smile, he was right about a lot of things, especially about how much of a great listener he is.

We all took care of Finn in his early days, we would always rotate, take turns on watching over him.

Mondays and Tuesdays he was with Grayson.

Wednesdays and Thursdays he was with me.

Fridays, and Saturdays he would be with Chris and Sundays, he would always be with Neil.

He's, our kid.

"I think I like someone..." I let out with a scorned expression as his face flashed with light.

Like he never thought he would hear that from me, and honestly, I shocked myself as well.

"You what?" He leaned closer to me with eager ears.

I shook my head with a sly laugh, "Don't make me repeat it, I don't even know if I'm in the right state of mind."

Finn sprung out of the couch, "When did this happen?!"

"In Greece." I replied.

"In Greece?!" He screamed at the top of his lungs before I

threw a pillow at his face, which caused him to come crashing down.

He pulled his body up, with a scowled expression, "Okay, throw a pillow at the kid who has cancer."

I couldn't help but die at the fact that Finn accepted the fact that he's ill, he wanted nothing more than to have a normal kid's life but forced to be trapped at his apartment because Chris is afraid something bad will happen.

I couldn't blame him; Finn means a whole deal to us.

"Who is it?" He gave a reserved look, which made me twitch. By the face he was modeling I could tell this wasn't a subject that he would let go quietly.

I stayed silent, which made his eyes widen even more.

"Is... it... a... he?!"

My eyes turned into saucers, "Oh god no!" I flung my arms around as he laughed, "I don't know maybe you and Grayson finally..."

My saucer eyes quickly turned into narrowed ones, "Grayson and I are not––" I shook my head as Finn smiled warmly.

"Then who is it?" He asked again.

I whispered Margo's name, a little too quiet, he wrinkled his eyes to the fact that he knew that I did it on purpose.

"William no offense but no one here cares about who you screwed over the summer but me, which is the only person you are telling. The plant over there cannot decipher what you are saying." He let out as I squinted.

"It's Margo Hamilton." I finally let out as his scowl turned into a massive grin.

"Oh... Margo Hamilton you say?" He twirled around his kitchen for a moment before pulling out a bottle of Pepsi and placing it in front of me and him.

"We are gonna need something a lot stronger than Capri sun."

CHAPTER 10

MARGO

I was ready to tell Liam the whole truth. And I had really hoped that he wouldn't freak out that I basically chose him over my flesh and blood.

He needed to know that I was choosing him. Of course, this was all new to me, so I was basically clammy all the way over to the party.

Liam and I are similar, we both wouldn't pass up a party before classes started up again. So, I knew I was going to see him there.

I had been nothing more but understanding, maybe he could explain the sudden radio silence that I had received the past couple of days.

I wore a black mini skirt and a corset, and black Dior boots, since my whole outfit was black, the blonde is the only pop of color.

As I arrived at the front of the party, I couldn't help but start shaking at the thought of seeing Liam again, but here in Hawthorne.

It made it real. Which is all I wanted. All the boys, the playing around, the bars, it was done because I finally had Liam.

"Hey Hamilton!" I turned to see Maya running towards me with a tipsy look on her face, "You came!"

I looked around at the packed party, "Maya, I'm pretty sure everyone came."

"Not your posse. I'm pretty sure that you are the only one here from your clan."

"They were busy, I can assure you no one would want to miss this." Maya led me into her large house, everyone was drinking and selected few were making out.

There was a destined couch where I'm sure if you would take a seat, you would get an STD. I was thinking about beating around the bush to ask about Liam, but I didn't care anymore.

"Have you seen Brookshire around?" I ask.

"Why?" Her face looks confused for a second before a smirk creeps on her mouth, "You planning on getting laid?"

What was that supposed to mean... wait I knew exactly what it meant but was it true, even now?

"No, he just owes me a favor is all." I answered as Maya turned around to kiss a random stranger.

"I think I saw him by the guest bedroom, talking it up with the sophomore girls in that one sorority. A majority of them are puck bunnies, their main target left early tonight." She continued, "So they are all trying to feed on the next best thing."

I stayed to examine the face that Maya kissed, only to be shocked that it was Brooks. All color drained from his face when he saw me, knowing that I would one hundred percent tell Adrianna the next day.

I walked away before he could get a word in, running into a random man who looked at me like I was a golden ticket in a Charlie Chocolate Factory movie.

"Oh, hey Marie," He says in a slurry voice I gave a scorned look.

"It's Margo, and you're drunk." I comment before pushing his body over to a random group of people who smelled like throw up.

Somehow all I had to do was follow the stench of cheap Victoria Secret perfume to see the many girls flirting up a storm with Liam.

He looked like he was practically forcing himself to stay in each and every conversation. I took a deep breath, straightening my skirt out before I took a leap of faith and approached him.

It didn't take long for his eyes to navigate towards mine, it was like he was drawn to them, and even if he only had brown eyes, I liked the honey undertones.

He immediately straightened up, as I gave an iffy smile, call me a bit crazy but he looked like he wasn't thrilled to see me.

"Raine?" He whispered looking around a bit agitated.

I felt a pit in my stomach sink to the bottom of the floor the moment he grabbed by wrist and pulled me into one of the many empty rooms.

"Liam––," I spluttered as I ripped my hand away from his grasps.

"What are *you* doing *here*?" He huffed as I couldn't help but squint at the confusion that has now settled inside my head.

I would've thought that he would've been happy with the thought of me surprising him. Was that not what couples do?

Are we even a couple?

I couldn't help but just stare into his gloomy eyes, which have now lost all color of honey. They looked angry, betrayed, and hurt.

"Are you not happy to see me?" I gulped as he turned around and paced around the large room.

I wasn't aware that my breathing had turned into huffs and my hands were shaking. Like one wrong word from Liam could break me, I wasn't sure if that was normal.

I had to remember, I'm a very understanding person and all good couples communicate. So, all Liam and I had to do was talk it out.

Except suddenly, I couldn't find the courage of telling the truth about the engagement that I was supposed to undergo.

.   .   .

LIAM

The original plan was to forget about Margo and leave her and my feelings for her back in Greece. That was a bit challenging when she barely gave me 24 hours to forget her.

What the hell was I supposed to tell her? I was never good at facing my problems.

"You seem surprised to see me." She spoke again while I turned around, my eyes tried hard not to catch hers.

I contemplated more on how to respond.

"I don't get it, Liam did *I* do something wrong?" She mumbled as her face fell.

I had planned to walking into this room and ending it with her, coldly, harshly and do what I always did... which was break hearts.

I, however didn't count on the factor that I couldn't think straight by being in her presence, and I grew to fucking hate how her face looked when she was upset.

But it was a fucking lie. She played me. She lied to me. And I wanted her to say it to me now.

"I thought you weren't leaving until then." I perplexed, "I thought you had plans." I continued.

Margo took a step forward, "Yeah we were supposed to hang out by the beach, but you ran to New York."

"I heard you had a family dinner, so I thought the plans were cancelled." I mutter as she took a paused hesitation.

I could see fear settle in her eyes, and yet she continued to avoid the subject.

Every step that she took closer to me, I saw Ben's fucking face. His smug face at the jewelry shop.

I took a look to her hand. No ring.

Maybe she decided to play me before continuing on. One more night with freedom before being fucking tied down.

Fuck. Why did she have to pick me?

"You know what Liam, I don't know what's going on with you, what happened from the day on the beach to now?" She exclaimed while her hands flew up to the air.

"Margo, don't do this to me." I ran my hand through my hair.

"Do what?" She shook her head.

I couldn't believe what I was hearing. Margo really wasn't about to tell me about her engagement. She really thought I could be fooled.

"You really have nothing to tell me?" I questioned her as she swallowed down the lies that were about to leave her mouth.

"No." She muttered.

Which was the only fucking word I needed to hear to confirm my thoughts that Margo Hamilton was nothing but a lying, manipulative, and desperate girl that picked the wrong guy to have a last fuck with before she gets strapped down.

She certainly had me in the first half, but it was a lie.

All of it.

And two can play it this game.

I took a moment to look at her up and down, my mouth curving up into a charming smile that I would flash any girl that I wanted.

"Sorry Raine," I began, "I totally broke my phone on the way to the jet, my mom called me before I left Greece, and she said it was an emergency. I was gonna tell you, but I didn't know how to, if you haven't told your parents about us." I added while shaking my head in dismay.

"Telling my parents will take a while." She addressed as I nodded.

I wonder fucking why.

She takes another breath before wrapping her arms around me, I sunk into the embrace, "What's the hug for?" I asked.

She looked up at me like I was her Lord and savior.

"I've just had a long day and I just wanted to see you." She sluggishly responded as I stayed silent.

I bet.

"What happened?" I pried as she peered up at me with glossy eyes, "Nothing that really concerns you." She wearily let out.

Another lie.

Margo Hamilton, I will make you wish that you had never talked to me at the beach.

I promise you that.

CHAPTER 11

MARGO

Liam held me like I've never been held before, his hand caressed the back of my head. Would it be too much for me to wish that I could stay in his embrace forever? Feeling protected?

"Can you spend the night with me?" I asked in a whispered tone. There was a deep pause before he spoke once more.

"Of course, Raine." He said softly, before kissing the top of my head.

He took my hand and led me to the large bed that was beautifully made.

Liam Brookshire looked absolutely handsome, and he was all mine.

He pulled away from me for a second before sitting on the couch, away from the bed, "You don't want to lay with me?" I laughed with a teasing tone.

Liam's face marled, he looked like there were an array of emotions that were trapped inside his gorgeous brain.

I tilted my head in a bit of a worry, did he not find me attractive anymore? Was the fire gone?

I mean, boys practically flew to the bed with me... which

sounded awful, but it was what I was used to. There were never good connections, just simply sex.

"I can't lay on that bed with you, while you're wearing *that*, Margo." He looked at me, up and down.

Liam sent shivers up my spine; he had never asked for me to do anything I didn't want all summer. I originally thought it was because he was not attracted to me. However, I'm not an idiot, I could see it on his face.

All summer he had never let go of that look on his face. The sparkle and need in his eyes were never hidden from my gaze.

Even now he's still fighting it.

He's still fighting the urge to want me.

"I could fight any man who looked at you tonight, Margo. God fucking trust me I would've, but I can't fight myself." Liam stammered.

"It's a losing battle." He trailed off.

I smiled to myself before I got up, I walked slowly over to him as he leaned back, which made enough room for me to sit on his lap.

Which I did, Liam looked at the door, "There are people outside." He mumbled while he ran his cold hands up my back, touching my bear skin.

I closed my eyes; euphoria flooded my bloodstream.

"I don't care. I want you," I let the words slip right out of my mouth, which was all the green light he needed before his mouth found my neck.

Liam's hand crept up my chest, squeezing. I let out a moan that I didn't expect.

"Fuck, Raine." He hoarsely groaned.

Liam's scent engulfed my nose, his calloused hands electrified my body. It was like I wanted to be consumed by him, which was a new feeling for me.

I never got horny or wet from the previous men that I dated or hooked up with. It was always me faking an orgasm or getting them off instead.

"What are you wearing?" He asked while taking a peak of my top's tag. Before I could answer, Liam bunched my hair together and tilted my head up to make eye contact with him.

"Chanel?" He answered his own question.

A moment of silence broke as he ripped my top open with his large hands, which made me release a large gasp.

"You're breathtaking, Raine." He whispered hoarsely.

I felt my center pulse, I'm pretty sure he could too. Liam pulled me up from his lap, only to pull me back towards him again.

He completely changed my position without me noticing, I was now straddling him.

My top ripped further, my breast spilled out and were now fully visible. He took a moment and cherished them and a second later he let out a shaky breath.

"Shit." He grumbled, before pulling me into his mouth.

Liam thoroughly sucked each of my nipples, making me groan as he let his tongue do Gods work. My mind couldn't help but explore the other options he could put his mouth to work on.

Without thinking I started to rock forward and backward, which made him pause on his tongue's assault on my tits.

My nails couldn't help but dig on his back as he moaned on the nape of my neck, "Hamilton, don't do that," He sternly warned.

I laughed and rocked faster, in which he picked me up, only to slam me down, on my back.

"You think that's funny?" He shook his head and took another moment to admire me before he got on his knees.

Holy mother of Jesus.

Liam placed his hands on both my thighs, I pulled away from him, but his hands gripped harder which kept me fastened to the couch.

"You're already soaked, Raine." I took a heavy breath out, shocked because that had never happened before.

I lifted my head up slightly and looked down. My eyes met with Liam's face in between *my* legs.

He looked about ready to ravish me, the simple look on his face was enough for me to be on the brink of an orgasm, and he hadn't even touched me there.

Once he does, I could already feel it coming.

My core tightened as he leaned closer to my pussy, I could feel his mouth so close, his nose inhaled the scent, did he think I smelled?

"Dripping wet for me, baby?" He whispered as I opened my mouth to say something.

My words didn't have time to escape before I jolted, his lips were on my clit, I needed to grab something to resist from the release that he was about to provide for me.

I reached for Liam's hair, which ended up being a mistake as it only pulled him in closer, his tongue explored inside of me. I couldn't help but just enjoy it and moan out his name.

"God baby, you taste so fucking good." He came up for a second for air before continuing his sentence.

"You taste like mine."

Liam's left hand finds my left breast, caressing as I felt my mound tighten as his tongue continued to work, "Liam–– wait–– no–– fuck." I lifted away from him, before he hooked his arms on both of my legs, slamming me closer to his mouth.

I gasped as his lips sucked, slurped, kissed, licked my clit, sending me to the highest point in Heaven. I tried to pull away once more, but his strong grip wouldn't let me budge whatsoever.

My orgasm felt like it continued on forever, but once I calmed down, Liam plunges two fingers inside me, causing me to jump.

He brings his fingers to my mouth, "Good job baby, taste yourself." He whispered as I took his fingers into my mouth without question.

Liam looked at me with a grin on his face, like there was a menacing event to come soon.

"Liam–– I don't think I can take another orgasm." I laid back as he laughs at my tired expression.

"Five times." He blankly stated.

"What?" I questioned as his hands pulled away from me and started to unbuckle is belt.

"We aren't stopping until you come five times." He asserted as my eyes widened.

There was absolutely no way that was possible, was it?

But I also didn't think it was possible for me to achieve an orgasm by a man and not just my own finger or vibrator.

Liam's belt unbuckled and clanked on the ground as he unzipped his jeans. I heard rustling and a condom wrapper being ripped opened.

I sat up to look, only wishing I hadn't.

Liam Brookshire was simply not average sized. I turned bright red; I could've felt my skin heat up at the thought of him inside me.

"Liam, I can't take that–– that simply wouldn't fit inside me." I abruptly specified as he shook his head, he lined himself up with my pussy.

"You can take it." He concluded, before slamming into me suddenly.

I gasped loudly throwing my head back like I had just been stabbed, he slammed forward and began thrusting hard and deep. Liam gripped my waist, which surely created bruises. He drove in faster, harder; my eyes began to roll back.

I had never felt anything so good in my whole life. My blood thundered through my veins; his arms flexed as I felt the room close in.

"Jesus," Liam gritted out, "Fuck Raine, I can feel every inch of you." He placed his head on top of mine.

"Me too, Charming." I groaned louder, "You're so big, Liam don't stop." I whisper as he slammed harder into me.

"The fuck that's happening." He rolled his hips upward, hitting my g-spot.

I felt my core tighten once more, squeezing him as he entered me in and out. My body feeling everything he had done to me.

I cried out as I orgasmed, Liam placed his hand on top of my mouth to quiet me down as he kissed my temple, "Baby you have to be quiet, there are people outside, remember?"

I close my eyes in ecstasy.

"Third orgasm." He leaned closer to my ear to whisper, "Let's make a fourth okay Raine?"

He pounded into me harsher, the force of his thrusts shook the couch. My tits hardened and Liam saw this opportunity to suck at them again.

Liam banged me like, he had been craving it for a long time, I could feel the need and want. He didn't even breathe, he just thrusted and rode the wave of pleasure.

"Margo." He stammered as I held my shaky breath in, tears formed in my eyes from the overwhelming amount of pleasure.

I stretched around him, my head hit the back of the couch repeatedly, as Liam reared up and slid deeper inside of me, his hands held me and positioned me to go even deeper inside.

I felt my legs start to shake uncontrollably, like with every time he slammed into my g-spot he was hitting me closer to the edge.

Liam took his hands and placed my legs closer to himself, they hooked behind his back, opening me further, "How close are you baby?" He groaned as I couldn't even speak.

"Close." I whimpered.

Liam groaned as he picked me up fully, flipping me over like a pillow. My face was facing away from him, and he placed me in a doggystyle position.

He gathered all my hair, and pulled back, my back arched as his dick entered me even deeper, I moan.

"So beautiful," He murmured, "So fucking mine."

I felt my body grew weaker as he pounded me harder, "Only me, Margo. No one else can ever have you like this."

I closed my eyes.

No one has ever had me. Not like you.

Liam gathered my wrists behind my back, he drove in deeper thrusting inside in a forceful lunge that took my breath away, my pussy started to quiver and tingle.

My arousal buzzed through my veins, as my legs shook at the uncontrollable wave of pleasure I was receiving.

"I'm coming--" I moan as he pulled my hair back further, fucking me into oblivion. I squeeze him as I felt his body harden, he was starting to falter.

I came back from my high, feeling very empowered and wanting to please him instead.

"Fourth." He remarked as I got up from the couch.

"I think you are forgetting that you need one more, Raine." He advertised as I shook my head.

I pushed Liam to sit on the couch, "Trust me I'm not forgetting."

I slowly got on top of him, my legs still sore and shaky from former events.

"Oh, fuck baby, are you going to ride me?" He asked as he pushed pieces of my hair away from my face.

Well attempt to... I've never done this before. But I wasn't about to tell him that.

I lifted myself from him, as his eyes glistened, I reached down to fist his cock, to position him at my entrance he nudged my opening.

I lowered myself on his erection as he threw his head back in pleasure. Liam curled his fingers around my hips and helped me push further down.

I sighed as I took him all the way in, I felt the sensation of fullness as he pulled my body closer to suck on my neck.

He didn't seem to mind at how slow I was going. He pulled away to look into my eyes, on the surface it was tension, but deeper I saw his light.

William Brookshire might have been the most beautiful man I have ever laid my eyes on.

He was all mine.

I rose up and slammed down, my head was thrown back and my hair streamed down my back. Liam's hand find itself back to my clit, rubbing it as I slid up and down more passionately every second.

He angles his hips a certain way that made me cry, my mouth wide open as a scream came out. Liam had flipped me, so I was now being fucked into the cushions. My legs shook uncontrollably, and liquid pooled beneath me.

Liam continued to fuck me relentlessly, his hand found my mouth to shut me up, and his other hand rubbed my clit even more as he slammed into me continuously.

Liam had made me come so hard, I squirted. His thrust had become messy, like he was on the brink of his orgasm.

He pounded harder as I lifted my hips to meet with his. His body jerked and for a moment he paused to close his eyes. He lazily thrusted inside of me to ride out his orgasm.

We were both out of breath, tired and succumbed. He collapsed next to me, giving me a passionate kiss.

I faced him with a warm smile.

"I'm so glad we waited." I muttered softly as I touched his face with my shaky hand.

Liam didn't say anything. He only closed his eyes and mumbled something I couldn't understand.

But I was too tired to pry, so I closed mine too.

CHAPTER 12

LIAM

I woke up to a warm body next to mine. I couldn't help but admire Margo's gleaming features before getting up to leave. I didn't want our first night to be like that, never imagined that it would've ended that way.

Good thing it was the last time it was ever going to happen. I truly hoped that she finds the most amazing sex ever with Benjamin.

Even though I could've probably inferred that he was going to be a steady log the entire time. I felt bad for her, in every way possible.

I got up from the bed as she rustled around, her eyes still remained closed as I gathered all of my clothing that was thrown to the floor last night.

I had remembered that I did however rip her whole top apart to admire her amazing body, so I did the gentleman thing and left her my shirt to wear.

Once I got dressed, I checked by phone to see that alarming amount of calls I had received from not only Grayson, but my mother.

The two most meddling people in my entire life.

I take a look back at Margo, wondering if she deserved this

treatment from me, and she did. How could someone lie like that?

It hurt me to leave her here all by herself, it hurt to know that she was never really planning on being with me. It tore me apart to know there was another guy in the damn picture.

It hurt to know I was played in broad fucking daylight.

I turned around and resisted the urge to wake her up and take her out for a coffee.

Instead, I took a scan outside for people who were still partying. I check the clock on my phone to notice it was only 3:00 A.M.

My phone began to ring once more, I take a look at the incoming call and see that it was from Grayson. I couldn't help but roll my eyes before answering.

"Yes, my love?" I flirtatiously muttered as I could hear his rough sigh.

"Are you home right now?" He frantically asked as I paused in confusion.

I leave the noise-filled party and got on my motorcycle to start making my way back to my house.

"I will be in a bit." I said as I could hear Grayson's car engine roar through the phone.

"What's wrong?" I asked before pulling out of Maya's driveway.

"I just need to be away from my family right now." Grayson mumbled as I took a small breath, "Okay I'll meet up at my house in fifteen."

Grayson never showed anyone his weakside, not even Chris or Neil. I felt we were always that way, we liked to keep our problems to ourselves.

His family was something that he never wanted to talk about. His mother was someone he never spoke about, how he always knew that Sara wasn't his real mother.

Don't get me wrong, she was an angel to Grayson in ways that only God himself could've sent his way. But there was still a really big line and border when it came to feeling like he was a part of their family.

He was just the half-brother in his eyes.

His mother was the other woman, and he was the child that had to go above and beyond for his father's approval.

Even if it broke and tore him down every day, he wanted nothing more.

Once in high school, Grayson had broken his arm during his private training for hockey, his father and Sara were present during one of the games. Grayson had to make sure he put a brave face on and play with his absolute hardest.

Only when that last buzzer rang and we won, Grayson had collapsed on the ice. His father just walked out of the arena, embarrassed that his son was such a failure.

Sara was the one that ran on the ice to take care of Grayson. I would never forget the look on Grayson's face when the color of his skin went pale. The bone in his arm had fractured even more that it tore his skin and was now visible to the naked eye.

He didn't scream, he never showed signs of pain, but he laid there in Sara's hands, bleeding out on the arena.

I never remembered much after that day; we never spoke of it again.

I finally had arrived at my house; I spotted Grayson's car parked in the driveway. He looked dazed and unreachable, before I knocked on his illegally tinted windows.

"Yo Gray!" I banged on his window, "You going to stay there forever, or are you going to get out of the car?" I kept knock on his car as he visibly got more irritated.

"Yeah." He grumbled while he stepped out of the car.

"You can stay here for as long as you need." I smiled at him as he just nodded with an out of the world look expression.

He goes on to tell me that he only wished to say in my house for a day or two, which I didn't really care. My mom had a room just for him made a long time ago.

I looked behind Grayson to see a pack of condoms, "You

spend the day with Emma?" I guided him towards my house as he rolled his eyes, "Why would I spend the whole day with Emma?" He sneered.

"Right... I forget you're a fuck boy." I mutter as he paused really quickly.

"Says you."

"You know maybe I thought you were going to settle. She seems really into you." I made a point as he rummaged through my fridge for a bottle of water.

"A lot of girls are into me." He scoffed, "What makes this one any different?"

I couldn't really answer his question since my head had been scrambled from the whole week with Margo.

"No one is the same as August." He continued on.

I never fucking liked August, I had a bad feeling about her, but I knew I couldn't tell my best friend that information.

"Has she reached out?" I asked faking my entertainment on the whole August subject.

"No." He said with a blank expression.

A moment of silence passed.

"But have you...?" I asked slowly as the smile from his face extinguished.

"I'm going to, tomorrow, after the game. I'm going to win her back." He sounded so happy with himself I could only predict the shit hitting the fan.

"I'll do whatever I can to get her back." He continued on.

I smile at my best friend, being supportive was something I could always provide for him.

"I know you guys never really liked her..." He addressed as I thinned my lips.

DING DING DING.

"We don't like her, she leached onto you because of your money, and she just ended everything for no fucking reason. You ended up in the dump because of that." I narrowed my eyes at him to show my seriousness.

"She was there for me with my whole family situation." He countered as I rolled my eyes. He kept going on and on about how much he wanted her back I was starting to gag.

Grayson started to see my very enthused face before he changed the subject, "But enough talk about me, let's talk about you."

"What about me?" I couldn't help but sound fucking nervous.

He narrowed his eyebrows, "Been hanging out with Margo, haven't you?" He smirked, "Don't think I haven't heard."

It seriously just happened an hour ago, nothing in Hawthorne could stay secret for under an hour.

But with the menaced look on his face, he looked like he was sniffing for trouble, and I didn't think that I was going to like what was about to come out of his mouth next.

"Keep me and her out of your stupid need for rivalry with Adrianna." I had made sure to say it in a way he knew I meant what I said.

"I'm serious." I turned away from him as he looked gob smacked.

"Wait, you don't actually like her, do you?" He sarcastically asked as I chucked a pillow at his face.

"Maybe I do." He threw the pillow back.

"You know you can do whatever you want." He paused, "Or whoever you want... but Adrianna will make Margo end whatever it is you two are doing."

There was no need for Adrianna to do that. I made sure it was the end tonight.

But why not have some fun for a little and confuse my best friend?

"I know what you're doing and it's not going to work." I grumbled.

"I don't know what you're talking about."

"Listen." I made a serious face as his eyes never left mine,

"Margo made my fucking summer in Europe unforgettable." I walked closer.

"We were together the whole fucking time, and it almost felt like maybe we could work as a couple here too. So, you and Adrianna are not messing this up."

Grayson looked mortified as well as shocked, "You're joking right?"

My satisfaction of the situation had been reached.

"Of course." I rolled my eyes, "Besides, you know I hate clingy girls. She was basically, up my ass the whole fucking time. it pissed me off."

Though it felt like venom that poured out of my mouth when I lied.

"There's my boy. For a moment there, I thought you were tamed." Grayson laughed softly, but still had the awkward tension.

He didn't looked convinced enough, I didn't even convince myself.

"I think I just stuck around because she's honestly a good lay. Fucking rocking body. She can take it well." I blew out a cloud of smoke from his cigarette.

I felt like I had betrayed Margo just by telling Grayson I had slept with her, but it wasn't my fault. This wasn't how it was supposed to go.

I took a look at Grayson's face once more to see if he had believed me now. That Margo was nothing more than just a summer fling.

He laughs, "You're a dick."

CHAPTER 13

MARGO

I felt like a freight train had slammed into me multiple times until it finally broke. My body was a living corpse, and each step I took I felt a part of me decayed.

Liam and I officially had slept together, and it was the best thing in the entirety of my sexual life. However, he was nowhere to be found in the morning. I only suspected that he had somewhere important he had to take care of.

I was never the clingy type of person, but I couldn't help but want to be near him every second of everyday.

I woke up surprisingly early to get home and take a well needed shower. I needed to rinse every dirty thing that was muttered in my ear last night.

As I laid in my bathtub, I couldn't help but just imagine Liam's hands all over my body once more. Until now I can't stop thinking about how he would take me in one of these dressing rooms in the mall and get his way with me.

I'm partly disappointed at the fact that I'm not the only woman that's ever had him this way.

I hadn't noticed that I had been entranced the entire fifteen minutes of my shopping in Victoria's Secret. Only my phone's irritatingly buzzing noise jolted me a way from my delusions.

Verina's name popped up, I could only imagine the news about Liam and I's rendezvous last night had spread like a wildfire.

"Hey V--," I beamed before I got interrupted by my worst fear herself.

"--Margo are you out of your *mind!*" Adrianna yelled as I squinted and pulled the phone away from my eardrums.

I had a tad feeling that she's heard about Liam and me.

I smile thickly as I walk closer to their location, since I was already at the mall near them.

I needed retail therapy.

"Well, good morning to you too, Anna!" I greeted as she stayed silent on the other line.

"Margo." She addressed calmly.

"Adrianna..." I asked slowly as I heard her take a loud breath to herself.

"Please tell me you did not conspire with the enemy and share a bed with the sleazeball, Brookshire." I could hear the hope and patience that her voice held.

I had finally arrived at the dressing room they had all gathered around. I hung up and continued the conversation in person.

"Me? With Liam?" I laughed hysterically, "Over my Christian Louboutin collection I would jump in a bed with that dick."

I couldn't lie to them. They could see it on my face.

"Don't lie to me, Margo Raine Hamilton." Adrianna stepped up and did not break eye contact.

It was like an interrogation, I looked behind her to see Verina holding up her phone, pictures of Liam and I had surfaced on the internet.

Well fuck, now I definitely couldn't lie.

I folded my hands together, my eyes squinted, "It was once! It was last night, and we were fooling around at Maya's party."

There was one thing that each of us knew from one another, and it was that we could never lie to each other.

We could certainly try but it would always end in defeat, I mean what would I have to lie about anyways?

Liam and I were going to be official, and I couldn't wait to tell everyone that I was his. He was mine. I felt so giddy I might die.

With him by my side, how could I possibly want anything more?

But oh boy... was that feeling short lived.

The next day...

I was always up earlier than anyone else. It was the first day back and I felt incredible, I turned to reach for my phone which was laid on top of my nightstand.

My parents had returned, and I hadn't gone back to them, I still slept in the guesthouse. For as long as I could remember, my parents had been noble. They always had done what was right and never hurt a single soul.

I figured that was the reason we went bankrupt in a way, my father paid everyone with good prices, and we stopped making profit from it. He was never in it for the money at first.

But like every human ever, we started getting used to the wealth. It was more uncommon not to have money living in Hawthorne.

I was taught never to be selfish. And for the longest time, I wasn't. The day I said no to my parents, the day I told them I wanted to marry for love was the first selfish decision I had ever made in my life.

I think it broke my heart more to know that I broke theirs. My goal was never to cause pain. Before I met Liam, I was for sure on board to get married for my parents sake.

But... have you ever had someone change your life in ways that are unspoken?

Have you ever met someone who saw life the same way you

did, and you not only fell in love with them as a whole… but their soul?

I had fallen in a deep hole of red and light.

As I got ready, I couldn't help but stare at my phone, Liam's name popped up, and I couldn't hide the smile that was emerging from my face.

"Good morning Raine," Liam uttered in his still sleepy voice that I had fallen for.

"Morning Charming," I replied as I heard his husky laugh, "How was your night baby?" He continued as I shook my head.

"Tiring." I took a breath, "I wish you were here, I missed you." I muttered as I could practically feel my heart jump out of my chest.

"I'm sorry Raine, Grayson needed me yesterday. I couldn't leave him." He answered quickly.

"It's okay Brookshire, I admire you for caring about him. I didn't know you two were such softies." I poked fun at the two best friends.

"He's my best friend, I would do anything for him." He replied as Adrianna popped in the back of my mind.

They were going to kill both of us.

"You know Anna and Prince are gonna kill us, right?" I brought up as he laughed once more.

"They can hate each other all they want Raine, but you and I have nothing to do with them. No one does. It's just you and me, sunshine." He assured.

I couldn't help but smile at his words. Only Liam could reassure me and tell me everything was going to be okay. He was right, we shouldn't care what anyone would say.

It was just us.

"I can't wait to see you in school." I addressed as he went silent.

I could feel my cheek redden from the embarrassment that has lingered on my body. Never in my life had I ever told a man I was excited to see him, but when I saw Liam, I felt actual lightning bolts strike my body.

There was a long pause.

"Liam...?" I asked to see if he was still there.

"I gotta go--" I heard his voice was rushed.

"Are you okay, did I say something wrong?" I asked with a shaky voice.

"No, you're fine. I just have to go." He sternly grumbled before he hung up the phone suddenly.

I turned back to look at the time, my eyes widened at the idea of arriving late to class, so I rushed into the shower and rushed into putting my uniform on. When I got downstairs, I realized that since I am officially cut off from my parents, I didn't have a ride to Hawthorne University.

No, I was not planning on getting inside a cab.

No, I was not planning on calling Liam or Adrianna.

I looked down at my Jimmy Choos and let out an adorned sigh, walking it is.

So, I walked until I got to the front of the building, my shoes had cuffs that I dreaded, and I felt my eyes start to water because of the great pain it took me to get here.

But my shoes were already ruined, I wasn't about to ruin my make up as well. Instead, a bunch of the freshmen were already waiting around the pit.

Eager for approval, and eager for the status they looked like they were ready to do just about anything I would ask them to do.

One being cleaning my heels before Adrianna got here. Before Liam catches me crying because of blisters and mascara dripping down my face.

I sat on the table, I gave one look to the two freshman, and I didn't even need to ask until they got down and started cleaning my heels.

Verina and Juliette came out of the students center with smiles on their faces, before sitting next to me. Juliette paid no mind to me, but Verina couldn't help her disgusted expression.

"What the hell happened to you?" She muttered as I rolled my eyes.

"Nothing is wrong with wanting to get some exercise and walking to school." I laughed as they both looked at me with weird faces.

"Yeah okay, you act like you're poor you can afford a limo, Margo." Juliette made a point without lifting her eyes from the page she was on.

"Again. Nothing is wrong with a bit of exercise." I repeated as Adrianna's limo pulled up.

"Well, there you are!" Verina yelled as Adrianna began to walk up to us with a scowled look on her face, "Well, here I am."

Adrianna's eyes zeroed directly on Amara, the one freshman wearing boots with her uniform. I could already feel the ridicule and disgust Adrianna was about to spew off.

As much as we understood it to be mean, we never cared. People looked up to us because of our wealth, our influence and our thoughts. As much as it was an unlikeable trait, we didn't care what anyone else thought about us. We cared about what the founding families thought.

A motorcycle arrived at the parking lot, and previous years, I would roll my eyes at the dark-haired beauty with the minimal tattoos.

Liam arrived like that every day. He would arrive with Neil, as they both rode on motorcycles. Grayson would arrive in the new car of the week. And the last of their group, Chris would arrive late on the bus.

As Adrianna kept going on and on about God knows what. My eyes couldn't steer away from Liam's face when he pulled off his helmet.

He looked just as magnificent as I remembered, only the moment his eyes reached mine, he looked away, ashamed.

Had something changed since yesterday or this morning that made him so hesitant with me?

Had I done something wrong?

I don't think I did, but if I did... I'm sure we could fix it.

"You too Margo?" Adrianna scoffed as I snapped back into reality.

I stood up and placed my hands on Verina and Juliette's shoulders.

I had absolutely no idea what was being discussed at this very moment and felt lost, but I wasn't about to tell Adrianna that.

"You know you guys should turn over a new leaf this year." Juliette muttered as I ran over to Adrianna's side.

"You guys?" I asked with shock.

"I am a lot nicer than Mrs. Flawless over here." I snarled while I crossed both my arms together.

"I'm nice." Adrianna said as all of us went silent.

"No, but apparently you're funny." I smirked as she ignored my sarcastic comment.

As the group and I walked around the halls, I pulled my phone out of my bag and texted Liam, to tell him he looked great today. Only my message wouldn't send.

My stomach sunk, as I looked up to see Anna and Grayson fighting, arguing, bickering, whatever you wanted to call it again.

As they spewed off insults at each other I couldn't shake my head away from the fact that Liam had blocked me.

I looked up once more to see his face with sent me some sort of comfort to know I could just talk to him.

"Hey, Liam..." I smiled at his beautiful face. I didn't care if my friends knew we were dating or not, like he said.

It was just us.

"I've been texting you like crazy." I added on as he gave a disgusted look.

He was about to embarrass the shit out of me.

He looked at me up and down, with a roll of his tongue, "I'm sorry, who are you?"

My heart had stopped.

And it broke, just from five miniscule words that came out of *his* mouth.

My hand tightened around Adrianna's, like if I had let go, I would have fallen to my knees.

"Was I just a notch in your bed post this summer?" I mumbled.

"A fun one." He smirked as his friends patted his back.

I took a glimpse up to Liam's face only to see no ounce of remorse. This was a lesson that I should've known, I knew I didn't deserve this.

And he knew it too.

Never again will I let William Brookshire into my life ever again.

And that is a promise.

"Asshole." Verina angerly muttered as Liam laughed, "I'm wounded."

Oh, how I would love to slap his face multiple times. But even if anger had been the surface of my feelings. I couldn't help but feel the breaking of my heart underneath.

I wanted to cry, let the pain from my blisters out, and let the heart break that Liam just caused me to spill, but I didn't. I stood tall and stared at him.

But before I could let a tear fall, I heard my named being called by a familiar voice.

Jackson Gollum.

"Hey, Margo..." A boy eased in front of me, but my eyes stayed on Liam's.

"Hey Jack." I forced a grin on my face as his cheeks turned bright red.

"I was wondering if you wanted to go out with me sometime." He smiled, and asked so nicely how could I ever say no.

"Really?" I smiled and looked at Liam's sour expression.

"Yes, of course..." Jackson beamed. I had felt my old self emerging from the ashes. I fluttered my eyelashes, twirled my hair with my finger as Brooks came up next to Jackson talking to Adrianna.

Before I knew it, Liam had made an angerly exit from our

vicinity, I was glad for it because I never want to see Liam's face ever again.

Liam and I had never labeled ourselves to be anything particular, meaning there was never a breakup nor a relationship. I didn't need his permission to go out with Jackson.

I also wasn't stupid; Jackson is one of the easily known assholes in the whole University to have a body count higher than the Empire State building.

I wasn't going to sleep with him but, Liam didn't need to know that.

All he needed to know was how widely I hated him and how bad he's lost me.

Honestly, if I can't make a boy act right, I'm going to make him wish he did.

I was way too fucking pretty to cry about a known playboy. I simply had no type of patience for Liam, or any guy.

Choose me or lose me. He lost me.

CHAPTER 14

LIAM

I had royally fucked up.

Fuck Jackson Gollum and his fake tan. I had a game today and now all I could possibly think about is Margo cheering on a fucking guy that's second string in football.

I couldn't even blame her; I couldn't even be mad at her. It was my fault. I was the one who ruined things and I was the one who chose to fuck it up.

That also doesn't mean I can't be pissed about the situation. She looked angelic today, I didn't even get to tell her. I blocked her number.

I knew I was going to do this; it was the plan. Why the fuck did it hurt so much.

Seeing her face fall, broke my heart more than I ever thought it could. Playing her like this pained me so much I couldn't go to sleep last night.

But I made my bed. I had to lie in it. Was she ever going to tell me about Ben, now?

Was she ever going to confess that she was actually the one playing me?

That she was the one actually pulling my heart strings?

Was it better to end things on bad terms or good?

At least now she didn't have to pretend to keep liking me, right? I didn't have to wait for the shoe to drop, for her to break my heart.

Because I did it first. But was it any better? I heart felt shattered anyways.

What if Margo Hamilton was the one for me and I made a huge mistake.

Was it too late to fix it?

A hockey puck slammed in the board right in front of me as I stayed still.

"Will!" I heard Finn scream from the top of his lungs as I delivered a scowl.

"You know the goal is over there right!" I stood up to meet his eyes from across the rink.

I had to pick up Finn from hockey practice since Chris was working before the game tonight. Finn never made the job easy of course as he repeatedly tried to hit me square to my face with the rubber puck.

"It's time to go." I sternly said as his eyes widened and skated over to me immediately.

"Who pissed you off?" He asked as he sat next to me, pulling off his skates.

"Who said someone pissed me off?" I glared as he paused to look into my hardened eyes.

"It's that pretty blonde girl isn't it." He smirked as I let out an irritating sigh.

"Shut up and get your gear off." I ignored his question as he laughed, "I knew you were going to fumble her. She's way too pretty for you, and she's got a killer voice."

I turned around quickly as Finn's face turned bright red.

"What do you mean she's got a killer voice?" I questioned as he laughed awkwardly.

"Oh, nothing I just heard is all." Finn stood up quickly and tried to run away before I gripped him by his jersey, I pulled him closer to me as he took a large gulp.

"Amelia listens to her songs on Spotify, okay!" He spilled out as my eyes furrowed.

Margo released music?

I couldn't help but smile at the big accomplishment my girl has made. She was like a singer, not just any singer but like, my singer.

"Wait since when do you talk to Amelia Prince?" I narrowed my eyes at Finn's face as he gave a long-awaited sigh.

"We're friends." He answered as I smirk.

"What type of friends?" I wink as he wiggled his way out of my grasps.

"Leave me alone!" He took his hockey bag and stomped away from me.

But before he slammed the doors, "Then leave my love life alone!" I countered as he turned back and gave me a middle finger.

I quickly pulled my phone out of my pocket a clicked on Spotify, I looked up Margo's name so quickly I was scared my phone would crash.

And there it was, all her songs. And it looked like she had just released a new one, titled *Greece*.

I wondered what it could be about. If I've lost all contact to Margo and if she refuses to ever talk to me then this could be the only way I would hear from her.

Hear her.

Even if it's from a distance.

I looked up to hear banging from the door, completely forgetting about Finn.

"Stop thinking about the girl you lost because of your stupidity and take me home." Finn pointed out as I roll my eyes.

"I wish I could, Kid." I sigh.

I wish I could.

MARGO

. . .

I had shopped all my problems away and bought lingerie for everyone to wear underneath the opposing team's jerseys.

Was this a ploy to piss off Liam and all his goons. Yes absolutely.

Ever since the embarrassing encounter with Brookshire this morning I had realized that there was no need to be crying over him.

Only to show him what he will be missing out on. Whether that meant flaunting my perfect pilates ass around hungry hungry hockey players who just want one thing.

I had convinced everyone to wear the lingerie I had picked out, even Juliette, which was a miracle might I add.

I had promised Anna that the only reason I was doing this was to make Liam jealous and to get revenge, but it still killed me inside seeing him.

I would never tell her that, however. Adrianna had her own battles to fight, and I could never bring up any of my problems to her.

She was already going through so much.

I'm her best friend, it's my job to help her carry the world around her shoulders when her spine is splitting.

But what happens when even I can't take it and I'm breaking too? Who's going to help her?

I promised her that I would be strong enough for the both of us, so I will.

Now, I'm not really a sports type of girl, unlike Juliette but I do know that the events of tonight were definitely out of the ordinary. Grayson had shattered the glass boards around Darius Sawyer.

Thankfully there were no casualties, but the fury on his face when he saw Adrianna wearing Sawyer's jersey was priceless. Liam's eyes darkened every time his eyes landed on me.

I wish I could say that it didn't give me everything I needed but it definitely did.

The minute the game ended, the two teams basically swarmed at each other.

Colton however made his way over to me, he pulled off his helmet and smiled at me, "I couldn't help but see that you have my jersey on." He bent down and whispered in my ear.

"Indeed, I do." I remarked as he shook his head, urging over to Liam who glowered over on the other side of the rink.

"Does your boyfriend know that?" He asked as I rolled my eyes in disgust.

"He is certainly not my boyfriend. He made sure of that." I proclaimed as Colton nodded.

"So, what's the goal? You trying to make him jealous?" He snuck a look over to Liam who was continuously brooding.

My lips thinned out, "Is it bad if I say yes." I confessed as he laughs softly.

"Hey Hamilton, I'd do anything to get a rise out of Brookshire. All you had to do was ask." He moved closer to me, and I found myself not pulling back.

"What are you doing?" I whispered as he smirked, "Don't worry darling, consider this a favor to be owed."

Before I could ask him about what he meant, Liam came stomping over at us with nothing but fury in his eyes.

"Any chance why you aren't on your side of the arena, Colton?" Liam seethed as I took a step back from the fire being fueled.

"Yeah, I came because Margo called me over, she and I have some unfinished business." Colton fired back as Liam turned his head to meet my gaze.

One more word out of Colton's mouth I already saw Liam's fist forming and ready to punch the moment Colton provoked him.

"That's enough." Grayson walked in between the both of them. However, his gaze only remained on Adrianna's.

Colton steps in front of me, "We are having a party tonight at a bar or club. You guys can come." He looks around, "Your hockey team can come too." His eyes met Liam's.

"I would love to end this feud." He spit out like it was venom.

"Fuck you." Liam gritted out.

The look in Colton's eyes looked deadly like he absolutely wanted to start something again.

Liam's face grew more irritated and upset, which only fueled my happiness even more.

"Unless you guys are too whipped by your captain that he won't let you party."

He knew what he was doing. What a smart guy honestly. I looked at Liam's tortured face as I pushed my body closer to Colton.

This was going to be fun.

Let's party.

CHAPTER 15

MARGO

As I watched Adrianna decline the offer of partying with us tonight, all the girls packed up in one car. There was visibly no more room for me to get in with them.

The rank smell of sweaty hockey players and axe body spray was also not that appealing to the nose. But my thoughts on getting even more blisters by walking to a club also made me even more nauseous.

I took a deep breath, my eyes made contact with Colton and his friends, "You want a ride Hamilton?" He asked while opening the door.

Before I could even answer, a muscled arm wrapped itself around my waist, "She's fine." Liam's voice emerged next to me.

Colton only winked and followed it with a smirk, "Okay Hamilton, I'll see you there."

As they drove off, I pulled my body away from Liam who looked at me with distasteful eyes. I couldn't even begin to list off the many reasons on why he has no right to be angry with me.

"I can live my own life, thank you very much." I spit out like it was venom in my tongue.

"We both know you are only with him because you are trying

to make me jealous, just like when Gollum approached you this morning." He shook his head with an egotistical laugh.

The nerve of William Brookshire was something that needed to be studied, because it made absolutely no sense.

"Not everything is about you, Liam." I counter as he looked into my eyes.

"Whatever Margo, you are not going to that party." He pulled all of his belongings up to his shoulders as I smiled at him.

"Liam you are either taking me to this party or I'm walking there. You cannot stop me from having fun tonight especially when I fucking need it." I couldn't help but feel my stomach drop, almost like I wanted to cry in front of him, but my mind wouldn't let me.

I didn't want to party. I just wanted to be with him. Which was revolutionary considering that I was known to be the party girl in the whole University.

Liam took a second to look at me and let out a large sigh, before getting on top of his motorcycle. He urged to his back seat with a scowl.

"I'm with you the whole fucking night." He snarled. I stood there shocked and confused before he continued with his proclamations.

"Get in before I change my mind." He turned his head straight ahead so he wouldn't have to look into my eyes.

If he ended things and he broke my heart, then why was he having a hard time looking at me without love.

This should be easier for him, he shouldn't be cockblocking me and he certainly shouldn't be caring about me.

I got on Liam's motorcycle; his hands urged my arms to wrap around his abdomen. I was quite sure that space was what we needed. Isn't space what every broken-up couple needed?

Not us. As much as I tried rejecting it, I found comfort being around Liam. I craved his touch and my body being enveloped around his arms.

I could feel myself shake as I inched myself closer to his body.

He started his engine and drove off, I felt him tense up like he wanted to resist that he was enjoying me being around him.

Was I truly that revolting that he couldn't want me?

Did the nights we spent together mean nothing to him?

Did the night of Maya's party mean shit?

I looked up at him, no emotions rested on his face. Which kind of gave me my answer. I am now a victim of Liam Brookshire's long list of women he has played successfully.

And somehow, I didn't hate him for it, only I was disappointed because I saw it coming and still wished for different results, hoped for a different ending. It felt so real for it not to be.

But at the end of the day, he did what he did, he did what he wanted, and he did it with a smug face and a laughing tone.

All those sleepless nights with him, all the kisses, the picnics, the laughter, the facemasks and the flowers went down the drain with our memories.

We were just how we were in the start, the beginning where we acknowledged each other's presence, but it didn't mean more than that, it was like our love and us as a whole were wiped from the face of the planet.

I wondered if this was how it was going to be for the rest of my life, I was either going to try and marry for love but at the end of the day I was too unlovable to want.

The second option was to marry for financial reasons and let my parents pick who would take care of me, even if it wasn't for love.

Why did the other option sound better?

As we arrived in front of the club, Liam got off his motorcycle first, then offering me a helping hand to get off, I didn't need his help and got off myself.

"Thanks for the ride." I snarked as I looked at the club, "Don't let Colton fool you, Raine." He voiced as I took a deep breath.

I had no intentions of being with Colton, let alone spending the night with him. But there also wasn't a problem making Liam sweat a little bit.

"I don't think my love life has anything to do with you now, does it Liam?" I dusted off my clothing as he went quiet..

"Now if you will excuse me." I took a deep breath before making my way to the club. I looked back for only a moment to see Liam stood next to his motorcycle; his gaze never left mine.

I wondered if this was how it was going to be forever. Him watching me from a distance, not knowing how he ruined something so beautiful.

I shouldn't care. Should I even still fight for it?

As the bouncer let me in, my first view was Verina doing shots on top of a table and Juliette talking to multiple guys. Even if Juliette was an Einstein, she knew how to impress guys, she fucked around but never dated around.

God forbid her father found out he would kill every man that ever peaked an interest at her. She was always the one that had gave us the advice that we so desperately needed.

But I couldn't talk to my friends about the arranged marriage stuff, nor the humiliation that I had received from Liam. I was way too embarrassed to talk about it.

Well except Anna, I told her everything. I might as well tell her that I was thinking about accepting my father's offer about marrying Ben.

A half an hour passed since Adrianna got escorted out by Grayson, and I was having zero fun, Liam had been watching me like a hawk and I couldn't help but think maybe there was something I could do to provoke him to tell me why he played me.

I've talked to countless men throughout the whole night, I wanted to get laid. I felt so stressed and aggravated about so many things in my life I couldn't control. I swirled my drink around with a straw, my eyes took a small peek at Liam who sat at a booth and was having a conversation with a random girl.

My heart ached at the thought of him being with another girl, worst my whole body ached at how good he looked tonight. My body rejected Colton the moment he bought me a drink, but somehow even if Liam stomped on my heart, my whole being still wanted him.

That didn't stop me from making out with Colton the whole night, I practically made him excited just by a couple of minutes of being on top of him.

I scanned to see Liam and the random girl making out, it didn't affect me, we weren't together. We didn't have to explain our hookups to each other.

I got up, my body went straight as I walked over to Liam with my Vodka cranberry, "Hey baby, ready to go?" I looked at him, and scowling at the girl who gave me the dirtiest look of all time.

I smiled at her before, sliding my body next to Liam's and accidentally pouring my drink onto Liam's lap.

He looked down at me with a knowing sigh and expression, he knew I didn't like him talking to her. And his eyes challenged mine.

"You should go." I turned my head over to the girl who already left the other seat empty.

"Oops." I sighed as Liam shook his head with a low laugh.

"Are you just going to scare off any girl that shows interest in me now?" He asked as I rolled my eyes.

"No, I'm just saving her from your lies and torment, Charming." I raised my empty glass at him as he leaned closer to me.

"Looks like you've had too much to drink." He noted.

I lazily looked at my drink, "I just want to be taken home, Liam. But I can't go home because my parents kicked me out." I yawned as his eyes sent a wrinkled look back at me.

"What?" He questioned.

"Oh, you know... I told them I didn't want to get married to this kid, because you made me fall in love with you, so they kicked me out because I betrayed them." I sighed a Liam's eyes turned lighter.

"They practically disowned me because I chose *you* over them. Isn't that stupid of me? Because not only did I lose them, but you also fucked me over!" I laughed louder as he shook his head.

"You didn't lose me, Raine." He mumbled as I pulled away from him.

I started shaking my head, "You could've just left me alone Liam, but I think you knew that." I sighed, "So, yes, I tried to make you jealous by being with Colton, and dancing and drinking all night Liam. But at the end of the day, it doesn't matter."

I got up from the seat, my eyes watered, "Can you please just take me home?"

Liam looked at me, like he regretted everything he's done for the past 48 hours to me.

He got up, "I'm not taking you to your house, you can sleep at mine." He said sternly as he made me sit back down on the booth.

"Let me just grab my coat and my keys from the bartender and we can go, okay Raine?" He tilted my head to look up at him, I nodded quickly.

He smiled at me for a little, it was the smile he would give me when we had picnics in Greece. He disappeared into the large crowd, and I waited for him to come get me, but he never did.

I sat there for about an hour everyone had left, but I stayed and waited for him. Until I couldn't anymore, my sobriety had come back, and I stood up to go up to the bartender.

"Hey, have you seen Liam anywhere, he said he would come find me, but he never did." I asked nicely as the bartender gave me a worried expression.

"Brookshire went into that room with two females, about thirty minutes ago." He muttered hesitantly.

I began to walk closer to the door to the room, "I wouldn't go there if I were you." The bartender warned as I opened the door.

I really wished I hadn't opened the door.

CHAPTER 16

LIAM

Margo had just spilled to me the entire truth and I couldn't be more relieved that she did. I didn't understand why on Earth she kept it a secret, but she did.

It took one day for me to realized how much I fucking missed her, one fucking interaction with Colton, I almost lost it.

If he hadn't left earlier, I would've beat him to death in the back-alley way for kissing Margo. But again, I couldn't be mad because I ended things with her, and I was also making out with a random girl to make her jealous.

But she was mine again, we could put everything behind us and just be together, like we wished for.

I walked up to the bartender only to be greeted by two women who looked like I was their next meal.

"Ladies, excuse me." I swerved myself around them as they stepped up in front of me.

This was nothing but trouble.

"William Brookshire, just the man we want to see." The one redhead had smirked while placing her hands on my arm.

The jet-black haired accomplice had slithered her way on my side, "I'm sorry have we met?" I asked, I was confused on what they wanted with me considering, I'm afraid I had never met them in my life.

"No, we haven't. But we know who you are." One of the ladies have muttered as I pulled away from the other's grasps.

"Excuse me?" I sounded reluctant to know who they were. Maybe it was for the best I let them get away without any questions.

They urged me to go to one of the club rooms, I looked at them, then back at Margo who sat by herself, waiting for me.

"Trust me, you'll want to come with us." The redhead laughed wickedly as I rolled my eyes and followed them to the room.

"What's this about." I implored as they took two seats in front of me, placing a diamond case, black iPhone in front of me.

"Before you think about deleting the videos or pictures, or breaking the phone, we have copies." One of the ladies implied.

They sat back as I picked up the phone and played the video. It was a video of my stepfather placing money in a safe and as I further swiped, pictures of his bank details getting large sums of money.

I took a deep breath, "You know... embezzling money is a crime Brookshire, your father sure does a lot of it." The dark-haired lady muttered.

"He's my stepfather." I clarified as they both rolled their eyes at my stupid remark.

"I don't think they'll care; they'll send him to prison so quickly along with your family's reputation going to the trash can. Your mother's dream about fashion and jewelry making are as dead as you finding a chance out of this mess." She retorted.

I never liked my stepfather one bit, and it's shit like this that makes me want to beat the shit out of him.

"Why are you telling me this, if you wanted him in prison then you would've gone to the police or FBI by now." I remarked as they smile.

"We don't really want to ruin your life Liam, trust us. We just want to ruin your little sunshine's life.

"Margo." I muttered as one of them winked.

"What on Earth do you want with Margo." I grit out, more annoyed and aggravated that they wanted to hurt her more than they did me.

"That's for us to know and you to never find out. And all you have to do is follow our directions, and we won't have to see your little angel suffer. You got it?"

I gulped, more afraid to leave her by herself for a long period of time, than whatever the fuck they were going to do with me.

"Whatever, make it quick." I lashed out as one of the girls lifted up their shirts and throwing it on the bed.

My eyes widened at what the directions were going to be next. She pulled out a condom from her pocket and ripped it off with her tiny fingers.

I backed away slowly as my body slammed on the door behind me, "I'm not sleeping with either of you." I expressed as the lady sat down and took the phone.

"That's too bad. It's the only price we're asking for, and these videos and photos will be forgotten." The other lady pulled her skirt down, and I only felt trapped in this fucking room.

Margo or my family. I thought to myself, this could send my mother down a depression, this could get me kicked out of college because of the fucking bad look it would put on my hockey career.

I sighed; my eyes closed for a moment before opening.

"Don't you sleep with so many women you're an expert, this shouldn't be an issue then." The red head muttered while walking up to me and grabbing my arm.

She led me to the bed, unbuttoning my jeans and I kept a stern face, her face came close to mine, "It doesn't count if you don't try, Brookshire." She snapped as I shook my head.

This was fucked up. Why am I being punished for my father's

mistakes, even when I'm out of the house and he isn't beating me to a fucking pulp, I still couldn't escape him.

They placed alcoholic beverages on the table in front of me, "Drink up Liam, we wouldn't want you to not have fun." The lady kissed me as the other unbuttoned my shirt.

I froze up, my hands shook the moment they touched one of the girl's bodies... this was wrong.

The door slammed open, my eyes find Margo's eyes which were set on nothing but me and the two women on my lap. Their mouths were on my neck, and I could only stare back in horror as she took a step back from the sight.

"No need for you to give me a ride home, I can call an Uber." She quickly muttered as I stood up, buttoning my shirt together.

I ran after Margo, who's face looked angered and disappointed.

"Margo please, let me explain." I let out quickly.

"No, Liam!" She screamed at me with conviction and power.

We were the only two people in the dark street, the light only shone on her face, which glistened with tears.

I could tell she was tired, and not just because she visibly looked tired, but she was exhausted.

Like she couldn't handle me anymore.

She couldn't handle us anymore.

Her face right at this very moment told me everything I needed to hear which was that she was done trying.

"I'm not doing this anymore." She let a tear fall to the ground, "I *can't* do this anymore." She said calmly, she looked deeply into my eyes.

"If they can have you, Liam. They can have you. If they can take you away from me that easily then you are all theirs. Our story ends here and that's okay." She wiped the tear away from her face as my heart broke.

"Our story has to end here because I can't take it anymore. It was amazing in Greece; know it was everything I could've asked for, dreamed of... even but we aren't in Greece anymore." She looked around and pointed at the "Welcome to Hawthorne" sign.

"This is our real life and, we can't be together in our real life. I don't really want to know why you were in there with two girls when you had me *waiting* for you." She laughed harshly.

"I refuse to know why you thought it was okay to block my number, humiliate me in front of our friends, play me, and betray me by going to hook up with two women tonight. I would rather fucking marry whoever my parents picked out for me than ever be with you Liam." She seethed as I could only listen.

"You made your play. I can't wait for the day you realize that you fucked up." She laughs off as her Uber arrived.

Margo didn't waste a moment and hopped in the car, before I could even explain myself. I wondered if I even should.

Maybe she was right. It was too hard, too painful for us to work. Maybe we were just destined to be a summer fling, nothing more than that.

I mean isn't love supposed to be something that God wants to stay together, without hardships?

She shouldn't have to be trying to make me jealous for me to get back with her, I wouldn't have to be breaking her heart because I was too scared that she would break mine first.

It was supposed to be easy, and it wasn't.

We were too hard.

I knew I fucked up the moment I sought her out in Greece, she was way too precious for me to lay my hands on her. I never should have, because now I know how she felt like. I know it felt to be cared and loved for by her.

God it was addicting.

But it was wrong. She has to be married to someone else, and I didn't deserve someone that *good* in my life.

Not when all I've done is cause her pain.

I ran back up to the bar once more and only found an empty room and an empty bar, the iPhone laid on the floor with the videos and pictures of my stepfather in them.

I tucked the phone into my back pocket, and my anger relinquished itself as I thought about the fact that I lost Margo tonight.

Before I thought about punching the wall or drinking my problems away, I ran down to my motorcycle and started the engine, my only thought was to get to Dead Cullen's bar.

By the time I arrived, I waved at Samuel who knew I had no time for his jokes and games. He let me in with no problem as I stomped my way to the upstairs lounge.

I knocked on the door with slight anger and hurry as Finn opened the door, shyly. He rubbed his eyes and his face looked tired like I had just woke him up from a nap or a slumber.

"Uncle Liam what are you doing here so late?" He groaned as he let me in without hesitation.

I rolled my eyes while plopping down on their couch, Finn yawned before giving me his undivided attention.

"You told me the next time I felt like punching something or someone, to come to you and talk about my feelings instead of acting on them, right?" I clarified as he gave me the deadliest look of all galaxies.

"I meant in daylight and not at two in the morning!" He raised his voice at me, I couldn't help but feel my lips thinned, and my eyebrows furrowed.

"Well, it's too late for that now, I'm here." I added as he walked over to the fridge and pulled out two juice boxes, he threw one over to me.

"It's about your girlfriend, isn't it?" He sat down across from me as I nodded my head.

"You should've said no, because one she *isn't* your girlfriend and second, you're the one that fucked it up." He explained as I looked around wondering if Chris was watching us from a distance.

"Watch your damn language, Finn!" I whispered as he rolled his eyes.

"What's the issue?" He looked at me as I practically looked like I shit my pants.

"She caught me with two women." I couldn't help the looked of guilt that emerged from my face as he gave me a disgusted look.

"Dude, you do realize that you are the problem, right?" He scowled as I shook my head.

"They wanted to hook up with me in exchange to keep quiet about my father's embezzlement." I explained further as he stood up frazzled.

"Isn't that a *crime*?!?" He voiced while the color drained from his face.

"Be fucking quiet Finn!" I whisper thickly as he sat back down, "She caught me and then we ended things there." I finished as he placed his hands in front of his face.

"Fight for her!" He advised as I gave him the same face I gave my calculous teacher, the look of *bitch please*.

"I don't think she wants me back, Finn. I'm afraid I actually lost her this time. You should've seen her face when she opened the door and saw me. It's something I wish I would never have to live through again." I asserted as he suddenly had a notebook and a pen in hand.

Finn looked at me and started to write sentences down, like a professional fucking therapist.

"I've solved your issue, Uncle Will." He looked at me seriously.

"Well, what's the issue?" I leaned in closer.

Finn's concerned face morphed into something gruesome, "You're suffering from dumb asshole disease, it's when you give up on a girl because you're too pussy to be better for her." He threw me a snarky remark as I just stared at him.

"What do you think I should do, then?" I asked as he handed me a list of things to do to win Margo back by the end of the school year.

"Get her flowers every single day?" I looked at him with curiosity and the look of concern.

He nods, "Make sure they are different every day. Girls like the idea of consistency, thus the bringing the flowers every day, but they also like a little surprise everyday so it isn't repetitive, thus having a different flower every day is also a fantastic idea" He beamed as I laughed.

"You really think that could work?" I couldn't help but smile.

"I think the definition of love is you don't give up even if things are bad, like ministers say, to have and to hold from this day forward, for better, for worse, for richer, or for poor, in sickness and in health, you love and cherish them till death." He shrugged as I gave a confused look.

"Why the hell do you know that?" I couldn't help but ask as he looked smug.

"Besides, isn't that like how you guys are with my brother, and how my brother is with me. You love someone or something you don't give up on them, you take care of each other. Even if it gets hard, you love even harder. Chris works his ass off every single day to pay for my chemo and to put food on the table." His eyes pulled away from Chris's room.

"You guys are always helping out with picking me up or taking me to my appointments. That's real love, even when I know I'm gonna die someday." He whispered the last part as I shook my head.

"You aren't dying Finn. I simply will not allow it," I took a sip of my juice box as he smiled at me.

I could see the hopeless look in his eyes. He always prepared himself from the day it would come, the day where the doctors can't do it anymore, or when he couldn't and wouldn't do it anymore.

He paused, "Hey can you do me a favor?" He asked.

I tilted my head as he continued, "I overheard Chris telling Gray that he was thinking about quitting hockey because he can't afford it, when really he meant he couldn't afford me."

I stayed quiet as Finn kept going, "I know he's been coughing up money from illegal fights to pay for my chemotherapy. He never gets time to rest, he's always coming home late and he's tired. But he's up before I am and he's back at work by then." He further explained as I frowned.

"Finley, listen to me. Chris loves you; we love you, and if I'm picking up what you are putting down, no I will not let your brother quit hockey. Yes, we will take care of him." I moved closer to him as he smiled.

"And yes, things will get better, Champ." I punched Finn's shoulder playfully as he grinned from ear to ear.

He coughed before proceeding back to the old subject.

"But I'm just saying Will, do you want Margo?" he asked point blank.

"She doesn't want me back, it's too hard Finn." I replied as he gave a big huff.

"That wasn't my question. Do you still want her back?" He asked again as I waited a couple moments to answer.

"Of course I do." I let out as he stood up.

"Then get her back and stop bitching and complaining!" He yelled at me as a smile crept on my face.

Then a light turned on in the hallway, Chris's body came into view as he opened his bedroom door.

His eyes adjusted and watched as we gave him a guilty look for ruining his beauty sleep.

Without another word, he looked at the clock and groaned. Chris shut his door for a moment, then opened it again, throwing a hockey puck at me and slammed his door shut once more.

"Ouch!" The puck hit my bicep as Finn started to holler at the look of my injury, "That fucking hurt."

"No cursing around Finn!" Chris screamed from his room as I gave Finn a dirty look.

Finn only smiled at me, he took his notebook from the table and threw it at me, I looked up at him.

"What's this?" I questioned as he fluttered his eye lashes.

"It's you and Margo, sitting in a tree..." He winked before I picked him up and threw him on the sofa.

God, I loved this kid.

CHAPTER 17

MARGO

"Margo." I heard someone groan.

Ring, ring, ring!

"Margo!" Someone screamed as my eyes squinted open, harsh light from a cell phone blurred my vision.

I looked up to see Verina and Juliette cuddled together as I laid on the cold floor next to Verina's bed. My phone had been the one disrupting their beauty sleep, as well as mine.

I slowly crawled outside her bedroom, to answer my phone which had my Father's caller ID.

"Hello?" I groaned as his loud voice erupted from the phone's speaker.

"Maggie Raine Hamilton. Where the hell have you been?!" He shrieked as I moved the phone away from my ear.

"Why do you care?" I whisper as he paused.

"You are still our daughter." He replied as I rolled my eyes.

I waddled around to Verina's kitchen to grab a bottle of water, only to catch a small glimpse of a flashlight on her balcony, which quickly disappeared.

"I thought that, that label had been revoked the moment I chose love over you two." I remarked.

"You don't know what being in love feels like." He muttered as I shook my head.

"You're wrong." I blanched.

I heard footsteps from the outside porch as I turned my head nothing appeared through the window.

Verina's house was fully secured, and I had no doubt that something would happen to the Mayor's estate.

"Maggie, I've gotten word that you and Liam are now separated, so was betraying us worth it for love or was it a stupid mistake."

My eyes closed in annoyance, "You asked someone to spy on me, haven't you." I snarled as he laughed.

"I will do anything to know what you are up to Maggie, so please stop being stubborn and come home."

I took a breath.

My parents were right. I was wrong. It was as simple as that; I mis profiled Liam and I underestimated him. He might've been lying the entire time, or he might have not.

But at the end of the day, we were done. What was the point of fighting my parents, fighting the offer of having a roof over my head and not having to walk to school every morning.

I had nothing to lose, so why fight the arranged marriage?

Why fight something that could not only help me but help my parents as well?

I pulled my phone closer to my face, "What exactly are you offering me father?" I sighed as he took another pause.

"Your mother and I want you home, you will live under our roof, we will have a family dinner with the Grimaldi's. Your engagement will be finalized soon. And you won't fight it."

I swallowed. My eyes started to water at the thought of my loss of freedom. Maybe that's why I've been fighting them. That's why I've been fighting it.

But never in my life will I ever betray my parents because of a boy again. I promise myself that.

"Okay." I said quietly as I could practically feel their happiness at me obeying their orders.

Before they could say anything else, I hung up on them. I turned around to see Xavier, walk in slowly through the balcony door.

"Ahem." I coughed out as he flinched at the sight of me.

"Margo!" He addressed with a guilty smile as I rolled my eyes.

"Xavier Du Pont, why are you only getting home at this time?" I folded my arms in front of me as he walked closer giving me a kiss on the cheek.

"Well, if you must ask, Michelle and I were out partying with some kids from Columbia University, I even met a guy on the football team." He winked as I tried to look uninterested.

"Xavier, it is dangerous to be out late, and could you even imagine if your parents found out, or worst, if Verina found out you were late because of some guy you just met." I lectured as he pulled out his phone.

"It is not even that late Margo." He defended as I huffed out.

"You know I care about you, but you and Michell need to be safer. There are a lot of creeps hanging around the outskirts of Columbia, and may I remind you. You have to stay out of trouble for your father's sake." I pointed at him as he continued to listen.

"I know what you're going to say Margo." He cut me off and I shut my mouth before he continued, "You have to watch what you do because of your father's upcoming election." He mocked.

I stayed quiet.

"It's worse enough that the mayor has a gay son, Margo. I know he seems like he's fine with it but deep down I know he wished for the son that he could've taught football to, not one that dates a football player." He took a seat on the island countertop.

"My family is so damn perfect, and I'm just a weighing disappointment. Verina is the golden child, she is the one they pay attention to, the one they are proud of, every step of the way, she gets the guys, gets the fame, everything." He looked at me in a sad manor.

"I know it sounds awful, but sometimes I wish and pray for the day she messes up, her downfall, where for a second our parents might think of me first. But that's a long shot anyways." He laughed off as my lips thinned.

What could I even say to make the situation better?

"I know, I'm probably the last person that you think would relate to you, because in the past you've made it clear that we couldn't have been more different. But can I tell you something?" I whispered as he leaned closer to me.

He was ready to dive deep into the lore I was about to drop on to him.

"Well for starters, I know you and Liam hooked up." He voiced as my eyes widened.

"What? How?" My face practically fell to the ground as he chuckled at the color that left my face.

"Margo, be for real right now. You two spent more than a few hours in one of Maya's rooms. Now of course no one really knew if you guys actually hooked up, but you reacting like that just confirmed all my suspicions." He winked at me as he took a sip from the water, I had poured on a glass for myself.

"To be honest with you, I saw it coming. You guys just seemed compatible, you both like to play around, the partying, the mind games you would use on men, you've met your match. Lastly, I think it's hilarious that if you two started dating, Adrianna and Grayson would have to spend time together." He smirked.

I knew Xavier had a fat crush on Grayson Prince, everyone kind of did. Well except for me, I was more into dark features, as much as I disliked Liam, I hated myself for being attracted to him.

But Xavier was right, Adrianna and Grayson hanging out would've been a funny thought or idea. Maybe in another planet, or another life things would've worked out between Liam and I.

Maybe if we were still in Greece, we would still be together.

But like I said to him, we weren't in Greece anymore, we're in our real lives.

It was time to move on.

"Yeah, I thought so too." I questioned as he gave a dirty look.

"Did he fuck up already?!" Xavier looked shocked as I nodded.

"I walked in on him with two girls on his lap yesterday." I elucidated further, "But earlier that day he acted like he didn't know who I was and also embarrassed me." I continued.

Xavier's face looked mortified as he flinched away, "I think I might have to reevaluate why I'm gay." He laughed as I joined in.

"Yeah, men are such characters aren't they?"

Chapter 18

Margo

The next morning, still with my stubborn attitude. I didn't come to my house; I stayed the night at the guest house. Since they barely check the damn thing, I could literally live here without the issue of getting caught.

I was planning on coming home tonight, make it official that I was basically agreeing to listen to my parents for the rest of my life.

I had a right to be pissed, but I also understood why they were making me do it, why I thought it was necessary. Especially now without Liam weighing down my other option.

I left the guest house pretty early and walked to the school yet again, I usually spend countless hours in the University's musical lounge.

It had every instrument you could possibly think of, the most valuables that money could buy. And it was my safe place, here I could create anything.

Hawthorne University had a big range of students, of course you had the athletes, such as the hockey team, people like Juliette. You had the future politicians, CEO's, designer's, entrepreneurs, attorneys, artists, surgeons, doctors, FBI's and even writers.

However, there were limited musicians. Only about seventeen students participated in anything remotely music related. Sure, there were dancers, and people in plays and musicals. But only a select few were into actually writing music and dreamed of playing it for the world to hear.

I never told anyone this, but I could play twenty-two instruments. But as any basic person would say, I preferred the piano and the guitar the most.

I lost count of how many hours I would spend at the music room in the University. I only knew that I used it the most often. It's the one place I knew that no one could interrupt me or disturb my peace.

Or so I thought.

As I turned my guitar, I heard the door slightly open and shut.

"I'm sorry, I probably took too long, you can have the room now if you want." I muttered without turning my head to see who the person was.

I only saw a glimpse of blue, which caught my eye and made me turn around only for my face to change from a smile to a scowl.

"Liam what are you doing here." I asked blankly.

"And with that." I gestured over to the flowers he had in hand.

"I knew I'd find you here." He commented with a small grin that made my heart melt.

"Well, you found me, I thought we made ourselves pretty clear last night. It's over." I murmured as he took a step closer.

"You don't understand Margo, I didn't know those girls. I had to do it, they were blackmailing me, and I had to do it for my father." He explained while he placed the flowers on top of the piano.

I rolled my eyes, "And even of that is true Liam, which by the way I can't trust you anymore. You embarrassed me in front of all our friends yesterday, pretending you don't know me. You blocked my number, and you ghosted me the day after we fucked." I clarified as his face looked glum.

"We can't be together." I simplified.

But he looked determined.

"We can't be together? Or your parents don't want us to be together?" He asked with conviction as I gave a large sigh.

"No, Liam." I said plainly.

"You screwed up, and I don't want us to be together because you broke my heart, and you might do it again." I exasperated as his face stayed the same.

"I know I fucked up, but I'm not giving up. No matter how many times you turn me down. I'm going to stay here because I know it's going to be you and me." He walked closer to me as I took a step back.

"You can try and show me that you hate me and that you never want to see me again. But I can see by the look in your eyes that you still want me, and you want us, but something is making you hide it." He placed his hand just right under my chin.

I tried to resist his touch, but as his hand tilted my chin, I couldn't help but meet his eyes. I could practically melt on his arms if I let myself.

"I think you're delusional." I slapped his hand away from my face as he smirked.

"I'll play along with your game, Raine but you'll lose. I'll win you back." He said with confidence as I turned around and grabbed my purse, I placed the guitar I was using back to its stand.

"Even if you don't believe me, Liam. Just remember, for every single time I reject you from now on, just know you had me already and *you* lost me." I said thickly as I continued to smirk.

"It's going to take a lot more than measly flowers for me to see you more than a liar and the same old playboy you were." I picked up the flowers he brought me and threw them in the trashcan as he laughed softly.

"You think that's all I got?" He raised his voice.

No, I didn't think that's all he's got. I knew Liam and I knew that he was right. He wouldn't stop at winning me over. But he also knew that by the look I gave him, I wouldn't stop at making it harder for him.

Game on, Brookshire.

Game on.

LIAM

Day 1 of Project "Get Raine Back."

Okay so that wasn't a complete fail. I knew my journey in winning Margo over wasn't going to be easy. But like Finn said, never give up.

I knew Margo was going to resist me right to the bone, which only made me want to work harder for her.

I was already planning my next move, which type of flowers I would bring her tomorrow. I was sure she would keep these ones since she threw the other ones away earlier today.

I shook my head to snap back into reality as Grayson walked us to the Hawthorne Café.

Which by the way, he suspiciously gathered everyone for. I didn't question Grayson's random endeavors.

Neil popped a cigarette out of his pocket as Chris continued to bandage his hand from his fight last night.

"Dude, you look like you're about to shit your pants." I laughed as we finally arrived in front of the café.

He rang the doorbell, as the door opened, my eyes widened at the rare sighting of Adrianna Cassian who opened the door for us.

"You look like you're the one who shit your pants." Chris snarked as I shouldered him to walk inside.

"Grayson." I addressed as my eyes met with Margo's ocean blues. She looked about ready to kill me, like she was ready to burn me alive.

"Sit." Grayson ordered as everyone in our group listened and walked over to the couch. Chris however stayed standing.

Margo's eyes never left mine as I sat down, I couldn't help but stare back. She wasn't kidding when she said she would try and resist me. But I also wasn't kidding when I said that I would make it hard for her to do.

"What was so fucking important?" I nudged.

"They were getting to that part before you opened your mouth." She sneered as I gave a small laugh.

"I wasn't asking you, was I?" I whispered as she turned her head with a sarcastic smile.

"Yes, well dogs don't ask, they listen." She spit back as my eyes widened at her response.

I only rolled my tongue inside my mouth and leaned back to listen to the rest of what Grayson and Adrianna were about to spew.

"We're dating." Adrianna revealed as everyone's face dropped to fucking hell.

A loud shattering sound emerged from my peripheral view as Verina Du Pont dropped a plant that she was holding earlier.

Juliette Livingston, the coach's daughter was usually cuddled up in a book, however she was bothered enough by the two words to shut her book fully closed.

Neil pulled the cigar out of his mouth with an exasperated expression, and Chris let himself fall on the couch with ease.

Margo's voice emerged after the years of silence.

"Excuse me?" She laughed at the mere idea of Adrianna and Grayson together.

But before I could say anything, Verina ran over with a yell, "I knew this day would happen!"

"I had more faith in you!" Juliette added whilst handing over a one hundred dollar bill to Verina.

"You two made a bet on me?!" Adrianna blanched with the look of annoyance as I couldn't help but laugh as well.

Of course, to me, this was because Margo and I would spend days talking about how we were going to break the news to our friends that we were together, you know considering the fact that Adrianna and Grayson hated each other.

I had a feeling Margo thought the same thing, as her eyes found mine again, but they didn't have the sassiness that they had earlier.

She quickly shook it off, as Juliette and Verina got scolded for holding a bet on them.

Margo walked over to Adrianna with her finger pointed, "This is so upsetting!" referring to the bet that was made.

Verina's eyes bulged so much they looked like saucers, "Margo shut it, you owe a thousand!"

The guys and I couldn't help but laugh at the chaos these four women had introduced us to in less than thirty minutes.

"Listen up!" Grayson loudly commanded as everyone jolted.

"We're fake dating." He addressed smoothly.

Adrianna quickly whispered something to Grayson's ear, that we couldn't hear.

Chris decided to ask a question like we were the students, and Adrianna and Grayson were the two teachers that would interrupt the class just to flirt.

"Why?" Chris asked.

Adrianna smiled at Grayson, "Oh yes. This is a wonderful story! Tell them, Grayson, tell them why." She followed with a smirk.

"Was this because of August? Let me guess, she wants you to prove to her you can be in a serious relationship, so you fake it to get her back?" I added as Grayson gave me a scary look.

Margo quickly added, "No, this is about Adrianna's campaign. It has to be, or to piss off your dad?" She asked Adrianna as I rolled my eyes.

Margo walked closer to Adrianna, "Because lets be honest, A, you have got to be joking, you can't possibly be up for this with a Prince!" She shot out as Neil started to smoke again.

"Well, it doesn't really look like they are asking for our approval." I smiled thickly as she sent me an annoyed look.

"It will only be temporary." Grayson said as I nodded.

Margo looked at me, "Of course *you* would agree if it was *temporary*."

I chose to ignore the dig she gave me. As I knew that she wanted to rile me up so that she could get more upset with me. But I meant what I said when I said that I will get her back.

"I forgot to mention, Raine." I leaned closer to her, "You look so delicious today." I said in a low whisper as the whole group continued to talk, my hand snaked on her lower back.

Margo tensed up, but she didn't remove my hand.

"And you look like an ass." She muttered as my mouth found her ear.

"An ass that wishes I could spread your legs wide open on this very couch." I huskily murmured as she gave a large sigh.

God, I loved it when she made that noise.

"I know you missed my tongue on you, Raine." I continued as she swallowed.

"You don't know what you're talking about." She denied as I couldn't help but smile against her ear.

"No guy is ever going to make you feel as good as I made you feel baby. And I know you're wet for me already." I looked as her eyes closed for a moment.

"Shut up Liam." She mumbled as I laughed in low tone before I pulled myself away from her intoxicating smell.

"What exactly do you need from us?" Margo shuffled making it look like she was paying attention to the conversation that was had.

I smiled before further explaining, "They need to make this believable so, obviously they are asking their trustworthy friends to help, sweetheart."

Margo turned her head, "By how, exactly?" She threw attitude my way.

Juliette stood up, "We know them the best, we teach them the other's dislikes and likes."

"Oh, I'll start." Margo smiled from ear to ear while she

grabbed Adrianna by the arm and pointed at Grayson, "She dislikes you." She blanched as I stood up.

I walked over to Grayson with a scowl, "You're no picnic either, sweethearts." I spit out as Grayson sent me an irritated look.

"Get your fucking hands off of me." He shook me off before he pulled Adrianna away from Margo's grasps.

Margo and I throw each other nasty looks, which by the way only made me want to kiss her even more.

She rolled her eyes at me as I winked at her.

"Now, I can't believe I have to say this, but you all have to get along. Even if we can't stand each other, you most certainly can try."

Margo took a second and looked at me like they were asking her to put down her dog.

"That is rich coming from the both of you! Do you realize that you two have been put against each other since I don't know..." Margo looked at me to continue the sentence with her.

"You were born!" We both exclaimed loudly as Adrianna and Grayson both flinched.

"Gee, thanks for the massive support, you lunatics." Adrianna muttered as Verina breaks out into a small laughter.

"This is obviously a satire." She turned to Adrianna and Grayson, "Right?" She looked unconvinced as they both shook their heads.

Chris stood up.

"No, this is sadly not a satire because Grayson would never touch Adrianna like that *just because*." He said.

Chris walked closer to the both of them, examining their every move, "Not even within a ten-foot radius." He finished.

Adrianna shot Grayson an offended expression, "What, do you think I have lice or something?"

Grayson shrugs, while looking at me, "Maybe mono."

Within that thirty second insult, Adrianna and Grayson

started to fight once more. Who could blame them? It was in their absolute nature.

I couldn't stop staring at Margo's beautiful face, she looked so angelic even when she threw me deadly stares once in a while. I snap back to reality only to hear Neil and Juliette spew off some random quote from a book.

I kind of looked stunned hearing Neil quote something, then realizing I've never seen Neil pick up a book his entire life.

"You read?" I couldn't help the look on my face looking surprised.

"Not a lot." He said plainly.

A flashback of a night in Greece, when Margo would read me her favorite fairytales just about when we would fall asleep. And I would tell her the cruel and scary original stories of the fairytales she did tell me.

They always ended up creeping the hell out of her, only made me happy because I always got to hold her when she was frightened.

I watched as Grayson put a necklace on Adrianna. She looked at him warily and then asked, "How much did you spend on this?" She scowled.

Grayson didn't answer so I yawned and replied instead, "You have like seven million dollars around your neck right now."

Adrianna's face turned bright red, my birthday was yesterday, and I didn't really celebrate it often. I never told anyone this but part of the reason I hated my stepdad was because on my birthday, my present was always a belt and a dark room.

Made me not want to celebrate it.

"My birthday was yesterday, and he didn't even get me anything!" I pointed out, only for Grayson to laugh.

"Your friendship with me is your present every year." He walked over to me, ruffling my hair I pulled away, my eyes zoned in on none other than Margo.

She looked upset which only made me want to hug her.

"What's wrong?" I whispered as she swallowed, "I didn't

know your birthday was yesterday." She muttered as I chuckled in a low tone.

"Why?" I bent down closer, "If you knew would you still have broken up with me?" I asked as she turned her head, her eyes met mine.

"No." She forced a smile, "We were never dating, thus there was never a breakup. We were simply just a summer fling."

I shook my head, "No Margo, we were more than I've ever experienced in my entire life." I whispered.

Before Margo could get a word out, Grayson and the whole group looked at me. They were ready to leave and were waiting on me.

I got up and left without another word.

If looks could kill, Margo Raine Hamilton would've committed murder.

MARGO

It was the next day, and I still have yet to return to my house. My parents have gotten antsy and haven't stopped calling or texting me, I figured that I would make them wait a bit longer.

After all, it wasn't a big deal. I've been at their backyard the entire time and they haven't even noticed.

Although the housekeeper, Jenny saw me enter the guest room, she promised she wouldn't tell a soul, and I believed her.

She also told me some extremely important news that ruined my entire day, possibly my entire school year.

Dean James had come for a surprise visit, informing my parents that last year, I was caught streaking by the campus frat houses. It was either I got expelled or I had a shit tin of community service to do.

What a shocker my parents got me the community service option and get this. I have to help the university's hockey team with their physical therapy!

Could I be any luckier?

Yes, there was sarcasm there, because as much as I loved watch hot boys playing the sport they enjoy and seeing them sweaty and looking good, I hated the idea of me seeing Liam every single day.

It was hard enough that I see him momentarily during school hours and frequently, after school hours because of this stupid deal Grayson and Adrianna came up with.

Today when I opened the door to the university's musical lounge, a bouquet of sunflowers laid on top of the piano. I walked forward only to read the note.

When I'm with you, it just makes sense.

- Liam <3

I couldn't help the smile that crept on to my face. But I also couldn't help the tear that escaped my eyes.

As soon as I snapped back into reality, I took the flowers down the hall to the arts and crafts center, found some trusty scissors and cut them all up.

My next stop was all the way over to Liam, who was standing around his motorcycle with all of his friends.

I threw the bag of cut up flowers and smiled at him before he gave me a knowing smile.

His smile read, that he wasn't going to stop, and I knew it.

He winked at me, in front of all of his friends, "You're going to fold eventually, Raine." He called out as I flipped him off.

I grinned back thickly, "If you think flowers are enough to get me back, you can shove each of them up your ass, Brookshire."

No matter what Liam would try I was going to resist harder.

"You want me to come with you?" I said with a groan as I painted my fingernails.

Adrianna had been moving back and forth in her walk-in closet, she pulled out every article of clothing she practically owned.

"Yes!" She shot out of her closet, "Will you please?" She asked while holding two different colored beanies.

Verina looked at the two different options, we both agreed on the white one. Juliette came stumbling in the room with a bowl of cereal.

Juliette took a look at me, "I thought you had a date?"

"I do." I yawned.

It was true I got asked out by one of the engineering majors today, I however got a message out of nowhere that he wanted to cancel due to a six foot, three inches of muscle threatening him.

I left that part out.

"You know that day I flashed an old couple when I was drunk on campus and streaked down the frat houses?" I mentioned as they all nodded their heads.

"Well, I have earned community service from the university. So, my dad thought it would be a great idea if I was helping the hockey team with their physical therapy."

Adrianna nodded her head slowly, "So like if they get injured, you would have to tend to their wounds?"

I started to gag at the thought of smelly athletes.

"You know we aren't bad; however, you are going to be helping out boys... so I could she the differences." She added before she poured the last of her cereal into her mouth.

"Yes, but also... this is a great way to meet many guys, even from different schools." I continued as their face didn't change.

"More like she likes guys that won't ever like her back." Verina laughs as I threw a well-earned glare at her.

"Says the one making it a decided plan to make Christopher Florence fall in love with her." I revealed as I looked to take a scoop of cereal from Juliette who then swatted my hand away, even when her bowl was already empty.

"Isn't he hot though?" Verina grinned from ear to ear, "Very mysterious!" She added.

"If by mysterious you mean you caught him with your greedy

eyes all by his lonesome at the party, then yes." Adrianna added before Juliette, and I broke into laughter.

"Chris is beautiful." Verina fell on the bed besides Juliette.

"Don't get attached to him." I couldn't help but advise.

Adrianna walked over, and pulled Verina back up, "Grayson mentions that Chris is not looking for a girlfriend. He keeps to himself a lot."

Everyone knew that Christopher was the kid that got a hockey scholarship to Hawthorne. Everywhere people went he was always working there. It was like he had no life, if we were out partying, he would be sometimes bartending.

I ran over to the three of them in the bed, "Oh so it's Grayson now?" I sat on the bed next to Juliette."

Adrianna had never called Grayson by his actual name; it was always Prince or some dumb nickname we created during our years of hatred towards each other.

"I've called him Grayson before," I point out as they all send knowing looks at each other.

"So, you were talking to Grayson?" We all said in unison with smirks, which caused Adrianna to roll her eyes.

"Very mature." She mocked all of us.

"But yes, well we were locked in the janitor's closet, and forced to talk to each other." She finished off quickly.

As minutes of chatter passed, Adrianna and I had to leave to go to whatever Grayson told her to attend and I was the willing accomplice in her mission.

I remembered that I left my lucky lip gloss in the room, so I had to quickly run up and grab it before I descended back down the stairs.

My bra kept unclasping, which to my demise I had to switch over to no bra at all.

I had a moment to look at myself in the mirror and fix any inch of me that I wasn't satisfied with, something my mother did to me before I descended down to a party filled with people I never met to get sent off to the highest bidder.

I opened the door to see a luxurious black car, I ran up to it in a hurry, Adrianna rolled down the window, "What took you so long?"

"My bra kept unclasping, so I switched." I smiled, before getting into the car, only for my eyes to target Liam Brookshire.

"Well, let's go!" He forced out as I groaned.

"Why is he taking us?" I asked.

Adrianna looked a bit annoyed, "Prince couldn't make it."

There was a moment of dead silence that I made a decision to butcher, "What do you expect us to do while you guys are skating around like figure skaters?" I complained as Adrianna grinned.

Liam kept his eyes on the road ahead, "Talk like you guys always do." He smirked at me before adding, "That shouldn't be a problem."

"You can flirt with the players." Adrianna turned over to me, and gave me a moment to spot Liam's narrowed eyes on the rearview mirror

"You bet." I grimaced over to Liam who looked even more agitated.

"You have no shot against the boys." He laughed as my eyebrows furrowed.

I leaned in between the seats, "Why not?"

Liam looked flustered as I leaned closer to him, "They are way too focused on the season."

His sentence only made me more excited, "I sense a challenge." I smiled.

Another silence beckoned and suffocated the car, Liam look fully about ready to pull over and give me a nice lecture by the sidewalk.

"The arena isn't far from the mall." Liam addressed as Adrianna scowled.

I look over at him with an annoyed look, "Grayson wants me to watch." Adrianna said.

"Grayson also wants a Bugatti, but his father will flip his shit if he buys another car." Liam shot back as I couldn't help a snort.

"Like that would create a dent on his card."

"No, but Grayson tends to splurge on things he doesn't need." Liam defended his best friend as I gave a sassy reply.

"And you don't?" My powerful gaze meet with his once again on the rear-view mirror.

"No," Liam smirked, "I tend to resist the things I want." He continued.

He thought he was being clever, well he wasn't.

"Too bad maybe that thing you want will end up being sold out." I snapped back as he gave a small little laugh before pulling the shift into park.

Adrianna got out of the car, she already started greeting Grayson by the front of the hockey arena.

Liam and I got out of the vehicle the same time, but before I could even pull away from the car, his hands gripped my waist and pushed me against the side of the car where no one could see us.

"I've been really patient, Raine." He grumbled against my ear as I couldn't help but feel the wetness form in between my legs.

"Patience is a virtue." I shot back as I could feel his hot breath against my neck.

"If I see you flirt with another guy in there. The moment I get you back, I will fuck you so hard, the only man's name you'll remember is mine." He murmured as I felt my knees weaken.

Liam held me up, and before I knew it, I felt a soreness on my neck that felt amazing at the same time.

Oh god, he gave me a fucking hickey.

It took all my will power not to tell him to keep going and push him away from me instead.

I groaned, "I hate you."

I placed my hand on top of the hickey I just received as he just shot an innocent smile at me, "No you don't, because if I put my hand in between your legs, we both know what I'll find, Raine."

I didn't even respond, before I walked over to Adrianna and Grayson, which left Liam behind.

Hours passed since the practice, and I found myself walking around the hockey rink.

I figured if I was going to spend more time here then I might as well be familiar to it.

I walked into an empty office, I walked around even more only to sport many team pictures or guys who looked like they loved each other.

One picture with Liam, Grayson, Neil and Chris stood out to me as they held the championship trophy. Everyone knew that hockey was a big deal in Hawthorne, I remembered Liam telling me that he practically killed himself in high school trying to get scouted by Hawthorne.

Grayson, Neil, Chris and he were a package deal. A bunch more trophies and medals were hung on the walls, glass cases filled with it.

As I continued down the hallway, I walked into what seemed to be the boy's empty locker room. I turned a corner, only to see several men, shirtless and absolutely ripped.

My eyes widened in fear as I back out of the room, my body slammed against a tall figure with rock hard muscles. My eyes shut momentarily because with my luck I knew exactly who was behind me.

"Look who's lost." He grumbled as I turned around slowly to meet him gaze.

"I'm not lost, I just went into the wrong direction." I shot out quickly as his eyes narrowed.

"You know for wanting to be away from me, you surely end up the same place I am quite often." He scoffed out as I ignored his comment.

Liam's eyes found the clock behind me, he placed his hands on my waist and pulled me to the slide quickly.

"Get your hands off of me." I whispered as he pulled away.

Only for a second it was silent, before a major herd of hockey players rammed inside the locker room like they were some sort of animals.

Liam leaned closer to me once more, "I just saved you from ending up like Simba from *the Lion King*, by the way." He pointed out as blew out a huff.

The last person who came into the locker room was Coach Livingston who looked like he had ran an entire marathon himself.

I tried sneaking out, before he spotted me by his peripheral vision, "Hamilton!" He yelled for the whole locker room to hear.

Everyone in the room instantly quieted and all their eyes directed at mine.

"Sorry I was just looking around, getting used to things around here." I muttered as he nodded.

"Listen up!" Coach Livingston screamed as Liam gave me a confused look.

"You guys probably know Margo Hamilton already, but if you've been living under a rock, she's the new physical therapist intern and she will take care of any of you with injuries and any of that sort." He further announced.

Two players from the team already started to approach us as Coach Livingston paused, "And they also have to be real injuries and not fake ones just so you can flirt and try and hook up with Miss Hamilton." He swatted them both away as I couldn't help but laugh.

"This is my assistant coach, Asher Reese." He points at a man with a clip board and then points at a woman with dyed maroon hair, who looked like she worked out for a living.

"And that is Trainer Ronni Cruz." He continued as I greeted her with a smile, "You will probably be hanging around her office the most." He informed me as I nodded intently.

"I really don't feel like introducing the whole team today, so you will be just meeting them along the way." He added.

"Thanks Coach Livingston." I smiled.

He looked at me with complexity, "Margo, you act like I haven't seen you in diapers with Juliette, you can call me Brian." He said with a small grin before he pat my shoulder.

I snuck a look at Liam who had a mixture of me being a part of his hockey team was the worst thing to ever exist and at the same time he looked like he had a plan up his sleeve.

"Lastly, Margo gets the Juliette treatment, making her off limits. If I hear one word from her that you have been harassing her, or word on the fucking arena that you have made a silly bet or tried anything, you are benched for future games. Do you understand me?" He raised his voice.

Juliette's dad was scary alright, I think it's what made all the boys stay attentive, but he always knew what he was talking about which made everyone respect him even more.

He was the most sought-after hockey coach in all of the East Coast. He was tough too, I remembered when I had to participate in soccer camp with Juliette for the summer. He made us do fifty pushups, then fifty burpees, with suicides if we couldn't score. If we failed, he would make us do it again.

So those are my credentials to know that if you were being trained by Brian Livingston, you were one tough cookie. But I also knew that all the boys in the team were picked and scouted for a reason.

They don't just let anyone join Hawthorne's Hockey team.

Liam's eyes lingered on mine for a while before they met with the other guys on the team checking me out already.

I just realized that this was the perfect battlefield for Liam and me. So many guys threw themselves at me and all he could do is watch. He wasn't allowed to hook up with me or he would be benched and lastly, I could watch him suffer through drills and at the same time.

I could watch him work out. Which by the way was one of my favorite things to do in Greece.

And I could also learn a bit more about hockey, I've always wanted to learn more anyways.

Liam walked closer to me with a smirk plastered on his face, "Looks like I'll be seeing you around more often, Raine."

God, he smelled so good, I wanted to kiss him.

"Not by choice." I muttered with a scowl.

Liam turned back to me with a menacing laugh, "Well maybe you shouldn't go streaking down the frat houses next time."

My eyes widened.

He was the one who snitched on me.

But before I could get another word out, Liam winked and disappeared into the large locker room filled with men.

CHAPTER 20

LIAM

Day 5 of Project "Get Raine Back."

I'm not going to lie to you, but this plan was a major bust. I've gotten so many flowers thrown, shredded ripped and slapped at my face it's starting to get embarrassing.

And I'm not the type to get embarrassed quickly.

After my daily ranting phone call from Finn about how nothing is working and how much Margo hates my guts, I decided to blow off some steam and skate around the hockey arena and practice some drills.

There were a lot of stuff I needed to work on anyways, while I was on vacation in Greece I completely forgot to train for hockey since a certain blonde daydream captured my attention.

I was distracted.

I still am distracted.

Grayson and the other guys didn't miss one day of training which kind of made me feel bad that I did. I've been trying to catch up, but Grayson trained like a fucking crazy madman.

No one really loved this game like he did.

I did it to get away from my stepfather, and he did it to

impress his father. Chris did it to distract himself from the fact that he didn't have a father, and Neil did it to piss off his father.

What a fucking circle of friends we are.

It was already late, and the light had dimmed inside the arena, the perfect time to think and self-reflect.

I was wearing my gray sweatpants with a Hawthorne sweatshirt and a windbreaker over it, I tied up my laces and began to skate around for what felt like forever.

I paused to see a certain blonde strutting down the hallway, carrying a bunch of water bottles and she bit down on a booklet. She had only been here for about one day and she had already been working overtime?

Margo walked over to the sinbin and laid out the booklet and the water bottles. I couldn't help but smile at her as she tried to figure out the ropes of inside the arena.

"You need help?" I asked as her eyes widened; her body jolted backwards.

"Liam!" She gasped, "How long have you been there!" She snapped as I gave a gentle smile.

"Long enough to see you struggling to walk holding all of those water bottles." I pointed out as she shook her head.

"So, you just stood there and chose not to help me." She muttered with an attitude as I leaned on the boards.

"I thought you said you didn't want me near you." I countered as she threw me a fake smile.

"And so far, you haven't listened to me one bit." Margo flipped through the pages of her booklet; she seemed pretty set on ignoring me.

I wasn't going to lie; did she not care that I was here late all by myself?

"Are you going to ask me why I'm here?" I muttered as she sighed over my question.

I rolled my eyes at her pettiness; she was giving me the silent treatment now.

"Well, what are you doing here?" I asked as she turned away from me, revealing the title of the book she was closely reading.

"How to learn how to skate for dummies?" I laughed as she pulled the book away from her face to death stare me.

"It does not say dummies!" Anger rippled out of her as I skated around in circles.

"How are you going to learn how to skate with a fucking book? You actually need to try it." I said matter of a factly as she slammed the book on the seat.

"Liam, please just do your thing and I do mine." She asked kindly as I grinned back at her.

"I'm just saying Raine, if you want to learn so badly, I could teach you and then you can return that god awful book that's probably teaching you nonsense." I skated towards her as she eyed me up.

She looked down at my skates and down at hers, "I don't even have skates." She informed me as I looked at her and rolled my eyes.

"Come with me." I got out of the ice and stood by the door as she hesitated to follow me.

"Come on, I don't bite Raine." I winked as she took a step closer to me.

Only suck, lick and kiss. I wanted to say to her. Those were the exact things I wanted to do with Margo Hamilton right now.

"Where are you taking me?" She asked with worry.

We approached a closet where the four of us kept things we valued the most. Even if it looked like a bunch of junk, Grayson, Chris, Neil and I kept things in here that we cared about.

I opened the closet door and pulled out a pair for size seven skates for a woman.

"I am not wearing one of your puck bunny's skates." She snarled as I couldn't help but chuckle at her comment.

I pulled out the tag that was still on them, her eyes found mine.

"I asked Ronni to buy skates for you when we were together

in Greece because I knew that I would want to teach you how to skate." I slurred as her eyes held a certain look to them that I hadn't seen since we were in Greece.

"Oh." Margo swallowed as if it was all she could say.

I felt the air thicken as I wanted to place my hand on her cheek, feel how warm she was.

But I held back, she followed me back out to the arena. She sat down to put her skates on, but I beat her to it, I bent down and started tying them up for her.

Margo swatted my hands away, "I can do it myself." She voiced as I gave her a look.

"Doesn't mean you should." I murmured before I took her hand and led her to the ice rink.

Margo started to sink into my arms as I pulled her further into the rink.

"Okay, I want you to just try standing on the ice with your skates, okay?" I instructed as she looked at me with hate.

Like if I would let go of her, she would actually haunt my dreams.

After I let go of her, she started to shake.

"Raine, just relax. You can do it baby." I coached as she started to panic.

"How am I supposed to relax when you aren't here!" She screamed as my whole body almost shut down from the alarm in her voice.

"You can do it." I said as she took a deep breath and stood taller.

That's my girl.

"That's good, now can you just try walking over to me, don't skate just walk."

Margo listened to me, she started to walk closer to me, but I kept backing away from her. I could see the frustration that grew in her eyes like she was desperate for my support.

Even if she couldn't see it, Margo was doing so well. I didn't think she noticed that her eyes remained on mine the whole time.

The majority of first-time skater's eyes are glued to their feet on the ice in front of them. But her eyes were on *me*.

I finally held on to her cold hands, she stopped shaking and her body started to relax once more. I began to skate backwards while I dragged her around with me to get her used to moving in a gliding motion.

We both stayed silent as I kept moving. Her eyes were now directed to her surroundings, not paying attention to the fact that we were on the ice.

"I'm going to let go now." I said as her eyes widened again.

"No." She said in a panic as I laugh, "Don't worry even if I'm not with you I'm watching you and I'll be there for you."

Margo took a breather before letting go of my hands, before she knew it, she started skating, obviously it wasn't professional or hockey style skating, but she was skating.

"I'm doing it!" She beamed as I couldn't help but smile at her sunshine of a face.

"See I told you; you didn't need that stupid ass book. You just needed me." I took her hand and led her back to where the ice ended.

Margo looked at me for one second before she jumped up and wrapped her arms around my neck. Her lips enveloped mine as I groaned into her mouth.

Margo pulled away for a second, "Just this once." She muttered as I picked her up from the ground, her legs wrapped around my waist.

I could get lost in her mouth, truthfully, I would die a happy man if I got to kiss her for the rest of my life.

It didn't take long for me to slam her body against the boards. Margo was already moaning for more as my fingers found their way under her skirt.

"Fuck." She writhed under my touch as I kneeled down and spread her legs.

I could hear her muffled moans, her hips bucked as I grinned from ear to ear. My hand finally came in contact with her wet and warm pussy. I relished her sweet smell before my lips parted.

Her head dropped back as she rolled her hips for more contact.

My breathing got heavier, and her chest heaved, she grunted, groaned and moaned lowly, trying not to make any noise. I took a second to look up as she licked her lips.

"Raine give me your hand." I commanded as she gave me her delicate hand.

I brought her hand to her wet center, making her moan louder at the contact.

"Next time you defy me, remember who makes you wet like this." I whispered as she started to rub herself in front of me begging for any sort of friction.

I grabbed her hand away from her, which caused her to jolt. I took her fingers in my mouth with a large sigh, I tilted my head back to savor her.

"So, fucking sweet." I muttered as her knees shook.

Margo moaned deeply as my mouth hovered over her clit, ready to feast until her phone began to ring.

Her eyes widened and her cheeks blushed scarlet red, she looked at the caller to show me it was Adrianna calling.

I smiled.

"Answer it." I muttered as she shook her head no.

"Answer it or I'm going to stop." I clarified as the look on her face looked absolutely mortified.

She swallowed before she answered her phone, "Babe?" She said with a shaky breath.

"Margo. Thank God." I could hear Adrianna pacing around as I sunk my teeth into her thighs.

Margo hisses down at me, without stopping me.

"Am I interrupting something?" Adrianna asked as Margo's eyes never left mine.

"No, of course not."

Margo's eyes widened even more as I smiled around her skin in my mouth, her head knocked back and hit the boards.

"Are you okay?" Margo asked with worry and fear as I moved Margo's hips closer to my mouth, I hummed against her folds and nudged her clit with my nose.

"Yes. Actually, Grayson and I got into a screaming match."

"Sounds typical, what's the problem?" Margo pulled my head closer to her as she set the phone down.

"Well, you know how much we hate each other, and I would rather stick a blade into my torso than ever be affectionate with him." Adrianna kept rambling as my tongue gave Margo's pussy a big lap.

"Your point?" Margo gritted, making me laugh lightly before I resumed fucking her with my tongue which kept driving her against the hockey boards.

Her hands gripped my hair and her right tit, she tried to silence her moan but only a few were successfully truly hidden.

"Well, I think I'm going to ask him to take my virginity." My eyes widened the same time as Margo's.

Margo's body started to shake as well as her legs as I sucked on her clit, her eyes rolled to the back of her head. She let out a gasp and a sigh.

"Adrianna." Her voice was shaky and not loud enough.

"Margo."

"Anna, you can't be serious," She exhales, "You can't possibly want Grayson Prince to take your virginity." Margo said as she thrusted her hips to my tongue.

"I don't want him too; I'm giving it up." Adrianna explained.

Truthfully, I didn't care what the conversation was about, I only cared about the girl who was on my mouth.

Adrianna went on a whole rant of something I couldn't even recall, my eyes only remained on Margo's.

"You like having your clit sucked like a slut, huh?" I moaned while I licked her folds. It was like my words further electrified her need for me.

She started to rub her clit with her fingers, "That's it Raine, such a good girl, riding my mouth so good."

I sucked and licked faster; she stopped concentrating on the call with Adrianna.

"Your virginity is very important. You should have someone that will cherish it with you for your first time, you do understand that Grayson is notorious for..." She paused, her eyes rolling back once again.

"...being a God and a Devil in bed." She sighs.

"I know." Adrianna continued.

Margo continued to have a conversation with Adrianna, as I teased and licked her. She started to grow impatient as I moved my hands from her hips.

I brought it over to her pussy, I held her apart and dove in, making her groan loudly. Her hand slapped on her mouth to stop any audible noise to come out.

Margo's body moved along with mine like she had been lost in the lust and the euphoria I had served her.

The next thing I heard from Adrianna's phone call was a brief meaningful advice from her.

"Oh, and Margo. Use a condom." Adrianna hung up immediately. As I took two of my fingers and fucked Margo's pussy.

"Come on baby, don't fight it, say my name when you come." I mutter as I went to a faster pace.

I felt her nails dig into my hair as well as her walls constricted around my fingers. I took my other hand and started to rub her clit, sending her to drop her mask and loudly moan.

"Liam." She moaned out as I felt her tighten around me, her legs stopped shaking and her eyes looked absolutely dazed.

The way she moaned my name tonight would be burned in my brain for the rest of my life. That was for sure.

I finally set her down back on the ice, she stood there looking like a damn angel. I got up and smiled.

"See I told you; you would get the hang of skating." Margo looked at me and grinned.

An actual smile with her teeth showing and everything! This was a very successful day of winning Raine back! Sure, I might've needed for her to come in my mouth, but it was still progress.

I licked my lips to savor the last of her sweetness. Only to infer that she wouldn't let me ever do that again, at least not for a while.

"I can't believe, I answered Anna's call while I was––" She got flushed as I smiled.

"While my tongue was on your pussy?" I finished as she pushed me back playfully. She got down and started to pull off her skates.

She stayed silent as I changed the subject, "Margo what else can I do to win you back?"

She pondered for a moment before a grin appeared on her face.

"Sing in front of the whole school." She challenged as I closed my eyes in annoyance, wishing I never asked.

"You can't be serious." I laughed softly as her face remained the same.

"Thanks for the lessons, Charming." She winked at me before disappearing into the two double doors on the hockey arena.

God, I'm forever ruined for any other female that looks at my direction.

Because that is the girl that I want, the only one I will forever want.

CHAPTER 21

MARGO

"Margo, come outside right now!" Verina yelled at me as Juliette pulled me away from the piano and practically dragged me to the front lawn.

"What is the matter with all of you!" I grumbled.

I only paused and stopped more words from coming out of my mouth the moment I realized that the whole student body was outside.

They were all staring at me, like I was an A list celebrity.

"Margo Hamilton." I heard a voice yell as I turned my head to the direction the voice echoed from.

Nothing but horror filled my eyes, when I realized the yell came from none other than William Brookshire who stood on top of a table, in front of everyone.

I pulled away from Juliette's grasps, walking closer to Liam, "Get down from there Liam." I whispered harshly as he shook his head.

"You said you wanted me to sing in front of everyone in the whole school, right?" He clarified as my face only turned redder than ever.

"William Brookshire, get down right now!" The panic in my

eyes started to reach the surface of my face as the whole Hawthorne hockey team emerged from out of nowhere.

Neil pulled out a microphone and Chris pulled out his camera.

I didn't think he would've actually done it, but he was up there, no embarrassment in his face whatsoever. Nothing but a big old smile.

"This song is for you." He pointed at me as everyone in the lawn started to gush at the idea of the grant gesture.

Before I knew it *When I was your Man* by Bruno Mars started blasting on the speakers.

I looked around only to find the whole music department of Hawthorne were a part of it. The hockey team were dancing in the background as well as other random students started pairing up and slow dancing.

I tried to fight the smile that emerged from my face, the whole school seemed to be in on it.

Liam jumped down from the table, brought the microphone to his mouth and started singing the well-known words, everyone sang along.

They pulled out their flashlights from their cellphones and started to serenate the whole school even when it was broad daylight.

Liam took my hand and guided me to the middle of the lawn and started to slow dance with me, to be honest, it was cute. He continued to sing and everyone else did with him.

"I'll do whatever you throw at me Raine," He announced as I shook my head in disbelief at his ambition to keep trying to pursue me.

I only threw him a disgusted look and began to walk away from the concert he was putting up for me.

But he ran after me, his hand captured mine, which made me turn back to look at him.

As the song ended, one of his friends handed him another

bouquet of flowers. This time they were different colored roses; he ended the song and handed me the flowers.

"Just for tonight, please wear my jersey to the game and just watch." He asked as everyone in the crowd was entertained by the question.

I waited for a moment; everyone was at the edge of their seat.

"Fine." I muttered.

I'll give him what he wants tonight, only because of the concert and the amazing head he provided last night. I tried my hardest to resist William Brookshire, but if he keeps pulling these stunts, I'm afraid he might actually win.

Win me back.

Adrianna had decided not to attend the boy's hockey game tonight. Grayson and she got into a screaming match during the whole concert Liam had orchestrated for me.

After she left, I couldn't help but think about why she was going through these lengths to piss Grayson off. I didn't understand that even Liam would keep embarrassing himself just to get me back when he lost me in the first place.

The bouquet of roses he had bought out for me had been sitting on top of my desk. Those roses probably cost a bunch of money, but he didn't care. He knew there was a ninety percent probability that I would cut them up and send it back to his doorway.

But he kept sending them anyways. It made me wonder the other lengths he would go through just to get me back.

I pulled out a notebook and started listing five outrageous things that Liam had to do for me to even consider getting back with him. If he didn't complete them all, then he wasn't taking me seriously.

Since I ran out of room in the front, I wrote in the back that he needed to let me know if he is agreeing to doing what was written on the list by meeting me at my parent's guest house before midnight.

If he doesn't show up by then, I'm making a promise to myself that I will forever close my heart to him and there will be no way for him to get me back after.

Even if it hurts to let him go, I had to do it for myself and for my parents.

I had landed on wearing designer boots, luckily for me Liam had two of his goons deliver his sought-after jersey for me to wear to the trainer's room.

It smelled exactly like him. I walked over to Liam's cubby and slipped the folded piece of paper on top of his picture with his family.

But it was ripped, the picture only consisted of him and his mother, his father seemed to be ripped off.

He never talked about his father; I could only infer that he wasn't a very nice man.

I moved the picture only to find a beautiful diamond bracelet with gold attaching each and every single diamond.

But before I could do even more digging, I started to hear loud commotion of men walking in.

I quickly ran out the back exit so I couldn't be spotted.

I remembered pointing out that diamond bracelet when we were in Greece. It of course was way too expensive for me to buy. I never knew he went back and bought it.

I took a breath; hearing Liam and Grayson's voice emerge from the locker room.

I had no idea if Liam was ever going to show me or tell me that he bought the bracelet for me. If he didn't, I wasn't exactly sure how I felt about the fact that I knew he did.

LIAM

. . .

"What on earth are you wearing right now." Grayson snarled at me as I looked down at my pregame suit.

"It's a Brioni." I informed as he gave a disgusted look.

"That's a Brushitty." Grayson threw back as I flipped him off.

We arrived at the locker rooms; we were always the first two people here. Usually, Grayson was but I'm rarely never late.

"So, have you started thinking about who the next team captain should be? You know once we're gone?" I asked as he looked around to see if anyone else was in the room with us.

"Well, we still have like two more years dude." He voiced as I started to unpack my bag.

"Yeah, but don't you think the Freshman are already showing off their skills to you and coach?"

"Yeah, your right I think I know which freshman you are thinking about." He smiled at me as I smiled back.

Grayson and I were always on the same page.

"I'm so glad you think that Khons is the best pick."

"Yeah, Duke has been showing the work." I muttered as we both realized we were not thinking of the same person.

Grayson dropped his stick and turned to me, "You think Duke Kean is the freshman that's been putting in the work?" He gaped as my eyes narrowed.

"You think Dustin Khons has?!" I laughed as he nodded his head seriously.

"Kean is insanely fast on the ice even with pressure and a puck." I defended as he rolled his eyes.

"That gets you nowhere without looking around and being a team player. He's always hogging the puck." Grayson pointed out as I rolled my eyes.

"Well, we'll have to keep watching them, won't we?" I blanched as Grayson slowly nodded his head.

"Watch them, we shall."

I kept my eyes narrowed to his before I caught a note on my cubby.

"Oh, by the way how was your karaoke thing in front of the whole school? Sorry I missed it I was preoccupied by a stubborn fake girlfriend who finds enjoyment of not listening to me." Grayson kept talking as I opened the note.

By the looks of it, it was in Margo's handwriting.

"Earth to William?" Grayson waved his hand in front of my face as I read the list of things Margo wanted me to do in order for her to take me seriously.

Which was ironic considering the fact that all of the things she had written for me to do were completely unserious.

"Eat twenty jalapeños without water or milk?" I read out loud as Grayson pulled the note from my hand.

"Add another tattoo to your body."

"Learn to name all of the fifty states in alphabetical order."

Grayson took a moment to reread the last one as he smiled before reading it aloud.

"Shave off your hair." He finished off as my eyes widened and my mouth dropped to the floor.

"That's a fucking joke, right?!" I exclaimed as he smirked.

"Nah I'm just joking with you, Will." He yawned as he passed me the note.

"She gave you free reign to pick whatever you want to do for the last one." Grayson muttered before he turned back to his locker.

He looked at me like I was crazy.

"All this for a girl?" Grayson asked as I rolled my eyes.

"You are literally fake dating Adrianna to win your ex-girlfriend back." I shot back at him as he hesitated to say something.

"You would get your nails done with me, wouldn't you?" I asked quietly as Grayson's head slowly turned to face mine.

"William Brookshire, you're lucky you're my best friend." He snapped as I smiled back.

I had a feeling it would be like this. Grayson was falling for Adrianna Cassian, but in my opinion, he's been in love with her ever since he laid eyes on her.

He always denied it because it felt like it was forbidden by his father for some odd reason. I've only ever seen Adrianna's father once, and it was when our parents had to tour Hawthorne University.

He seemed scary and easily irritated but he was always on side quests, on his phone or taking care of some other business.

I knew Grayson like I knew the back of my hand. This wasn't just about getting August back. He didn't know it himself, but every now and then I could see his eyes linger on Adrianna's every move.

As if she tripped or anything he would be there to catch her.

"You wanna drive with me to Philly tonight?" I asked as he shook his head.

"I can't. I suspect that I'll be getting a visit from Cassian." Grayson said in a sing song way that made my eyebrows wrinkle.

"You can ask Chris, or maybe even Neil." Grayson suggested as I nodded, "Why, what did your father do to piss you off now?" He finished as I laughed.

"Stepfather." I corrected him before continuing, "I just heard about some shady shit about him from a few people and I want to know if he's staying out of trouble. Besides my mother also wants the divorced papers signed."

Chris and Neil walked in together.

"Well, if it isn't the married couple." Neil snarked as Chris blew out a laugh.

Grayson and I looked at each other then flipped both of them off.

"Were we interrupting anything?" Chris asked as Grayson shook his head in dismay.

They made fun of Grayson and me because we always spent an abnormal amount of time together. No shame. I love my best friend.

"What's that?" Chris walked over to the opened note in my cubby.

"It's a list of things I have to do in order for Margo to take me seriously." I answered as they burst out in laughter.

"Get nails done?" Neil's eyes widened as I shook my head in shame.

"You're actually going to do this?" They asked in unison as I pulled the paper out of their gremlin hands.

"Yes, I will. If this is what she wants from me then so be it." I breathed out as all three of them looked at me like I was some sort of lost puppy.

"What has she done to you?" Chris looked at me in disbelief.

"One day you'll understand boys. When you fall in love, and you see your whole future, but you can't imagine it without her." I preached as all of them ignored me fully.

I rolled my eyes.

Gee. I sure do love my friends.

CHAPTER 22

MARGO

"GO LIAM!" I heard shrieks come out of several girl's mouths as they stood up and intently watched Liam skate around during the game.

The team was losing and yet the girls still kept screaming at the boys.

Verina and Juliette had sat next to me as I rolled my eyes repeatedly and ignored the eye contact, that Liam would hold with me from across the arena.

"Shouldn't you be over there?" Juliette muttered as I turned to look at her.

"Am I?" I stood up, not sure if I was supposed to.

"Margo! You are technically part of the team now. Get over there!" Verina pushed me into one of the many girls that looked like a copy and paste of each other.

Of course, with my luck the girl I slammed into was holding a poster which was specifically made for Liam.

"Did they just say you're like a part of the team?" The girl beamed as I smiled thickly.

"Uh... yes." I muttered, as I slowly walked away from her, she followed me.

"Do you personally know Liam?" She asked as I nodded.

"Well tell him to return my calls!" She shouted as I ran away from her as quickly as possible.

Oh my god, these girls were crazy.

As I approached the team, they started unloading and walked over to the locker room. I could hear Grayson screaming already.

I certainly wouldn't want to be in that locker room, that's for sure.

Ronni's eyes found mine, she started to wave me over, I walked closer to realize she was making an ice pack for a player on the other team.

"Thought you were never going to show." She said as my face turned bright red.

"I actually have been here and completely forgot about the intern portion." I explained further as she laughed.

"Trust me, it's a lot peaceful on this side of the arena than that side. You have screaming girls around you wishing the best of luck to their favorite player."

"Unlucky for you, your boyfriend is a heavily picked heart-throb around here." She made a point as I laughed lightly.

"Uhm, no he's not my boyfriend." I corrected.

Ronni looked at me up and down, then behind me to where the players started to walk out of the locker room.

"Then how comes you two look at each other like you are made for each other?" She asked as I turned to Verina who suddenly appeared.

"What are you doing here!" I snapped at her as she laughed, "Take a chill pill, I just wanna see what you're doing."

"Nothing right now, no one is really injured except for that guy." Ronni pointed at the opposing team member who laid on their back with the ice pack on their arm.

"You girls can chill and watch the game from this side for a while." Ronni advised as we both nodded and walked over near the benches.

Verina's eyes automatically scanned around to look for

Christopher Florence. Which has been her newly found obsession.

As we wait around there, the team starched out, Grayson approached both of Verina and I with narrowed eyes and a mission.

"Where the hell is she?" He demanded an answer.

"Why do you care?" I smirked as his eyes darkened even more.

"She's at Brooks' game, isn't she?" He scowled as I stayed quiet. I didn't want to add to Grayson's disappointment as a part of me already understood that he knew that Adrianna wasn't going to attend.

Liam skated over to Grayson and me, "Don't worry man, we can still win this, even without your girl." He patted Grayson's shoulder.

Grayson looked about ready to throw hands, he looked laser focused on the scoreboard and the fact that they were losing. Liam looked at me with a wink as I avoided his eye contact.

"Learn your states yet?" I muttered while a smirk as he smiled.

"You are so incredibly lucky to know that I remember the fifty nifty United States song we learned in elementary school." He shot back with an innocent smile as I looked at Verina who gave him a fist bump.

"You're gonna have to work a lot harder to get me to stay away from my future wife." Liam smiled widely at me before he skated away.

I shot a look to Grayson as he put both his hands up.

"Don't look at me, I can't take your side. I always help my best friend win, even if it's winning a girl back." He quickly muttered before he skated away from Verina and me.

"I mean there is absolutely no way he is getting his nails done right?" I throw a look at Verina who didn't back me up.

"I don't know Margo... he seemed to look pretty determined and not only that, his whole friend group may have big egos, but they are definitely secure with all their masculinities." She rattled off as I looked back at Liam and Grayson skating around.

I really did hope that Liam would finish the list.

But that was really up to him.

I just saw someone's legs break.

I watched as Ronni and other people pulled Twain's body into a stretcher. I knew that he received a concussion, but everyone knew he might've just lost his whole ability to walk.

Grayson didn't even look like he felt bad. None of them did. I walked past Liam who looked like he was on a mission to leave the place.

To be fair, the game was done, and I knew that players were either tired or ready to party somewhere else.

"Liam, how's Grayson?" I asked as he tilted his head.

"How could Grayson do something like that?" I shook my head as Liam paused.

"Whatever happened, Grayson didn't mean to break his legs Raine. Grayson also wouldn't have striked like that if Twain didn't provoke him into doing so." Liam finished his sentence quickly before I pulled him back with his arm.

"Where are you going?" I grew worried he wasn't going to meet me by the guest house.

"I'm a mysterious man, Raine." He joked before he threw a wink at me.

He certainly was, and I guess all I could really do was trust him.

That wasn't as easy to do than say.

CHAPTER 23

LIAM

ater that night.

"Do not get crumbs in my car." I grumbled as Neil paused his action of stuffing a burrito down his throat.

"We just finished a game; I need to refuel the body man." He panned out before he threw me a cold look.

Silence.

"Listen, you need to chill out." He continued.

I took a deep breath in and a deep breath out. Neil was right, I've lately been snapping at so many people. I've been snapping at coaches, professors, and even some teammates.

I haven't thought straight ever since I found out about my stepfather's embezzlement.

I had no clue what the fuck those two girls' problem with Margo was. And the fact that I haven't had sex since I had been with Margo.

"You're right. I'm sorry." I apologized.

Neil smiled back at me, I often forgot that wasn't his normal personality when he talked to other people. He was always cold and mean.

When in reality he was a soft baby who just indulged in so much food on the daily.

"Besides, we both know Grayson and Cassian are probably spending the night together, Chris and the Du Pont girl are starting to hang out as friends. We are the only two bachelors left, it's so obvious that Hamilton doesn't give two shits about you anymore man." He finished off his burrito.

For a man who was eating a stuffed ass burrito he sure had a lot to say.

"What do you mean Chris and Verina are hanging out?" I asked, quite shocked.

"Well, you know she was trying to pursue him and he like straight up rejected her. You know how he is." Neil rambled on.

Chris didn't believe in true love. Sure, he believed in caring for someone and loving family and friends, but he doesn't believe in the act of falling in love.

He's always made it clear; he didn't trust easily and ultimately, I understood that you need to trust in order to love.

"How has Chris been doing in the fights?" I turned my car and drove into the driveway of my old Philadelphia mansion.

Neil took a second to respond, "He hasn't lost any yet, the prize money has gone up to six hundred thousand right now and it isn't even close to finals."

"Yeah well, rich crooks and stupid people will pay for anything just for some enjoyment. You think that's enough for Finn's treatment?" I turned off the ignition and got out of the car.

Neil slammed the passenger door, "I just don't understand why Chris won't let us give him money. Finn is our brother too at this point, I say we get a say in how he gets the money for his treatment."

Deep down, Neil and I also knew that it still wasn't our place to tell Chris how to raise his brother. He had every right to, he was the one who changed Finn's diapers, fed him, clothed him, and took care of him when he was sick.

As Neil and I both approached the large double doors, Neil gave the door one push and they both opened without a hassle or a lock.

My stepfather sat on the tall chair in front of the fireplace, he was smoking a cigar, and he looked like shit.

"William!" He greeted me.

"Killian." I addressed as Neil closed the door behind us.

"So glad to know that you look cozy in a house that you probably paid for, by embezzling money."

My stepfather stood up, pulling a bottle of scotch out of the cabinet, and took a large swig of the alcohol.

"When is your mother coming home?" He had the nerve to ask as I stomped over to his body quickly, before Neil pulled me back from causing some major damage.

Thank God, I did bring him; we both knew if I didn't, I would've committed some type of murder. My stepfather wasn't a good man, I knew he wasn't a truthful businessman, neither was he a truthful husband or father.

He brought countless of women home every night when my mother was on trips around the world to launch her jewels. While he was acting the supportive role, he was having countless affairs.

I couldn't even say anything because my mouth would meet with his fists, and my body would be met by his belt. It didn't take long until I knew I could fight back.

"We both know she isn't coming home, Killian." I muttered while throwing a file front of him, "Sign those divorce papers and I won't turn you in for embezzlement." I mustered off as he gave a vicious look at Neil who guarded the door.

He grabbed the pen that I rolled over to his hand, I looked at his menacing smirk.

I halted, as he read over the words on paper.

"Funny how she sends you as the guinea pig to get these papers signed." He lazily signed the papers.

"If you pull more illegal shit Killian, trust me when I say I will watch you rot in prison." I seethed; while placing my pointed finger on his chest, I gave him a slight push which set him back for a little.

"I'm very flattered you want to watch me, but don't forget

William. When I go down, you and your mother go down with me. You are still my family, and you are associated that way."

I threw a sappy look at Neil before he turned around. That was when I let my anger seeped through me, I clenched both my knuckles so tight I saw my veins popped up more than ever.

Next thing I knew, my fist came in contact with his nose, and his body made contact with the hard floor.

"Looks like I did teach you something well." He spat back.

Harsh memories of Killian snapped into my brain. I envisioned a time back then when he damn near snapped my neck. A day after he lifted me up by my throat and slammed me down on the cold concrete floor.

He always took pride on giving me a great education, but he continuously failed to talk about how he would stab my hand with a pencil when I got an equation wrong.

And he wondered why the fuck I moved out so quickly.

"Did your speech get inspired by the *Hunger Games* or something?" Neil gave a contemplating look as we watched my stepfather's nose, bleed out on the ground.

"What are you talking about?" I turned to Neil with confusion as he shrugged.

"You know Katniss's speech to President Snow. If we burn, you burn with us." He recited with passion as my father, and I gave him a dumb founded look.

We stayed silent for a second before my stepfather speaks up again, "You can hit me all you want William, but it isn't going to change the fact that you still need me to keep being relevant in our high society."

I gave him a second to catch his breath before I pulled him back up by the neck.

"My mother and I don't need you Killian. We are better off without you, and if you do some more illegal shit, since you signed those divorce papers... we couldn't care less what you fucking do." I threw him back on the ground.

Killian laid there and stayed down. He was never a father to me in anyway, only ever a man who would bully the fuck out of me and claimed it was because he wanted me to be better than him.

I knew I was better than him, because I had never laid a hand on a woman who didn't want it. I would never willingly and repeatedly abuse a child who did nothing to deserve it.

I would spend my life making sure I was better than him, but a piece of me lost that when I intentionally hurt Margo when I knew she didn't deserve it.

"Are we done here?" Killian gritted out as he tried to stand but failed.

"Where are my hockey sticks?" I muttered before I spotted them on the other side of the house.

"You don't get to have them." He snarled at me as I maneuvered past him to grab all of them.

"You said I could have them when I turned twenty, well guess what, my real father's property is now mine." I pulled a few of the hockey pucks from the unlabeled boxes as well.

Neil opened the door and threw me the car keys before he slammed the door shut, which left my stepfather with a distained frown.

"I'm surprised you've been so cool tonight." Neil muttered as he got into the car, and I dumped all the hockey equipment in the trunk.

I slammed the trunk closed to look at him, "What are you talking about?" I got in casually as he threw a confused glance.

"You know... it's getting late, I don't think you'll make it on time." He rubbed the back of his neck with an anxious laugh as I grew more confused than ever.

"What are you talking about, we don't have a curfew Vanderbilt." I start the engine as he narrowed his eyes at the note in my cup holder.

"I just thought you were adamant in getting Margo back so I thought you would do the list." He stated as I tilted my head.

"I am going to do the list." I said plainly as he looked even more horrified to break some awful news to me.

"It's 11:46 p.m. Liam." He acknowledged as I looked at my watch, "Way to state the obvious." I threw back as his lips thinned.

"Neil, what the fuck is it?" I slammed on my brakes as he handed the note Margo gave me earlier today.

"You didn't read the whole note, did you?" He looked absolutely petrified to continue speaking as my hands frantically opened the note and flipped it around to the back.

"She wrote that you needed to meet her tonight before Monday at her parent's guest house to agree or she'll close her heart to you forever." Neil explained as I reread the note over and over again.

It felt like I was having some sort of breakdown where I didn't even know what to do, I didn't know what to think. The only thing I knew was that I had about fifteen minutes to get to Margo's house and I was in butt fuck Philadelphia.

"Fuck, we gotta go." I backed out of the driveway so fast and stepped on the gas when we hit the road.

"Liam we can't get to New York in fourteen minutes." Neil sounded adamant in making me slow down. He knew it was impossible; he was always the logical speaker in the group.

I kinda wished I brought Grayson. He would be hyping me up and feeding into my delusions that I could've made it. Even when I knew I wouldn't.

"We have to try." I breathed out as my speedometer read ninety-eight miles per hour.

I didn't care about whether I would receive speeding tickets or if I would be getting pulled over.

I had one destination, and it was to Margo fucking Hamilton.

CHAPTER 24

MARGO

It was 12:08 a.m. and Liam didn't come.

I mean I just didn't understand, I thought he wanted it to work. He's been trying so hard all this time but every time it really counted, he disappoints me.

I couldn't help but imagine that was how it was always going to be, he would always be disappointing me no matter what.

I couldn't keep giving him trials, I should not be giving him more than a second chance. I just had to face it and let go of whatever I thought could be and focus on what is.

I slammed the door closed to the guest house, and marched over to my parent's front door, where before I could even open the door, or ring the doorbell my mother opened it quickly and freely.

"Finally, you have come to your senses!" She pulled me in for a warm embrace.

I swallowed my pride and the urge to just scream at her for siding with my father. But I couldn't blame her, not really.

She pulled away, and a view of my father was noticeable as he sat at the head of the dining room table like he always did.

I stepped into my home like I was a guest, a visitor.

My father stood up and nodded at me, "Welcome home Maggie," He muttered without making eye contact.

Tell me that your father and daughter relationship has forever been ruined without telling me your father and daughter relationship has been ruined.

He couldn't even look at me.

What was worst was that I felt like I physically couldn't even talk to him anymore.

My mother guided me over to my room, where everything was left as it was, except there were new shopping bags and new designer clothes that sat on my bed.

I felt immense anger that made me go back outside to the dining room table, "You can not buy me back!" I screamed at my father who looked taken back at my attitude.

He only stood up once more and buttoned up his suit, "They weren't from me Margo. They were from your future husband, so if you don't mind... you should get cleaned up, they will be here in a little to finalize the engagement."

I felt tears built up and I ran straight to my bedroom, I slammed the door shut in front of my mother's bewildered face.

Who was I kidding, my parents deserved to be mad at me. They had every right to be upset when I was the one who betrayed them. It was all my fault they were still struggling when they could be building new businesses and clubs by now.

I knew Liam and I were done for, forever. But a part of me still wished he arrived on time.

But I should've learned my lesson the first time.

I have been staring at the salmon and broccoli on my plate since the Grimaldi's have arrived. It had been an hour since we got introduced and sat to have dinner.

A very late dinner may I add.

I couldn't help but sneak a look up at my future husband to be, he wasn't ugly, he wasn't rude, he wasn't everything horrible in one person.

But he wasn't Liam.

It was a bad mentality to have, comparing men to Liam but it was how I could somehow operate. Maybe it was a good thing he was nothing like Liam.

Our parents have been having long conversations about God knows what, we've been eyeing up the four main spot of awkwardness.

The food in front of us. The painting above my father's chair. The small glances at the clock and lastly, the balcony that led out to the back of the house.

I've yawned about a billion times already and I couldn't help but wish that I could just excuse myself to go and sleep but my father would've absolutely killed me by now.

"Shall I excuse myself and Margo, over to the balcony?" I heard a deep voice speak up.

My eyes zoned in on Benjamin who walked over to my side of the table and held out his hand or me to grab.

Our families looked ecstatic about the idea of him leading me out of the dining room and talk.

I hesitated before I reached for his hand, but when I did it was like we were automatically transported over to the balcony outside of my living room.

The balcony was always one of my favorite places.

The white tiles, the marbled stone, and the night sky. It was always perfect, I only wished that Liam was here to enjoy it with me.

"Sorry it took longer for me to pull you aside for a chat." He said nervously as I laughed.

"At least you did it."

Ben looked like every woman's dream man. He was tall, brunette hair, he was muscled, he came from a successful family, and he was a gentleman.

In a world where I didn't fall in love with William Brookshire, I would've hit the jackpot with Ben.

He fidgeted with his fingers. I couldn't help but laugh, Adrianna would do the same thing when she was anxious.

"You, okay?" I asked.

Ben's eyes met mine, "I'm quite nervous." He admitted.

"No need to be nervous I'm not going to be mean or anything Ben." I assured him as he laughed awkwardly.

"You are beautiful, Margo." He whispered it like it was a secret.

I smiled.

"I know that our situation isn't ideal." He made a point as he started to pace around the balcony, "And I know that you probably aren't too fond of marrying a complete stranger but, I promise there is never any pressure, and you can always back out if you want." He explained.

I couldn't help but feel comfortable around Benjamin, he looked genuinely concerned.

"I want this," He motioned to the both of us, "To be special, and we can take it slow. Since we've never really done an arranged marriage before, I figured we can learn from each other." He continued to ramble as I leaned forward.

I pulled him in and landed a kiss on his lips, they were soft. I felt a field of flowers surround us and a cozy cloud that pushed us in further together.

This was the safe option.

I pulled away from him, his hand remained on my cheek.

"Woah." He looked flabbergasted as I let out a small giggle.

"I'm gonna remember that for a while." He looked dazed.

Then he snapped back into reality, "I like kissing you." He pointed out as I felt my cheeks turn a hue of red.

"That was terrible, sorry... I meant I like you, not just your kiss. Not that the kiss wasn't good-- erm, it was amazing, but it wasn't like the best thing about you." He was fidgeting with his hands once more.

"Ben, calm down. As my future husband I would hope that you don't freak out because your wife is kissing you." I muttered as he nodded his head.

"Margo, I know we just met like an hour ago, and we probably have to spend the rest of our lives together. I just hope that one day... I earn your love like I would if we weren't getting married with an arrangement." He smiled at me.

"If you do wish to say yes to this engagement, I promise you I will treat you like you deserve, and I will not take you for granted."

There were so many green flags in Ben, everything a girl could ever want was right in front of me, telling me that he would care about me, and respect me.

He was my age; he was good looking, and he would help my parents with their financial status.

While Liam had given me everything, I couldn't dismiss the amount of pain he had caused me. How he would never be one to propose to me, help my family. He wouldn't give me what I needed in life.

He had never had to care for anything else other than himself and hockey. I deserve more than what he could offer and what I needed was in front of me.

"Just know you have free range to say anything..." Ben muttered as he pulled out a red box from his back pocket. Before I could process what was happening, he was on his knee, with the box out, being presented to me.

He wasn't Liam.

Liam isn't showing up Margo get over it!

"Will you marry me?" Ben asked with a golden glare in his eyes.

I looked at the ring, before my eyes settled back on Ben's face.

He was full of hope, admiration, and need.

He was here now, on his knee asking me to marry him.

"Yes."

LIAM

"No, you already named that one." Neil sprawled out as I hit the steering wheel.

"I did not name Connecticut yet!" I defended as he pointed at his list on his phone, with the looks of Connecticut already being called out and crossed off.

"You did so." He retorted as I rolled my eyes in pure annoyance.

"Start from the beginning." He knocked his head back as I coughed out to restart.

"Okay, Alabama, Alaska, Arizona, Arkansas, California, Colorado, Delaware--"

"You missed Connecticut." Neil cut me off as I honked the horn with my forehead.

"I thought you knew the song!" He asked as I gave him a death stare.

"I do know the song!"

"Clearly not." I checked the time of destination being three minutes away.

"Who needs to know the damn states anyways!" I yelled as Neil gave me a thin smile.

"You do." He muttered, "Because your girlfriend put it on her very amazing list."

I knocked my head back in annoyance as he continued to speak.

I wish she was my girlfriend.

"How are you so sure that she would even consider giving you another chance?" Neil asked as I stayed quiet.

I wasn't sure if Margo would ever give me another chance after tonight.

"God Neil, I don't know! I don't know anything anymore when it comes to her. She has completely blindsided me. I can't talk to other women. I can't breathe when I'm around her. I don't know what else to do other than learn these damn states just so I can have her back." I quickly let out as he gave me an apologetic look.

Neil inhaled and exhaled heavily, "What if you can't get her back Will?"

That was surely the dreaded question.

"That can't be an option, she's the love of my life. I can't imagine being with someone else other than her Neil, and I know you don't know how that feels like but damn it's all consuming."

"Why don't you tell her that?" He suggested as I slowed down.

"What?" I asked.

"No games, Will. No jokes. You show up to her house, and you tell her how you feel. The raw emotions, who gives a fuck? You really think she's your soulmate then you tell her anyways." He looked at the note.

"Fuck the deadline, you show up anyways because if you two were really right for each other then you two will be together." He continued as we turned the car quickly and finally reached Margo's house.

I turned to look at Neil who was smiling at me like a dumb chump.

"Don't smile at me like that." I muttered as his face turned into a disappointed pout.

"Come on, you're going to take my advice aren't you." His eyebrow wiggled as I gave him a small and tiny punch.

"Shut up." I paid attention to the road ahead of me.

"Good because we are here." Neil settled back up as I place my car in park mode.

God Margo, please wait.

"Remember." Neil looked at me before I slammed the door closed, "From the heart!" He rolled down the passenger side window with a wide grin.

I ran as fast as I could to Margo's guest house, which was behind her parent's house, by the big ass balcony that she loved. I pulled out my phone, to check if she had returned any of my calls.

Sadly, she hasn't. But like Neil said, who cares. All I need to do is tell her how I feel, hope for the best that--

And there it was.

It was 1:57 a.m.

I was outside her guest house with a perfect view of her balcony where she stood, getting proposed to by Benjamin Grimaldi.

And she said yes.

I felt like my whole world crashed down on me all at once. The sky turned a shade of red as I just stared at her with no emotion.

I just lost.

Only now there was no fucking game. It was just me who played myself.

This was a living nightmare I swear I had experienced before; except I couldn't wake up from it.

Margo Hamilton was no longer mine, not that she ever was before. I heavily think that she could never really be anyone's. She doesn't want to be owned. That's why I fell in love with her.

I watched her as she smiled at him, the smile she would throw at me, that I took for granted. I will forever kick myself for taking her presence for granted.

Her parents came out with celebratory smiles and hugs, like she had always wanted.

I on the other hand, walked slowly back to the car, Neil's smile withered with every step I took.

"What happened?" He peaked his head out the window.

I smiled lightly, in a way of defeat.

"I lost the girl man."

I could really only smile and hide the scowl on my face, after all... I lost her fair and square.

CHAPTER 25

MARGO

Isn't it such a beautiful day?

The birds were chirping, my parents and I aren't arguing.

I mean hell, we even had breakfast all together as a family, with my dad's smile back on his face and my mother's newest Chanel being handed to her by her personal buyer.

"Oh Maggie, remind us how he asked you again!" My mother ran over to me while she pulled my hand over to her eyes and settled her orbs on my beautiful ring finger that adorned a massive diamond ring.

"Mom, I told you at least a billion times." I verbalized as she gave a sigh of relief.

"We're just so happy you've come to your senses Maggie. This was the right choice honey." She mumbled as I shook my head.

"Have you talked to Adrianna?" My father spoke up as he wiped his mouth with a napkin.

My eyes widened in remembrance that I was supposed to tell her the moment I said yes, however due to the fact that it was late, and she had her early appointment today, with her therapist then I figured she was already asleep.

"No, and I am on my way over to her house now actually." I

got up and hugged both my parents goodbye before jetting off to Adrianna's mansion.

Of course, my day was going smoothly before the moment I took three steps out of my driveway only to see Liam, who leaned against his motorcycle.

Suddenly, clouds of misery gathered around my self-esteem and the sky, I pulled out my sunglasses and flounced my way from Liam.

But of course, me ignoring him was not a part of his agenda.

"Hamilton." He addressed as I walked faster, but before I knew it his body found itself in front of mine within seconds.

"You're nine hours late, Brookshire." I remarked as he knocked his head back.

"Margo, I didn't see the back of the note, I swear once I did, I was rushing back from Philly to your house." He explained as I let out a breath.

"I understand." I gulped down as he's face filled with relief and happiness.

Liam held my hand, and pulled me closer, "I would've been there on time if I could, Raine."

Liam was right, he could've been there if he could. But he wasn't. I was always a firm believer in second chances, and I've given Liam twice as many as I could. And yet I was always the one that ended up scathed.

He never had repercussions, consequences. Other people always got hurt and never him.

I pulled away, and the light on his face drained.

"That doesn't change anything Liam, you didn't show, and I made my decision." I stood my ground as he shook his head.

"Just because I was late you want to throw what we have away." He hissed as I felt water build up around my eyes.

"You threw us away the moment you left me by myself in Greece with no explanation, no contact and no respect." I snapped.

"So don't tell me about throwing us away when I still came

back here for you, and you had girls all over you and you miss the last chance I give you." I continued as he, himself backed up.

"You seriously think that you belong with a fucking Grimaldi, Margo?" He fumed, "Seriously?"

"Aside from you?!" I gawped; Liam paced away from me as I stood in place.

"Margo I'm trying, don't you see that?" He paced back.

"It's not enough Liam!" My voice heightened before I took a breath to compose myself.

"I already said yes to Ben. There's nothing you or anyone else could say to me to make me take it back. He has been nothing but a gentleman and––"

"––And what?" Liam interrupted.

"Margo, you and I are meant to be together don't you see that?"

"You. Didn't. Show. Up." I closed my eyes and seethed as he gave a large breath. Those were my terms, and you didn't meet them." I said plainly as he stood there and just looked at me.

"I didn't know––" He exclaimed as I cut him off.

"––That doesn't matter anymore! You say we're meant to be but maybe that's not true! You say you care about me but there are so many obstacles that show that it's hard." I acknowledged.

"Loving isn't supposed to be hard; it's supposed to be calming. You and I are too hard, you hurt me too much and I can't let myself spiral down this pattern just because you are my kryptonite." I confessed.

"So, what?" He paused; he looked frustrated.

"Are you just giving up on us because it's too hard?" He settled as I shook my head sideways.

"No Liam, I'm letting you go. I have a future with Ben, he's made it clear he is willing to let me take it slow, under my conditions. So, I'm giving him a chance."

Liam looked down at my hand as the diamond ring glistened.

"So please, give up." I finished.

I didn't want to tell the rest of my friends yet, so I pulled the engagement ring out of my hand and down to my Birkin.

"I'm not going to stop fighting for you Raine." He admitted.

I paused for a second.

"No matter how long it takes." He continued.

Without another word, I passed Liam, with my eyes on the sidewalk, and tears draining down my face.

LIAM

As I made my way over to Grayson's bedroom, I couldn't help but think about whether riding my motorcycle into a volcano or facing Margo again would be more destructive.

I should've never approached her, only because now I know that she wants absolutely nothing more to do with me.

But she still spoke to me, meaning that she still wants me in a way.

I mean she could've picked anyone, and she picked fucking Ben Grimy Grimaldi. First off, I'm pretty sure he ate paste until middle school. I've always hated his family, he and his brother waterboarded Grayson and I at the Vanderbilt's brunch.

I didn't bother knocking before barging into my best friend's abode. To my mistake, my eyes feasted on places where the sun didn't shine.

"Yo! Knock!" He yelled at me while wrapping a towel around his waist.

"I'm guessing that's why Adrianna tried desperately walking out of your house by the back door, dropping packs of condoms." I laughed off while flopping down on one of Grayson's chairs.

He did nothing but roll his eyes, "So did you guys..." I shrugged as he gave me one of the deadliest stares to man.

"No. We didn't, and we aren't going to, it was a mistake." He shook his head.

"Why do you say that?" I grew intrigued as Grayson put clothes and started packing for hockey practice.

"Will, if you could've seen her face. It was like... I shouldn't even be allowed to touch her man. I felt like I was destroying everything that God sent down to be the purest."

I let my eyebrows wrinkle, "She deserves better than me, and I can't be a better guy for her, I just can't." He continues as I coughed out.

"Uh, yeah you're right she does deserve better, that's why this is a fake thing remember, you don't actually like her, you want to be with August remember, or did you miss the memo by looking into Adrianna's doe eyes." I laughed as Grayson licked his lips to prevent further words to escape.

"Whatever you did Gray, break it off tonight." I mumbled as he nodded.

"So, what are your plans with Hamilton?" Grayson looked over at me as I flipped through the pages of our ECON textbook.

I looked up slowly, "What do you mean?"

"Well, that list, did you throw it away?" He asked.

"Are you kidding me Gray, this is the ultimate test on me getting her back, it's only overtime. Sure, she's made it absolutely clear that she wants nothing to do with me but, I will do whatever it takes to get her back, and I mean whatever, even if I hurt myself." I grumbled.

"You sound psychotic." His face grew disturbed.

I smiled, "Or you, my friend, aren't crazy for a girl yet."

I could only grin at Grayson, he didn't know it yet, but Adrianna was slowly wrapping him around her finger, slowly but surely.

"I think I never will be." He sodded as I rolled my eyes.

"I think we both know that you are wrong in that department. Adrianna has been bugging you since the moment you saw each other."

Grayson threw his head back, "Let's not forget that Margo and you didn't push each other in the pool during P.E. class in elementary."

At that moment I realized that maybe it was written in the stars that Margo and I were inevitable, we were supposed to happen. Even if Grayson and Adrianna can't see it, they were born for each other.

Before Grayson picked up his keys, his phone rang. My eyes caught Margo's name in his screen, which made me swipe his phone from his desk.

"Hey Raine." I smirked at Grayson as he rolled his eyes.

"What are you doing picking up Grayson's phone?" She snapped back as I couldn't help but smile.

"You know you miss me. Besides, why do you need to talk to him when you have me." I asked as she stayed silent.

"I was planning something as a group thing, for Adrianna and Grayson to look like they enjoyed each other's company."

"So would that mean that we would be hanging out together too?" I asked with a grin on my face, Grayson's eyes rolled to the back of his head.

Before I could even get an answer, Margo hung up.

She wants me.

"You do understand that she hates you right?" Grayson made a point as I threw our textbook at him.

"And you do understand that so does Adrianna, right?"

While he might've been right in the fact of Margo hating my guts, I cannot forget the nights where we were completely in love and that nothing else mattered.

That was what was keeping me going, that one day everything was going to be worked out.

Whatever it takes.

CHAPTER 26

MARGO

Before we left to go to the bar, before everything went terribly wrong, I told my friends about my engagement. I finally told them about Ben.

The first thing they asked about the situation was if I was happy, and of course the normality of them telling me that if he ends up hurting me, they will hurt him.

I also told them that Ben could've been there. But of course, I never actually asked him to join or come to the bar.

We weren't that close yet.

Besides, something about last night, went terribly wrong, as Adrianna had now been off the rails wanting to party.

She even wanted to lose her virginity which by the way, I am heavily against.

But I could only do so much to stop her, and she was not in the mood to discuss her choices of her fight with Grayson that pushed her over edge.

So tonight, the girls and I planned for a great night out, in one of the clubs my father owned, as much as I was on her side of vengeance and the act to getting back at Grayson.

I was still very much rooting for her and Grayson to make it work. Thus, me tipping him off earlier when I saw him skating around by himself.

I told him we were going to out, that obviously doesn't mean that things were going to work out to the best they can. I only had a cup of Vodka and a dream.

But before I could even think about partying, I was dreading the walk towards the trainer's office.

It was my first day on the job, well community service hours that is. I was irritated of the fact that I might be seeing Liam's face most of the time.

But a bit glad that my eyes got to roam around to other hockey players. But I would never want to use this job as a way to take advantage of the masterpieces that I found myself looking at.

Ronni was bandaging a kid's hand being completely helpful, aside from me who just sat there and watched her do her magic.

"You know you can't just watch there all the time, right?" She laughed as I straightened my back.

"You just look like you would do it a lot better than I would." I threw her an innocence smile.

"Next one is on you princess, and don't worry I'll be right here the entire night." She patted the kid's back who jumped off the table.

"Thanks Ronni!" He beamed as I smiled at him.

A group of smaller kids came prancing their way over to the door and suddenly my heart rate shot up.

"You'll be okay, the kids are the easiest to deal with." Ronni consulted as I nodded.

"Hey Ronni, can you please wrap my arm, it hurts after that amazing slapshot I did." The little kid talked about his sport with so much happiness and fulfilment.

"We can sure wrap that up Link, but you mind if I watch and let Margo over here wrap it up for you?" Ronni whispered as I prepared the tools and bandages.

"Is she new?" One of his friends whispered to Ronni as she laughed.

"Charlie, Link, Brahm, Joshua, and Mark, this is Trainer Margo, she will be helping me with fixing up your injuries from now on." Ronni presented me like I was a cuisine dish.

Would I have to know all of their names soon?

That was not part of the job description.

"Sup, Margo." A curly redhead winked as I rolled my eyes.

"You must be Charlie." I acknowledged whilst I ripped a section of tape for the bandage.

Link steadied up for me as I wrapped the bandage slowly but tightly on his arm. He started to whistle which I didn't mind; I had a feeling it helped him calm his nerves that a complete stranger was wrapping him up.

"Is that snug enough for you?" I questioned as he nodded his head.

"It's really comfortable, Margo. Thank you!" He smiled.

A part of my heart warmed, I enjoyed helping and making sure he was okay.

"Who's next?" I looked back at Charlie who yawned.

"What can I do for you Charlie?" I sat down beside him as he shook his head, "I just need an ice pack ma'am."

"Coming right up." I swung the freezer door open, pulled out an icepack and threw it at him.

"See you're a natural." Ronni winked as I laughed.

"This is nothing, I'm not so sure that I'll be any help when something seriously bad has happened."

Ronni shook her head, "The hardest part about this job is making sure the kids and players can trust you first."

Before I could even acknowledge what, she said, the kids rushed in and wrapped their arms around me, "Thanks Margo!"

Even the quiet one, Mark waved at me, "See you tomorrow!"

And just like that, they left.

As I got up to fill up my water bottle with cold water, my vision blurred for a moment, as I heard familiar voices from the main room.

Neil, Chris and Liam had all perched up by the counter where Ronni sat. They looked like they were making good conversation.

"There she is." Liam muttered with a smile as I tried to sneak off to the back door.

"Hey." I smiled back as he coughed out not really knowing what to say.

Liam followed me back to the back room as I grabbed a few things from inventory.

"Heard you guys were going out tonight." He walked along with me as I nodded.

"I don't really see how that's any of your business." I fired back as he laughed it off.

"It's not. I'm just saying, how is your fiancé going to feel about you going out and partying, probably wearing just a mini skirt that middle schoolers use as duct tape for an art project." He pointed at my shorts as I pulled away.

"Last thing I remember, you liked it when I wore my skirts, short and tight. I think it even made you weak in the knees Brookshire." I bent down for a moment to pick up a bag of ice.

"Yeah, I liked it, but it doesn't mean I like it when other men see what's--" He cut himself off.

"--Yours?" I smiled.

"I think you forget that I'm not yours anymore, and I never will be again." I continued as he looked like someone just blew out his birthday candles.

"I can still do the things on the damn list, if that means you're mine again." He pleaded as I shook my head.

"That list expired a while ago Liam."

"We also know that Ben isn't what you want, he also can't give you what you need." He asserted as I closed my eyes remembering the godly orgasm I received from Liam, the night before.

"What do I need?" I turned around to face him.

Liam's eyes zoned in on me and my fingers were itching to touch him, just have him here, but myself control has stepped into overdrive.

"We both know Ben hasn't touched you yet, my question is why not... and second question is, what if he can't please you like I can?" Liam's hand found itself on my waist.

A feeling of tension and butterflies circled itself around my stomach, like I needed him to consume me. I hated that no matter what, I would feel this certain way towards Liam.

I took several deep breaths, before I pushed him away from me.

"Ben and I actually have tremendous chemistry. Better than whatever we have. And lastly, please have some decency and stop going for women who clearly aren't available to you." I grumbled before running out of the room and slamming the door.

Chris and Neil sat outside with Ronni, who was wrapping up Chris's hand, which looked severely injured.

I just needed to let off steam, the worst part is. Liam was what I needed to let off the anger and stress I had stored in my body.

Ben looked like he's never touched another woman in his life, and we were barely acquainted for me to even want to have sex with him. I just needed to do something to make my stress go away.

Of course, partying with Adrianna and the girls was definitely one way of doing it.

It was approaching midnight and the girls, and I had not stopped dancing. Adrianna had been flirting it up like a storm with plenty of random guys at the bar, not that it helped.

Verina and Juliette had been up on tables and the bar counter just dancing. Everyone seemed to be enjoying themselves. Verina had invited me to take shots with her and it was one of the few things that got me to forget how awful I had been feeling.

Grayson had already stopped by and fished answers out of me

before running into Adrianna's little room with that random guy. He practically pulled her out of the club and punched the living daylights out of that guy.

I really don't remember his name so he will be continued to be classified as "that guy."

No matter how many times Grayson says that he didn't care about Anna, he still found himself to save her, every single time.

But since Adrianna got escorted out by Prince himself, I was still stuck here with Verina and Juliette.

I still had the drinks and the music to keep me occupied for a while.

I was numbing everything down, but sadly my eyes couldn't believe what they were seeing. Liam and Neil were here, by the VIP table that I had for myself and the girls.

"What are you doing here Liam?" I screamed so he could hear me.

The music was loud, so he screamed back, "What do you think I'm doing here?"

It was an obvious reason why he was here, "Yeah well you aren't going to stop me from having an amazing night." I muttered back as he took a seat by the bar which had a perfect view of the whole club.

"I have all night Raine, I'm not taking my eyes off of you." He placed his black card down.

"You don't let random guys buy your drink, I will buy anything you want," His eyes claimed mine, and travelled their way down to my body.

This sent shivers down my spine as I smiled at him, I knew he could fight, I also knew that he was not a type of guy that liked to be messed with when it came to a public setting.

He was always goofy when it came to himself and his friend group but that wasn't the case when it came to being out in public with just me.

He was like a bodyguard. My own personal protector.

"So what? You're just gonna watch me the entire time?" I laughed at Liam who stayed put on the bar stool.

He swallowed, his Adam's apple bopped, which made me want to run my tongue across it.

He stayed silent, which only made me enjoy what I was about to do, a lot more.

"Verina, could you tell the DJ to play something more... scandalous?" I whispered as she grinned.

Verina and Juliette had dared me to dance in front of everyone earlier tonight and I hadn't found the nerve of doing it until now.

Where Liam could only look and not touch, I was going to enjoy this.

The DJ started playing a very seductive song, and I quickly hopped on the stage with the multiple dancers. My eyes stayed to Liam's. His eyes started to falter the moment he understood what I was doing.

But not once did he break eye-contact, instead his eyes remained on mine as I got rid of my layers, when I began to undress even more, he began to walk closer, but he never uttered a word.

Only watched closely as I twirled around the stripper pole, that was accessible to me. While my eyes stayed on his and just only his, I didn't care about of the plenty of men that gawked at me.

I even heard Verina and Juliette whistle, and cat call me from a far. But the only thing that mattered to me was Liam's locked gaze on my body and my eyes.

It was like it physically pain him to see me show off and not have me to himself.

Which was what I wanted and needed from him.

To know that he's lost me.

His body stood tall and angry. "I'm taking you home now Raine." He grumbled as I laughed.

"Yeah right."

Liam's eyes promised me that he wasn't joking and actually meant what he said.

He wanted me home quickly and effective immediately.

"Tell Verina and Juliette that you're leaving now." He ordered as he pulled me towards him, all the male gazes on me as I followed him out the door.

"They look like they want to stay," I looked at Verina and Juliette who were still dancing and having fun.

"That's great because Neil is watching them, you are going home." He opens the car door, and I couldn't help but just follow his instructions. It was confusing to me on why I was following his orders when I was fully sober.

"You are such a party pooper." I mutter as he rolled his eyes and turned on the car.

We had been sprawling the whole week, so many insults had been thrown, so many jabs at each other had been said. I missed the days where it was just us in love but that was long gone.

As he drove me home, I couldn't help but think that maybe it was okay to just have a decent conversation with him, no screaming and fighting.

"How was your first day?" He muttered as my face turned to complete shock.

Were we thinking the same thing?

"It was so fun; I actually might enjoy it... the kids are adorable, and they are very sweet." I let out without a second thought. I was shocked that I was speaking in full sentences to him.

"I'm glad it gives you joy." He smiled as I threw him a condescending look.

"Why are you being nice?" I asked with a confused look as his eyebrows furrowed.

"I can't be nice?" He threw back as I stayed silent.

"I know the only thing that makes this easier for you is for you to hate me Margo and that's fine, but I don't want you to hate me." He turned a corner and stopped into a parking lot.

"Why are you pushing me away, when I know you want us to work out." He asked as I stayed silent.

"What are you afraid of? You need Ben's money? Fuck Raine, I can give you double." He looked at me with hurt and resentment in his eyes.

"It's not that easy Liam." I muttered as he knocked his head back.

"I miss you so much Margo, it hurts." Liam clutched his heart like he was in physical pain and God, I missed him too.

"Please just tell me, if you are truly done then I understand because I can't keep looking like a fool. If there is still a chance, I will be sure to make it known I'm a fucking fool and I will keep trying. But if it's all just fun and games and we truly are over then... I'm done." He laid it all out for me right then and there.

His heart was out in the open and I just stared at him.

Until.

"I'm planning on telling the group that I'm engaged tomorrow, because truly there is no going back. The wedding date is going to be soon and there's really nothing to stop it." I let out as I could hear his heart break piece by piece.

"So that's it then." He asked.

"It's over?"

He said it this time like he was waiting for confirmation.

"I need you to tell me it's over Raine, because then maybe I'll stop trying to find something in this." He pleaded.

And I could only stare, "I can't tell you that I want it to be over because that would be a lie, Liam." A tear shed.

"But I have to tell you it is, so we can both move on. Which is what I think the right decision should be."

"Great." He pulled out of the empty parking lot and drove straight to my house.

I tried to hold in the tears that were waiting to be released.

"I still love you, Liam." I whispered as he stayed silent.

Only for a second, before I opened the door, his hand reached for the nape of my neck and enveloped his lips on top of mine.

I could taste the salt from my tears, I could taste him and the tension there was to the kiss.

It was like we were gripping for each other; we were each other's lifeline.

I bit his lip; my arms didn't want to let go but it did anyways.

"Goodnight, Raine." He whispered before kissing the top of my forehead.

"Goodnight, Charming." I muttered before exiting his vehicle, he watched me walk into my house before driving off.

I kind of wished that we stayed together for the night, but it defeated the whole goodbye portion of the conversation.

Of course that was never going to last long term.

CHAPTER 27

MARGO

As I slowly walk into my house, I was startled by the sound of loud footsteps approaching me.

Ben had sat down on the grand ottoman, staring straight into my very drunk body with fury in his eyes.

I had totally forgotten that I had accepted his proposal, when all that ran through my mind was Liam and his determination.

Even if I did just end things tonight, that didn't mean that it was truly over.

"Where have you been?" He raised his voice as I stumbled towards him on the couch that sat next to the ottoman.

"I'm sorry I just went out with a couple of my friends, it got late, and a friend took me home." I defended as he rolled his eyes.

This was definitely a side of Ben that I had never saw.

"Did I give you permission to go out?" He sneered as my whole body took a step back from him.

"Excuse me?" I let out a small huff as his eyes narrowed down on my body.

"Do I really have to repeat myself to your thick head?" He stepped closer as my body stayed completely still.

It was like I was getting hit by the worst-case scenario.

"Margo, I don't think I gave you permission to go out." He once again repeated it.

"Ben, who are you to think you can speak to me like that?" I walked closer.

His smile grew more wicked.

"I think that I'm the guy that looks picture perfect to your family." He let out.

"I'll just tell them that you aren't who you say you are." I said it so vigorously, so ready to bust him and so ready to bust out of this planned engagement.

"Oh, but you can't." He said it so plainly.

I couldn't say anything more.

"I'm the guy that's saving your father from going broke, Margo. My family has your family under a leash… and frankly… I have you on a fucking collar." He grinned.

I'm pretty sure my eyes filled with horror as he walked closer towards me. His hand reached under my chin; he lifted it up so my eyes could reach his.

"I basically own you now Margo. The one thing that Willian Brookshire can't have. I have all to myself, and that means you do as I tell you." He bent closer and whispered in my ear.

"So that's it?" I laughed.

"What is?"

"You're only messing with my life because you want pay back for Liam. You want something that he can't have." I felt defeated in a way that made me want to crawl into a shell and never leave.

Ben walked backwards and took in the view of my body.

His hand grazed my upper thigh, which raised my skirt. He did it with a twinkling eye and a menacing smile.

I felt something churn inside me, like I felt sick to my stomach.

Of course this would happen to me.

"Why?" I asked him.

"Why did I pick you to mess with?" He laughed, "Because, why the fuck not?"

I could only stare back, I could only really look at him with shock, resting on my face.

Liam was right, Ben was a horrible person, and I couldn't do anything about it because my family needs him.

"But trust me Margo, I'm not a monster... I won't make you do anything." He muttered.

I gulped down a lump that formed in my throat.

"If I do fuck you, I want you to want it." His voice slithered around my brain like venom.

"I would never." I spit out quickly.

"Oh, you won't?" He grimaced before he walked closer with a closed fist.

My heart was pulsing, my head was experiencing a rush that I never thought I would feel in my whole entire life.

It was fear, as soon as Ben's hand lifted, I knew where it would land. His hand made direct contact with my face.

It was like I saw a billion stars flashing around me in the room.

"What was that, again?" Ben pulled my body closer to him by my throat. His hand was wrapped around my throat so stiff and so threatening.

I couldn't speak, only look at anywhere else but his eyes.

"What was that again, slut?" He said it in a more intense intent.

I wanted to cry, but I couldn't.

I was sure many people have it worse than I did. I mean I'm best friends with Adrianna for God's sake; nothing measures to that kind of trauma and pain.

I needed to be strong, and I needed to go through this marriage because my mother and father are counting on me to do so.

I couldn't back out now, especially when I disappointed them this summer because of Liam. Nothing can get in the way.

No one can get in the way of what my family has built.

"I said I would never." I pulled away as his hand grew tighter around my neck.

My air way was being blocked, and I could feel my face turning a hue of purple from the lack of oxygen and this discomfort of his grip.

I could tell it was going to leave a bruise tomorrow morning, and I would have to wear a scarf.

"Get away from me." I forced out as he let go, only to wrap his hand around my wrist and squeeze.

"How about you listen to what I tell you to do from now on, Margo." He grinned from ear to ear as I felt a single tear run down slowly.

I was in pain.

Not just emotionally.

CHAPTER 28

LIAM

Buzzzzz. Buzzzz. Buzzzzzz.

I felt like I was going to be sick.

I felt like I wanted to punch something and at the same time wanted to experience any other type of pain because nothing else hurt more than what I felt internally right now.

It felt like she ripped my heart out of my chest and stomped on it a billion times.

When did I ever let myself be this intrigued, this focused and this fucking caught up on a girl.

A girl that is completely unavailable now for my fucking information.

She practically told me to fucking leave her alone. She put in on a billboard with bold fucking letters.

The guys had wanted to meet up at Neil's place which was not really a place that we would hang out often, but I needed it.

Chris finally took a break from his fighting and hung out with us.

Buzzzzz. Buzzzz.

"What else did you want again?" Neil asked me as I looked at the mirror.

"Can you add a bit of rain to it?" I asked as he nodded.

"Why did you want a lightning and thunderstorm again?" Chris asked me as Neil looked up from his tattoo pen.

"I had this thing where I was afraid of thunderstorms, I shouldn't be afraid of anything." I muttered as he nodded.

"And the rain effects?" Neil further pushed as I stayed silent.

Margo's middle name is Raine. I thought to myself.

I knew that a new tattoo felt as if it was way too much for a coping mechanism, but it covered most of the internal pain I felt.

It crossed one of the things in Margo's list for me to do.

"Hey, can I have some of that fried rice?" I asked Neil as he took a small bite of his chicken.

"No." He sneered as Chris, and I gave each other a look.

As the back window creaked open only for a baby kitten to be discovered.

"Woah a cat." Chris muttered.

"No shit." I laughed as the cat continued to walk closer.

I would've loved to pick up the kitten as it sauntered over next to me, with its bright blue eyes.

The kitten was brown, but not a regular orange, brown. This cat was coffee colored.

The cat's bright blue eyes reminded me of Margo.

She shouldn't be on my mind this much, but I can't help being so obsessed and in love with her.

Even if I can't be with her and she broke my heart.

"We should give it a home." Chris muttered as he pouted.

"I would love to take it but I'm allergic." Neil sneezed as I looked at Chris.

"I'd love to take it, but I can barely afford Finn and I; I can't take a pet." He defended.

Since Grayson wasn't here to defend himself, I looked at the kitten and didn't mind taking it to find a home.

"I'll find a place for it, temporarily." I mutter as the looked at me with concerned filled faces.

"What is it?"

"Well... I would never expect you to be the one to find time just to find a home for the cat." Chris said as my eyebrow raised.

"Yeah, why do you want the cat?"

"When did I say I wanted to cat?" I defended, "I just said I'll find a home for it, so leave the subject alone."

They both looked at each other and shrugged.

"How have the fights been?" Neil wiped some ink off my tattoo as Chris looked up from the kitten, he was holding.

"It's been good, the training has been extremely hard, balancing hockey, school and work at the same time has been very challenging especially trying to take care of Finn as well." He explained as I snuck a piece of chicken from Neil's plate.

I waited for him to finish.

"But... Verina had been a really great help these past few weeks." Chris couldn't help but blush.

He's always been a clean-cut type of guy, he works his ass off, grinds his gears during hockey, and maybe has two hours of sleep every night.

I had never seen his life been detoured because of a girl. I've never seen him give a second glance to a girl. I mean sure, I knew Chris has his moments and he would easily get one.

Which he does, but never anything serious. He had never gave an inkling that there would be a chance of anything else the next day.

"You've been spending a lot of time with her lately." I added as he looked down at his phone and a wide grin had appeared on his face.

"We are very close friends... she makes me feel like maybe the world isn't out to get me, you know?" He laughed as I nodded.

"Does she know about your fights?" Neil asked while taking a closer look at my tattoo for the finishing touches.

Chris had stayed silent as Neil, and I gave each other a funny look.

"Don't you think she should?" Neil looked up.

"She would be involved in something that could get her in trouble, I wouldn't want her to know about it." Chris took another bite of his fried rice as I snuck another piece of chicken from Neil's plate.

"Oh, so it's okay that we know about it though." I narrowed my eyes as he rolled his.

"Correction, I tried to hide it from you guys too, but you guys sneakily followed me around and ended up watching the illegal underground fights." He pointed at me, as I pretended, he pointed at Neil.

I took another look at Neil's chicken that was laying there waiting to be eaten, he only had two left, and I had already been snacking the whole time he was working on my tattoo.

"All right, you're done." Neil pulled away from me, I hid my face away from him, as I was chewing on his second to last piece of chicken.

"Is that my fucking chicken?" Neil stood up as well as I did.

"It looked really good." I smiled at him before he started to run after me, circling around Chris and the kitten.

"Oh, come on, I'll get you more!" I shouted as he only held anger in his eyes.

Chris only stayed sat and quiet.

"Chris, can you say something!" I yelled for back up as he smiled at me menacingly.

"Maybe you should just shut your mouth and stop bitching and complaining. What did you expect? You took his chicken that he has been talking about for weeks." Chris made a point as I continued to run around.

"Come on!" I ran near Chris for protection.

He threw me a horrible look, "I'm going to get back to my fried rice now and it's going to taste a lot better when I'm not looking at you two fighting like Finn and his friends."

Neil and I paused.

We both turned our heads towards Chris.

Chris's face had waved a white flag before Neil, and I jumped on top of him.

Even if I had a horrible encounter with Margo, I could always count on my best friends to keep my head up. No matter how bad it hurt.

CHAPTER 29

MARGO

I had finally told the whole group about my engagement with Ben. No surprise that Liam wasn't very fond of the news, we ended up bickering like how we used to.

Also, not to my surprise, Adrianna and Grayson had announced their debut as a couple. A real couple now, they never looked so happy.

She was excited to attend his game, and this time I'm quite sure that she would actually come and make it.

I, however, have no choice but to go because of my jail sentence. I don't really know why I'm even overreacting when I actually kind of enjoy it.

I never really realized how much I enjoyed it. A place where I can just be by myself. I never appreciated it until now, especially since Ben and his family are now spending a bit more time at our house because of the wedding preparations.

"You ready for tonight?" Ronni yawned while she sat, with her phone close to her face, with a wide smile.

"I mean, I surely wouldn't want anyone to get injured." I said with a simple expression.

Ronni had been spending time smiling and giggling at her phone for quite some time. She has recently gotten into a relationship with a barista that worked the Hawthorne Coffee shop. Ronni's new girlfriend was everything that you would want a partner to be.

They are everything, the communication is excellent, they want nothing more but to be in each other's presence. I mean that's what all couples should be right?

I find myself comparing my relationship with Ben with other people's which of course isn't right. But I can't help it. I feel like we were doing everything right and yet... I don't gravitate towards him.

Isn't your boyfriend supposed to be your best friend?

I mean fiancé.

I don't get giddy when he does something romantic, I don't look for him in a crowded room. I don't admire his eyes even though they are a dashing color. I don't feel anything but an ache in my heart.

Ever since that night I hadn't been able to look at Ben the same, I had bruises on my waist and my wrists were covered with hues of purple and pink. I couldn't help but feel so embarrassed. Everything hurt.

But telling anyone would be a bad idea, he would be charged, and his parents would back out of the engagement. My family needs this opportunity.

And I would do anything and everything to not disappoint my family, especially after I picked Liam before, and it was a huge mistake. I would never want to put a wedge between my father and I ever again.

Even if I'm in pain.

A girl walks into the trainer's office. Ronni looks at me with yet another smile, "You got that Hamilton." She stood up and left from the back door.

I twirl around to grab a first aid kit before I walked over to the girl who had tears in her eyes.

"Hey sweetie, are you––" I start my sentence.

"––No, I am most certainly not okay." She snarls at me as I take a step back.

"Well then what can I do for you." I smile.

She lifts her leg up, a giant opened scab presented itself to my eyes. I couldn't help but gag internally. It was bloody, dirty, and I just knew that, when I would disinfect it, she would be screaming at me.

"Okay take a seat on that." I point at the high trainer's bed.

By the time I turn back around, she hopped on it, in no time.

As I pull out the necessary items, I would need to clean up her wound, the door opens and of course to my luck, Liam walks right in the door with another kid.

I completely ignore him, after all, we said goodbye. I wasn't really sure how to be friends with him. I mean we were never really friends in the first place.

"Okay, what's your name?" I ask the girl as she still blubbers with tears.

"Alexa." She speaks.

"That's a very pretty name, how did you hurt yourself darling?" I continue with the brilliant questionnaires so that it would take her mind away from the fact that I was about to put rubbing alcohol on the scab.

"Well, I figure skate." She starts off as I could hear Liam and the young boy behind me, taking a seat in the waiting area.

"I was trying to impress this boy I like; his name is Eric by the way. And I was doing beautiful moves I've been working on all year, but I don't think he really cared." She continued with a frown on her face.

"Is Eric perchance a hockey player?" I ask as she nods her head.

"Hockey players are usually not thinking of much else other than being on the ice." I suggest as she stays silent.

I didn't really know if giving love life advice was a part of the job description, even if my love life is nowhere perfect. I would like to think that I had a few words of wisdom to share.

"Alexa, you shouldn't care about boys just yet, let alone making sure they see you." I pat down her scab with a wet cloth.

"Trust me when I say, the right boy will always seek you out in a crowded room. You don't have to beg for his attention or beg for him to pick you out of the millions of other girls."

I couldn't help but hear the two boys behind me laugh.

I turn around, "Is anything funny?" I ask as the little boy next to Liam stands up.

"Nothing." Liam quickly mutters.

"No, if you have anything to say, say it." Alexa points at both of the boys.

"I just think you are a bit overreacting, Lexi." The boy says at Alexa.

"You two know each other?" Liam asks, as I was about to ask the same question.

"Chase. He's Eric's best friend and he was the one who hit me with a puck." Alexa answers.

There was a slight pause, Liam and I made direct eye contact.

"How am I overreacting?" She continues.

"Eric doesn't really give two craps about you, and your figure skating. I can vouch and say that no guy on the team cares whether you fall or not." He says in a rude tone.

"You don't know that." Alexa comments while folding both of her arms in front of her.

"I do." Chase scowls.

I smile for a second, seeing how annoyed the two kids are at each other, bickering. It kind of reminds me of an old married couple.

"Eric might just not tell you anything." Alexa defends herself once more.

Chase gets irritated, "He doesn't care whether you wear your white skates or your pink ones Lexi. He doesn't care whether you put your hair up in a bun, or if you do your stupid Dutch braids." He turns red with each word that comes out of his mouth.

"I was finally talking to him, before your stupid puck hit me!" Alexa starts to scream a bit louder.

"It wasn't my fault! You guys could've found a different place to talk." Chase gives a huge sneer, "Accidents happen all the time around the ice rink."

Liam and I smile at each other, knowing the situation now.

Chase likes Alexa. But Alexa doesn't have a clue, and she likes his best friend.

This is a big problem.

"Why don't you just apologize, Chase." Liam slowly approaches him.

"No way! It's not my fault she was having a conversation in the middle of the ice rink." He grumbles as Alexa glares.

I finish up, putting a huge band aid on Alexa's knee.

"You should just apologize anyways." I turn around to Chase.

"I didn't come here for a lesson; I came for an ice pack." He says with an attitude, walking over to the freezer and pulling out a bag of ice.

Alexa thanks me, then gets down from the chair. She walks in front of Chase with a small smile.

I had no idea where on earth this was going, I can't lie and say I wasn't interested.

"You don't have to say sorry to me Chase, just know that karma will get you!" She blows him a kiss before walking out of the office door.

Chase looks at both Liam and I, looking absolutely gob smacked.

"She's cute, isn't she?" He places a huge smile on his face before exiting through the door as well.

"I can't believe that just happened." I turned around to Liam who was also laughing.

"I can understand why you like working here so much." He remarks, while taking a seat where Alexa previously sat.

I grin, walking over in between his legs.

"What can I help you with today, Charming?" I look at him while tilting my head.

"Careful, you should word that differently." He winks at me; I couldn't help but roll my eyes.

"You're just a natural flirt, aren't you?" I back away from him as he laughs.

"No comment." He slurs.

Liam takes off his sweatshirt, revealing a big bruise on the side of his abdomen. My eyes widen in horror, my body felt winded just looking at it.

Seeing Liam hurt in any way makes my heart drop to my stomach, even if I knew I shouldn't care.

It's hard to turn off feelings just like it never happened, but I can't erase the wonderful memories that I got with Liam. I'm sure that it's hard for him to forget as well.

"So, you're wearing your ring." He coughs out as I swallow.

"Well, if you were my fiancé, would you want me to hide the fact that I am engaged to you?" I question while grabbing more ice from the ice maker.

"If you were my fiancé, you're ring would be your dream ring, that you couldn't hide from anyone." He glowers.

Liam knew what my dream ring was. A beautiful white gold band, blessed with diamonds throughout and of course a radiant 5 carat diamond.

"Doesn't he know you like radiant cut?" Liam says with a condescending tone.

I walk back closer to Liam, my eyes meet his again, "Like you were ever going to commit and buy me a ring."

He smiles.

He smiles at me like a damn fool.

"Well, it doesn't matter, it's a cute ring. It'll have to do." He whispers.

I shake my head, "I'm sorry, are you the one that's engaged?" I laugh with a sarcastic tone.

He rolls his eyes.

"How did you even get this bruise, Liam?" I ask, while placing the ice on it, which makes him tense up.

"Motorcycle accident." He cringes as I twitch, dropping the ice on the floor.

I slap his leg, "Are you kidding me William? Be careful." I sigh as I catch a smirk on his face.

"You still care about me, Raine?" He looks at me painfully as I roll my eyes.

"I care about all my friends." I counter.

He put his hand on his chest, pretending that I just shot him with a gun.

"You're breaking my heart, Raine." He says.

I get up, pulling him up by his collar, "Will you shut up and get going. I have a date in half an hour and I'm already running late."

Liam's hands wrapped around my waist, pulling me closer to him, "Or you can stay here with me."

I knew what Liam was doing. He was flirting with me like he would with any other girl. Because if he wasn't, it was like he was giving me special treatment. He wanted to treat me like he was treating every other girl.

I was the only girl that Liam ever took seriously in a way. At least that's what I assumed. I can't really see him with anyone else other than me.

Which sounds very selfish. I know that one day Liam would get over me, not because he has to, but because I know he eventually would meet someone that was destined to be with him.

It wouldn't be hard; it would be easy.

Liam finally stood up, smiling like he had a plan, yet nothing happened.

He put his sweatshirt back on, "I'll see you tonight, Raine."

I stare at him, "Goodluck, Charming."

He turn his head back at me, "I don't need luck, I just need you."

. . .

LIAM

I had been sitting outside of the parking lot for about three hours.

Margo sat by the big window, drinking champagne and had been pulling out pieces of bread from the dish that is originally offered for the table.

She had mentioned to everyone this morning that she was getting dinner with Ben, which is very understandable since he is her fiancé.

But what isn't understandable is the fact that she has been sitting alone for three hours.

No fiancé was in sight.

It was like she was waiting for someone, yet at the same time it looked like she didn't want anyone to show up.

Which Ben was doing a really great job at.

I knew that the hockey game starts at 8:30 p.m. and it was 7:37 p.m. I was supposed to be at the arena by 7:30 p.m. but I couldn't leave Margo alone knowing that she was being stood up.

I finally couldn't stand it, and I made my way over to Margo's table.

Her eyes had been set in front of her glass of champagne. Margo had not paid any mind to anyone else around her, that is, until I sat down on the empty seat in front of her.

"What are you doing here?" She whispered with aggression.

I only smiled, "The question is why have you been sitting here for three hours alone, when you said you had a dinner?"

Margo stayed quiet.

"He's coming." She says out of nowhere.

"What else is more important than being here with you?" I remarked.

Margo averted her gaze towards my eyes, which she used to avoid.

"You are as sharp as a circle Liam." She grumbled.

"How?"

"There are some things more important in life than just being with your loved one. Other people have responsibilities, things that are asked of them to do. Which you have no idea about." Margo said with persistence.

"Men like Ben, are providers. They don't have to be on time, they don't always have to be there for me, but I expect them to take care of me and my family." She continued on.

I've never seen Margo so full of annoyance and emotion. She was right, I was immature in that way. I didn't have anyone else to take care of except for myself.

I tend to think of the other things in life, other than being stable, because I've never been unstable.

"How much is he worth." I asked.

"100 million." She replied, her eyes down casted as she fiddled with her nails.

"Margo, even your family is worth more than that. You don't need someone to provide for you." I advised as she flinched.

She stayed silent.

I had no clue what went on in her mind.

"I'm worth 500 million." I grumbled with a smirk.

Margo's eyes found mind once more but this time she wasn't serious, she had a smile plastered on her face.

"You're very irritating, you know that?" She chuckled.

"No actually, I'm pretty sure when I walk in a room, people are in awe," I muttered while I took a sip of her champagne, "It's a gift." I bragged.

Margo's eyebrow raised, "I think it's a gift when you leave the room."

I couldn't help but laugh, she always knew how to banter with me.

"Why don't I give you a ride back to the arena, for the game." I wiggled my eyebrow which made her let out a small giggle.

"You know just in case I get injured; I wouldn't want anyone else to treat me other than you."

Margo started to gather her things, "I'm telling Ronni you said that." She said in a threatening tone.

Before we started to walk out of the front doors, Ben's face decided to greet us.

"Ben!" Margo screeched.

"And where does my lovely fiancé think she's heading off to?" He snaked his arm around her small waist.

Margo tensed up.

A fit of rage filled me in a quick second, "Maybe you shouldn't hold her like that, she looks uncomfortable."

Ben dismissed my words by just ignoring me.

"How about I handle my fiancé any fucking way I want, and you run along," He hissed while grabbing Margo by her wrist so tight that she yelped.

I swear my eyes filled with fury before I ripped Ben's grip away from Margo's wrist.

I held on to Ben's hand, squeezing tighter and tighter until he started to struggle.

"How about you think about the next time you grab your fiancé like that, how bad it would feel if my fist rammed in your fucking skull." I shook him away from me.

"Let's ask Margo who she would like to leave with then." Ben laughed.

I swallowed a lump in my throat, because I knew the answer. Margo was going to pick Ben, she's picked him before, and she would pick him again.

She took a deep breath, scared of her own answer.

"I'm sorry Liam. I'll see you at the game." She muttered softly before she walked out of the door with Ben.

Ben took a moment to look behind him before he left with Margo, his eyes locked on to mine.

I had no idea why I felt like all of this was a fucking game. It was my fault really; Margo came here alone, and Ben came here to get his fiancé.

The only person that shouldn't be here was fucking me. The only person that was way out of line was me. I only stood up for Margo because I thought she was in danger.

Yet again she made it clear she didn't need my help. She didn't want me at all.

I agreed to her terms before but I'm so fucking stubborn to accept it. But it was time for me to accept it.

If she wanted Ben, then it was her decision. I had to start looking out for myself again, just myself.

LIAM

I've recently been hitting the gym way more often than I should, and I knew that my legs were feeling weak and swollen throughout the week, but nothing would make me sit out this game.

Grayson being my best friend and all, won't stay quiet about the fact that he's noticed my weaker right side.

"You might need to get that checked out." He hinted at me.

I stood up, straightening my helmet, "Nah, coach might not let me play. I need to play this game."

Grayson looked away from me, but only a second passed where he wasn't up my ass.

He skated towards me, "I will not let you play if you are genuinely injured."

I knew that Grayson was going to keep his eyes on me the rest of the night now. But all I could really do was lie, I didn't want him to bench me.

"I'm fine." I taunted as he nodded.

I could tell by Grayson's face that he knew something was wrong, he's my best friend after all.

The one person I would trust with anything in my life.

I didn't want him to worry about me, I knew I could handle myself. He had to focus on playing well since Adrianna was finally in attendance. I've never really seen him smile like he did when he sees her.

Leave it up to Mr. and Mrs. Perfect to be together and break the hearts of most girls and boys here in Hawthorne University.

I had skated to the goalie, only to spot my mother's face.

Why was she here?

She's never watched my games before.

She of course came in, modeling the look of a mother who just ransacked the Hawthorne Hockey merchandise store.

When did she have time to get a customized jersey?

I rolled my eyes at my own mother who made her way over to sit in the VIP section up front, my eyes scanned further through the crowd and made eye contact with a girl.

I quickly looked away from her. If I wanted to truly get over Margo, I needed to make sure that I was focusing on nothing but the game, nothing else.

Nothing good ever comes when women were stuck in my head. This reminded me that I had to learn how to let Margo go, it's not like she was available anyways.

We were losing and I felt more aggravated each passing second of the game.

Grayson and I had been getting absolutely slaughtered throughout the whole time.

The screamed of excitement and school spirit didn't even help as I felt like every moment I got the puck, two players kept coming for me.

And if I wanted to pass, they were surrounding all my teammates.

I knew I wasn't focused on hockey like how Grayson was. Don't get me wrong, I love the sport, but I wasn't obsessed with it to a point where I would sweat blood and tears for it.

Maybe that was the problem with me, I needed to focus on something else other than many of the other things in my life that's been going on.

I felt my vision starting to tunnel, like I could only see maybe a few feet away from me.

I knew we were losing.

I felt the chill of the ice as more of the players around me skated, it stung my face.

The atmosphere of the arena had me on the edge, the crowd roared like there was no tomorrow. I spotted the puck on the ice, my vision finally settled.

I noticed an opening, one of the players from the other team had been distracted by Neil coming at him with full speed. I had an inkling that this player didn't have good defense.

I speed up with my full capacity and caught up to him by surprise, I capture the puck with my stick and passed it over to Chris who was trying to make it across the arena.

My eyes narrowed to one of the players who was on their way to attack Chris, Neil skated behind us for another layer of protecting but instead of going for any of us he changed his direction to Grayson.

Grayson looked like he had been struggling getting guys off his back. They had been targeting him from the first period of the game.

I rammed my body to push one of the many guys who skated towards Grayson. But to my luck another opposing play had cross checked me.

My body slammed so hard on the ground I felt my energy

drain. The guy's body weight continued to crush my body, until I had been held in such an uncomfortable position, I couldn't help but scream in pain when he put pressure on my knee.

I felt nothing but a rip, as everyone in the crowd stopped cheering, my teammates looked like they were filled with rage. It only took a second before they started to fight the opposing team.

My ears started to ring and felt my eyes drift in, and out of the world. I later heard the referee's whistle. I opened my eyes back up to see medics coming to place me in a stretcher.

It only took one second before Grayson skated over to me.

I knew exactly what he was going to say, and it was that he shouldn't have let me play because he had a bad feeling.

"I shouldn't have let you play." He blamed himself; I could see it in his eyes.

I couldn't help but just laugh off the immense pain I received.

I attempted to look around, "It's better to be me than anyone else on the team, Prince." I inclined.

It was true, Grayson lived and breathed hockey, Chris needed to get scouted, so he had a brighter future, and I knew that Neil didn't want to go into politics for the rest of his life and found love within the game.

Grayson looked far too upset to keep the game going.

But I explained the reason why I was okay with the injury happening to me.

"I don't want you doing shit on the ice one you get taken care of." He said in a sternly voice.

I couldn't help but grin back.

He looked irritated, "I'm fucking serious." He warned.

I rolled my eyes at my best friend, as our coach approached us, "Coach wouldn't let me anyways." I glowered.

I saw Ronni approaching near as the medics started to get me off the rink.

"Is Margo here?" I quickly asked Grayson.

"No, I don't think so Brookshire."

I shook my head, I laid back down, "With her fiancé, isn't she?"

Grayson looked at me with sorry eyes, "I'm not sure."

I sigh, "You don't have to lie to me."

I think I bickered more than I wanted because of my state of injury. Grayson had to leave and continue on with the game as I got rolled away with Ronni.

CHAPTER 30

MARGO

I got thrown in the passenger seat by Ben, forcefully.

"Ben, he didn't mean any harm." I cautioned.

I saw nothing but fury and vain in Ben's eyes. He walked angrily over to the driver's side of the car, locking all of the doors.

The car had all of its windows tinted and I was normally very happy about that decision. Every wealthy family in Hawthorne is worth a lot of money, and danger was never, not considered when being in a vehicle.

I never thought about being in danger inside of the vehicle and Ben was nothing but dangerous.

He turned his body towards me, his large hand wrapped around my throat and squeezed my airway. Ben's other hand pulled my hair, forcing my eyes over to his.

"Don't ever embarrass me like that again." He raged.

I felt my heart drop to my stomach, tears in my eyes started to run down my cheek.

It was like I was trapped in a nightmare; I was about to live the rest of my life in constant fear of Ben, he was unpredictable and only gave his outburst of rage towards me.

I felt helpless, I was never a girl to walk around anyone in eggshells but by the grace of my luck, my fiancé who I thought was a wonderful guy turned out to be a monster who liked to hurt me.

Ben squeezed tighter and I couldn't back away, I just sat there all tensed up.

"I'm sorry." I mumbled in a low voice, the most I could get out while he had his hand wrapped around my neck.

Ben loosened his grip but forcefully kissed me.

"Margo, I don't want other men touching you." He growled as he lowered his slobber of a kiss down to my neck.

I felt sore, like I would bruise again, such as my wrists.

I could only cry silently as he released my hair from his rough hold. I felt helpless and scared of anything that he was capable of.

I was scared of what he would do to me, my family and what he would do with Liam.

I knew Liam could always handle himself, but I also never experienced such fear from someone like I did with Ben.

Liam had only ever made me feel safe, even if he hurt me, he was never one to make me feel unsafe and scared of him. He would never lay a hand on me, not if I didn't want it.

Ben had a reason to be jealous and threatened by Liam. Not only because we have history but because Liam was a type of man that many men would always compare themselves to.

He was wealthy, he was built, he has a family, friends that would do anything for him, he had a hound of ladies that surrounded him everywhere he went.

He is talented in hockey and even if he acted stupid, he was one of the smartest guys I knew.

"I forgive you, Margo." Ben pondered, before he put the car in drive. My heart started to slow down as he drove.

I never started a conversation with Ben ever since he put his hands on me. I only turned to face the right passenger window and stare out in the abyss.

I would sometimes find my reflection in the window of the car, and when I did, I didn't even recognize myself.

"I have to go and attend this game." I shuddered as he gave me a quick look of annoyance.

"You're not going." He asserted.

Ben looked dangerous in this very moment, like nothing on this earth could ever get to him or scold him that he was acting irrationally.

I couldn't talk, it was like my body wouldn't let me without his permission. I wanted to call for help, every bone in my body wanted to ask for forgiveness so that he wouldn't put his hands on me again.

But I couldn't, it was like I physically couldn't do anything about it. I was helpless, I could only be strong so that I could help my parents.

This was all for them.

We arrived back at my house, I shakily walked towards my room like it was my only place of solitude, but I was wrong. The moment I had opened the doors, suitcases and boxes of Ben's items have laid all around my room.

"You're moved in?" I asked with a tremble as he grinned.

"Since I'm your husband to be, we need to jumpstart, don't we?" He looked at me with a malicious gleam in his eyes.

Ben's phone began to ring, which made me twitch when he moved his hand to grab it from his pocket.

He turned away to answer his call, I turned back around to notice an abundance of shopping bags that filled the closet.

Top of the line brands were laid across from *Hermes, Chanel, Ralph Lauren, and Loro Piana.*

"You like them?" He came up behind me in a gentle manor, placing his hands on my waist like he didn't bruise them earlier.

I winced as he kiss the top of my head, "You got gifts." I said in a low monotone.

Ben turned around, "Of course I would get my fiancé presents, I would be a terrible future husband if I didn't."

He was sick and twisted, all of his rage had subsided, and the only thing left was his gentleness that, I was introduced to the first time we met.

"I have work to get back to, at my father's office, I'll come home tonight, and we can have some wine in the balcony. I'll have the help set it up, it could be romantic." He suggested while he straightened his cuffs.

I nodded, dreading the rest of the day.

He walked out of the room, I followed him out to the front doors, Ben placed a soft kiss on my cheek before he left. I wiped it off the moment he left the driveway with his fancy Bentley.

The help looked around, guarding my every move. I soon realized that Ben had made sure to let them know that I was never to leave their sight.

It made sense that they would be given this advice. It just hurt because they were my help first before Ben, who apparently took over the whole household.

My phone began to ring, seeing that it was from Adrianna. I answered from the second ring, "Hey Anna." I uttered.

"Hey Margo, I know that you probably wouldn't care anymore or that you do care but you're in denial." She started as I rolled my eyes.

"Just get to the point." I begged as she took a deep breath.

"Liam's at the hospital." She confessed as I felt my whole body weaken.

"What?!" I faltered, "What happened?" I felt my chest heave like I was panicking for a second.

"Grayson just got informed that he slightly tore his ACL during the game when the other team were on him like crazy." Adrianna expressed as I ran to my room to grab my bag and put on a sweater for more comfort.

"I'm on my way." I replied to her whist I ran to the garage. I looked at one of my drivers who have driven me around since I was in middle school.

I rung up the phone, and got into one of the available vehicles, "Look Barry, I know you were given strict instructions from

Ben to keep me in the house, but I really need to go the hospital this very moment because of Liam." I pleaded.

Barry looked at me from the rearview mirror and started the engine. I felt my smile reach my ears as he shook his head, "I will always have your back first, Miss Hamilton."

I ran in the hospital lobby with one vision in mind and it was to see that Liam was safe and okay.

"What room is Liam Brookshire in?" I asked as the lady in the front desk completely ignored me by taking a sip of her coffee.

"Yeah, and I'm pretty sure that Doctor Torrez was with Doctor Aang last night, they've been getting pretty cozy." She muttered to her other coworker.

I tapped my foot with the impatience written all over my face, "I'm sorry but could you just--" I continued but their conversations cut me off once more.

"Wasn't she with one of the nurses last week though?" Her coworker said in shock as the lady nodded.

I felt a bit of rage fill me as I took a deep breath, "Just please tell me what room I could find Liam Brookshire." I grumbled.

The lady looked at me, "Only family is allowed to visit him, no girlfriends allowed sweetheart."

I gave a sour expression, "I'm not his girlfriend."

"Are you part of his family?" She asked.

"Well-- no." I stuttered as she laughed.

"So, you aren't his family, you aren't even his girlfriend, then no room entry." She asserted after she took another sip of his coffee.

I slammed my hand on the counter, "Listen lady, if you don't want me to make a complaint to Doctor Alica Du Pont that your service here is horrible and you can't take a moment to listen to me, because of both of your gossiping, then I suggest you give me the damn room number.” I threatened as she typed on her computer with fear in her eyes.

I normally wouldn’t use my connections to get ahead… that’s a complete lie. I knew Verina’s mother owned the hospital and knew it would help me in the long run.

But I was sure she wouldn’t mind.

“Room 202.” She glowered at me as I made my way to the elevator.

As the elevator door opened my eyes met with Grayson and Adrianna, who looked like she had just gotten some action.

“Margo!” She affirmed as I squinted my eyes at her.

At the end of the day, I really didn’t care because it wasn’t the reason I was here to begin with.

“Is he okay?” I asked as Grayson looked at me with concern, “Yeah, he’s in surgery so we’ve just been hanging around.”

“So, we have no idea if he’s okay or not.” I swallowed my nervousness down, but it was apparent that it was still visible in my face.

“No, we don’t, but it was just a minor tear, the worst that could happen is that it might take a longer time for him to get back on the ice.” Grayson pondered as I took a deep breath.

The elevator reached the destined floor. My eyes reached the waiting room to meet with Chris, Verina, Neil, Juliette, a little boy, and Liam’s mother.

“Where have you guys been?” Neil hesitated to ask as Grayson and Adrianna only sheepishly smiled at each other.

“You two are gross, you can’t keep your hands away from each other for more than three hours?” The boy says as Grayson rolled his eyes.

“Give me a break Finn, she’s my girlfriend and I don’t have to keep it a secret anymore.” Grayson disclosed as Liam’s mother looked confused.

At the same time, she looked at Adrianna in awe, but I didn’t think it was much to ponder on.

I sat down on the empty couch as everyone gathered around me.

"Margo I'm sure, he'll be fine." Verina sat next to me, she put her arm around my back.

There was no point in hiding the fact that I was scared something could go horribly wrong.

I placed my hands in my hair, Juliette sat beside me on the other side, "Yeah Liam has an eighty nine percent chance of being completely fine." She trailed off.

"I know he'll be fine guys I'm just worried is all." I groaned as they all sat in silence.

"I should've knocked one of the members out like Grayson did." Juliette dryly muttered as Verina shouldered her to shut up.

"I'm not fucking licking that!" I turned to Neil who voiced out to Chris while slapping the lollipop out of his hand.

Chris's face turned into complete anger, "Neil. What. The. Fu--."

"--Language!" Grayson yelled over to him as Chris paused.

Chris's head slowly moved to meet Neil's eyes, in a very scary way.

"Oh, here we go..." Grayson mumbled, he leaned on the back of his seat.

"That was my last lollipop, you had no right to--" Chris screamed at Neil in an extremely angered tone.

"Will you both shut up, you're both doing my head in." Grayson yawned out while his legs spread apart, leaning his elbows on the back seat.

"Let the children play." Finn insisted.

"You're acting like a baby Chris; It's just a lollipop." Neil muttered as Chris did everything in his power to ignore him.

Chris subtlety mocks Neil by mouthing everything he said in a petty way.

"Will you two knock it off!" Finn yelled at both of the boys.

"Can't you see that this is a very serious moment." He breathed out.

"Margo clearly looks frightened, because Will is in surgery. Grayson obviously is trying to act calm because his best friend is on an operating table, you guys are acting childish because Liam isn't here to be the one cracking the jokes." He clocked all of them as they sat there and stared directly at him.

Everyone was silenced. Including Liam's mother who was shocked to hear Finn yell at grown adults.

It was safe to say that Liam not being near our presence making his stupid comments or annoying jokes put all of us on edge.

Almost two hours passed. Adrianna had fallen asleep on Grayson's lap as he ran his hand through her hair. Finn leaned his head on Verina's shoulder and her head was laid on Chris's.

Liam's mother had been pacing around while Neil was on a call with someone in the other room, Juliette had picked up one of the magazines on the coffee table to read.

I felt like I had been looking at my watch and the ceiling for eternity.

Two doctors finally had walked out to greet Liam's mother.

Liam's mother looked at me and waited for me to join her before the doctor would be able to deliver any news. I smiled at her as she held my hand.

"Liam did a great job with the surgery." He mentioned.

"Since it was just minor it wouldn't take long for him to recover with doing the right types of physical therapy and medications." The other doctor had noted.

"What type of exercises would he need to do and what types of medications?" I asked.

I knew it wasn't my job to make sure Liam recovered but I

couldn't help but want to help, and I would do anything to make sure he was well and alright.

"We can give you the list up at the front desk." The doctor muttered as I rolled my eyes.

Those ladies at the front desk, wouldn't help me even if I was dying on the floor.

"He is just resting now but anyone can visit him." The doctors included before they walked off.

"You should go see him first." Liam's mother hinted at me as I shook my head.

"No, you are his mother, you should be the first thing he sees when he wakes up." I reckoned as she smiled at me before entering Liam's room.

I looked at Liam's mother's mannerism and how much she reminded me of someone I knew, she looked like an angel and everything that Hawthorne parents wanted to be.

She was successful, gorgeous, and kindhearted. I don't have any clue how on earth she raised Liam to be egotistical and annoying at times. But yet I'm the stupid girl who fell in love with him and practically almost had an attack when I found out he was at the hospital.

I sat back down on the couch; my movement had woken everyone up. Grayson shot up and woke Adrianna.

"Did the doctors say anything?" He questioned.

"Yeah, he's going to be fine, his mother is checking on him right now." I reported back as he calmed and sat back down.

Liam's mother walked back out, looking defeated.

"Is everything okay?" I wondered as she shook her head.

"He refuses to take any of his pain medication," She walked towards me and Grayson.

Grayson stood back up, "Does he want to see me?" He guessed as she pulled out her hand to stop him.

"No, he just asked for Margo." She remarked as Grayson fell back down to his seat upset.

"Awh, you've been replaced." Chris laughed at Grayson as he threw him a middle finger.

I stood up and walked into Liam's room. He was laid on the hospital bed looking irritated and annoyed.

"Liam, thank god you're okay." I breathed as I ran up to his bedside.

"You can't miss me that much already." He winked at me like a dumb doofus he was.

"I hate you for getting hurt." I pushed his shoulder as he winced in pain.

"You have to take your pain reliever, you know; I will shove it down your throat if I have to." I laughed, in a joking manner.

"I don't need to take any medication." He groaned.

Liam raised his hand to find mine which rested on his chest. He held on to it like I was what he needed to wind down.

I sat down on the chair beside of his bed, not retrieving my hand from his grasps.

"I don't need any pain reliever; I just want you next to me to hold my hand." He whispered as I pulled the chair closer to his bed.

"Okay."

It didn't take much time for Liam to fall asleep.

I heard rustling, the three boys, Grayson, Neil, and Chris stood by the doorway looking restlessly at their best friend.

They didn't say anything much, only stared at Liam holding my hand as he slept.

I didn't know my role in Liam's life anymore, I didn't know what his role was in mine either. I wasn't sure if we were mature enough to figure it out.

All I knew was that when we needed each other, there was nothing standing in our way to be with each other.

We were each other's peace, and I was okay with that.

CHAPTER 31

LIAM

A week later.

I had been avoiding Margo for days. I knew sooner or later I would have to face her. I had started this big plan of maybe getting a little bit injured during that last game, so that I could hang out with her a little more in the physical therapy room.

I wasn't exactly hoping for a tear in my ACL. This plan completely backfired because, ever since I finished with surgery... I had done some thinking; I wanted to stay away from Margo.

I had realized that I had turned into a complete mad man for this girl. I got her different flowers every day. I memorized all the fucking states.

Yet I knew that if she asked me to get on my fucking knees, I would be a goner.

I'm not saying that it's a bad thing to do anything for a woman you love. I thrive to do that for my future wife, but the issue was that I'm acting like this for a girl, that is to be married to another man.

I'm doing this for a girl that I'm not even with.

Which gets to be really embarrassing when I think about it.

But here I was, I stood outside of the physical therapy office.

Before I knocked, Margo opened the door. She looked like she had just seen a ghost.

That wasn't a far comparison, I hadn't seen her since I woke up and asked her to hold my hand after surgery.

I hadn't texted her back. I hadn't called her back.

I had pretended like she didn't exist.

The first thing I wanted to tell her was how beautiful she looked but the only thing I was able to spew out was…

"Weather looks nice today, doesn't it?" I laughed cooly, while I scratched the back of my head.

"It looks miserable outside." Margo stared at me with a confused face.

Margo wore loose, low-rise jeans with her Manolo pumps. She had a tight long sleeve shirt that accentuated her slim waist and sharp collar bones.

Since her jeans were low, my eyes caught on to her tan lines from summer. I would've thought that they would've faded by now, but it was like they would stay on her forever.

"I think the sky looks nice when gloomy." I struggled to find more words.

Margo turned her head to look out the window as a bolt of lightning struck the thundering sound roared through the building.

"You hate thunder and lightning." She said plainly.

The look on her face said it all, like for our type of relationship right now, my fear of thunder and lightning wasn't a fact she was supposed to know about me.

But she did, because she listened to everything I said.

Margo shook her head lightly, brushing off the entire conversation prior.

"So, at least you're standing." She averted her gaze down to my knee.

"I can walk too, just a little bit wobbly." I commented while I walked into her office.

Margo stayed silent.

This was definitely the most uncomfortable interaction we have had.

"Okay so, I think we should start with stretches." She nervously suggested.

I had noticed that Margo started to walk around the office like she owned the place, like she was now so comfortable she did things with ease. Whether it was getting ice to make an ice pack, wrapping someone up or clicking the dials on the telephone.

She pulled out a book, quickly scanned over it, before she suggested for me to start with stabilization exercises.

She poured a bunch of resistance bands on the floor.

"Okay so you are going to hook the band on the bar right there," She pointed, "While facing the bar you will loop your ankle on the resistant band and try to−−"

"I got it." I interrupted as she widened her gaze.

"If you need help, I will be just right here." She stated before she hopped on the top of her desk, next to the bowl of grapes.

"How many times do you want me to do this?" I asked as she tilted her head.

"Until failure, then you rest for two minutes, then you can start again." She voiced.

"This is going to be a long fucking day." I whisper under my breath as she rolled her eyes. Margo pulled out a remote and turned on the television.

"Okay I'll turn something on, to pass the time then." She sneered at me while she opened the Netflix tab on the television.

Margo was on her way to click on the movie, *A Walk to Remember.* I rolled my eyes, for her to visibly notice.

"Come on, you liked it when we were in the hotel." She jabbered as I couldn't help but laugh.

"The movie is bullshit. She deserved better." I defensively coughed out while I continued on my exercises.

Margo threw me an ugly look.

"I don't want to hear it; I wasn't the one bawling the whole ending of *Titanic.*" I claimed as she stood up.

"If you didn't cry during the *Titanic,* you are a complete psycho!" She yelled back.

"All I'm saying is if Rose didn't move her lazy ass over just a little bit, then Jack could've definitely made it. She's selfish and she's the reason he died. They could've definitely fit on that wooden plank." I went off while I fixed my knee's form.

Margo face looked baffled.

"Rose was going to kill herself in the beginning! Who stopped her?" Margo threw me the stronger resistant band.

Probably a sign to go a bit harder on my exercise since she observed that I was cruising through the easier resistant band.

"Jack saved her! In the end, Jack died for Rose... while Rose lived for Jack." She folded her arms together.

"It's a phenomenal story." She threw me a dirty look.

"Aside from a girl who died from her leukemia treatments." I looked back at her.

I couldn't help but spot a smile appear in Margo's lips.

I, myself had a grin plastered on my face.

"Fine then what do you want to watch?" She huffed as I looked back at the television.

"Little Mermaid, who could go wrong with the queen of the sea." I shrugged as she fixed my posture.

"Ariel is not the queen of the sea, Moana is." She debated.

"Uhm, how?" I probed.

"Moana left her village, to save the ocean and to return the heart of Tefiti. Meanwhile your queen of the sea left her entire kingdom and her family for some guy she didn't even know!" Margo snapped back.

"Whatever, everyone knows that the first queen of the sea is better." I protested as Margo's face visibly looked more red.

"That's not true." She said angrily.

"Okay, then tell me, who the second guy who walked on the moon was, without looking it up." I snobbed as she crossed her legs.

"This is a really good time to have Juliette's brain." She gave me an irritated look.

"Did I just win the argument?" I asked Margo with a look on disbelief on my face.

Margo looked up at me slowly and threw me another thicker resistant band.

She was going to make this harder for me, wasn't she?

"No." She remarked, with a gloomy sigh.

I think... just maybe... I had a plan.

As I sat on the bench all of practice I started getting FOMO.

If I skated to the other side of the rink and back, maybe coach would let me join in on some drills.

The smell of the hockey locker room was obviously never ideal but the feeling of being around the team and the mist of the shaved ice that gets blown towards me whenever someone made a complete halt.

"If you even think of getting up and skating at full speed I'm going to tell Margo." The daunting yell from Grayson's direction made me pause.

God they are so annoying.

Grayson, Neil, and Chris skated over to me with disapproving looks.

"Are you guys more friends with her of with me?" I placed my eyes over to all of them as they rolled their eyes in unison.

"Quit acting like a baby, we want you back on the ice more than anyone, but we can't let you get on here when you aren't ready." Neil said before shooting water all over his face.

"How do you know I'm not ready?" I folded my arms together.

Grayson laughed.

"Because of Margo's logs." Chris popped in.

"Logs?" I say in a questioning manor.

I knew Margo was always taking notes on her stupid little iPad, but I never paid much attention to the things she would write.

"I want to see these logs." I stood up, rather shakily.

"No." Grayson plainly uttered.

"Why not?" I challenged with a pinched expression.

"It's your progress, and her inner thought on how you've been improving. Margo mentioned that if you asked to see them, you aren't permitted to because it might affect your own idea of your pace." Grayson finally let out with an exaggerated sigh.

What could Margo possibly be writing about me, that I didn't already know. It would've had to be something bad or else Grayson would've one thousand percent told me... right?

"I'm fine." I smiled before I tapped my knee.

Everyone ignored my little proclamation.

"So, is everyone available to come at... what time did Adrianna say again?" Neil asked.

"I think, Dove said six." He said it so proudly.

Grayson Prince was inevitably whipped by Adrianna Cassian, and I definitely saw it all coming.

"I have work until seven, but I could still swing by, we might end early because it's a weeknight." Chris added.

The rest of the team disbanded; Coach Livingston made sure to pat my back before heading out as well.

"Do we have to attend this?" I couldn't help but ask this rather jarring question because at the end of the day I knew what the answer was.

"Come on, it's just a movie." Grayson threw on his very convincing smile.

"What movie are we even watching?" Neil asked.

Grayson shrugged as well as Chris and I.

It had now been a weekly tradition that the girls had started, they would watch chick flicks together and eat ice cream like everything was right with the world.

Recently, we found ourselves attending as well, not by choice but because these girls are manipulative and have easily tricked us into going.

I don't think the boys and I would ever actually admit that we somewhat enjoyed coming over, having to stuff our faces with snacks and watching another movie that's starring Julia Roberts and Richard Gere.

Last week's *Pretty Woman* changed my life for the better. I am also quite deeply upset that Julia Robert's smile hasn't cured world hunger yet.

"I thought I saw Adrianna looking up movies earlier during class, maybe it's that one with the guy and the girl." I mumbled.

Neil didn't take a moment before he smacked the back of my head.

"No shit, there's a guy and a girl. You are so incredibly dense." He hung his head.

"Can we make them watch *Fight Club* or something?" Grayson yawned as I opened a bag of chips that I pulled out of Chris's bag.

"No!" Neil said with urgency.

He quieted down quickly, "It seems to me like, you have been enjoying the movies the girls are making us watch." Grayson probed.

Neil only rolled his eyes as I skated back towards Chris who slipped a look at his bag of chips.

"Okay I might've enjoyed the last one we watched." He confessed.

"I enjoyed it too." I said with a defeated look.

Grayson and Chris laughed.

They always thought they were better than us, more masculine might I add. Even though, I knew they enjoyed watching *Notting Hill* more than anyone.

A moment of silence passed as all the boys sat down next to me. This felt like it was a forced intervention.

"Is there any reason why you all look like your parents died or something?" I laughed.

In the contrary actually, if their parents passed away, there would been smiles galore that filled the arena.

"We're worried about you." Grayson put his hand on my back as I stood up in confusion.

"For what?"

"Well for starters you've been hanging around Margo and we've discussed that this might not be a good idea since she is getting married, and you are supposed to be getting over her." Chris reasoned.

I looked at all of them with a look of demise and a bit of annoyance.

They were telling me something that I've tried to tell myself. As if I hadn't heard it enough.

"I'm hanging around with Margo because *news flash*. I am injured." I threw an irritated look.

"We could see if Ronni could help you out instead." Neil added.

I shook my head, "This is sounding ridiculous. You guys don't think that I can control myself around Margo? I'm not an animal; I know that she's getting married. I know that she rejected me more times than I could even count." I was pacing around like a damn teacher giving a lecture.

"You don't think I know that I have to stay away from her?" I ended.

"I just think that--" Grayson opened his mouth.

"--No, you don't get to talk." I disrupt him.

"You don't get it, Prince. You got your girl. You have hockey, despite you hating your family, you choose to ignore the fact that they would do anything for you." I started.

"Adrianna loves you like she loves to breathe. You and her

look at each other like you guys were made for each other's gaze."
I kept going.

"Margo and I look at each other like that too. And I know I'm not the only one who sees it because, I only have to look at her to get my heart to relax. You know how much of a privilege it is to look at someone you love and for them to return the favor with nothing in the way?" I finally lost my breath.

They all stared at me, defeated.

"I was just trying to help." Grayson stood up with an angry look in his eyes.

A look I had only seen when he was truly upset with someone.

"Guys it's not that serious." Neil stood in between us.

"Of course you would say that, for you nothing is ever serious." I mouthed off.

"What's that supposed to mean?" Neil's posture had turned rigid.

"What else do you really have to worry about Neil, aside from the fact that yes, your parents are up your ass about an internship with the Mayor?" I snapped.

"Oh yeah? Let's face it Will, you never would've lost Margo if you weren't acting like a fucking dickhead in the first place." Neil walked toward me.

He was right of course.

"We all need to calm down." Chris stood up, again always being the sensible one.

"I was calm before, Will brought up my family." Grayson muttered.

"Then stop discussing my life like I'm a science experiment, I can handle my fucking life with Margo. We aren't fucking, we weren't really friends in the first place so why be nice to her?" I rasped.

"That's not what we're trying to tell you--"

"If you want the old Liam that just fucked any girl in sight before summer then good job. You fucking got him back. Lay off my back about what I should do with Margo because frankly, how I run my life is none of your business." I turned and walked away from my friends.

We had never gotten in a fight like this. The last time we fought was in grade school, I had broken Grayson's favorite hockey stick and hid it.

We had fought because he thought I couldn't handle myself around Margo.

I got mad because in the bottom of my heart, they were right.

This fight was not about some lousy hockey stick that I had broken. It was about Margo, which to me is so much more important.

CHAPTER 32

MARGO

"Close, you just need to lift it higher and keep it there." I placed my hand on Liam's knee as he stiffened and pulled away.

I quickly retracted my hand from his skin.

He lifted his knee higher but failed to keep it up. He looked at his knee with anguish and irritation as he slammed his hand on the table.

"Fuck this." He stood up and walked over to my desk, pulling his water bottle to his mouth.

"Liam, for me to help you... I'm going to need to lead you through the stretches for you to do better on your form... meaning that I would *have* to touch you." I lightly mentioned as he faltered.

"Who said I won't let you touch me?" He looked over at me with a smug face.

I froze.

"Oh, I don't know, you turn into a gargoyle every time I touch you." I made a point as he walked up to me quickly and interlocked my hand with his.

He then brought our interlocked hands in front of my face, "I don't have a problem with touching you Margo, I'm not a nine-year-old." His words filled my ear drums with venom.

I wasn't sure what point Liam was trying to pull with me, not that it mattered. Things with us pretty much ended the night of the game where he tore his ACL.

He hadn't show me any idea that he liked to spend time with me versus not wanting to spend time with me.

I wasn't really sure which one I wanted. It was selfish for me to wish that he would still give me the attention I used to receive before.

"Sit down." I commanded as he threw me a look of disbelief.

Liam just stood there and looked at me.

"Let's make a pact." I offered.

"A pact." He said it in a tone were it was a combination of a question and a *are you serious, right now?*

"Yes, a pact. We are friends, are we not?" I asked as he hesitated to answer.

"Okay, I'm intrigued, keep going." He mumbled as I took a breath.

"No kissing." I first mentioned as he did nothing but smile.

"No checking each other out." I added.

"I'm a big girl Liam, you can date other people, I'm pretty sure I can handle it." I sneered.

"Do you *want* me to date other girls?" He laughed as I took a deep breath.

"Yes!" I panicked.

"No!" I corrected.

"That's not the point. The point is, there is no chance that you and I will ever be more than what we were." I stuttered.

"So, you can either move on, or you can stay and play with yourself." I finished off.

I understood that how I spoke to Liam was a bit harsh, but it was the truth. There was no other way around the fact that I was going to be married and one day we would just be memories of each other.

"No having sex." I whispered as he shook his head with a low laugh.

"Oh yeah?" He licked his lips.

"Stop that!" I slapped his arm as he winced.

"What?!" He defended while petting his arm.

"You can't look at me like that."

"How am I looking at you?" Liam folded his arms together.

"Like you want to fuck me on that desk." I answered blatantly and with a rushed tone.

Liam leaned closer to me, his voice was husk and low, "I do want to fuck you on that desk."

I felt shivers down my spine and my mouth salivating. This was exactly why I set the rule of not kissing or having sex because, one taste of him I would be back to square one.

I knew I couldn't resist Liam, and I would hate to think that for the rest of my life I would still be wanting him, even when I couldn't have him.

I couldn't hide the fact that my face had turned red, and my chest was heaving. Whoever said they got through rehab easily have not gone against the temptation of William Brookshire and his stupid way of words.

"No flirting!" I got up walking away from him.

"What?! I can't help it, Raine!" He begged.

Without flirting, Liam's charisma would've gone down to a low percentage.

"I didn't say no to flirting for everyone, I just can't have you flirt with me." I narrowed down as he rolled his eyes.

"Don't you get it Raine?" Liam's eyes searched for mine in a far.

"What?" I asked, but I knew the next words that were about to come out of his mouth.

"I don't want to flirt with anyone else other than you." He said it in a whispered tone.

How do I reset my heart's factory settings to always wanting Liam when he says things like that?

"Fine. We can be friends that flirt." I flashed him a look of annoyance.

"That's risky, Raine." Liam stayed at a low monotone as my legs trembled.

"Can't be, because we can't kiss, we can't have sex." I swallowed, "All risk, no reward." I finished off.

"Do we have a deal?" My voice broke as I muttered.

Liam took a second to look at me, his eyes penetrated mine.

"I can't not check you out," His eyes continued to glaze down my body.

If I was being completely honest, I couldn't not check him out either. It would just be wrong not to look at one of the most perfect people God had created.

"Fine. The other rules stand. And you have to start dating other girls. You take them out, you bring them to dinner, you have sex with them and we're both happy." I reasoned as his eyebrows furrowed.

"How would that make us both happy?" He looked exasperated.

Because maybe me knowing you are fucking other women would help *me* get over you. I wanted to say out loud, but I didn't.

If I had told Liam that I wasn't over him, he would do nothing but try and win me back, and I couldn't afford for him to know that.

If I had to be a bit heartless towards him, I would do it. It was for the best. For the both of us.

"Friends that flirt." He said, trying to make sense of the whole agreement.

"Yes." I gasped out.

Liam walked over to me; his eyes settled on my trembling lips. I suddenly felt my heart beating, my pulse raised and my eyes looking up.

"You must be having some pretty great sex with Ben, for sex to be off the table for me and you." He whispered.

Ben and I were having no sex whatsoever, and it was going to stay exactly that way.

I hadn't had sex since Liam and I at the beginning of the semester.

"Great sex." I forced my eyes away from him.

"It's a shame he's not seeing you in these jeans then," Liam's words slithered around my throat. It was like I was getting suffocated.

I couldn't help but knock my head back slowly, my back had been against the wall. Liam's arm was propped on the same wall that I leaned on.

His head bent down; his lips close to my ear.

"Why?" My breath shook.

"Do you really want me to tell you?" Liam leaned closer to me; I could recognize his smell.

I felt my nipples harden; I was sure he could see them too. Most of the time, I knew how to control myself. When I'm at home by myself I knew how to embrace my pleasure. I used my vibrator and clicked the stop button for it to stop.

But at this very moment I had no idea how to stop the pleasure from my stomach to build up.

Liam wasn't one of those guys who didn't know a clit from a cucumber.

All I had to do was hear Liam's voice for me to get this turned on, I felt my center get wetter.

"*Mhmm.*" I let out a small whimper.

That was all Liam needed for his eyes to sparkle.

"You're so pretty, Raine." He murmured on my right ear.

Liam switched over to my left ear, "Say it back," He paused before speaking again.

"*Tell me you're pretty.*" He slowly murmured.

The worst part of it all was Liam had touched me one bit and I was getting off to him.

"I'm pretty." I groaned, my eyes stayed closed.

"Not good enough, Raine." He purred.

"You're so so pretty." He rasped.

I felt waves of pleasure crashing in my stomach, my hips wanted to buck forward, but there would be nothing. My clit was aching for the pressure, only I wasn't being touched by anything.

"I'm so so so pretty." I gave in with a sobbed moan.

I absolutely should not be getting off to my thoughts of Liam. He stayed playing with my imagination, I'm going to have to start sleeping with a dream catcher.

"Such a good girl." Liam lazily said as my hips bucked forward, my clit ached for more. Every muscle in my body wound with so much tension, I wanted to cry for the pleasure of release.

With one brush of Liam's fingers on any part of my body it would've been game over.

I couldn't help but moan again. "Careful, Raine. Anyone could step in at any given moment." He warned me as my clit felt the tiniest friction from my jeans.

I opened my eyes to Liam looking straight down at me, his left hand close to cup my face. My doe eyes watched his body dangerously close to mine.

"Look at me like that again, and I might think you want me to fuck you on that desk." He said so casually as I bucked my hips forward.

"I'll look at you however I want." I shot back at him as his lips curved to a menacing smirk.

"Feisty." He laughed as my clit pulsed at the sound of his deep voice.

"Fuck." My body froze up, my pussy was so wet and aching I couldn't stop from squeezing my legs together.

"Come on Raine, let go... you deserve it." He cooed.

That was the last thing I heard before thunder came and struck me, my hands gripped Liam's shirt, as my body kept bucking. I clenched my eyes shut and heard my moans that travelled lightly on the air.

I felt my body start to calm down from the high as I fell on to

Liam, who in which did not falter whatsoever. He was ready to catch me.

"No risk, amazing reward... huh." He grinned as I rolled my eyes taking his hand and shook it.

A pact had been created.

The doorbell rang, Adrianna's face was met with mine as I pushed of Liam's body.

"Anna!" I laughed, trying not to look frazzled.

Liam only waved back at her.

"Are you ready to go?" She smiled at me as I nodded my head, grabbing my keys and my jacket.

"Liam are you not coming?" Adrianna had asked as I turned my head to look at his face.

"No, I don't think the guys want me there right now." He laughed awkwardly as my eyebrows furrowed.

Had they gotten in a fight?

"Nonsense, and besides, they aren't your only friends. We're your friends too. So, it's either you get in that car or we're knocking you out and taking you with us" Adrianna folded her arms as I laughed.

"Fine, I'll go. Only because I wouldn't want you to get charged with kidnapping and I wouldn't want you two to hurt yourselves by trying to pick me up." He insisted as he also picked up his keys.

"Hey, Grayson has been taking me to the gym. I could bench you." Adrianna gloated as I shook my head.

This was going to be a long ass night.

CHAPTER 33

LIAM

We finally arrived at Adrianna's house.

Adrianna ran around the house, preparing popcorn, sodas, alcohol, other assortment of snacks and a fruit platter.

Margo and I sat on the stools.

I wasn't exactly quite sure how Margo and I were going to handle this. I hate to give her credit, but she was smart for making a pact.

This was an amazing way for her and I to be friends and not fuck each other. Sure, what just happened a couple minutes ago, wasn't an ideal way to show that there was a method to our madness.

But I swear now, I won't mess with her any further.

"So, Liam, how is your recovery?" Adrianna asked me like she was a mother.

I took a look at Margo who threw me a face to urge me to answer her best friend.

"It's been fine, Margo's been helping a lot." I assured as Adrianna smiled at me.

"That's good, I'm sure you'll make a full recovery soon." She added.

"Where is everyone?" I was afraid to ask, but it came out of my mouth anyways.

Adrianna gave me a look as she shut the fridge.

"You don't have to beat around the bush." She laughed, "You miss your boyfriend." She probed while she placed a wine bottle on the countertop.

"I don't miss him." I said with a look of defeat.

"Yes, you do." Adrianna laughed.

"Why, has he said anything about me?" I questioned with a bit of an embarrassing tone.

Grayson and I haven't talked in a week. Which I didn't realize was such an inconvenience.

I had to find someone else to work out with, that wasn't Neil or Chris. I didn't know who to call when the New York Rangers lost. I had no idea who to call when we had our chemistry exam.

We couldn't sit together during the exam. We couldn't even cheat off of each other, which sucks because I was good with the multiple choice and he's good with open ended.

"No, he won't talk about it." Adrianna yawned.

"What even happened between you guys?" Margo turned her body towards me.

He tried to give me advice about you.

"Nothing much important." I ran my hand through my hair.

"Right." Adrianna stumbled to a halt.

"Well, whatever it is, might be resolved to night because they just got here." Adrianna walked over to the door and opened it.

"Baby!" She greeted Grayson with a kiss.

Grayson picks her up with one hand and spun her around as he held a bouquet of flowers.

"Are those for me?" Adrianna asked as Grayson kissed her cheek and handed her the flowers, "No they're for the fish in your backyard pond."

I looked over at Margo as she looked at Adrianna and Grayson. I understood that look way too often. She was watching the Adrianna and Grayson show.

The show where the Hawthorne's favorite couple not only looks perfect but their love for each other is perfect.

"What is he doing here?" He looked directly at me.

"He's our friend, he's a part of movie night." Adrianna spitted out like venom.

Grayson never spoke back to Adrianna anymore when it came to things like this. Don't get me wrong they still bickered but if you wanted a definition of *whipped* you can take a good old look at Grayson Prince.

"He's your friend now!?" He asked Adrianna as I stood up.

"I told you, me coming was a mistake." I informed as I grabbed my coat and started walking over to the door.

"Will you guys knock this off? You guys are best friends. A stupid little fight and what?" Adrianna threw her hands up.

"You guys just forget that you two practically were raised together?" She continued as I took a breath out, putting my hands on my hips in annoyance.

"Stop acting like children and admit that you two miss each other." Margo piped in as I turned my head to look at her.

Adrianna and Margo looked at each other as Grayson and I avoided each other's gaze.

"You don't have to leave; we can still have a good night. We don't have to talk to each other." Grayson made a point as I looked over to Margo who smiled at me.

"Don't worry, you can bother me." She suggested as I nodded my head.

After a few seconds, Neil walked in with a box of pizza and later came, Juliette and Verina. The idea of talking to Chris grazed my mind before I forgot that he wouldn't be here until later.

I kind of looked forward to watching a movie with Margo. We used to do it all the time back in Greece, of course we never really paid attention to the movie, but this was a great revisit.

The girls have decided to watch the *Dead Poets Society*. Grayson and Adrianna were cuddled up as usual. I would usually spend my time with Neil at this point and Margo would spend time with Juliette and Verina. It was a weird idea that Margo and I just laid together.

As friends of course.

I placed a cup on the coffee table, which made Margo move it on a coaster, "I didn't buy Adrianna these coasters for show, *use* them." She whispered.

I laughed at Margo's stupid quirks. I always knew how technical she was. She liked things a certain way, her phone kept beeping every five-minute interval.

I knew who the calls were from, I had an idea that she didn't want me to see. Every time it happened; she would point out something obvious in the movie so that my attention would move away from her fiancé's call.

"I really like Neil in this movie; he's such a sweetheart." She murmured as I shoved her softly.

"You've said that already." I stated as she threw me a full face of attitude.

"Whatever, give me a bite of that." She motioned over to the half-eaten slice of Hawaiian pizza that I held up to my face.

"No." I pulled the slice away from her as she tried to swat at it.

"No?" She warmly huffed as I shook my head.

"No, I'm not going to give you a bite because I know you're not going to like it. Then you're going to ask me how the fuck I could possibly put something like that near my mouth, and I don't want to listen to that when I want to watch the movie." I teased as she rolled her eyes.

"You're lucky I don't spike that pizza with kiwi right now." She said with a quiet tone.

"Ah yes, kill me. That's always a good idea." I laughed.

"Neil would've gave me a bite." She beckoned as I turned my body to face hers.

"I could do more than give you a bite." I urged as her body stiffened.

"Are you always this revolting?" She taunted as I couldn't help a smile form on my face.

"I try to be, but especially when I'm with you." I swore as she directed her eyes over to the group on the other side of the room.

"Why does Neil look like he's about to shit himself?" She asked me as I shrugged.

She looked at me then back at Neil, "Uhm, Neil why do you look like you're about to shit bricks?" She jabbered as I laughed.

Neil looked away from the movie, his face looked like he had just been stunned by a ghost.

"I'm not really comfortable with a character having the same name as me." He said fearfully as Grayson and I couldn't help but burst out laughing.

The moment we realized we laughed at the same thing; the laughter died off very quickly.

"I have a bad feeling about this movie." He added.

"No, I'm sure that's just you." Juliette giggled as I looked at Margo and Adrianna who held in their laughter.

"How could something possibly go wrong, look at him he just put on an amazing play and his dad is probably going to understand that he's talented." I consoled as he nodded his head.

"No yeah, Liam's right." Grayson added as I placed my eyes back to the movie.

"You know... these group of guys reminds me of your friend group." Margo asserted as I shook my head.

"Knock it off." I remarked as her eyes narrowed.

"I don't know what you're talking about." Her tone went up.

"You and your best friend need to stop urging me and my *ex best friend* to reconcile." I expressed.

Margo placed her hand on her chest looking hurt, "Oh my god! You called him your *ex best friend;* things are really in the doghouse." She made her voice louder.

Grayson's eyes directed themselves towards our direction, his laying positioned changed as he shot up.

"Ex best friend?!" He blubbered.

I rolled my eyes, "Gray, you know I didn't mean it."

"No, but you said it." He folded his arms together.

Like a child who was ready to throw a tantrum.

"Well, what do you want from me, we're fighting!" I yelled as he shook his head.

"Not permanently! You just called me your ex best friend." Grayson spluttered as I couldn't help but laugh.

"Okay I'm sorry!" The words spilled from my mouth so quickly as Grayson's face formed a smirk.

"You're forgiven." He looked content as I gave the deadliest stare back at Margo who threw me a wink.

"See now you're all good." She whispered as I slapped my hand on my forehead before Neil screamed on the top of his lungs.

Margo jumped closer to me; she was now sat on my lap. I looked around and saw Adrianna gripping Grayson's arm. Verina and Juliette jumped away from him.

"You all *lied* to me!" He stood up and looked astounded.

"What are you talking about?" Grayson asked as Neil looked at me with sorrow filled eyes.

"Neil Perry just killed himself because he felt trapped by his father." Juliette informed us all as I looked at Grayson.

"Hmm... how fitting." We looked behind Neil, to hear Chris's voice pop up.

"You guys are watching my favorite film on Earth." He added whilst placing his bag next to the coat hanger.

Chris looked at me and Margo, then Grayson and Adrianna, "So I'm guessing you guys made up. And I'm guessing that Neil just reached the point in his life where he realized that he was named after Neil Perry from the *Dead Poets Society.*

"I understand him so much." Neil shook his head.

"He's literally me!" He insisted as we all grew quiet.

"Well let's not say that out loud, what happened to Neil Perry was a travesty and I'm pretty sure I cried for days." Chris reported as Neil moved closer to him.

I looked at Margo who realized she was still sitting on me; she moved back to sit beside me.

"If I died, would you cry that much too?" Neil asked with a pout.

Chris went silent for a moment.

"I don't think I would cry at all." He rolled his eyes as everyone in the group cried of laughter.

By the end of the movie everyone's laughter had turned into tears.

I will forever thank the *Dead Poets Society* for reuniting me and my friends. And a second lousy thank you to Margo for reconciling my best friend and I.

"Thanks." I whispered as she stared at the screen of the television.

"We're friends now, remember?" She looked at me with a smile.

"I guess so Raine." I sighed as she brushed her hand on mine.

I couldn't help but wonder if she wanted to hold my hand, but it didn't matter because she was snuggled up next to me and that was all I really cared about.

CHAPTER 34

MARGO

A week later.

Liam and I had been making amazing improvement as friends, and you know... his physical therapy. Whichever was more important.

I mindlessly strolled around as Liam did knee ups.

"Too slow." I remarked as he sped up his speed.

"You're revolting." He said with a controlled smile.

"I hear a whole lot of talking, and not a lot of grunting!" I said in a sing song voice as I took a sip of my coffee.

I twirled around him as he laughed at a low tone, "What I'm hearing is... you miss hearing me grunt." He continued to exercise as I ignored his comment.

I took a look over to the desk; Liam's phone had been ringing for the past thirty minutes and each time it rang, my blood pressure rose up.

I knew it wasn't his group of friends. Grayson and the other guys were practicing on the ice from my viewpoint, they had no access to their phones.

Sure, it could've been a family member or another person that isn't of a women species. But I choose to be insane.

"You need to ask me a question or something?" Liam finished his work out before he walked over to take a drink of water.

"No, why?" I defended myself.

He turned around and leaned his body against the wooden desk.

"Are you sure there is nothing you would like to ask me to reduce the probability of that vein on your forehead from popping?" He folded his arms together as I turned back to look at him.

"You're phone needs attention, or should I say..." I picked up his cell phone and took a look at the name, "Sammy." I practically choked while saying the name.

"No way... are you jealous?" He asked with mock astonishment.

"If it's the Sammy that I've heard of, then absolutely not. No one has anything nice to say about her." I smiled thickly.

"Sammy Rodriguez?" Liam questioned.

Sammy Rodriguez was the scum of the Earth. She body shamed Juliette and Verina last year, then slept with the girl that Juliette was dating at the time.

Later on, Sammy then ended up befriending Juliette again only to home wreck and have sex with Juliette's boyfriend at the time.

Sammy was very well known around the campus as the *Hawthorne Hoe*. As much as I disliked Brooks, all the credit for making up the nickname was all on him.

As much as I would love to stick up for all women like others would, Adrianna, Juliette, Verina and I believed in a different system, which was looking out for our best friends first.

Obviously, we weren't monsters, at least we were working on that. If a girl looked like she needed help, or she was feeling uncomfortable by another man or woman we would step up and help.

But I would always stick up for my friends first no matter what.

Sammy had not only stole Juliette's past two relationships, but she body shamed Verina. Verina practically hadn't sized up from a double zero, ever since she heard about Sammy's comments.

You might find this hard to believe but, at some point in the first semester, Sammy was a part of our friend group. Until we noticed that she craved a lot of male attention. She yearned for it like she would beg for water in a stranded desert.

Not only would she act like a complete moron near guys, but she was also incredibly selfish and inconsiderate of other's feelings. She didn't care if a man had a girlfriend, she didn't care whether her words and actions hurt someone else.

The only thing she would ever care about is herself and if that body count of hers could stay in double digits by the time she reached twenty-one.

"I advice for you stay away from her." I yawned as he tilted his head.

"Is she crazy or something?" Liam continued to click on her contact.

"That and if you want to get an STD." I reassured him as he gave a disgusted look.

"Noted." He said.

"Are there any other prospects?" I asked.

Liam looked at his phone with no excitement, "Yeah, a couple."

"I could practically see the infatuation and excitement spilling out of you." I said with false cheerfulness as he threw a glare at me.

"What can I say Raine, it's hard to get over you." He sounded slightly brittle as I couldn't help but laugh at the awkward silence.

"Well, time for you to get over it, Charming, now list them off so I can give you my well needed advice." I smiled as he gave an exasperated sigh.

"And you'll be unbiased?" He turned around and pulled his phone closer to his face.

"The point of giving you my opinion is so that I can't be unbiased." I looked at him.

"Fine," He gave a skeptical glance, "Justine Morcant?"

"She doesn't just fool around; she wants a partner." I answered.

"What makes you think I don't want something serious?" Liam gave me a weary look as my lips thinned.

Liam smirked, "Neely Sung?"

"The one that's still obsessed with her ex-boyfriend?" I inquired.

"Mae Candelaria?" Liam glanced upwards in annoyance as I mentioned how she was known to have slept with her step-brother.

As he kept naming random girls from Hawthorne, the more he showed impatience. With the amount of times he had rolled his eyes, I was surprised they haven't gotten stuck on the back of his head.

"I could hook you up with one of my friends." I voiced as he laughed up a storm.

"I would rather you not be involved in any of my future rela-tionships, so you playing cupid is definitely not happening." He gave me a withering look.

My face could say it all, I was annoyed at his intense need to find a partner so quickly. Sure, I was the one who told him to find other girls but, in my head, I envisioned him to just sleep with them and leave.

Which obviously wasn't a good thing, but I couldn't help but face the wrath of jealousy that boiled in my body.

I wanted to feel anything, instead of just a slap in my face when I got back home to Ben. So I didn't care about how angry it would make me to know that Liam was dating again.

I stuck around campus so much, I was glad no one ques-tioned it.

I would just say I liked spending time at the trainer's room, which I did. But avoiding my home address was the real answer. I was happy that Ronni had been taking time off so that I could continue working.

My volunteering hours had almost finished because of the amount of hours I logged in with helping Liam and his damn knee.

Which honestly could've been the best thing to happen to us and our relationship together.

"Fine, I get it. You want to find your Cinderella on your own." I gave a heaved sigh.

I went to look at my clipboard and noticed all of Liam's physical therapy had only one more day to go before he could get back on the ice.

"Looks like you could be back on the ice by the next game." I expressed as his eyes widened and his fists shot up in the air.

"No way?!" He exclaimed as I laughed.

"Yeah, you come in for your last hour tomorrow. Then, I just need to write your evaluation, and you are going to be saying your farewells to the trainer's room... I hope." I said with skepticism.

"Yeah, trust me I will try and not be back here any time soon." He assured me.

"Geez, just tell me you hate me next time." I joked as Liam walked closer to me once more.

His hand came up and fixed my hair, "I know you hate it when your hair looks nothing more than perfect." He noticed as I hesitantly pulled away.

"Any plans this weekend?" I coughed out as he smiled.

"No, not much just hanging out with the guys. I might visit Chris's brother; I haven't seen him lately." He informed as he packed his things.

I realized that when Liam and I had made this pact, it was solely so we could work together through his physical therapy. But since it was ending, it was a hard pill for me to swallow knowing that we might not have the same relationship after.

He was hardly going to see me and one day when he does find another girl, there was no excuse for us to still be friends.

Because at the end of the day, we could preach to the choir that we were just friends, we knew deep down it was the last rope of hope for us.

He started walking up to the exit with a wide smile, was he not a bit sad that we weren't going to hang out anymore?

"Thanks for all the help, Raine." He winked before exiting.

I shouldn't feel like he was stepping on my heart but that's what it sure felt like.

CHAPTER 35

LIAM

"Samuel!" I greeted as his face stayed stern with the look of resentment.

"How is my favorite bouncer!" I added as he continued to ignore me.

I haven't seen Finn in a long time, nor have I been in the bar.

"Is the runt here?" I asked as he took a second to look at me up and down.

"What is it?" I questioned as he did nothing but deepened his weary look.

"I thought Grayson said that you were in rehab or something." He registered me with disapproval.

I rolled my eyes, "He's overdramatic, I was in recovery from my torn ACL not for alcoholism."

Samuel's face changed from stern to skeptical.

"For the first time, you don't look like shit." He muttered as the comment set me back for a second.

"And you finally took my advice about that ugly V-neck you wore," I laughed.

Samuel coughed with a sigh of impatience and annoyance.

"Yeah, the runt is here," He finally told me as I winked at him, placing five hundred dollars in his pocket.

"Thanks for being the best." I ended before walking through the double doors.

Slamming into a girl.

Her drink spilled on the ground, and without hesitation she fell on her knees to clean it up with a bunch of napkins that she pulled from her pocket.

"Oh my god, I'm so sorry." She apologized.

I also fell on both of my knees, which surprisingly didn't hurt much anymore, "No, I'm sorry. I should've been paying attention to where I was going." I coughed out.

"Let me help you with that." I pulled more napkins from the side table and patted down the floor.

"Thank you." She whispered.

I had looked up, and my eyes had been blessed with a mirage of light brown hair. She looked down and kept on patting the floor, which only accentuated her long eye lashes.

"Wow." I abruptly mumbled as her eyes finally looked up and made contact with mine.

She had beautiful hazel eyes and a striking smile.

She quickly stood up and threw away the used napkins and grabbed the mop on the way back.

"You work here?" I asked as she tilted her head.

"Yes, I'm new." She answered rather with a short tone.

I held out my hand, "My name is Liam." I introduced myself as her smile widened.

"I figured," She mopped the floor, "You're friends with Chris." She continued.

I scratched the back of my head as she laughed, "Don't worry I'm not a stalker, he mentioned that you would be coming for Finn."

She looked over at the booth with Finn sitting all by himself with a juice box.

"So, you're the guy that Finn won't stop talking about." She placed the mop back down; her eyes scanned my body like an x-ray.

"Sadly." I awkwardly laughed as he shook her head.

"Don't worry, I've heard nothing but great things." She led me over to the booth. Before I sat down, Finn pleasantly hugged me before he went back to sit on his side.

"Well hopefully, you'll hear better things about me through dinner, Saturday night?" I asked in a courteous manner.

I couldn't help but notice her cheeks turn a hue of red.

She walked away laughing.

I turned my head over to Finn who looked about over my attempts of flirting with the new hire.

"So, you've met Sabrina." He sighed.

"Sabrina's her name?" I smiled, interested in the next words that were about to leave Finn's mouth.

"You can't play with her Will; I actually like her." He said with a sad grimace as I threw him a skyward of disbelief.

"What makes you think I'll just be playing with her." I folded my arms as he raised a single eyebrow.

"I've changed!" I tossed my arms.

"What about Margo?" He interrogated me as I huffed.

"What about her?" I scowled as he took a sip of his juice.

"Your first love, the girl you've been trying to win back for months?" He informed, "Does that help ring a bell?"

I couldn't give a look at Finn other than the look of disturbance, at how much he just violated me.

"Margo and I are just friends, barely even. She told me to get over her and that's what I'm doing. It's nothing to get back at her, it's not to make me feel better" I explained.

"This is me, asking a girl out because I think she's pretty and I want to get to know her more. I can't keep dwelling on the past when I know things have changed."

"I've changed." I sighed, "And so has Margo."

Finn didn't give up his skeptical look.

"We aren't the same people who fell in love during summer. She's getting married, which is the ultimate reminder of her being unavailable." I continued to convince him as his eyes started to squint.

"So, you're moving on?" He challenged.

Through the several weeks I've spent with Margo, I've realized the many ways she had power towards me. When in reality she shouldn't, she wasn't my girlfriend. Therefore... she had no business caring about me, more than just as my trainer.

But even that was about to end, I noticed that the more I pulled back from her, the more she started acting like my love interest again.

Which was something we were trying to avoid, she was getting close to me again and it was not my problem anymore.

I had to move on, and if I had to be a tad cold towards Margo to do that, I would.

"Yeah, consider Margo wiped from my heart." I pressed as Finn nodded.

"I got it!" I screamed as Margo and Ronni looked at me with happiness.

"Way to go Liam, I always knew you were going to be a quick recovery." Ronni encouraged me as I smiled from ear to ear.

"It's still a bit weak but once I get the hang of being on the ice again, I'm sure I'll be good as new." I explained as Margo walked over to me.

"Liam be grateful that your recovery was fast, you can't wish for too much. Don't rush your knee, but you are right, it will feel better on the ice in a few more practices or sessions." She muttered.

"I think since your knee got injured on the ice, it feels different than stable ground." She remarked as I took a seat.

Ronni's phone began to ring, "Margo, way to go. You can write up his evaluation and can you close up for me when you guys are done." She asked while walking through the door.

"Congratulations on your recovery Liam, and Margo I enjoyed having you as a PT, if you want to continue volunteering you should contact Coach Livingston."

Margo nodded before Ronni closed the door.

The whole time Margo and I's relationship hadn't changed. I wasn't quite sure how to explain it. We weren't having sex, we weren't fighting, I refused to flirt, and I just stayed quiet unless it was a question about my knee.

Don't get me wrong, I still cared about her, but I had made sure she knew there was now a fine line with us. I had promised myself that I would no longer dedicate my life to just trying to get her back.

She's engaged. That's the bottom line. Unavailable.

"I know you're excited, Charming but trust me, you still have to be a bit careful." She reassured me once more before I started to take my skates off.

I shook off Margo's touch as I sauntered over to put my sweatshirt on. I noticed two cups of coffee on the table, I looked back at Margo who made her way back towards me.

"I got you a vanilla latte to start the day. I know you like it." She smiled at me.

One thing about Margo that I've struggled to overcome was how hard it was to not remember me being in love with her.

"I've decided to cut out caffeine from my diet, since I've been cutting, I wanted to cut out a lot of things to help with my recovery." I added as she looked embarrassed.

"Oh okay." She muttered.

I heard multiple voices from outside, "Great, your fan club is outside." She fiddled with her bracelet as I couldn't help but grin.

"Are you jealous?" I smirked towards Margo who rolled her eyes.

"Of what?" She laughed, "All the girls that throw themselves at you?"

"Precisely." I searched Margo's eyes.

I walked towards her, "You have nothing to be jealous of, Raine. You've pretty much given my heart a run for its money."

"I'm not jealous." Margo walked up to me; a question was waiting to be answered.

"That brings up a question I've been meaning to ask, though..." She lowered her tone as I tilted my head.

"Have you been going on dates?" She slurred as she fixed her sleeves, "Or like been... uhm... hanging out with other girls?"

I couldn't help but smile at her jealousy, it felt great to be wanted by Margo once more. It had been a long time for her to show an ounce of hatred towards the girls that fawned over me.

"Careful Raine, you're looking like you miss me just a little bit." I whisper as her eyes widened.

"Nonsense, I'm with Ben and I'm very much happy." She glowered while she walked away from me.

One thing I admired about Margo is that she stood her ground, but it was rare for her not to falter around me.

"How's the sex?" I mused as her face dropped from my question.

"I don't believe that's any of your business." She blurted with irritation.

I took a good look at Margo, and noticed she looked way more tensed up than all the other times that I would rile her up.

"He doesn't satisfy you the way you want to be satisfied." I grinned at her as she faced away from me, her face turned red.

"Ben satisfies me just *fine*." Margo publicized.

I didn't believe her one bit.

"Maybe you should practice that line in front of the mirror, so that you would believe it first." I looked at anywhere else but her, "You know... before you try convincing me."

"You're infuriating." She expressed as I bent down so I could meet her gaze.

"I thought that was the reason you liked me." I joked with her.

"Exactly Liam, I *liked* you. As in past tense, it was a mistake." She voiced.

I also understood that Margo was trying to break my heart throughout this process as well. She would mention Ben any time she got, just to shoot me where it hurt.

She would repeatedly go on and on about how much she regretted giving me a chance over the summer and how we were never meant to be more than what we were.

We should've just kept it as benefits. Margo was the best sex I've ever received in my life. And not to toot my own horn but I think that I'm the only man that's ever made her orgasm that many times in one round.

Which I know she still reminisces about.

But what I really didn't understand was why she was still sticking around. If she was so happy with Ben, why did she frequently avoid her house.

She says they have a blast when they're around each other yet I know, no one's ever made her laugh more than I could.

It was like she had something to prove to me. I had no idea whether she actually wanted to intentionally hurt me.

"So, you are over me." I wondered as she took a second to respond.

"Absolutely."

I went back up to my own original height, yawning, "Then yeah I've been seeing a girl."

I hadn't been with another woman since I've been with Margo, my first date with Sabrina was tomorrow night, so technically it wasn't a lie.

"Then why haven't I met her yet?" She looked at me with a face full of doubt.

"Well, why would you need to meet her?" I drawled out.

Margo's mouth opened to say something, but nothing came

out. It was like she thought she had a good response but went back on it.

She had no right to tell me who I could or couldn't date. That's where I think she pondered on because for a moment in time, she did have a right to know.

"I don't need to meet her. I just would imagine if she was important enough, you would've invited her to hang out with the whole group." Margo trailed off while picking up the other coffee cup.

"She's met Chris." I notified, "That's all I really care about her meeting for now." I continued as Margo stared at me with a straight face.

"Oh." She mumbled.

There was a pause, like Margo had gotten a new perspective on things. She looked like I had just set fire on her favorite pair of Christian Louboutin.

As much as I would've liked to kiss her. I had to remember that I had come a long way, and getting one taste of Margo would set me all the way back to summer.

I couldn't afford to have the same feelings I had for her again. Maybe I was in denial, because I knew from the bottom of my heart, Margo would always be it for me.

But of course, I knew I was wrong.

I could live with lying to myself for years if it meant that Margo was happy.

She couldn't be happy with me, and I had to accept it.

Margo opened the door as a swarm of girls ran in. One in particular came up to me with a donut and a cup of coffee.

"Hey Liam, I got you a donut and a coffee." The random girl choked on her own words as I smiled back.

"Thanks sweetheart, I appreciate it." I took the coffee and looked back at Margo who gave me the deadliest death stare.

As the girl left, Margo shouldered me.

"Cutting caffeine from your diet, huh?" She sneered before dropping the vanilla latte that she got me into the trash can.

"You want me to say no to her?" I asked as Margo rolled her eyes.

"Do whatever you want Liam. I don't care anymore." Margo walked out of the door, not caring if I was following her.

It was for the best that she ended our relationship like this. Just two people who happen to know each other from mutual friends.

CHAPTER 36

MARGO

There is actually no way that Liam was seeing someone else, was there?

I mean I did tell him to, but was there an actual possibility that he was.

"Has he mentioned anything to any of you?" I grumbled as the girls, and I walked around Fifth Avenue.

We had one mission, and it was looking for dresses to wear to the ball, Verina had already purchased one from Paris which was getting shipped soon.

Technically it was just me and Juliette on the hunt. We dragged Adrianna to come along even though she despised the idea of going.

She had barely talked at all the whole time; I knew her and Grayson were hitting a rough patch.

"Why does it matter, I thought you two were just friends." Juliette yawned.

That's what I thought myself, except I couldn't stop thinking about Liam being with another girl.

"We are *just* friends." I defended as Adrianna and Verina rolled their eyes.

Juliette pulled my arm and sat me down at a random café seat. I was sitting in front of all three of them.

"You need to knock it off Margo." Adrianna announced which took me back for a moment.

They were about to lead me through an intervention. I knew this look all too well. I was acting crazy, and they were about to tell me, straight to my face that I was mental.

"We don't care whether you want to believe it or not, Liam is over you." Juliette added on.

Well, those words stabbed me in the heart. I was hoping they were going to be a bit nicer to me.

"You are getting married for God's sake!" Verina proclaimed. She picked up my left hand and pointed at the ring that adorned my finger.

"You are wearing an engagement ring. You gave up Liam the moment you said yes to Ben. And Ben has been nothing but nice to you. He doesn't deserve you, still giving your attention to another man. Especially William Brookshire." She said with a hoarse sigh.

I tend to forget that I never mentioned all the things that Ben has done to me. I would never tell anyone that he hurt me in many ways not just physically, but I'm pretty sure he destroyed my emotional spirit as well.

He would slap me if I said the wrong thing. He would shove me when he didn't agree with my comment.

There were countless times I had fallen down the stairs and sometimes I like to convince myself that it was my fault. In reality, I knew he's pushed me.

He chokes me when he doesn't want to hear me say anything. There are a kaleidoscope of patterned bruises everywhere on my body that I have to hide with an enormous amount of concealer and foundation.

He's gotten inventive the past few weeks with using objects to knock me out before we went to bed together, the next day he would present me with a new gift to shut me up.

I was in pain almost every day of my life and I had to stay silent for my father's sake.

It angers me when my friends brought him up like he was everything glorious in the world, that he was perfect. Though, I could never be angry with them because I had been keeping the secret.

"I can't help it." I sighed.

They all pouted, "We know you love Liam. We see the way you two look at each other, but Margo... you treating him like he's your boyfriend when, there really is no hope for you guys is cruel." Adrianna whispered as I nodded.

"I'm trying so hard not to be selfish with him." I lowered my gaze to the ground, "But it's like someone is ripping out my heart piece by piece, every time I look at him and the look, he gives me looks nothing like how he looked at me in the summer."

Adrianna exhaled heavily, "If you love him, you let him give his love to someone else, even if it hurts."

I knew at this point, Adrianna wasn't talking about me, she was talking about herself.

She hadn't talked to Grayson in a long time, he had completely ghosted her. It was way out of the ordinary, everyone knew that Grayson wouldn't want to live in an earth without her.

At least that's what we did think, he hadn't called, texted, or talked to her in days. He has completely avoided eye contact with her in campus, hadn't attended any of the movie nights.

Adrianna had held out hope but as the days went on, the look of love in her eyes started turning into heartbreak.

I understood why love would fail for me and Liam. I really did, there were many things that fought the idea of us ever being together.

But when it came to people like Adrianna who deserved nothing but love. I really resented God for causing my best friend pain.

"Don't you want to give Grayson a piece of your mind, Anna?" Verina asked as Adrianna shook her head.

"If he wants to talk to me about it then, he will. I will not seek him out first." She replied.

Adrianna checked the time, "I have to get back to my house, it's getting late."

We all stood up to send our goodbyes to her, as her driver picked her up from the curb. Juliette checked her phone with a slight look of disappointment.

"I have practice too, so I'll catch up with you guys later." She said in a hurry before running off.

I looked at Verina who laughed, "Okay well, we haven't hung out just the two of us in a long time."

It was true, I haven't hung out with Verina in a while.

"Well, you're always off with Florence and you never have time for me." I shot back as she rolled her eyes.

"You spend all your time cooped up in that trainer room all the time with Liam no wonder your back to falling for him." She gave a weary sigh.

Verina was the only one who understood me at this very moment, her and Chris were only friends because he wasn't capable of anything more. Obviously, that didn't stop her feelings from blossoming.

"I need you to do me a favor." Verina's mouth quirked up in a smirk as my eyebrow rose.

These were never good.

"––Hear me out first!" She placed her hands up in the air as I sighed dramatically.

"Fine."

"Every Wednesday and Friday, Chris disappears out of thin air, like I have no idea where he goes. He claims he picks up checks from his mother to help with Finn, but I hired people to look into it for me. He hasn't received help from his mother for years." She whispered.

Verina sighed heavily, "I think he might be up to something no good. I'm worried for him."

I listened intently to Verina who looked like she was about to be sick out of her mind.

"What do you want me to do?" I asked as she smiled.

Verina's two bodyguards held on to two different duffle bags in silence, my eyes registered over to Verina's.

"Oh, please don't tell me those are dead bodies." I whispered in a panicked tone.

"No!" She slapped me.

"It's worst."

CHAPTER 37

MARGO

"This is absolutely insane!" I yelled as Verina as she put her pointer finger in front of her lips to quiet me down.

Verina had dragged me all the way back to campus, in a storage closet, nevertheless. The two duffle bags that the two guards were carrying were two hockey uniforms that two members of the team owned.

Cole Smith and Toni Santiago.

Verina's brilliant plan was to put on the hockey uniform and disguise ourselves as players so we could eavesdrop on the guys in the locker room.

While I admired Verina's dedication to the role, I was seriously rethinking it due to the fact that the uniform and the locker room smelled absolutely rancid.

"You're the goalie." She threw me a bigger stick, "I'll be right defense." She smiled as the helmet shield fell in front of her face.

"Make sure that your helmet is on at all times." She instructed as I could hardly move in the uniform.

"Why don't you just ask Chris?" I looked at her as she gave me a dramatic look.

"You really think he's going to tell me? And besides don't you want to hear what Liam and these boys talk about?" She probed, whilst walking towards me.

It would be intriguing to hear what the others would talk about. Technically, I was doing it for Verina, it had nothing to do with me.

"If Adrianna and Juliette find out we did this, we will not hear the end of it." I expressed as she pulled my helmet down, which covered my face even more.

"Which is why they won't find out." Verina shrugged before she opened the door.

Verina shoved me out of the closet, my eyes easily grazed by a handful of chiseled men. She walked out behind me, with a grin on her face.

All the guys barely paid attention to us as the room was filled with conversations about many different topics.

Two of Verina's bodyguards had taken Cole Smith and Toni Santiago in a vehicle so we wouldn't run into them.

Verina spotted Chris and the rest of the group, by their lockers quickly, she pulled me over like her life depended on it.

Liam had his whole uniform on, except this shirt. All the guys had everything on except their helmets. They sure did look larger in person.

Verina paused the moment Chris pulled off his practice jersey and his shoulder pads, his abdomen was adorned with bruises.

For a person that worked in a bar, mall and did hockey he was surely beat up. I knew those bruises all too well, they were from inflicted pain, they were meant by the person that caused them.

"Where the hell, did he get those bruises?" Verina asked me, concern filled her eyes.

"You sure you're still good to fight tonight?" Liam asked Chris as he didn't even answer.

"The question is, are *you* good to fight tonight, you just got healed. I wouldn't want to set back your progress." Chris asked with a sense of guilt.

"I'm fine, besides I think I'll win tonight." He said with excitement.

"Why are you in such a happy mood?" Grayson laughed while he put his helmet on.

"He has a hot date tomorrow with Sabrina." Neil patted Liam on the back.

I felt like I slightly lost my balance, Verina's eyes sought mine, filled with comfort.

"Are you sure you didn't double check with Margo to see if your new girlfriend is good enough?" Chris asked as Liam rolled his eyes.

"Margo has nothing to do with my love life from now on. I'm pressing the off button on that light. I'm moved on, and if she isn't moved on by now then that's not my fault." She trailed off as he pulled a jersey on his body.

"That sounds a bit harsh." Grayson said.

"She's engaged for God's sake. You guys tend to forget that. Fuck, I think she tends to forget it, I can't do anything about it now." Liam looked impatient as Chris's lips thinned.

"I'm looking at my future and she's not a part of it. I'm putting all my eggs in Sabrina's basket. I can't be bothered with Margo anymore." He glanced up at his friends who stayed quiet.

"Aye aye, Brookshire." Neil saluted, followed with a laugh.

"Don't get me wrong," Liam breathed out, "I still care about her, but I don't love her anymore."

I'm quite sure I hadn't breathed out since Liam began to speak. My heart ached more than ever; my body physically hurt more than any type of pain that Ben would inflict on me.

"I'm sorry babe." Verina whispered as I smiled through a tear that fell from my face.

"It's fine. That's not the reason we're here anyways." I pulled away from Verina's warm embrace.

I brushed off the words that Liam said from my mind. Because in reality, he was right. I wasn't a part of his love life anymore. I shouldn't be upset, I shouldn't be mad, or sad for that matter.

This was the end of Liam and I's chapter and that was okay.

I snapped out of it, my eyes moved away from Liam and back to Verina's. Her eyes have not left Chris's body, the moment we stepped foot out of the storage closet.

Chris had mentioned something about a fight, no one dropped the location, yet which was a tad bit annoying.

"Chris why don't you invite Verina?" Neil asked.

Verina looked eager for his answer.

"Why would, I?" He shrugged.

"Well, you guys have been spending a whole lot of time together, call me crazy but maybe she can be a lucky charm during your fight, kind of like how Adrianna was Grayson's lucky charm." Liam teased Grayson by shoving him over.

"Yeah. Now he plays like shit, because they're broken up." Neil laughed as Grayson threw his water bottle at his friend.

"Verina is nothing more to me than just a friend. You know I don't have time for a relationship, there's no way I could balance it with Finn and work." Chris muttered.

Verina swallowed a lump in her throat.

"Besides, I wouldn't date a girl like Verina anyways. I need someone with dreams, passion. She doesn't really care for much other than herself and the clothes she wears." Chris lamely mentions.

"We haven't been hanging around. She's been following me around, I know she has a crush okay, I can't just tell her to fuck off." He finished.

"Why not? You've told other girls to fuck off before." Grayson asked.

"Well as much as I don't see Verina as a girl I would romantically be interested in, I would consider her a close friend." He answered.

Verina looked at him no longer with awe in her eyes but betrayal and disappointment.

"Why does this fight have to be in the middle of a shady place in Brooklyn?" Grayson asked while he picked up his stick.

"Brownsville isn't that bad." Liam muttered.

"It's literally known for its high murder rate. It has a high risk for violence and gang activity. Thus, it being called *The Kill Zone*." Neil mentioned as the group quieted down.

They all picked up their hockey sticks and started to walk towards the exit. Grayson rammed into Verina for a second.

"Yo, sorry Cole, I didn't see you there." He laughed, "You kind of look like you got smaller, you need to start bulking more." He finished before he left the locker room.

Verina turned and faced me, "Okay, Brownsville in Brooklyn tonight." She informed as I laughed.

"There's no way we are actually following them there still after what they just said about us right?!" I shook Verina by her shoulders as she breathed out.

"I know what they said was awful, Margo." She paced, "But even if Chris practically friend zoned me, I still care about him whether he accepts it or not, I care if he gets hurt."

"You're going to go after them tonight aren't you." I asked her but it was a rhetorical question.

"You are either coming with me for back up, or I go alone. It's your choice, I'm not forcing you to go with me if you don't want to." Verina smiled at me.

She knew there was absolutely no way I would've let her go by herself. I was only going for her, and not for Liam.

As far as I'm concerned, William Brookshire was just someone I formally knew.

CHAPTER 38

LIAM

I couldn't help but be excited at the fact that my knee was almost fully healed. I was back to playing hockey, I had no heart ache about Margo, and I was hanging out with my best friends.

Chris, Neil, Grayson and I entered through a sketchy tunnel that led to an abandoned warehouse in Brooklyn. There was fire that was lit up and crowds of people that were circled along the cage.

Blood on the floor, people in gurneys. Most people would be scared of places like these, but my friends and I can't help but love the smell or sweat, blood and tears.

On Wednesdays and Fridays Chris would get a call about a fight, he was the best out of all of us and a lot of powerful men would bid money on these series of brawls.

Chris was one of the most paid ones, random men placed hundreds–– maybe even thousands of dollars on the table.

Every week, Chris got to pick either, Grayson, Neil, or me to be on his duo match. We would both have to fight two other men.

Was this dangerous?

Sure.

But all that ran through our heads was that, it helped Chris put food on the table.

It helped Chris pay off his debts, taxes, and it helped him with Finn's chemotherapy costs. We would do nothing but fight until we got that money.

Neil's hangout area had a gym that we would go to, to work out when it came to fights. Chris would help us train after hockey practices if he didn't have work.

I sometimes wondered what type of energy Chris ran on, because it definitely wasn't sleep.

"Okay, it looks way more occupied than the last time we were here." Grayson mentioned in a low monotone.

He looked like complete shit. Ever since Grayson had been shackled by August's pregnancy, he had been nothing but a total jerk to everyone else.

I was surprised he even showed up today when he hadn't left the fucking hockey arena running through drills and laps nonstop.

But at the same time, we never missed a fight with Chris, call it our love language towards him.

"Who are we fighting against?" I asked as Chris nodded over to the two men who looked like they had just crawled out of jail.

"Don West and Makati Sibonakaliso." He attempted to pronounce as I raised an eyebrow.

The boys and I settled on one corner of the cage opening before one of the announcers walked over with a big wad of cash.

"Hey Angelo," Chris greeted as he shook Angelo's hand.

"Hey Florence, so listen we got a rare bid tonight from a man named Kai Romano. He's bidding at least fifty thousand on tonight's fight if you win." The announcer whispered as Chris's mouth dropped.

"That's like six months of Finn's chemo treatment paid off." I beamed as Chris grew skeptical.

"What does this guy do to be spending that much money on an underground cage fight?" Chris inquired.

Angelo shrugged his shoulders, "I heard he owns a shit ton of buildings and companies all over the world. But who cares, if you win tonight, it's a big reward." Angelo smiled.

Chris looked at our two opponents once more, before looking back at Angelo, "How much is tonight's payout?" He asked.

"Five hundred." Angelo muttered.

Chris handed over a stack of cash over to Angelo.

Angelo patted Chris and I's shoulders, "You guys got this, the two guys are ex-convicts trying to get some cash to start up their lives again." He informed.

"What were they in jail for?" Grayson asked as Angelo shrugged.

"All I know is that they might play dirty, so be careful out there, try not to bleed on the cage I just cleaned it up." He finished of his sentence with a skip and a jump over to his announcer box.

"Well, what's the plan?" We looked at Neil as he examined the two opponents we were about to face.

Neil grins, "The one with the bald head, I've been watching him practice his jabs. There happens to be a very miniscule hesitation on his right foot every time he steps forward, I believe he had an unfortunate childhood injury that weakened him."

Chris turned to look at the one with the bald head, "Okay, his right foot. I got it."

"How about the other one?" I asked as Neil tilted his head to watch the other opponent.

"The other one was sparring with another person while you were talking to Angelo. He's slow with his hits, even slower when he's on defense. Make sure to keep attacking him, he wouldn't be able to keep up with the blocks." Neil finished off as I smirked.

"See this is why you are a part of our group." I shouldered Neil as he gave a withered look.

"Don't forget, they're ex-convicts. Not ballerinas." Grayson muttered, "Keep an eye out for something they might pull out of their sleeve or waistband." He added.

"You think he might pull out a shiv or something?" I stuttered as Grayson nodded.

"We can only be cautious." He admitted as I turned around, Chris's body had already been in the cage, waiting for the whistle to blow.

MARGO

Verina and I stood outside an old warehouse that made our skin crawl. We heard small noises from things that could only come out during the dark.

Street signs glistened faintly, as two figures moved throughout the alleyway.

"This should be it," She carefully whispered, "The entrance should be through there."

She pointed ahead of us, which led to nothing but the dark.

"Are you sure, there looks like there's nothing over there." I slightly adjusted my jacket, "I mean this just looks like it's just, an abandoned warehouse."

"I think that's the point" She said, with a dismissive gesture. "I don't think they would advertise a big illegal fight club with a big sign in the front of the building."

I rolled my eyes at her as she started to creep along the perimeter of the warehouse, she avoided the main doors with the big bouncers that looked about the sizes of two semi-trucks that leaned against the walls.

"Careful with that pothole." She warned me as I sighed in annoyance.

Verina navigated her way through a side alley, which was dimly lit by a flickering streetlight. I continued to follow her through a rusted metal door, she tapped it twice and then paused.

She knocked another time.

"I don't think it's going to open for us." I calmly suggested as she looked at me.

"Well, what's your plan?" She queried as I looked around, I spotted a small metal trash can and picked it up.

I held my breath from the disgusting smell before I threw the trashcan toward the doorknob with so much force that, the knob broke off.

The door creaked opened.

I looked at Verina who looked stunned that my idea had worked. To be quite honest, I was shocked as well.

The hallway that we entered was narrow, the air was thick with the smell of sweat and something metallic. There were faint cheers from afar as the rhythmic thud of fist on flesh grew louder as we walked closer.

"Okay this definitely has to be it." Verina assured herself.

My jaw tightened, "Let's go."

The hallway ended in a large dimly lit space. There was a room where the crowd was alive with movement, and full of noise. We spotted a makeshift cage made out of metallic railings and thick ropes that stood in the center.

It had been surrounded by a roaring crowd. Our eyes centered on Neil, Grayson, and Liam who stood next to the cage.

"Where's Chris?" She asked me as our bodies froze.

"You're not going to like the answer." I muttered as I pointed over to Chris who was in the cage. He was bare-knuckled and bloodied. They traded punches and jabs under harsh yellow lighting.

Everyone in the room seemed to live for the fight. The crowd's energy was electric, and a mix of exhilaration and danger was in the air as we watched Chris knock his opponent out.

A whistle was blown as Chris hopped out of the cage with a smile on his face and tiny splatters of blood on his bandaged knuckles.

"Florence won against West." An announcer yelled as the crowd cheered louder.

"Up next, Brookshire versus Sibonakaliso!" He alarmed everyone as people started to walk over to his desk with an enormous amount of cash.

"Bets on Brookshire on the left! Sibonakaliso on the right!" He screamed louder as I jumped backwards.

I felt overstimulated and anxious. At least Verina knew Chris won already, safe and sound. I still had to wait and watch Liam fight a man that looked like John Cena.

A whistle blew, we move deeper into the crowd, we weaved between spectators clutching their cash and drinks. My heart raced as I watched Liam in the cage with his opponent.

Of course, I had seen him throw a punch or two, but I had never seen him like this. I was worried about his knee.

"Stay close," Verina murmured.

We edged closer to the cage; we tried to be careful not to draw attention to ourselves. The crowd's cheers surged as Liam delivered an upper cut and for a moment everyone's focus was on the fight.

I glanced back up at Liam's opponent who was about to pull out an object from his waistband to help gain an advantage in the fight.

"A knife!" I yelled in a warning tone to Liam who looked around in search of my voice.

His opponent swung at him with the sharp object, Liam quickly punched the sharp object out of his left hand and threw it away from anyone's reach.

He then punched the other man so hard that the man's tooth came flying out. The man landed on the floor, unable to get up as the crowd screamed louder than ever.

Liam just knocked someone out. The whistle blew, the announcer began to yell, "Brookshire won against Sibonakaliso!"

I smiled.

"Who are you two?" A tall and lean man with a tattoo of a blue snake coiled around his left arm grabbed the both of us.

"Let go of us, we are here with our friends!" Verina kicked the man.

The man turned back slowly; his sharp eyes narrowed as he sized her up. "I don't know you," He said flatly.

"And I don't really care what you have to say. All I know is that you're going to be a big reward, when I turn you into the boss myself." His expression flickered.

I looked around and noticed that Verina wasn't in my line of sight.

Panic began to rise inside me as he placed added pressure to my wrist which was already bruised up from Ben.

He began to pull me away from the cage, he led me through another set of doors and into a quieter corridor. My heart pounded, half from fear and half from hope.

I had tried to punch him but none of my efforts moved him at all.

The door clicked shut behind us, the man turned, his expression grim. "No one can hear you, shut up." He voiced.

CHAPTER 39

LIAM

"Liam! Liam!" I heard a faint voice from a far.

As my opponent crashed on the ground as my eyes found Verina screaming from the crowded room.

This wasn't a place that she should be at. I hopped out of the cage, my body rammed through everyone just to get to Verina and the guys behind me followed.

Chris got to her first, for him to supposedly not like her, her body was easily cradled in his arms.

Tears streamed down her face as she had a wave of panic.

"Some tall guy took Margo." She cried.

Suddenly my eyes went into a blurred rage. My body heaved like an angry animal. My fists bawled up, and I couldn't hide the worry on my face.

"What." I said, not meant for it to sound like a question.

"He was tall, he had a tattoo with a snake–– that's all I can remember." She said with a hurried tone.

Verina gripped on to Chris's body like he was her lifeline. One look at Grayson and Neil, they already started searching for her, I didn't have to say anything.

What on earth was going through her right mind to be in one

of New York's most dangerous towns. I shook my head in annoyance and distraught.

I turned my head and took off, I only knew of one man that Verina described, he only came here for one purpose, and it was to gather girls and trade them off for brothels.

I ran through the swarmed crowds, my legs had led me to a dimmed room, so much rage still filled me that I just kicked the door once, it broke.

There she was. The man had his hand wrapped around Margo's wrist. She looked so fragile next to him, like a porcelain doll next to Godzilla.

Margo hadn't registered my presence yet as she screamed, yanking her hand away from him.

My heart pounded in my chest; without a second thought I lunged at the man. My fists flew at his figure. He quickly threw Margo to the side; she was caught by Neil and Grayson who followed me, apparently.

My adrenaline surged through me as I threw a punch at the man's nose, then threw another punch at the side of his face. He had managed to land a few blows of his own towards me.

I looked back at Margo's terrified face. My rage intensified as I looked at her bruised wrist. I tackled the man to the ground and pinned him down.

"You stay the fuck away from her." I shouted with fury. The man underneath me struggled, but my determination had not disappeared yet.

I squeezed my fist tighter and pounded his face with my knuckles. I landed multiple hits as he groaned in pain, his blood had splattered all over my face, the floor and down to his chest.

"Liam, stop you'll kill him in two more hits." Neil informed me as I raised my right fist next to my face.

I threw one final, powerful punch.

I got up and stumbled next to Margo who held my body close, I could feel her shaking.

"Are you okay?" I asked.

She nodded.

The man laid there; his body twitched a few times before he coughed up more blood.

"Leave." I demanded as he weakly stood up and ran away stumbling.

He left through the back door, I turned towards Grayson, Neil, Chris, Verina and Margo.

"We need to call the police." Margo freaked out as she pulled out her phone.

I pulled her phone away, "No, this whole fight is illegal. We can't call the cops."

"Well, we can't just let him get away!" She screamed at me as I sighed.

"We just did." I said plainly.

Margo went from looking worried and scared shitless to a hue of red, plastered all over her face.

"You guys shouldn't be here." I put my hands on her shoulders as she shook her head.

"*YOU* shouldn't be here!" She said with mock astonishment, "Do you understand how dangerous you fighting in that cage is! Let alone you just got your knee healed up!"

I felt my jaw tighten as Margo continued to yell at me.

"What I do now is none of your business." I hissed as her body pulled back from me.

It looked like she just heard a sentence that she never thought would leave my mouth.

"You've made that really clear." She plainly muttered.

I couldn't help but explode, my heart was ready to jump out at her and yell.

"Did I tell you to come to this fight?!" I asked.

"No."

"You aren't my girlfriend anymore Margo!" I exclaimed as her mouth quivered.

"This feels like a back and forth with you." I laughed.

"You gave away the rights to care about me this much, the

moment you said yes to Ben's proposal. But you can't help but be selfish. I don't want to be your toy that you play with when you feel alone Margo." I licked my lips and threw my hands up.

A brief silence passed as she looked at me with pure heart break in her eyes, I knew the look all too well. I gave her the same one before.

"It's just not my job anymore." I said with simple directness.

"Okay." She choked out.

"What are you doing here looking for me, when you should be with the man you're going to marry." I finished as she closed her eyes.

She moved her gaze, away from me to the ground.

"You're right. I don't know why I thought it was okay to come." She said in a voice, soft with affection. "So maybe I should just go."

Margo walked out of the back door, seconds later Verina followed her out.

I took a breath.

"That was a bit--" Neil opened his mouth.

"--I know." I sighed.

"You nearly killed a guy." Grayson mentioned as I looked at him with a withering expression.

"That makes the both of us." I muttered.

CHAPTER 40

MARGO

I pulled my jacket tighter around me as I turned the corner and walked away from the warehouse. The street lights did not look like they were getting brighter. It was late, and I knew that I shouldn't have left the rest of the guys.

I fumbled my phone for a second before I tried to open my speed dial to call a driver to come pick me up. But I paused forgetting the fact that Ben couldn't find out that I snuck out of the house this late.

The streetlights flickered, the ground casted shadows. The cracks on the pavement grew larger. I quickened my pace, no longer had the view of the warehouse.

My footsteps echoed through the streets. I turned another corner; chills ran down my spine. The hairs on the back of my neck stood up. I felt someone watching my every move. I turned my head and glanced over my shoulder but saw nothing but a flickering streetlamp.

My body shook, still feeling unease. My pace started to grow faster. My eyes scanned the surroundings once more.

Suddenly I saw a glimpse of a man with a black hoodie, my feeling of being followed had grew stronger.

My heart started to race, his footsteps behind me, matching

my pace. I pulled out my phone, the second on speed dial had been Liam.

I clicked his name, with in one second, he answered.

"I know you're mad at me but Liam, someone's following me. I don't know where I am." My voice shook as I spoke.

I could hear Liam gather all the boys and yelled at them to get on their motorcycles.

"Raine, share your location with me again." He asked.

I clicked on the location icon; panic began to set in for me. I considered running but I knew it would've drew more attention to me.

"Okay, I shared it." I whispered.

I felt Liam's worry over the speaker, "Take a deep breath, try and stay calm. I'm getting you." He assured me.

I spotted a small gas station up ahead. It was maybe a block far, and I decided to wait for Liam there. I was slightly hoping that there would be people inside. I walked faster, the footsteps behind me quickened as well.

I felt my pulse pounding in my ears, and the fear tightening in my chest the longer it took for Liam to get me.

As soon as I reached the store I glanced back and caught another glimpse of a shadowy figure ducking into an alley. I quickly rushed, the bell above the door rattling loudly.

I tried to steady my breathing as I approached the counter.

"Can I help you?" The cashier asked, eyeing me with concern.

"I think someone is following me," I whispered, my voice trembled.

The cashier's expression didn't change, "It happens all the time in Brownsville, I have no idea why you are walking alone in the streets, let alone at night."

I miss Hawthorne.

I pulled my phone with shaky hands. But even before I could turn it on, the door slammed open, Liam's face gave me comfort. He rushed over to me, and I couldn't help but wrap my arms around him.

Liam was hesitant to embrace my hug, I opened my eyes to see Verina and Chris behind him. Liam finally gave in and let me melt into his embrace. His hand had crept to cradle the back of my head.

"Don't leave me, please." I trembled.

Liam didn't say a word, he only sighed.

Liam led me out of the gas station, and revealed a tinted car, "I thought you guys came here on your motorcycles."

"Yeah, we did but I don't trust that something will happen to you while we are on an exposed vehicle." He glowered.

The car ride back to his house was silent, the tension thick in the air. I couldn't bring myself to say anything, my mind racing with the events of the night.

Liam's presence was the only thing keeping me grounded. His eyes, focused on the road, occasionally glanced at me, concern etched on his face.

"It's cold." I muttered, hoping that it would start up a conversation.

Liam sighed and took my hand and placed it on the steering wheel, "Drive for me." He asked as my eyes widened.

Liam let go of the wheel as I continued to steer for him, with my left hand. I watched the road ahead as he pulled his sweatshirt off of himself.

He finally took a hold of the steering wheel again, before handing me his sweatshirt.

I sighed in relief as I put his sweatshirt on, smelling his cologne and the warmth of his hoodie.

We pulled into his driveway, the house looming in the darkness. Liam got out first and opened my door, offering a hand to help me out. I took it, grateful for the small comfort. We walked up to the door, the silence between us almost unbearable.

Liam paused before opening the door, turning to look at me. "You're safe here," He said softly, his voice was a soothing balm to my frazzled nerves. I nodded, unable to find the words to express my gratitude.

Inside, the house was dimly lit, the shadows casting eerie patterns on the walls. Liam led me to his room, the familiarity of the space providing a strange sense of comfort.

LIAM

Margo and I had arrived at my room. She looked horrified and tired all together. I couldn't blame her. We haven't talked the whole ride to my house.

"Why did you agree to take me to your house?" She asked me plainly as I avoided eye contact.

"You asked me not to leave you." I muttered.

Margo walked into my room, her eyes scanned around and spotted a bouquet of flowers on my desktop.

"You're still going on your date?" She asked as I didn't answer.

Margo walked closer to me, my skin felt her presence get closer and closer. She turned me around, her eyes softened.

Her expression was a mix of longing and regret, she took a deep breath and turned my face so that I could make direct eye contact. She took a deep breath; her voice was barely a whisper.

"Thank you for... saving me. I know you don't have a reason to anymore. You shouldn't be saving me anymore but, it's a force of habit." She shook.

I swallowed as she kept her eyes on me, "What is it, Margo?" I asked her as a tear fell from her eyes.

"I was so scared Liam," She buried her face into my chest, "I know you're staying away from me because of my engagement, and I should be staying away from you but despite everything––." She sobbed.

"––I miss you. I miss us." She cried as I cradled the back of her head with my large hand.

I was taken aback by her confession, my heart pounded in my chest, which I'm sure she could hear loud and clear.

"Margo, you chose to move on. You chose someone else." I mumbled.

She shook her head, a tear slid down her cheek as she looked up at me, "I want you, Liam."

Her words hung in the air, heavy with meaning. I watched the turmoil in her eyes, the same that mirrored my own. I wanted to believe her, to give in to the hope that she gave me.

But she was still engaged, and it was a constant reminder of the walls that we had built between us.

"We're just friends now Margo." My voice shook, I knew I was lying through my teeth.

"Fuck the pact." She said, breathless.

Margo pulled me down, her lips enveloped on top of mine.

She groaned, as I gave into the kiss. Her lips were soft and urgent, tasting of salt from her tears.

This was home.

Margo grabbed on to my jacket, as she pulled me closer, the kiss felt more longing and desperate. It was like a silent plea for the connection that we tried to suppress, that we both ached for.

I felt her heart race, every fiber of my being screamed to pull her closer, to never let her go. The world around us faded, and all that remained was the warmth of her body against mine and the electrifying sensation of our lips moving in perfect harmony.

"Margo, don't." I warned as I pulled away.

She looked at me with hurt filled eyes.

"I've been very good with keeping my hands to myself from you, resisting you in every way. If you kiss me again..." I paused.

"If I kiss you again, then what?" She asked.

"If you kiss me again, I don't want to hear you begging for me to stop." I said plainly as she stood there.

She pulled away for a second before she clutched my jacket back and pulled me in ever deeper into another kiss.

She was making ups for all the lost time, all the desires she's had for me, all the bottled-up emotions.

"I warned you." I groan against her lips as I felt her lips curve.

"I don't care." She said breathlessly.

My hand moved to her waist, drawing her nearer until there was no space left between us. The kiss grew more passionate, more intense, as if it were our only way to express the myriad of emotions that words could never capture.

At that moment, nothing else mattered. Not her engagement, not the pact we had made, not the chaos that had ensued. All that existed was the undeniable connection that neither of us could deny.

Her breath hitched as we finally pulled apart, our foreheads resting against each other. Our eyes locked, and in that shared gaze, I saw the same hope, fear, and love that mirrored my own. For a brief moment, the impossible seemed within reach, and the barriers that had once seemed insurmountable began to crumble.

I threw her on the bed, as she started to back away from me, I pulled her legs towards my face as I got on my knees.

"Be gentle––," She whispered as I laughed cooly.

"Me thinking about how Ben has touched you, is not going to get you a gentle fuck, Raine." I scolded before I slapped her thigh.

I kissed her thigh before I slapped it again, my hand wandered around and felt her panties, soaked.

She shivered around my touch as I looked back up at her ecstasy filled face.

I inserted two fingers in her, as her eyes rolled to the back of her head. I brought my face closer to hers, licking and sucking on her neck as she moaned.

"I miss you so much, Raine. I miss how wet you got for me... your moans." I whispered as she bit her bottom lip.

I felt her constrict; her face contorted to a bit of pain, I paused.

"Why are you so sensitive?" I asked seriously as she opened her eyes and met mine.

"Ben and I have never––" She started, her face turned red.

"You two haven't done anything?" I asked with disbelief as she nodded.

"But that would mean the last time you had done anything with anyone... was with me?" I asked her.

Margo swallowed, then nodded.

That just got me hornier than ever.

"Oh baby... you just earned yourself an even rougher night." I muttered by her ear as she sighed in relief.

I pulled her back into a kiss, my fingers started up again and fingered her slowly. My thumb found her clit, I slowly rubbed until she bucked her hips towards my thumb.

"Good girl, just like that." I whispered as she felt moving her hips.

My other hand didn't waste a second before I ripped her clothes off of her, she fumbled with my zipper, opened buttons and ripping off fabric that was too hard to take off properly.

"Fuck." I growled; my nostrils flared as my eyes took in and drank Margo's naked body.

As I looked at her, all of my progress of trying to get over her had gone back to zero percent.

Margo didn't resist; I pushed her legs further apart. I took it all in, she was beautiful. I licked along her slit which made her pull back. I wanted to taste every inch of her. I wanted to make her come so hard tonight that she'd squirt all over the comforter.

I pulled away for a second, grabbed a towel for my closet and walked back slowly to her frail looking body. She looked horrified, but not because of me but because she was letting her guard down once more.

Margo moaned and tugged at my hair, if only she knew that even if I hadn't been with her like this in months. Every single night I would imagine this in my dreams.

I curled my fingers around her clit. I teased it with my tongue, licked and sucked. I twirled my tongue around her folds, her clit peeked out even more as I played with her.

I looked up at Margo, her eyes were closed, her chest was heaving heavily.

"Raine, keep your eyes on me as my tongue fucks you."

Margo opened her eyes, her face form a hue of red.

I used my pointer and middle finger to separate her folds and blew cold air. Her arousal glistened as she whimpered.

"Liam please..." She begged as I dove back in.

I stroked the tip of my tongue along her lips, I gently parted them and swirled around her clit before I moved back down inside her.

Margo's mouth was open in disbelief, her eyes rolled to the back of her head. She began to close her legs but it only took a small nudge for her to part her legs further, and revealed more of herself.

I bent down further, my tongue dipped inside her. She was so wet that it was the only thing that I could feel on my tongue. I brushed over her tight opening; my tongue had circled along her opening.

Fuck I wished that I was back inside her.

"Please––," She whimpered as her fingered played with her nipples.

It only took one look of Margo doing that, for me to pull her down on my face, burying her pussy into my mouth. I sucked her clit, as she cried out in surprise and full of pleasure.

I ate her out messily, smeared all of her juices all over my cheeks and my chin. She buried herself deeper into the covers as she moaned loudly.

I couldn't decipher anything that she was saying only that she was enjoying herself.

She wasn't just wet, but she was soaked, she coated my whole mouth as I fingered her.

Her thighs tensed up, her pussy clenched and her face had contorted like she was being sent to the heavens.

There was a long groan that escaped her parted lips. I griped her ass, my finger dug in as I pressed her pussy against my mouth.

Margo shuddered, her eyes were rolled, and her nails had scratched my scalp. I groaned and shoved my tongue into her tight opening, I eagerly lapped along her arousal, and I fucked her with my fingers, curled.

"I can't––," She started to pull away as she pulled me up to kiss me.

"Can't what?" I asked as she breathed like there was an elephant on top of her chest.

My chin and my mouth were covered in her lust. She licked her lips; her expression had turned stunned and embarrassed.

"Raine, we should stop." I paused, suddenly remembering that she had a ring on her finger.

"Liam, no." She pulled me closer, "Please I just want you."

"Margo." I looked at her as a tear fell from her eye.

"Please. Forget about the ring," She looked at me before she pulled the ring off and place it on my nightstand.

Margo's hand had fiddled with my waist band, she pushed it down as my dick had sprung up. She tensed as she lined her opening up with my cock.

My head had knocked down to the nape on her neck as I held myself up over her.

Despite how tight Margo was, she was dripping wet, that I slipped in easily. I looked down at my cock as it parted her. She opened her mouth to moan, then bit down to my shoulder.

Which turned me on even more.

"So, fucking tight," I said with a bit of a grin, "Nobody's touched you like this since me." I whispered.

"Nobody ever will." She whispered. Her eyes conveyed happiness. I wasn't really familiar with the look until I noticed it was the same one, I had only given her.

"I love you, Raine." I confessed as she smiled then kissed me.

CHAPTER 41

MARGO

My lips crashed against Liam's. There was nothing but happiness that filled me as he confessed his love.

"And I love you, Charming." A smile tugged my lips.

He dragged me closer, his fingers stroked my back, then up to my neck. His other hand had tangled themselves in my hair.

I moaned into the kiss, desperate for more.

His hands further roamed my body. He tugged at my nipples, I arched into him, my hands mapped out his strong back.

Liam pushed to his feet and ripped his shirt over his head. He grabbed a condom from the drawer in his nightstand, and ripped it open with his teeth.

He put the condom on, but I couldn't help but admire his physique.

I sighed as my eyes scanned and watched his tattoos, I placed my hand delicately on top of the thunder and lightning.

Liam was now on top of me again, he parted my legs wide with his thighs, his dark eyes full of need and want. He kissed me, which eased him.

Liam finally entered me again, my eyes closed.

"Fuck, Raine. I missed you." His lips brushed my ear, his voice was raw.

We connected in such a profound way. The way he looked at me was the way I wanted to be looked at. He held my heart in his hand.

With every thrust, I felt more like we were made to be together. We had our ups and downs, but there isn't even a question that he didn't live in my mind, heart, and my soul.

His voice was in the back of my head, keeping me going through every hit, slap, bruise that was given by Ben.

Liam kissed me like I was his salvation. I started to tremble, my walls tightened around his cock. I saw stars dancing before my eyes.

Liam took a breath, exploding inside of me, our fused lips stayed connected to swallow each of our moans.

We both separated and breathed out in unison.

"We can be friends that kiss." I uttered with a laugh as Liam turned to kiss me.

"Shut up, Raine."

And so, I shut up.

LIAM

Margo and I both lay there, our breaths slowly returning to normal. As the morning light crept through the curtains, it casted a soft glow over the room.

I turned to face her, a sense of hope bloomed in my chest.

She placed her hand on my chest, she twirled her finger around my tattoo, "When did you get these..." She mumbled as I smiled, "When you gave me your list."

She smiled, "But you hate thunderstorms." She whispered, in a way it sounded like she was teasing me.

"I do." I said plainly.

I picked up her hand and guided it through the rain, throughout the tattoo.

"But the rain, makes it bearable." I whispered as her eyes held a sparkle.

"The tattoo is... me?" She sprouted up, "You call me, Raine!" She exclaimed and I laughed.

"I guess you got lucky."

Margo came back down and curled into bed with me again, her heat had calmed me.

"I can't believe it; you're here with me. Just you and I again, together like we are supposed to be." I breathed out as she sighed.

But it wasn't a sigh of relief. It was like there were words that were lodged in the back of her throat.

"Liam," She started, her voice was soft yet firm, "I need to tell you something."

My heart thudded in my chest as I waited for her to continue. Margo sighed deeply; she looked away from me.

I pulled away from her grasps. I could tell this wasn't going to be good.

"I can't leave him, Liam. I can't leave my fiancé."

The words hit me like a punch to the gut, I sat up and stared at her in disbelief. "What? But after everything we've been through, after last night... I thought..."

Margo sat up too, she pulled the sheet around her. "I'm sorry, Liam. I really am, but I can't just walk away from him. This is a lot more than just a marriage to me, this wouldn't be fair to my parents."

A wave of anger surged through me. "Fair? What about what's fair to me? You let me believe we had a chance, that we could finally be together!"

Margo's eyes filled with tears, but she held her ground. "I never meant to hurt you, Liam. But I have to go back to Ben."

I got out of bed, pacing the room. "So that's it? You're just going back to him like nothing happened?"

She stood up, her eyes pleading. "I don't want to lose you, Liam. I want you in my life, even if it's just as friends." She walked towards me, "You even said it last night, we can be friends that kiss."

"THAT WAS A FUCKING JOKE!" I screamed.

I shook my head, unable to look at her. "I can't do that, Raine. I can't just pretend that what we have doesn't mean anything."

She reached out to touch my arm, but I pulled away. "Liam, please..."

I turned to face her, my heart breaking. "No, Raine. You made your choice. You just can't help but keep using me."

"I'm not trying to use you Liam." She whispered in a husky voice.

I couldn't look at her.

My mouth wouldn't open to let words spill out.

But at this point what did I have to lose? I already screamed at her earlier.

"What are we doing?" I finally said as I turned around.

"You tell me." She breathed out, "You tell me that I shouldn't care about you when I know you still care about me."

Margo looked at me with the same glistening blue eyes that I fell in love with. There was hope that was laced in her expression.

"We can just be friends." She muttered as I rolled my eyes.

"Just friends? Who are we kidding Margo, I look at you like you are my whole world, and I know you look at me the same way."

"I can't not have you." Her voice shook, "I need you."

She took a step closer, her breath wavered as she closed the distance between us. "I can't do this, Margo." I said, "You're asking me to have an affair." My voice trembled as the weight of my words knew they were heavy.

"We can't pretend like there isn't anything between us Liam.

You can date as many different girls as you want but you can't replace us."

Her eyes filled with tears, a spark of defiance laid on them, "So this is what that's about." I laughed.

"Margo I'm pretty sure that you didn't fucking care how I felt with our whole, *friends that flirt* ordeal until you found out I was seeing someone new." I accused.

"It's not that." She said.

"You didn't care, until for one second you found out that I might be moving on and, was a little bit less miserable?" I glowered as she took a step back from me.

"Are you calling me selfish?" She criticized.

I shook my head, "Yes. I am."

There was a silence that blew in the room.

"I don't understand why you can't just leave Ben, be with me. Why can't we just be together? Why does it always have to be so complicated?"

"You made it complicated." She whispered.

"What?" I tilted my head.

"YOU LEFT ME IN GREECE, LIAM!" She screamed at me with anger filled pupils.

"You left me all alone! I come back here, and two girls are on you! You act like you didn't know me and I get punished for trying to move on, from the heartbreak that *you* caused me. I was supposed to let it go that quickly?" She seethed.

She laughed like she was fed up.

"You are the selfish one, to think that I would just go back to you so fucking quickly. Things now aren't that simple; we aren't in Greece anymore. You can't lie your way into my heart." She fought back the tears.

She took another step back, "We've both got our own lives, our own responsibilities. I have other people to think of, than just you. I can't throw everything away because of your beck and call."

"We've both made mistakes Margo." I calmly said.

"I know that. You've hurt me, I've hurt you. I just––," Margo walked back closer to me.

She shook her head, frustration etched on to her face, "What about us? What about how we feel? How do we ignore this?"

I took Margo's hands and held them.

I sighed as I ran my thumb across her cheek, "I don't know Raine, maybe... it's for the best that we don't see each other anymore. If this is how we are acting when we are together, we *can't* just be friends."

"Liam, I'm asking you please don't do this." A tear fell down her eyes.

"I'm exhausted, Margo. You hurt me over and over again and I'm just supposed to take it. You have so much control over me that I answer at your beck and call." I confessed.

"You have so much control over me that I have sex with you when you told me to forget about how you are going to be married. You have so much control over me that my heart physically pains when I hear your name."

She looked at me with a mixture of sadness and anger, but I could tell that the anger wasn't towards me.

"You have so much control over me that, I have a fucking date tonight with a really awesome girl and I'm over here begging for you back."

"You want to talk about fair? This isn't a game anymore. You are fucking piercing a knife into my heart over and over again."

I let out a breath.

"I'm done being controlled by you, Margo." I pulled my shirt on.

"This," I gestured to the both of us, "This isn't love. This is torture, this is anguish, and this is fucking toxic."

"Leave me alone from now on Margo." I seethed.

"I can't." She argued as I looked at her.

"Then leave Ben!" I yelled as sobs fell down her cheek.

"I can't, Liam please." She begged as I closed my eyes to relieve the pain, she was causing me.

"You don't love me enough." I said thickly as she cried.

"But I do love you, Liam." She answered as I shook my head and pulled away.

"Then, stop loving me." I said plainly as her hands pulled away from me.

She opened her mouth to say something, but stopped, as if I would burn her if she laid a hand, back on me.

"Okay, If that's what you want. I guess there's nothing left for me to say."

Margo gathered up her things.

I stood in silence for what felt like an eternity, the weight of unspoken words hung between us. Then, without another word, Margo turned and walked away.

CHAPTER 42

LIAM

Months later...

"Come on Liam, have some fun." I heard Adrianna yell from the middle of her foyer.

The music had been blasting, everyone had been dancing and twirling around like she was the happiest person in the world.

The months that passed since Margo had left, felt like a big blur. Life had moved on since Adrianna had gotten into the big car accident.

Her and Grayson were stronger than ever, and I don't think anything could really tear them apart.

We also had found out that we are twins, that's right, as in... we split from the same egg, developed together and share the same birthday.

But not really because, I was born before the clock had stroke midnight, and she was born after.

I never realized how amazing it would feel to have a sibling, not that I grew up without my own. Grayson, Neil, and Chris were my brothers.

But Adrianna loved and cared for me like she knew that I was her brother for the full lifetime.

She would set up time slots where our family could meet and have dinner, just talk, like a functioning family.

My mother enjoyed getting to know her daughter and I couldn't believe that my father was Damon Cassian.

That must've been the reason I was so good at hockey.

Grayson had walked up to me, "You can't just sit there forever, come on, your sister wants for you to dance. And as her boyfriend it is my job to make sure that the love of my life gets everything she wants."

I laughed. We hadn't changed our routine, this evening we all gathered at Adrianna's house once again for a casual get-together, an attempt to reclaim some sense of normalcy.

Margo hadn't come by in a while, however. I would only see her around campus, she would help out Ronni at the trainers office, but I avoided it.

My knee had been all healed up and there was really no need for me to be going back there all the time. I wasn't going to lie and say that I didn't miss her.

But the way we ended things wasn't really something that we would bring up the next time we saw each other face to face. Which as normally when I would run into her and Adrianna.

Laughter and chatter filled the room, yet I couldn't shake the feeling of emptiness from Margo's absence once more. Without her laughter and stupid jokes, there was a void that no one really dared to mention.

As my friends and my sister, have tried their best to lift my spirits, the memory of me telling her to leave me alone and to stop loving me was a really big thing to forget.

I didn't talk about her anymore, the only things that I focused on was hockey, my family, and my friends. Of course there was Sabrina who was a great girl, but I could tell I couldn't give her one hundred percent of what she deserved.

Maybe I just won't date anyone ever again.

As Grayson walked off, Adrianna caught my eyes.

Adrianna's smile faltered; It wasn't long before the conversation took a more serious turn. She noticed my distant gaze and put a hand on my shoulder.

"Liam, you alright?" She asked, her voice full of concern.

I nodded slowly, trying to muster a smile. "Yeah, I'm just... thinking."

She gave me a knowing look. "Is what you're thinking about possibly my blonde angel best friend, that goes by the given name Margo?"

The sincerity in her words struck a chord, and for the first time in months, I felt a glimmer of shock at the sound of her name.

"We can talk about her you know, I mean I'm not exactly stupid in the factor of loving. It took a while for me and Grayson to get together." She reasoned.

Grayson had followed up behind her, "You have got to stop sulking Liam."

Adrianna threw Grayson a look that could kill before hitting him in the crotch, "Hey, be nice to my brother."

Adrianna smiled at me before winking.

I couldn't help at laugh at the dynamic duo. The other four members of our group had finally stumbled back into the house, covered in snow.

"Guys! The snow!" Adrianna complained as Grayson grabbed a mop.

Everyone's laughter filled the room, "We made snow angels!" Chris beamed.

"Yeah, can you believe that he's never made a snow angel?" Verina exclaimed.

Neil and Juliette looked like they were avoiding each other, "What happened to them?" I asked.

"He threw a snowball at me." Juliette complained as everyone in the group laughed.

Neil folded his arms, "Oh live a little, it's just snow, besides you threw one back at me, a lot harder might I add." He pointed out as Juliette, threw him the middle finger.

Before anyone could react, Neil scooped up some snow from Chris's shoulder and threw it back at her, "Neil, when I catch you, I swear to god!" She shrieked.

I couldn't help but laugh at her betrayed eyes.

Chris, being the instigator, grabbed a handful of snow from his hair and tossed it into the air, we all watched it disperse over the group like a flurry of playful confetti.

"Snow fight!" Verina declared as her eyes gleamed with mischief.

Adrianna had terror on her eyes as she watched the snow fall to the ground, leaving a mess on the floor. She grabbed a cushion from the nearby couch and used it as a shield, "Don't you dare, Grayson Nicholas Prince."

Grayson smiled, at Adrianna's warning.

"Did she just use my full name?" He asked me as I grinned, "I think she did."

Grayson grabbed a handful of snow from Verina's shoulders and grinned as he was looking forward to throwing it at his girlfriend.

I took a step back, raising my hands in mock surrender, "Alright, alright, let's not turn the living room into a snow battle-field." I said.

I couldn't help but chuckle at the sight of my friends covered in snow and merriment.

This was the first time I've seen a genuine smile plastered across Chris's face.

Verina, determined to keep the fun going, lunged at Chris with a pillow, sending him toppling onto the couch with a surprised yelp.

"Truce, truce!" He pleaded, holding up his hands yet again.

As the group settled down, breathless and laughing, Neil took a moment to glance around at his friends, his heart swelling with affection. "You know, you guys are so fucking annoying," he said softly, his voice filled with genuine warmth.

Juliette, still brushing snow off her clothes, shot him a look of mock indignation. "You were the one to pelt me with snowballs first!"

"I never said I regretted it." Neil teased, earning himself another playful shove from Juliette.

Adrianna, still held onto her cushion shield, she slowly lowered it and looked around at the group, her eyes sparkled with happiness.

"I trust no one." She said, her voice sincere.

I playfully shoved her as she landed on top of Grayson on the couch.

"Except for me?" Grayson grinned before kissing her.

"You two are disgusting." I gaged as they picked up two pillows and lunged them at me.

MARGO

I watched them from a far, my heart hurt knowing that I couldn't hang out with them anymore. I had told Ben that I had a soul cycle class just so I could get out of the house.

I stayed hidden, well not really. I stood outside of Adriana's double doors. I felt a pang of sadness and longing as I watched my friends share those carefree moments.

It felt as though an invisible barrier kept me apart from them, a barrier erected by circumstances out of my control. Ben had become increasingly possessive, discouraging and sometimes outright forbidding me from spending time with anyone but him.

The more I tried to bridge the gap between us, the more he tightened his grip, isolating me further from the people I loved. I had barely seen Adrianna, he forbid me to hang out with them after classes, I was instructed to go straight home.

Each laugh, each playful insult exchanged between my friends seemed to echo around me, reminding me of what I was missing.

I missed seeing my friends, I missed seeing Liam, even if he told me to leave him alone. But instead, I stood there, a silent observer of a world that felt like it was slipping away from me.

My heart sank further when I saw the genuine happiness on their faces, realizing that even if I joined them, it would never be the same. Liam wouldn't be able to look at me.

As I turned away, the laughter and joy faded into the background, I knew I had made my choice. All I could do was watch from afar, my heart heavy with the weight of my decision.

Even when Ben wasn't around me, I could still feel him suffocating me, right when I would arrive back at home it would be him wrapping me around his hand.

I got back in my car; my eyes watered a little bit because I knew I was about to drive back home, back to my prison.

I drove back and finally arrived at the front of my door. I heisted to walk back in, but I had no choice.

Right as soon as I walked back into my own house, a pair of hands grabbed me by the neck.

Ben's cold eyes met mine, fury blazing within them. "Where were you?" he demanded, his voice low and dangerous.

I stammered, trying to find the words that might diffuse his anger. "I was just—"

"Don't lie to me," He interrupted, tightening his grip on my neck. "I know you weren't where you said you'd be."

Tears welled up in my eyes as I struggled to breathe, my mind raced to find an explanation that might appease him. But I knew it was futile; he had always seen through my lies, no matter how small or well-intentioned.

"I... I went to see Adrianna," I admitted, my voice barely a whisper. "I just wanted to see my friends for a little while."

His anger only intensified, his hold on my neck unrelenting. "You think you can just go wherever you want, see whoever you want? Your'e mine, Margo. You belong to me."

The words cut deep, but I couldn't muster the strength to

fight back. I could only nod, my vision blurring with tears as I accepted my fate.

Ben finally released me, shoving me away with a force that left me stumbling. "You don't fucking listen to me." He snarled.

"Do I need to show you why you should keep listening to me?" He bent down on the ground and slapped me.

I yelped as he grabbed me by my hair and pulled me to the bedroom.

I had never felt so much pain before in my life. I felt some of my hair bring ripped out of my scalp as he dragged me to the bed.

Ben pulled me up by my hair and pushed me on the bed. "Take your clothes off." He seethed as I cried.

"No." I sniffled as he grabbed me by my jaw and squeezed, "Take your slutty outfit off, or I rip it off." He whispered with anger as I resisted him.

Ben laughed, a cynical type of laughter, he ripped my tights off, along with my shirt. He exposed my nipples and sucked on them.

His hand found my pussy and forced his fingers inside me. I cried and yelped for help, only to know that there was no help around.

None one could hear me, no one was around that didn't work for Ben. He's fired all of my prior help, scared that I they would help me.

I felt his fingers inside of me, only I tightened because of the pan and restriction not because it felt good.

He griped my waist as I tried to get away. Ben's forearm was exposed, a tattoo gleamed, one that I had seen before.

A tattoo of a snake.

Trauma had hit me like a freight train.

It was the same tattoo that I had seen on the tall man that had tried to kidnap me.

Ben pulls out his belt, he threw me on the bed once more so that I wouldn't face him. My ass was face up; I was vulnerable. "You want to keep defying me?" He yelled.

I heard the whip of the belt, my whole body constricted as he whipped the belt on to my ass.

I let out a cry as he slapped my face.

"Shut up. Don't think I know you're still in love with Brookshire." He sneered.

I closed my eyes, wishing that this wasn't really happening to me, but it was.

"You don't think that I don't have you followed every fucking time you leave this house?" He belittled.

More tears had gathered.

"You are so fucking stupid, Margo. I was never going to fuck you like I'm about to, but you need to remember that you can't do anything that you want anymore. You have me to please and me only."

"Do you understand?" He asked as I cried softly.

I had to figure out a way to get out of this, any way to get out of this never-ending pain and fear. I couldn't tell Adrianna or Liam about it. My parents would never forgive themselves if they found out they traded me off to an abusive, rapist.

"Yes." I muttered as he slapped me again.

At this point, the slaps, the punches, and the grips didn't hurt. It was the new things that did, which only made it worst.

"You don't talk to Adrianna, Liam, Grayson, Verina, or fucking any of them do you understand?" He laughed, "Or else something might happen to them. You wouldn't want to be the cause of that would you?" He asked.

My heart felt heavy as he threatened my friends. It wasn't just my life on the line anymore, but it was my friends lives as well.

I already knew that Benjamin Grimaldi was an awful man, only now I knew that he wasn't just willing to hurt me but my friends.

Which was something that I couldn't endure.

So, for the next days, I took the abuse, the yelling, the pain, and I stayed at home.

Only it wasn't because of fear, but because I was going to dig up dirt on Ben.

Chapter 43

Liam

I walked Adrianna to class as Grayson had been called in by coach to the hockey room.

"So how are your classes doing?" She asked me as I jolted up.

"What?" I nervously scratched the back of my neck as she rolled her eyes.

"You definitely have dad's hearing." She let out a harsh sigh as I laughed.

We walked as she nervously glanced up at me, "You aren't acting weird because of me, are you? I'm not coming off too strong with the whole sister thing... because you've been acting different lately." She muttered.

I forced a smile, though I could feel the weight of the secrets pressing down on me. "Yeah, just a lot on my mind with practice and all. Don't worry about me."

She nodded, though her eyes betrayed that she wasn't entirely convinced.

As we neared her classroom, Adrianna waved to Margo, who was standing by the door. "Hey, Margo!"

Margo glanced up briefly but didn't return the greeting, her attention quickly diverted elsewhere. Adrianna's smile faltered for a moment, but she quickly brushed it off.

"That's weird, she never ignores me." Adrianna looked confused.

"Did you guys get into a fight? Is it because of me?" I asked as she shook her head.

"No, something's wrong." Adrianna alarmed, "We'll talk about it later."

"Okay." I replied, giving her a reassuring squeeze on the shoulder.

I really hoped that the reason Margo had ignored Adrianna was because of me. Because if there was any other reason, I wouldn't know about it.

Margo never ignored Adrianna, which had to mean that something was going on behind the surface.

And it couldn't have been good.

MARGO

I felt like a bitch ignoring my best friend, but I had to keep remembering that it was all going to end soon. I just had a feeling that Ben wasn't as nice and squeaky clean as he let others believe.

I had to prove it to everyone. I had to do it for myself, and my friends.

I waited for the sun to set, as the moon cast its silver glow over the quiet neighborhood. My determination solidified even more as I couldn't shake the gnawing suspicion about Ben.

He had left the house because he had to go do some unfinished work. Stealthily, I crept to out the bedroom window, carefully unlatching the lock with my practiced hands.

Every creak of the floorboards seemed amplified in the silence of the house. I paused, listening intently for any signs of movement from any of Ben's hires.

The steady hum of the heater and the muted sounds of the television downstairs were the only indications of life.

I slipped on a pair of my running sneakers; I had a feeling it wasn't a stilettoes night. I grabbed nothing but my phone then, I took one last glance around my entire room, taking a deep breath to steady my nerves.

I pushed the window open and swung my legs over the sill, landing softly on the grass below.

I made my way through the backyard, and I ducked behind the large oak tree, using its shadow for cover. The gate squeaked as I opened it.

I winced, freezing momentarily. I felt Ben's presence as he closed the front doors.

I knew I was taking a risk, but I had to gather evidence against Ben. I had to protect Adrianna and the others from whatever he was hiding.

With a final, resolute glance back at my prison, I stepped closer to Ben's car and jumped in the trunk hoping that he would lead me to whatever he was up to.

As the car started, I felt the engine's vibrations through the trunk. The confined space was claustrophobic, and I had to remind myself to breathe steadily. The car started moving, and every bump in the road jostled me, intensifying my anxiety. I could hear the faint strains of music playing from the car radio, but it did nothing to soothe my mind.

The drive seemed endless, each minute stretching into an eternity. I tried to focus on the task at hand, reminding myself why I was doing this.

But it didn't change the fact that I was horrified of what Ben might've been capable of.

The car finally turned off, I pulled the lever to open the trunk of his car, only to sneak off before he left his vehicle.

I remembered this place; I was back in Brownsville. The place I was kidnapped and followed the same night.

Back to the night where I was kidnapped by the guy that had the same tattoo as Ben.

I took a deep breath, trying to steady my nerves. The abandoned warehouse loomed ahead, its dark windows, like hollow eyes watching my every move. The memory of my previous encounter with the place made my heart race.

Carefully, I walked to the back of the building again, I avoided the broken glass and debris that littered the ground. The entrance was ajar, its rusted hinges protesting as I nudged it open just enough to slip inside.

The interior was the same, it was dimly lit by the moonlight filtering through the cracks in the walls, casting eerie shadows that danced across the floor.

I moved silently; each step calculated to avoid making any noise that could alert Ben to my presence. I knew he was hiding something here, and I was determined to find out what it was.

As I navigated the labyrinth of corridors, the stench of mold and decay filled my nostrils, making it difficult to breathe.

Finally, I found what I was looking for— the door was unmarked at the end of a long hallway.

I heard someone call Ben's name as he walked out with an angry look plastered on his face.

My heart pounded in my chest as I reached for the handle, praying that it wasn't locked.

To my relief, the door creaked open, revealing a small, cluttered room filled with papers and old furniture.

As my eyes adjusted to the dim light, I scanned the room, trying to make sense of the chaos. My breath caught in my throat when I noticed a large corkboard against the far wall, covered in photographs.

I stepped closer, my heart thudding in my ears.

The photos were all of me.

Candid shots from different times and places—at school, at home, even on my morning walks with my friends.

There were photos of me at Greece, before I even knew Ben.

Each one was meticulously pinned to the board, and some had notes scribbled beneath them, detailing dates and locations.

A chill ran down my spine as I realized the extent of Ben's obsession. He had been watching me for a long time, documenting my every move. I felt violated, my privacy shattered by this disturbing shrine.

There was a picture of me inside Verina's house having a drink with her brother. I remembered hearing a noise on the balcony that night only I assumed it was Xavier.

Despite my fear, I forced myself to keep looking, hoping to find some clue that would explain Ben's motives. My eyes landed on a recent photo, taken just a few days before my kidnapping.

It showed me and Liam in his bedroom; Ben knew that I had cheated on him.

I felt my heart drop to my stomach. I felt a surge of anger mixed with terror.

Why was he doing this?

What did he want from me?

I felt footsteps approaching, and quickly walked into a dark room, I closed the door behind me.

I felt horror creep up my throat as I turned on the flickering light, only to display the dozens of drugged women, who laid on the floor.

I wanted to scream but let my hand cup my mouth to keep me from screaming. I pulled out my phone quickly and texted Adrianna a quick *SOS* before dropping it on the floor.

Lost in thought, I didn't hear the footsteps approaching until it was too late. The door behind opened, a hand had wrapped around me and slammed the door shut.

I spun around to see Ben standing there, a twisted smile on his face.

"Enjoying the gallery?" He sneered, stepping closer. "I've been waiting for this moment."

My mind raced, searching for a way out. But I was surrounded, by Ben and his other friends I was guessing.

There were three other men who surrounded the room. I wasn't going to get out of here alive.

CHAPTER 44

LIAM

We had set up a meeting in Adrianna's house for everyone to come so that we could get to the bottom of everything.

"Okay, how are you so sure that she's just not mad at you." I asked.

Adrianna threw me a stupid glare, "I haven't done anything for her to be mad at me."

Adrianna crossed her arms and leaned back against the kitchen counter. "Liam, something must have happened. Margo wouldn't just ignore me out of nowhere."

I sighed, rubbing the back of my neck. "Maybe she's going through something and doesn't know how to talk about it?"

Adrianna shook her head. "No, that's not like her. She's always been open with me with anything."

"Anything?" I asked with a little laugh as she gave me a dead-liest glare.

"Yes, anything. And trust me, I knew all about your Greece vacation and how you left her there."

My lips thinned, "That was a mistake."

"It's always a mistake when it comes to your group."

I sighed out, ignoring her comment before a thought struck

me. "Did you guys have any disagreement recently? Even something minor?"

She frowned, thinking back. "Not that I can recall. We were fine the last time we talked."

I pulled out my phone, scrolling through the messages. "What if someone said something to her about you? You know how rumors can spread."

Adrianna's eyes widened. "Why would someone do that?"

"Well, you guys might be the most popular and known girls here in Hawthorne but that doesn't mean you guys aren't also the most hated." I muttered as Grayson, Chris and Neil swept behind Adrianna.

I shrugged. "It could be anyone. Maybe someone is jealous of your friendship."

Adrianna bit her lip, her mind racing. "I need to talk to her, find out what's going on."

"What's going on?" Grayson asked before he landed a kiss on top of his girlfriend's forehead.

"Margo ignored me today, I waved, and she didn't say anything. I think something might be wrong."

"Let's go to her place," Grayson suggested. "If you're right, she'll tell you what's bothering her."

Adrianna nodded, determination in her eyes. "You're right. Let's go."

"Only I don't think her home is prone to any visitors right now." Verina mumbled as we all turned to look at her and Juliette who finally arrived.

"Why?"

"I tried to go there last weekend and one of the maids said that we weren't allowed to visit anymore." Verina answered.

"Who said?" Adrianna stood up.

"Orders from Ben." Verina finished as Adrianna looked like anger had struck her again.

"It's got to be Ben. It had to be him, that's why she's acting like this. I think he might be hurting her some way or blackmailing her." Adrianna voiced as we all looked at her with crazy faces.

"I'm not crazy guys. I know my best friend, I also noticed that she hasn't worn any short sleeves in a while." Adrianna paced around.

"It's a bit crazy, I don't think Ben would hit a fly." Juliette muttered nervously as I looked at Neil.

"No, I'm pretty sure it was Ben who tried drowning me at the Archibald's Wedding." He forced out as Adrianna's face grew more scared.

"How are you so sure she's being black mailed?" Grayson asked his girlfriend, who threw an ugly look at him.

"Gee, I don't know, maybe because you were blackmailed to stay away from me." She mocked as Grayson threw his hands up in the air and shut up.

It was getting late, and I grew more concerned.

Adrianna's phone beeped; relief had crawled on her face.

"Oh, thank god, it's from her. She isn't mad at me." She muttered as everyone let out their breaths.

Only for a second we had peace, Adrianna's face dropped like she had seen something she wished she hadn't.

"Margo texted me an *SOS*." She frantically said.

"What's wrong? What did she say?" I asked, my heart pounding in my chest.

"She just sent me the letters *SOS*. That means she's in serious trouble," Adrianna replied, her voice shook.

We all rushed out of the house and piled into Grayson's car. The atmosphere was charged with worry and urgency as we sped towards Margo's last known location.

The usually busy streets seemed to stretch endlessly, adding to our anxiety. Adrianna kept checking her phone, hoping for another message from Margo, while the rest of us remained silent, each lost in our own thoughts.

Adrianna ran out, looking everywhere but only found Margo's phone, broken on the ground.

"Anna, we can't do anything we have to call the police." Verina yelled as she fell to her knees.

I got out, and walked towards Adrianna, "We'll find her Adrianna. Trust me I will find her."

MARGO

I was thrown into a cell, Ben yawned as I shivered on the cold ground.

"Why would you do this? To get revenge on Liam? He and I are broken up, you can't hurt him anymore if that's what you want." I yelled as he rolled his eyes.

Ben smirked; he leaned against the wall with an air of disdain. "You think this is just about you two? About my jealousy? You're more naïve than I thought," He sneered.

"Then what is it about?" I asked as a flash of despair hit his face.

"Liam killed the love of my life." He grumbled.

"I don't understand, he didn't kill anyone. Nor does he know who the love of your life was." I defended Liam as Ben grew more impatient.

"We were dating when she met him. Her name was Ally Stevens. She used to work for Liam's family back in Philadelphia, served him every day." Ben walked around as his eyes stayed on the ground.

"She fell in love with him, and he didn't care. Instead, he brought countless of women back home in front of her. Liam didn't reciprocate her love, so she killed herself." Ben finished.

I struggled with the ropes that tied my wrists together, "It sounds like your lover was clinically insane and obsessed like you are." I gripped as he laughed.

"So, I devised this beautiful plan to find the one girl that Liam

Brookshire loved and would do anything for. And hurt her like he hurt my sister." He ranted.

I stared at him, trying to process everything he had just said. The room felt colder, and the gravity of Ben's twisted plan weighed heavily on me. "You think hurting me will bring her back?" I asked softly, hoping to reach some shred of humanity within him.

Ben's eyes darkened. "No, but it will make Liam suffer. He will feel the pain of losing someone he loves, just as I did."

"If you wanted to kill me, then why didn't you just cut to the chase. Instead of abusing me and torturing me for fucking months."

Tears welled up in my eyes, not out of fear for myself, but for Liam.

Ben walked closer to me, his face was in between the cold bars, "I know you saw the dozens of women down in the basement, Margo. I am a powerful man, that is capable of powerful things."

"I don't even have to kill you; I can just send you off with all of them as they get sold to some pretty nasty guys that I do business with... ones that own brothels... ones that love blonde beauties." He whispered as his fingers caressed my cheek.

"You don't understand, Ben. This cycle of pain and revenge won't bring you peace. It will only destroy you further." I begged, not knowing how on earth I would be able to get out of this.

He looked away, the flicker of doubt crossing his face for a brief moment before his resolve hardened again. "You're wrong. This is the only way."

"What are you going to tell my family?" I asked with a shaky breath.

"That a very tragic accident had happened." He muttered.

I swallowed, "You aren't going to get away with this. Liam will come find me."

Ben smiled; his eyes held a sense of mischief.

"For your sake, I hope Liam doesn't come find you." He

expressed with content, his hand had reached behind his pocket and pulled out a gun.

My heart raced as Ben's hand hovered next to my face, I could smell the gun and his confidence. Ben pulled the trigger, making me close my eyes and let out a cry.

I turned to see the bullet pierced through the wall.

"Or it's his life instead." He finished off.

CHAPTER 45

LIAM

It had been three days since Margo had gone missing.

The group had met up every day since she had gone missing, Grayson and Neil had staked out the front of Margo's house and there was no sign of her.

We haven't seen her in school, and Ben hadn't returned to Hawthorne at all.

Grayson and I had hired some of the most professional police force to find her and, like I suspected they were shit at their jobs.

Everyone had fallen asleep on my bedroom floor as I stayed up on my desktop, unable to fall asleep.

I could not shake the feeling that Margo was in serious danger. Every lead I pursued seemed to dissolve into nothingness, leaving me in a fog of frustration.

My thoughts were constantly plagued by the haunting image of Margo's face, her eyes pleading for help.

As I sat in the dimly lit room, I stared at the wall adorned with a chaotic array of notes and paperwork, my phone buzzed. The screen displayed an unknown number, and my heart skipped a beat. With a deep breath, I answered the call, hoping for a breakthrough.

"Liam?" The voice on the other end was cautious and unfamiliar.

"Yes, this is Liam. Who is this?" I replied, trying to mask my impatience.

"You and Chris are coming to the fight tonight, aren't you?" The voice continued, hesitant and wavering. My heart pounded in my chest as I gripped the phone tighter.

"It's Angelo, you remember from that night?" He mentioned as my heart stopped pounding.

"This week isn't really a good week for us to go out there Angelo, can't you find someone else to fight?" I asked as he pleaded to stay on the phone.

"Sure, I got a good prize for you." He disregarded my words, I couldn't help but sit up from my chair.

"I'm not interested, Angelo." I said firmly as he coughed out, and put his phone on speaker.

I heard a lady scream from a far. A familiar sounding scream.

"HELP! HELP! HELP!"

My breath caught in my throat as I recognized the voice. It was Margo. My worst fears were confirmed, and adrenaline surged through my veins.

"Tell me everything you know," I demanded, my voice edged with a mix of hope and urgency.

I then heard gunshots, that were being shot throughout the rest of the phone call.

"Come alone."

Angelo's voice was strained and provided an address and abruptly hung up, leaving me with a glimmer of hope. I sprang to my feet, grabbing my jacket and keys, and dashed out of the room.

As I raced out of the room, my heart pounded.

My mind raced as I got into the car and started the engine. The address Angelo had given me was etched into my memory, and I couldn't waste a single second.

The streets blurred past as I sped through the city, my thoughts solely focused on Margo and the danger she was in. The engine roared as I pushed the car to its limits, weaving through traffic with a singular purpose.

I realized that the address given to me as far too familiar. I never knew the actual address of the warehouse in Brownsville, because we just went.

I took a deep breath before entering the abandoned building.

I pushed open the creaky door and stepped into the dimly lit warehouse. The air was thick with dust, and the only sound was the echo of my footsteps on the concrete floor.

My eyes scanned the darkness, searching for any sign of movement.

"Margo!" I called out, my voice echoing through the empty space. There was no response, only the hollow sound of silence. As I moved deeper into the warehouse, the sense of urgency grew stronger.

Suddenly, I heard a faint noise coming from one of the far corners. I hurried towards it, my heart pounding in my chest. As I approached, I could make out a figure huddled on the floor. It was Angelo on the floor, dead.

I further looked and caught Margo, her hands bound and her face pale.

"Margo, I'm here," I whispered, dropping to my knees beside her. "Are you okay?"

Her eyes opened slowly, and she managed a weak smile. "I knew you'd come," she said, her voice barely audible.

I quickly untied her hands and helped her to her feet. "We need to get out of here," I said, glancing around nervously. "It's not safe."

"No Liam, you need to leave me *now*." She warned me as I tilted my head looking confused.

"Oh no, he can't leave just yet! We haven't celebrated his return." I turned my heard and saw Ben, who walked over slowly with a gun in his hand.

My eyes narrowed at his weapon and shielded Margo away from it.

"No Liam, go please!" I heard Margo cry out as I stood my ground.

"I'm not leaving you." I said sternly as Ben laughed.

A cynical laugh that drew my attention to his tattoo.

"You are the sex traffickers' boss aren't you, the guys that would take women from the fights. They would bring them to you." I remembered as he winked at me.

"Now you know what my day job is, William." He grinned.

"You're fucking crazy." I exclaimed as Ben brought the gun up and shot my shoulder.

Pain seared through my shoulder as I staggered back, clutching the wound.

Margo screamed; her eyes wide with terror as she reached out to steady me. Ben's laughter echoed in the dimly lit room, a chilling sound that sent shivers down my spine.

"You're not going anywhere," Ben sneered, raising his gun again.

Summoning every ounce of strength, I lunged forward, knocking the weapon from Ben's hand. "Run, Margo!" I shouted, grappling with Ben as she hesitated, torn between staying and fleeing.

"Go, now!" I urged, as I struggled to overpower Ben and his other men.

With a final, desperate glance, Margo turned and bolted towards the door. I fought fiercely, but the pain in my shoulder made it hard to keep up. Just as I felt myself weakening, I heard footsteps approaching from behind. A wave of relief washed over me as I saw Grayson storming in, his eyes blazing with determination.

Grayson's arrival was just the beginning of our rescue. As he punched Ben, I noticed more figures entering the room.

Neil and Chris, with fierce purpose etched on their faces, sprang into action, they tackled the other men who were about to overwhelm me.

Neil moved with precision and strength, quickly disarming one of Ben's henchmen and turned Ben's gun to face himself.

Chris, was a skilled fighter that I knew fought many of these other guys before and won, took on two men at once, his swift movements making it hard for them to keep up.

"Grayson!" I called out, struggling to stay on my feet, the blood from my shoulder grew more apparent as I heard sirens from a far.

But I didn't care about the pain that seared through me. I pulled Ben towards me and swung around, my fists connecting with Ben's jaw in a brutal uppercut, which sent him sprawling to the ground.

Ben didn't say anything but only fell on the ground, I couldn't tell if he was down for good or if I had just knocked him out.

I felt the immense amount of pain that rushed through me once more.

The room spun around me, the adrenaline masking the full extent of my injuries. But as the immediate danger subsided, the pain in my shoulder grew unbearable.

It was as if a searing hot knife had been driven into my flesh, and every movement sent a fresh wave of agony coursing through my body.

I felt my head pound as well as my heart weaken.

Next thing I knew, I was hitting the floor, blood splattered everywhere as I heard Grayson's screams and the police infiltrating the whole perimeter.

"Stay with me Brookshire."

Then I saw black.

CHAPTER 46

LIAM

I woke up in a soft bed, I felt battered and foggy as I peeled my eyes open.

I watched as Grayson laid besides me, sleeping.

It was light outside; I figured that several hours had passed. There had been a big bruise on his arm, but something told me that I looked a whole lot worst.

We were alone in the hospital and disappointment filled me. I tried to sit up and was tortured by a fierce throbbing pain that shot down from my shoulder.

I glanced down to see my upper arm and shoulder wrapped with bandages.

Grayson stirred, he gave me a relieved sigh, "Finally."

"What, you know you can't get rid of me that easily." I whispered.

"I hate you." He mumbled as I laughed, then winced in pain.

"Yeah, you have got to stop spending so much time in the hospital bed." I explained as he rolled his eyes.

"Between you and Adrianna, is this going to be a thing. I have to worry about both of you being accident prone?" He joked as I laughed.

"We *are* twins." I made a point.

"What did I sign up for, my best friend and my girlfriend are going to end up sending me to the emergency room for how much I worry." He breathed out as I shook my head.

"Speaking of twin, I'm guessing she gave me the blood?" I asked as he nodded.

"Well, I would've offered mine but I'm afraid I would kill you because we are incompatible." He informed me as I flipped him off.

"I'm glad you were the one I woke up to." I concluded as he gave me a look of annoyance.

"We both know that's a lie, and before you ask... yes Margo's okay. She has been guarding your bed almost all night, but Adrianna forced her to come out and put food in her system." He noted as I let out a deep and awaited sigh.

"What ended up happening after the police got there?" I asked.

"Well, Angelo passed away. But I'm sure you saw that... you knocked Ben out pretty cold from what I remember, he's going to jail for sexual assault and a lot of other illegal shit."

"All the women on the basement that were kidnapped, I'm pretty sure all the police officers were doing everything they can to find their rightful homes."

"Margo got checked out, you aren't going to like this, but it turns out she's been getting abused by Ben for months. She was riddled with bruises, and she was close to overdosing on pain relievers."

I felt my heart drop and my blood pressure rise.

"Ben is not going to get out of prison for a while. Trust me." Grayson finished off as I exhaled.

Ben was lucky I was far from him, or else I would've killed him myself.

"Is she okay now?" I asked as he nodded.

I swallowed as I watched Neil and Chris walk back into the room with bags full of food.

"Oh, thank god you're okay, I was wondering who would end

up eating all of the food we bought." Neil teased as Chris came up and gave me a small hug.

"I'm really glad you guys are here," I said softly, feeling a warm sense of gratitude for my friends.

Neil grinned, "Of course. Where else would we be? Plus, someone's got to make sure you don't overdose on hospital pudding."

Chris laughed, as he placed the bags on the table. "And to save you from the questionable cafeteria food. We got your favorites!"

I smiled, and felt a tear of happiness threaten to escape.

What would I do without my best friends.

Neil pulled out a sandwich and waved it in front of my face. "Alright, no more talking. Time to eat!"

As we all settled in, the room filled with the comforting aroma of familiar foods and the sound of our laughter.

"Hey, no stealing my fries!" I protested as Chris tried to sneak one from my plate.

"But they taste better when they're yours," He replied.

Neil chuckled, "Here we go again."

As we chatted and joked, the hospital room seemed a little less sterile and a lot more like home.

My parents came into view as they entered in the room with Adrianna.

They brought in a bouquet of vibrant flowers and a stack of my favorite books. "We thought you could use a bit of color and some light reading," My mom said with a warm smile.

Adrianna beamed as she hugged me, "Don't you ever scare me like that again." She slapped my uninjured arm.

She earned a kiss by Grayson as I nearly gagged.

"You guys are going to make me sicker than the medication I'm taking." I joked as Grayson pulled his middle finger out.

"The doctor said that since your shoulder only got shot, it should heal pretty quickly and completely. You will be able to use your arm like before." He primed as I nodded.

The door opened once more, my beautiful, blonde angel had walked in with a small and scared smile on her face.

Margo's presence quieted the whole room, I knew it shut me up, seeing her angel like hair and porcelain skin, and baby blue eyes. She was the epitome of pureness.

"Well, that's our queue to go." Grayson announced as everyone dispersed out of the room.

Which left me and Margo, all alone.

CHAPTER 47

MARGO

I wanted to be with him, I wanted to be there when he woke up and hold his hand while he was conscious.

I wanted and yearned to tell him that I was tired of the games and tired of pretending that I didn't think about him every second we were apart.

I had lost my heart to Liam Brookshire.

I sat down beside him, my hand trembled slightly as I reached for his. The warmth of his skin against mine felt like a lifeline, grounding me in a moment that felt surreal.

His eyes fluttered.

"Thank god, you're okay" He whispered, his voice hoarse but filled with an emotion that made my heart clench.

"I should be the one saying that" I managed to say, my voice soft. "How are you feeling?"

"Better now," He replied with a weak smile, his thumb gently caressing the back of my hand. "I've missed you."

"I've missed you too," I admitted, my eyes welled up with tears. "More than you know."

For a moment, we just sat there, holding hands and gazing at each other, the world outside the hospital room fading away. It felt like we were the only two people in existence, bound by a connection that defied explanation.

"I thought that I had lost you, Liam." I said finally, my voice broke. "I love you."

His grip on my hand tightened, and he pulled me closer, his lips brushing against my forehead. "I love you too, Raine. But we are still going to need a bit more time."

"Why, I want to be with you now." I muttered as he closed his eyes.

I looked down at our intertwined fingers, his other hand had crept down my chin to make my eyes lock with his.

"Raine, I know what Ben did to you, it explains the bruises, the hesitation in your body language." He breathed out.

I felt tears running down my cheeks. I was upset that he knew, I was upset that anyone knew. I was so embarrassed that everyone had the knowledge that I was beat to a pulp every night.

I broke down.

"I didn't know what to do, I kept it a secret because I thought it was the only solution to help my family. We were going broke, Liam." I heaved out.

"What was I supposed to do?!" I cried out as he moved closer to me.

"I don't know what I would've done in your situation... I can't give you advice. I just know that I would've raised hell on earth if I knew before he was in jail." Liam seethed.

"I don't need justice Liam, I just need you." I swallowed.

"You have me Raine, no one has ever had me like you have me." He voiced.

I smiled.

"I'm scared that you won't be able to deal with how badly I was physically hurt by Ben." I let out as he hushed me.

"That's why I'm telling you to take time, Raine." He mumbled.

"You say you want me, you already have me. I'm not going anywhere, I can't leave you, I don't think it is humanly possible for me to leave you." He laughed as I raised our holding hands up to my lips and kissed his palm.

"You don't have to scared of me going away. You can't lose me that easily Raine, if you don't recall my pining." He reassured as I rolled my eyes.

"But I did almost lose you, you were badly injured." I explained.

Liam looked around the hospital, "But I'm alive and I'm sure that I'll be spending more time with you at the trainers office, if you'll have me."

"I'll check my schedule." I joked.

Liam lifted our hands over to his mouth and kissed my bruise that was located around my wrist.

I sighed as a tear fell.

"We can get through this together, Raine." He grinned.

As I rested my head on his chest, and listened to the steady beat of his heart, I knew that no matter what challenges lay ahead, we would face them together.

And for the first time in a long while, I felt a sense of peace.

"I can get through anything with you, Charming." I breathed out.

CHAPTER 48

MARGO

I felt like I couldn't breathe, my fingers trembled slightly as I turned the key in the lock of Liam's house.

I had offered to drop off the box of things he'd left at the hospital, insisting it was no big deal. But now, standing in the quiet hallway, I couldn't ignore the pang of unease in my chest.

My relationship had shifted lately warm, meaningful moments interrupted by uncertainty. I wasn't sure where we stood anymore.

I knew I still loved him; the only thing that was in the way was now gone and I offered him my whole heart.

It was up to him to figure out what he wanted to do with it.

The door creaked open, and I stepped inside. The familiar scent of Liam's cologne mixed with something new, something... distinctly feline?

I froze, staring at the living room. There, perched regally on the couch like it owned the place, was a small brown cat. It blinked at me lazily, tail flicking over Liam's favorite throw pillow.

"Oh my god," I whispered, my hand flying to my mouth. I felt my heart do a somersault.

One of Liam's helpers came from the kitchen, a dish towel slung over his shoulder. "Hello, Miss Hamilton."

I didn't respond. My eyes were glued to the cat, who was now stretching luxuriously before hopping down to investigate my shoes.

"Liam," I said slowly, my voice catching. "Is this... is this what I think it is?"

"Mr. Brookshire took this cat in weeks ago, but I think he's grown quite accustomed towards it."

He rubbed the back of his neck, looking sheepish. "Uh, yeah. Meet Coco."

"Coco?" My voice cracked on the word. I bent down, letting the cat sniff my fingers before it nuzzled into my hand.

"He remembered?" I whispered.

I straightened, my eyes shimmering as I looked at the cat, "That was so long ago. I didn't think that Liam would even--"

"I'm sorry ma'am?" The man asked as I laughed, tears filled my eyes.

"Our first date," I interrupted gently, stepping closer.

"I told him about how I would wish for a cat." I laughed, a tear slipping down my cheek. "I didn't think he was paying attention."

"Mr. Brookshire, pays quite great attention to everything you say," He said, his voice full of warmth. "Although he was about to bring Coco to the shelter last week, but something stopped him."

I glanced down at Coco, who was now purring contentedly against my leg, and then back up at the man.

"He adopted a cat because of something I said months ago?"

Coco meowed loudly, as if to seal the moment.

I missed Liam, the only reason he was injured was because of me.

I still wasn't convinced that he would never hurt me again but seeing Coco, now I knew that Liam was in it for the long game. I just wish he would come home.

LIAM

. . .

It had been a few weeks since Margo had confessed that she loved me.

Those words remained imprinted in my mind, a beacon of hope during the dark days that followed. Margo visited me every day, bringing a sense of normalcy and warmth to my hospital room.

But I was finally ready to play and this time I had one hundred percent promised myself that I wouldn't end up in the hospital again.

As my recovery progressed, I remembered how much Margo's laughter helped ease my annoyance and distaste for the world.

She had started to work at the trainer's office again, she took care of me, offered me water when I didn't ask, she made sure to root for me when I played.

As the days turned into weeks, I found myself eagerly awaiting each visit from Margo. Her presence was like a balm to my weary soul, and her unwavering support gave me the strength to push through the final stages of my recovery.

Margo arrived with a surprise before my game. She handed me a hockey stick, neatly wrapped. I smiled at her as she beamed.

"These are for your comeback," She said with a soft smile. "And a bit of a flashy gift to show off, Coach Livingston is kind of sick of seeing you injured."

Her words filled me with a renewed sense of determination and a bit of laughter. I knew that with Margo by my side, I could conquer any obstacle.

My heart swelled with gratitude and love as I stepped on to the hockey arena.

I knew that Margo was trying to be patient. I was happy that she was taking her time, and it was really what I needed from her at the moment.

I needed to make sure she was okay before we could go

through with being together. I was happy to be a part of her journey as well.

I couldn't tell her that I had something planned for us. That I was all in for her, that I'm quite sure that nothing ever will pull us apart.

MARGO

I sat across from my parents, I trembled as they watched over me. I forgot about how close I was with them.

I didn't understand why I still felt like something was missing. Why it was still abundantly clear that I was depressed and unhappy.

I hadn't spoken to them since I got engaged to Ben. They left me all alone and I was so angry with them that I had no support system through my whole engagement.

My hands shook as I held on to the end of my skirt, I fiddled with it to ease my nerves. It had been months since I've heard their voices– my parents, the two people who had loved me the longest... they were supposed to be my best friends.

But they didn't know what I had been going through.

I had realized since my conversation with Liam, I needed to figure my shit out before I could even be capable of being with him, and he was right.

I had finally given into the desperate, gnawing urge to hear their voices. Maybe it was because I had reached my breaking point. Maybe because I could still feel the bruises beneath the long sleeves of my sweater.

Maybe because I couldn't do this alone anymore.

I missed my mom and dad.

"Margo," My mother's voice, gentle and warm, filled the silence.

My throat tightened. "Mom."

A pause. Then a sharp inhale. "Margo, sweetheart, I'm so sorry." She got up from her chair and ran over to me, enveloping me within her arms.

"Mommy." The words barely made it past my lips before the lump in my throat swelled.

"We should've never made you think that we needed you to be married to save us."

My father's voice joined in the background. "I'm going to sue the Grimaldi family for all they've got."

"I don't need revenge dad, I just need you to hug me please." I sobbed.

I squeezed my eyes shut. I hadn't prepared for this, hadn't rehearsed the words, but there was no more time to hide behind silence.

"I— felt so alone." My voice cracked, and then the dam broke. Tears spilled down my cheeks as the words rushed out. "Mom, Dad... he hurt me. Ben hurt me *so much.*"

Silence. A suffocating, horrified silence.

My mother's grip tightened around the my body like she needed to take my pain away. "He controlled everything for months. What I wear, where I go, who I talk to. And when I don't listen, he..." I sucked in a shaky breath. "He punished me in inhumane ways."

My father's voice was low, dangerous. "Maggie, you are safe now." He reached out for my hand and held on to it.

"I just wanted to help you out so much, especially when I disappointed you because I fell in love with Liam. I didn't want to disappoint you again, so I went through with it." I cried as my father walked towards me.

"We've got you Maggie," My father said firmly. "We are so sorry for making you think you had to do that."

Relief coiled in my stomach.

"Margo, honey, listen to me," My mother cut in softly, as if reading her thoughts. "You don't have to be afraid anymore. We love you. We are going to help you."

I covered her mouth, stifling a sob. I had spent so long thinking that they wouldn't know about the abuse that I had endured. I had been prepared to be suffering in pain for the rest of my life and one would know , thinking I had no way out.

But now, for the first time in months, I felt something other than fear.

Relief.

CHAPTER 49

MARGO

I looked around the audience as there was no sign of Liam.

I felt my heart hurt at the fact that maybe... he had left me again.

I desperately searched the stands, hoping to catch a glimpse of his familiar face, but the more I sought, the more my hope dwindled.

My eyes locked on to the keys of the piano tighter, my knuckles white with a mix of anticipation and anxiety. He had promised to watch me.

I had finally found time in my schedule to play in a large crowd. I watched as Adrianna, Verina, Juliette and the guys *except* Liam beamed at me.

The piano's first notes filled the air, and I began to play, my fingers danced over the keys with a practiced grace. Each note was a piece of my heart laid bare, a melody of longing and hope.

As the music enveloped me, I could almost forget the emptiness in the stands, the missing face that meant so much.

Time seemed to stretch and contract in the oddest of ways. One moment, I was acutely aware of every second that passed without Liam's presence; the next, I was lost in the music and allowed it to pull me into a world where only the melody and I existed.

But reality's grip was relentless, and my eyes would steal glances towards the audience. The faces of Adrianna, Verina, and Juliette offered some comfort, but it passed. The vacant spot where Liam should have stood, gnawed at my spirit.

My fingers faltered slightly, a discordant note slipping through. Panic surged, but I gathered myself, pushing through the anxiety. I had to finish this performance, if not for myself, then for all those who believed in me.

And then, a movement caught my eye. My heart skipped a beat as I saw a figure at the edge of the room. The figure moved closer; my pulse quickened.

It was Liam. He was here.

A small smile playing on his lips. Relief washed over me, and I felt a surge of happiness.

The crowd dispersed as I stayed and stood in front of everyone. Liam walked closer and my breath hitched as he took another step towards my direction.

He finally closed the gap between us.

"I didn't think you'd come," I whispered, my voice barely audible over the cheers of our friends that stayed behind.

Liam smiled, "I know that it hasn't been easy giving me space and not knowing where the hell I've gone the past week." He voiced as I nodded.

"I was worried," I confessed, "But seeing you now, it's like the missing piece has finally clicked into place."

Liam's expression softened as he reached out, his hand warm and reassuring on my shoulder. "I'm here now," he said gently, "I never really left, but yes I did... just know this time I have a really good reason."

We stood there, enveloped in a silent understanding, until the voices of our friends broke through our bubble. Adrianna, Verina, and Juliette approached us, their faces lit with curiosity and relief.

Adrianna raised an eyebrow, a teasing smile on her lips. "So, are you two ready to rejoin the land of the living, or do you need a few more moments?"

Liam laughed, the tension draining from my body. "We need a few more moments." He replied, glancing at Grayson, who nodded in agreement.

CHAPTER 50

LIAM

Grayson had walked towards and handed me a flower, one that Margo had grown very familiar with.

Her grin had maxed out as I held on to the flower.

"Do you remember this?" I asked as she laughed.

"It's a saffron crocus." She informed me as I grinned.

Margo held up her hand to stop me from talking, with an unserious face, "Do you have a speech prepared or something?"

I rolled my eyes, "Yes and you're ruining it."

"Okay I'm sorry, keep going." She put her hands up in mockery.

My eyes twinkled as I turned to the group, still holding the saffron crocus. "This flower has seen better days, but it's still standing," I remarked.

I turned back to Margo with a meaningful look. "Just like us."

I bridged the gap between us, "I've missed this," I confessed, "Missed you. And I flew all the way to Greece so that I can bring this back."

Margo's face showed nothing but happiness, "I've missed you too. I promise, I'm not going anywhere this time."

Margo laughed, "Oh yeah? Do you have another trick up your sleeve?" She mumbled as I rolled my eyes and snapped.

This prompted Neil to walk up next to me.

He held out twenty full pieces of jalapeño peppers.

Margo's eyes had widen, only because I had come to the conclusion that she had now remembered what on Earth I was up to.

"Liam, you don't have to do that." She warned as I laughed, "No I have to, I'm prepared."

I bunched up all of the peppers into one hand and stuffed them into my mouth.

I crunched down on the fiery jalapeños, their searing heat erupting in my mouth like volcanic lava. I could feel the burning sensation radiating through my entire being, but I refused to give in.

Margo's eyes grew wide with a mixture of amusement and concern as I continued chewing.

"You're crazy!" Margo exclaimed, shaking her head in disbelief.

"Crazy for you." I forced out as she laughed.

Margo's hand hovered near her face, her smile both impressed and incredulous. "Liam, you're going to regret this later."

I could barely respond, the heat had set my tongue ablaze, but I managed a confident nod. Swallowing the last of the peppers, I gave a triumphant grin, even as sweat beaded on my brow.

"I'm not done," I said, my voice slightly hoarse from the spice. I lifted my shirt and showed her my new addition of art that was now permanent on my body.

"You know that this tattoo is because of you." I muttered as she nodded.

Margo's eyes twinkled with mischief. "Alright, Mr. Tough Guy. Can you name all fifty states?"

I wiped the sweat from my forehead, took a deep breath, and grinned. "Piece of cake." I declared, though I wasn't entirely sure of my chances.

"Go on then," She urged, crossing her arms and raised an eyebrow.

"Okay, here goes nothing," I said, gathering my thoughts. "Alabama, Alaska, Arizona, Arkansas..."

The group gathered around, intrigued by my latest stunt. As I rattled off state after state, my pace quickened. "California, Colorado, Connecticut, Delaware, Florida, Georgia..."

Margo watched with a mix of skepticism and amusement. "Indiana, Iowa, Kansas, Kentucky, Louisiana, Maine, Maryland, Massachusetts..."

Her laughter was infectious, and it spread among the group. I kept going, determined to finish the challenge. "Michigan, Minnesota, Mississippi, Missouri, Montana, Nebraska, Nevada, New Hampshire..."

My voice grew hoarser with each state, the residual burn from the peppers still lingering on my tongue. "New Jersey, New Mexico, New York, North Carolina, North Dakota, Ohio, Oklahoma, Oregon, Pennsylvania..."

"Utah, Vermont, Virginia, Washington, West Virginia, Wisconsin, Wyoming." I finished off as she stood there agape.

The group erupted in laughter and applause; the camaraderie stronger than ever.

"Okay then Liam, what's the last stunt you have for me?" She asked as I swallowed.

A loud noise echoed throughout the auditorium.

Margo turned to the doors and watched as both of her parents walked into the room.

Adrianna had ran up and handed me a small box, then I quickly got down on one knee before she turned to look at me again.

Margo's expression changed as she saw me on my knee.

"I got your parent's blessing, I knew how important it would be for you." I muttered.

"Liam you don't have to." She cried out for a second as she wiped away her tears.

"I want to, I live for you Margo and I can't go another breath without you being mine." I pleaded.

Tears welled up in her eyes as the realization of what was happening dawned on her. I cleared my throat and began,

"Raine, will you marry me?" I asked her with certainty as she grins.

Margo's hands flew to her mouth, and for a moment, the entire room held its breath. Then, with a voice shaky but filled with joy, she nodded vigorously, managing to whisper, "Yes, yes, a thousand times yes!"

The group erupted in laughter and applause; the camaraderie stronger than ever.

Mrs. Margo Raine Brookshire has a pretty cool ring to it.

EPILOUGE
LIAM

"That is one of the ugliest things I have ever seen." I muttered as Grayson wobbled around looking for a better ring.

"Never in my life did I ever think that I would be buying an engagement ring with you in our twenties." He sodded as I folded my arms.

"Yeah, I was thinking maybe you would wait until you were... I don't know... uhm fifties you would be getting married to a gold digger or something." Neil said matter of a factly as I threw him a mean look.

I rolled my eyes, "Thanks for the vote of confidence, Neil. Really appreciate it."

Neil chuckled, "Hey, just saying, you never know what life has in store. We never thought anyone could really get with Margo, she never showed any interest in any guy here at Hawthorne."

I sighed, watching Grayson sift through the display case. "Well, let's make sure this ring is perfect. Raine deserves nothing but the best. We have been through so much." I voiced.

"Agreed," Grayson said.

Neil picked up a rose gold, yet elegant ring. "How about this one?"

I studied it for a moment, then shook my head. "That's not it, it's too much. Margo is just perfect."

"Okay little red riding hood." He rolled his eyes.

This wasn't just a ring for show. My heart was pounding, though I would never admit it. It wasn't the kind of nervous I get before an exam or during a big game. No, this was a different beast entirely—the "about-to-commit-to-forever" kind of nerves.

"Relax, man," Grayson said, slapping me on the back with a grin. "You look like you're about to face a firing squad, not buy a ring."

"Yeah, bro," Neil chimed in, leaning casually against the door-frame. "It's just a tiny piece of metal with a rock on it. No big deal."

"You're not helping," I muttered, my hands shoved deep into my jacket pockets.

Chris, ever the mediator, stepped between them and threw an arm around Liam's shoulder. "Ignore them. This is huge, and we're here to make sure you don't screw it up."

I took a closer look at all of the sparkle of diamonds and the faint scent of lavender from strategically placed candles. A woman in a tailored suit appeared with a professional yet friendly smile.

"Mr. Brookshire...Welcome to Brookshire Jewelers. Looking for anything in particular?" She greeted, her gaze flicking between the four of us.

"Is my mother here today?" I asked as the lady held up her hand like it was a gesture to wait.

My mother popped out of the back door.

She gave me a warm hug, her eyes sparkling with excitement. "Darling, what are you doing here, this is an engagement ring jeweler." She warned as I looked at her with a still look.

"Oh, I see..." She smiled at me as I looked around.

"You're going to find the perfect ring," She said, her voice full of confidence that I didn't quite feel yet.

"Why don't you tell me a little about your fiancée-to-be?"

I coughed out, "She's... amazing," I said, my voice soft but full of affection. "She's smart, kind, and she's got this laugh that just…" I trailed off, a shy smile tugged at my lips.

Neil groaned. "We get it. She's perfect. But what does she like?"

"Yeah," Chris added. "Classic? Modern? Glittery? Simple? We need details."

"Uh…" My brows furrowed. "She likes… flowers? And fashion?"

Neil snorted. "Great, we'll get her a fern-shaped ring with a sewing needle on the side."

"Neil!" Chris scolded. "Don't make him overthink this more than he already is."

My mother coughed politely, redirecting her attention. "It sounds like she appreciates thoughtful, meaningful things. Perhaps something elegant and timeless, with a personal touch?"

"That sounds right," I said, nodded eagerly.

My mother looked at all four of us and nodded. She led us to a private viewing room where the rings were displayed under soft, flattering lights.

As we followed her, Neil whispered, "Remember, no pressure. It's just forever."

I shot him a glare, but my heart lightened a bit. We entered the room, and the sight of all those glittering rings made my pulse race even faster. Each one seemed to beckon with a promise of love and commitment.

My mother's reassuring presence beside me helped to steady my nerves. She always knew how to make everything seem achievable, no matter how daunting.

Grayson, immediately started pointing out rings. "How about this one? Look at that sparkle!"

We followed her to a glass case, where rows of sparkling rings lay nestled on velvet cushions. The jeweler began pointing out options, but before I could absorb any of it, Neil leaned over, squinting at a massive diamond.

"How about this one?" Neil said, he pointed to a ring so large it looked like it belonged on a trophy. "Go big or go home, right?"

"Unless you want her to get robbed," Grayson muttered. "That thing probably costs more than any New York citizen's house."

"Worth it for true love," Neil said dramatically, clasping his hands over his heart.

Chris rolled his eyes and pointed at a sleek, minimalist band with a small diamond. "This one's nice. Clean, simple, won't blind anyone when the light hits it."

"It's a little... boring," Neil countered. "You need something with the wow factor."

"The wow factor isn't everything," Grayson said. "It should reflect Margo's personality."

"Exactly!" I said, latching onto the lifeline. "Something... like her. Not too flashy, but not boring either."

"How about this?" The jeweler interjected, pulling out a ring with a delicate gold band and a single round diamond surrounded by tiny emeralds. "It's timeless, but the emeralds add a unique touch."

My eyes lit up. "No, but the one next to it."

The group fell silent as I stared at the ring. For the first time all day, I looked sure of myself. "I think this is it," I said softly.

I stared at the ring I was pointing to; my eyes couldn't look away from the more understated piece with a delicate design and a single, stunning diamond. It seemed to call out to me, much like Margo did.

The ring looked like the night I saw her on the beach all by herself, the diamond looked like it would glisten with the moonlight.

My mother's eyes widened. "Oh, that's beautiful. It's simple but has so much character. I pieced it together in Greece, when I went there for a branch extension."

I smiled.

Chris, who had been silent, looked at it and nodded slowly.

"It's perfect," He said, and for the first time, I felt a wave of calm wash over me. This was the one.

"It didn't even look like you needed our help." Grayson said confidently, ignoring the way I looked at him.

Neil clapped his hands together. "Finally! Mission accomplished."

"Not bad, bro," Chris said, giving me an approving nod.

Grayson smiled. "She's going to love it."

I felt a strange mix of relief and exhilaration. As we walked out of the store, Neil threw an arm around my shoulders.

"You're gonna crush this proposal," He said. "Just don't cry too much, or she might say no."

"Shut up," I laughed. But as my friends teased and joked, I couldn't stop picturing Margo's face when I would asked her to marry me.

And for the first time, I wasn't nervous—just excited.

THE END.
Thank you for reading!

About the Author

Liana Tiamzon is a young upcoming author who writes about a beautiful town filled with amazing characters. She creates love stories full of heartbreak and plot twists whether they be platonic or romantic. She grew up in the Philippines but currently lives in Pennsylvania. She enjoys listening to music, watching romantic movies, and reading about love. She loves finding new friends and including introducing them in her romantic fictional stories.